THE MUTINY GIRL

KAREN S. GORDON

For Margarita

1

FRIDAY

Vance Courage could not understand how his sister, Kathy, found any solace, or *positivity*, as she liked to call it, posting their news on Facebook. Even harder to get was the fifty-nine people who *Liked* their dad's death. Some had clicked on the crying emoji. But *Likes*?

How can you Like *death if you haven't tried it?*

That's what Vance wanted to write. But it would upset Kathy, and he'd vowed to keep his trigger finger off the keyboard. Too bad more people didn't exercise the same discipline. He plopped on the grungy floral sofa inside his tiny apartment, put his feet up on a plastic orange crate, and watched the *Likes* pile up. He hated every one of them. The comments were worse than the *Likes*:

OMG! So sorry for your loss!

What happened?

Lost mine last year, know how u feel

Preying for you and ur famly
Thoughts and prayers GF
So sorry for you Kat
Thots and prayers sweety
. *Time heals all wombs*
We're here for you

Someone posted, *Some good will come of this some day you'll see it!*

He shook his head at the screen. The same words and phrases in slight variations popped up over and over and over like the continuous video loop he'd seen at the gun show where he'd bought his 9-millimeter Glock. The salesman said the video was about three minutes long because that's the attention span of the average male. The guy was right. One hundred five *Likes* piled up before he snapped his tablet shut.

Everywhere he went, people were glued to their mobile devices like chewing gum for the brain: walking their dogs, sitting across from friends in restaurants, watching a movie at their local theater. How trivia could be so riveting was a mystery. The posts were just a bunch of stuff written by people with nothing better to do than brag or complain, and God knows he had his own stuff to bitch about.

Kathy had given him the tablet for his birthday, and his oldest nephew pre-downloaded the Facebook app and created his profile. He started out with five friends over a year ago: his sister and her four boys. His loser brother-in-law, Larry, sent him a Friend request, but he'd ignored it. More than a year later he still had the same five.

"You isolate too much," Kathy said when he looked less than enthused after unwrapping it. "This way you can keep up with our family." It was a quasi-delicate way of reminding him that he didn't have one of his own.

The tablet grew on him after he installed the MatchMeUp

dating app. Kathy and the boys took scads of pictures and posted them immediately to their accounts. He wondered how she'd feel if she knew the only reason he checked her posts was to see if there were any good pictures of him he could recycle as dating chum. He'd learned to copy, crop, and paste pictures from her Facebook timeline to his dating profile.

He glossed over their blurbs about school plays, softball games, vacations, and birthday parties. He scoured their newsfeeds looking for flattering pictures of himself. He'd read an email blast by an online dating blogger saying if he wasn't getting a lot of new hits from the kind of women he'd like to date, he should freshen up the pics. Otherwise, the blogger wrote, his online profile would get stale.

Online dating was intriguing in the beginning, especially when he got his first email from an attractive brunette. She turned out to be a fake email from a Russian porn site. His enthusiasm waned further after a series of disappointing dates.

Then the slimy marketers, experts at exploiting the most basic of human wants, started spamming him several times a day. They sent enticing emails about a "special someone" who was trying to connect with him. He knew he was being suckered, but the 50%-off deal was too tempting. Getting back out there might be a welcome distraction. While reactivating his account, a Facebook *Friend* request lit up on his tablet. That was odd. He didn't get requests, other than the one from Larry he'd never accepted. He clicked on it.

A thumbnail appeared above the new invite. Daniel Ruiz. He accepted it.

Now there's a blast from the past.

He hadn't heard from Sergeant Daniel Ruiz for at least twenty years. He clicked on Sarge's social media profile and started reading. He was a grandfather. Had three kids. All girls. Had recently gone on a cruise to Nassau, Bahamas. Was retired from the Fort Lauderdale PD. Was active in the local Fraternal Order of Police. And he was divorced. That was a surprise.

His profile picture wasn't of him or his girls. It was an old black-and-white photo of a young woman, scanned with crinkles and scratches across her beautiful face. Something ticked in the limbic part of Vance's brain when he looked at it. He couldn't quite place the feeling or the photo.

An instant message popped up on his tablet. How RU doing man?

Great and u

Blip. Sarge was quick. Retired and bored. You married yet?

He was looking for "n" for "never" when another question blew up.

What are you doing these days?

He was irritated and closed one eye to focus. Rather talk Give me ur # I'll call now

As soon as he pecked it out, his cell lit up. "Hey. Long time. What's the occasion?"

"¿Qué bolá contigo?" Sarge asked.

"I'm pressing *one* for English. You know I hate that."

"Yeah, you don't hate it. You just don't understand it. Nice to know you haven't changed. You should try embracing your culture. Voluptuous women and good cigars."

"I don't like the smell of cigars. Plus, I wouldn't know the difference between one from Havana and one from Idaho. I like to think of myself as the last American living in Miami."

"Don't get too used to the idea. Soon we'll be taking over the free world. In case you haven't heard, a pair of Cubans ran for president. So what if they didn't make it to the *Casa Blanca*? Still got two in the Senate. And you're as Cuban as the one from Texas."

"Don't take this personally, but don't remind me. I'm burned out on politics."

"I called to say sorry about your dad."

"Oh," he said. "Thanks. How did you know?"

"Saw it on your Facebook page."

"How did you find me there?"

"Are you serious? Um. I typed your name in the place where you search for people and a *muy* handsome guy came up, one that looks just like you."

"My sister puts everything out there. It's kind of embarrassing."

Sarge hesitated. "Is she your younger sister?"

"Yeah. She has a bunch of kids. All boys."

"You'd be surprised. Read an article that said posting stuff releases dopamine or serotonin or something. Makes people feel good; it does something to brain chemistry, like sex and online dating. Addictive."

The online dating comment hit a nerve. "I prefer beer and wine."

"You always did. Meet me for a drink later?"

He looked at his watch. "I've got to be at the funeral in an hour. I promised to go to Mom's house after the service. I'm definitely going to need a sports drink after. What about Tavern in the Grove?"

"My favorite dive. What time?"

"Five thirty."

"I got a better idea. I'll pick you up. We can sit in the parking lot at the bar and drink single malt out of brown paper sacks if you want."

"How chivalrous."

"I'm a Latin man. What's your address?"

He chewed on his bottom lip. He didn't want to tell him because he had a pretty good idea how Sarge was going to react.

"Geez, Glenvar Heights, nice," Sarge said. "Glad to see your career as a lawyer is panning out. I better bring my weapon."

"There're worse neighborhoods."

"Not above the poverty level."

Before he had the chance to agree, Sarge ended the call.

He saved his contact information. When he picked up his tablet and opened the cover, his brain went into overdrive. Sarge's profile picture was of the girl who was murdered at the Hotel Mutiny. It was hard for detectives to give up on a cold case, even ex-detectives. This one had been bothering him, too, ever since he'd left Miami PD to go to law school a couple of decades ago.

HE FELT the dagger eyes piercing him as he skulked down the church aisle to the front pew reserved for immediate family and sat down a few feet from the casket. None of his relatives were subtle about his tardiness or unkempt appearance. They twisted in their seats and glowered at him. He hid behind a pair of cheap wraparound sunglasses. His father had passed suddenly from a heart attack, and he hadn't had time to process it.

"Ju could have pressed jur slacks," his mother, Isabel, whispered in his ear, the y-words always spoken as j-words.

His pants were rumpled and his white shirt wasn't very white. He should have polished his shoes, too. And worn a jacket, maybe even a tie. Not a shining example for his nephews.

Kathy was already there with the boys; she'd separated them with two seated on either side of her. She squinted and wrinkled her nose, irritated. She needed them to behave, and he loved being a bad influence.

"Hey, Uncle Vance," Cory whispered, leaning over his grandmother.

"Shh," Kathy hissed.

"Sorry," Vance mouthed to his mother and sister as the service began.

The priest had delayed it waiting for him. "Death is nothing at all," the priest with threads of gray hair and a bulbous nose began, sounding theatrical, as if he were auditioning for something. "I have only slipped away into the next room. I am I, and you are you. Whatever we were to each other is what we still are."

Cory mouthed "WTF?" to his younger brothers. The kids covered their faces with their hands to keep from laughing. His sister and mother didn't see it.

But Vance did, and it took a lot to keep from laughing along with them. He *was* a bad influence. He winked and grinned at the kids. Then he stared straight at the altar.

The priest continued. "Play, smile, think of me, and pray for me. Call me by my old, familiar name."

Why was Sarge suddenly back in the picture? Not so much as a Christmas card in over a dozen years and now a same-day invitation to an old haunt.

His mother reached over and grabbed his hand. She squeezed it, then let go, dabbing at her welling tears. If the service wasn't so weird he might have cried, too.

He looked around. There was no one present from his father's side of the family. Dr. Jim Courage's lineage could be traced to the *Mayflower* on his grandmother's side. No one remotely descended from the Pilgrims was in attendance, only his mother's very extended Cuban family.

He lied about it at school, his ethnicity. He looked just like his dad, fair-skinned with the sort of medium-brown hair that streaked gold in the summertime.

"*Oye*, there's your *madre*, Vance." That's how the kids at school who knew he was half-Cuban teased him.

"She's not my mother. She's the housekeeper." He denied it to gain acceptance, to avoid being bullied like the other Cuban boys. All these years later he still felt guilty for saying she wasn't his *madre*. The housekeeper. The memory filled him with self-loathing.

"Let us pray for him. And let us pray for his family."

A relative on his mother's side who owned a floral shop in the colorful Calle Ocho business district had made the funeral flowers. There was an enormous spray of roses covering the casket flanked by wreaths on rickety metal easels. When the priest raised his arms, his robe caught the edge of one of the gigantic arrangements. It toppled forward. The congregation fell silent, then erupted into a choir of gasps. A woman raced to the altar with the urgency of an EMT. He had so many relatives on his mother's side he wasn't sure how the one fixing the flower crisis was related to him. His dad told him he'd be happy to have his ashes scattered in Biscayne Bay. But funerals were for the living. And the living consisted of his mother and her relatives, and they all fully expected a costly extravaganza.

SIX MALE RELATIVES, including Vance, began lowering the coffin into the ground using handheld slings. A powerful gust of wind came from nowhere. It blew so hard it unbalanced one of the pallbearers. Like dominoes, the men holding the slings wavered, and the casket swung above the grave. One man tottered perilously close to the edge before regaining his footing. His mother slapped the lavish coffin with her open palm, uttering something unfamiliar, primal.

Afterward some in the reception line picked roses from a large wicker basket atop a folding table and dropped them into the open plot. Others genuflected and crossed themselves forehead to navel, left shoulder to right. Others just walked past silently. Hankies and tissues weren't just for tears. Men mopped their brows and women dabbed their upper lips. Mid-May in south Florida could introduce summer with the subtlety of a sledgehammer, and today was one of those days.

After the casket was lowered into the earth, he stood grave-side with Isabel, giving her time to settle down, to compose herself. The sound she'd let out earlier was one he'd never heard before, and it was replaying again and again in his head. His father's coffin had just about pulled a half a dozen men, including him, down into the hole. His mother's strange shriek had alerted the dogs in the neighborhood. They'd been barking and howling until the roar of a front-end loader drowned them out.

The tractor driver sped toward the open grave, taking a wide berth around a white Cadillac SUV idling in the *No Parking* zone across the street. The operator popped out of the tractor seat as it flew up and over the curb. The sound of metal gnashing the concrete startled his mother back into the present. She covered her ears.

It was too loud to talk with the tractor growling a few feet away, the impatient gravedigger goosing the gas, his way of hurrying them so he could finish the job.

Vance reached for his mother's hand and gently coaxed her away. "Kathy and the kids are waiting in the parking lot to drive you home."

Walking slowly so as not to rush her, he looked back once. The scene morphed into a construction site. The operator dumped a bucket of dirt into the open earth. The scent of burning diesel filled the air. The white Escalade disappeared.

"Ju're coming to the house." Her look said she was not taking no for an answer. "Some friends and family are coming, too. Plus, I have something I want to give ju."

He ARRIVED at his mother's, not surprised the entire residential block was jam-packed with cars. His dad used to joke about it. *If you marry into a Latin family, you'll never have a place to park. And neither will your neighbors.* It might have been funny if it weren't so true. Even a small soiree meant both sides of the street were packed for as far as the eye could see.

His parents' modest Mediterranean Revival home backed up to a canal leading to the Intracoastal Waterway. Isabel loved the red clay tile roof and white stucco exterior because she said it reminded her of home. Cuba. When his folks bought the house going on fifty years ago, Coral Gables was respectable, but hardly ostentatious.

When the neighbors got wind that the Cuban family with the WASP surname planned a get-together, one of them preemptively called the police. It was one of the ways Coral Gables had changed. It was now snobby. And it was also a lot more expensive. Teardowns were selling for more than five hundred dollars a square foot. The new generation of home-owners waited anxiously for the old crop to die or move to assisted living so new people with more money could bulldoze the bungalows and erect lot-filling McMonstrosities.

When he reached the house, Kathy was in a spirited debate with a moon-faced Coral Gables female police officer named Gonzales with spiky auburn hair atop a tiny head. She looked like a tick about to pop, and the buttons on her shirt looked like they were about to let go too.

"Google Miami Parking Authority on your phone." Kathy held hers up menacingly.

He intervened. "Sorry, Officer. The ladies are touchy about parking."

"So I've heard. We've had several calls. Been here before."
She sighed.

"They always call," Kathy complained. "It's a public street.
There's no law against it."

Officer Gonzalez rested her right wrist on the butt of the gun
strapped to the shiny utility belt digging into her flesh. She
appeared to be in no mood for a showdown. "Looks like
everyone is legally parked."

He looked around sheepishly. Several neighbors had gathered outside their homes. He'd listened to their complaints
before. They didn't appreciate paying over a million dollars for a
house overlooking a pop-up parking lot. His sister was usually
mild-mannered, but not today.

"What are you all looking at?" she shouted. She turned
toward the cop. "I'd like to report them as stalkers."

"They live here." Gonzales furrowed her brow. "Legally you
can park on the street, and by law they can stare at you."

He was embarrassed. He felt sorry for Officer Gonzalez, who
headed across the street to talk to the woman with the surgical
duck lips, standing akimbo, her manicured claws gripping her
bony hips. He saw both sides of the dispute and privately sided
with the neighbors. His first generation Cuban-American relatives weren't into carpooling or economy cars.

He'd parked the dusty Nissan Cube titled to him—in lieu of
fees a client couldn't pay—two blocks away. He'd intended to sell
it, but the air conditioning went out on his car last summer right
after the warranty expired, so he'd sold the Range Rover for twenty
grand to pay bills. The Cube was part of a bug extermination fleet,
and the four-foot-long cockroach mounted to the roof couldn't be
completely removed without tearing a hole in the top. One giant
leg cut at the knee remained. Kathy's kids dubbed it Edgar. Parking
Edgar that far away had an upside. He'd been glared at enough at

church and wasn't up for being the focus of a neighborhood watch group. The car was humiliating, but with a little luck, the new online ad campaign he was running would jumpstart his law business and he could buy something normal to drive.

"*Vance, Vance, Vance,*" all the aunts, uncles, nieces, and cousins—mostly women—chimed when they saw him come through the door. Unlike him, his Cuban relatives were demonstrative and fussed over him. The house was full, standing room only. The reassuring scents of cumin and coriander, grilled onions and bell peppers flooded his head with happy thoughts. His mouth watered.

"We're so happy to see ju but so sad about jur *popi.* Jur mother is so lucky to have ju here." Aunt Sophia leaned on her cane and reached up with one gnarled hand. He loosened at the knees, lowering himself, making it easier for her to reach his face. She clamped a thumb and forefinger softly on his cheek and smiled warmly at him. His heart sang. The heck with the neighbors and the minor inconveniences his tight-knit family caused. He supported her shoulder as she rebalanced herself, needing both hands on her walking stick.

Marrying his dad-the-doctor had elevated his mother, Isabel, into instant upper-middle-class living. If there was any resentment between the two sisters, he'd never seen it. Sophia, six years older than his mother, had taken on the role of mama to Isabel and their much younger brother, Antonio. Their own mother, Marta, had died of cancer during the Cuban Revolution. Their father had preceded her in death by only a couple of years, details of which were never discussed. Sophia was just nineteen years old when she'd fled Cuba in 1962 to live with relatives, escorting her younger siblings to Miami. His Uncle Antonio was too young to remember his mother. His father died before he was born.

Sophia and Antonio—"Tony"—were regular fixtures around

the Courage household when he was growing up. He'd heard his father treated Tony when he suffered a medical emergency when he was nine years old. Uncle Tony was the big brother he'd never had. His dad tolerated the arrangement. Other than the story of the surgery to remove Tony's appendix, Dr. Jim Courage showed no obligation to play father to Tony. By middle school, the sisters were worried. Tony was getting into trouble, running with a new crowd—the kids from the barrios where he lived with his big sister.

Sophia's cloudy eyes met his and she studied him. He had to look away because when she looked at him, she saw Tony too. She used to talk about it. It had been a long time since he'd disappeared, and she didn't want to talk about a ghost anymore. That's how she put it: ghost. Twenty years, that's how long his uncle had been missing and how long he'd been an FBI Ten Most Wanted Fugitive.

"Ju need to eat something, Harry!" Salvador, an exuberant second cousin, corralled him. "*Oye, flaco, ju look pale.*" *Flaco.* Thin man. Sal was a personal space invader, and Vance had learned long ago how to sidestep him. It didn't work this time when Sal used an unexpected blocking move.

Harry was a famous jazz singer from New Orleans. Vance looked a lot like him—deep blue eyes, easy smile, good crop of medium-brown hair, sharp cheekbones, symmetrical features, a prominent nose that enhanced things—Sal was convinced he could pass for Harry Connick Jr.'s brother. He wasn't as sure about the resemblance as Sal was.

"Harry, ju look out for *your* mama, no? Ju the family lawyer —ju take care of business for jur mama."

"Of course." He looked for an opening and, when he saw one, darted past Sal to check on her. She was busy in the kitchen, a faded floral apron hanging from her delicate neck. He'd failed her for not marrying and having six kids. She used to bring it up all the time, and he was relieved the day she stopped.

Neither of his parents were enthralled with Kathy's husband —Larry the tire salesman at the local dealership—who'd made it to district manager. But Larry fathered four boys, and that was more than enough to cancel out their son-in-law's shortcomings.

Isabel spoke in barely a whisper. "Are ju hungry?"

He pulled a plate from the counter and loaded it with food. "Where are Kathy and the boys?"

"She wasn't feeling well, so she just left."

Kathy seemed perfectly fine confronting Officer Gonzales. No sense bringing it up. He put his plate down and got a beer from the refrigerator.

Sophia shuffled into the kitchen. The two sisters huddled near the sink, speaking Spanish in hushed tones.

"I have something for ju. Jur dad wanted me to give it to ju. What ju say?" His mother put two fingers on her lips, thinking. "Personal things."

Sophia carried a wooden cigar box, balancing it on her cane. She handed it to him. He lifted the lid a little and peeked inside as though a pair of white doves might slip out. No birds, just old papers and photos. He put it on the small table near the kitchen window next to his beer and food.

"Ju take it with ju when ju leave, no? I'll remind ju," Sophia said. "When ju leave, I make sure ju take the box with ju."

"OK." He was in heaven, gorging on red beans and rice, caramelized plantains, and his favorite, *ropa vieja*, shredded beef on tortillas.

When he was leaving, Sophia hobbled to the door, carrying the box he would have forgotten. "He wanted ju to have it. And here, take this, too. It's jur *popi's* . . . last will. Ju know what to do, right?"

Isabel stood next to her as if in solidarity, letting her older sister Sophia take the lead while she dried her hands on the old apron.

"I know. I was listening before." He took the box from Sophia and tucked it under his arm. He kissed her softly on the cheek. He hugged his mother with one arm. Her eyes welled again. He put the box down and used his thumbs to catch her tears. His throat tightened. "I'll call you," he said, picking up the cigar box and sliding the blue-covered document beneath it. He didn't have to look back to know they were watching him from the doorway. When he saw a neighbor scowling at him from a big picture window, he jogged the rest of the way to the car.

His phone buzzed. He fumbled for it in his pants pocket. Sarge came up on caller ID.

"Hello."

"*¿Dónde demonios estás?*"

"I'm pressing one for English now. Beeeeep."

"Let me translate nicely. Where are you?"

"I'll be there in ten."

"Hurry up, man, before I get robbed or killed."

"It's not that bad."

"You're right, *señor*. It's worse than that. Maybe you should relocate to Homestead. You'd get more bang for the buck."

"That depends on how you define bang."

"Very funny. Get your skinny pink ass over here. There's nothing good about this place. You live in 3B, right? Whoever lives next door sure is nosy—what my ex likes to call a curtain-twitcher."

"I wouldn't know." He shifted in his seat. "I try to ignore my neighbors."

"Me? I want to know who lives near me. Hurry up, *gallego*."

He was still laughing when Sarge ended the call. *Gallego* was vintage Sarge, Cuban street slang for a guy who can't get laid.

He pondered an old regret on the drive to his place. Maybe

he should have stayed with Metro instead of going back to the University of Miami to get his law degree and with it, a big pile of debt. If he had, he'd be on a cushy police pension. When he'd first opened his small solo practice, he thought it would be rewarding helping the less fortunate. Working pro-bono cases. Bettering the world.

It wasn't. Far from it.

He pulled into his apartment complex and parked Edgar between two older trucks with landscape trailers chained to rear hitches. He stowed the cigar box and legal document under the driver's seat.

Sarge zipped in behind the Nissan, perpendicular, blocking him in, and rolled down the passenger window. He looked incredulous. "Don't tell me that thing's yours. *Ay, yi yi!* Is that a cockroach leg?"

He couldn't deny it. There was nothing he could say to defend it. Sarge would never understand taking a car with a plastic roach leg on the roof in lieu of cash.

Sarge reverted to his old self. "You're one hot date. *Un hombre caliente.*"

"Should I punch you in the nose for English?" He climbed into the Jeep Renegade. "I need a drink."

"You'd think I'd get a little nicer greeting after all these years." Sarge stared at the underwear swaying from a makeshift clothesline strung from a tree roped off to second-and third-story handrails. "I gotta say I'm a little surprised you live here."

Last time he saw Sarge, he'd bumped into him at the grocery store. He'd just graduated law school and was being romanced by the big firms in Miami.

"Well, I guess things just don't work out the way we think they will. I figured by now you'd have a fancy place in Coco Plum." Sarge paused. "There's an upside, I guess. You don't have to worry about anyone ripping off your car." He sniffed the air. "Smells like someone needs another beer."

"Well, at least my rent's cheap." Vance looked out the Jeep window, up at the apartment next door and didn't see any curtains twitching. "You're right. Someone needs another beer."

2

FRIDAY NIGHT

THE SEATBELT CUT a diagonal swath across Sarge's belly, making its shape changeable, like a shallow canal cutting into a very big bowl of Jell-O. The driver's seat was as far back as it would go, otherwise Sarge might not have had enough elbow room to turn the wheel.

"I'd rather smell like beer than cheap cologne." Vance cracked open the passenger window, letting some heavy air in.

"Hey, now. It's not cologne. It's Axe body spray. Drives the ladies wild."

"Right. I'm flattered you freshened up for our date."

"At least I make an effort." Sarge craned his neck back and forth, looking for a break in traffic to make a left out of the shabby apartment complex.

Like lots of Vance's friends and family, Sarge was a first generation Cuban-American. Vance noted that Sarge still had the unruly eyebrows the prosecutor pressured him into styling before he testified at an important trial back when he was still a cop. Sarge had told him the attorney said his eyebrows made him look sinister. The hair on top of his silky brown head was long gone now, and he wore a tidy salt-and-pepper fringe cut, trimmed neatly above his ears. He was either growing a goatee or had missed a patch shaving. And it looked like he'd whitened his teeth.

Sarge wore thick-framed black glasses in all his Facebook posts. He wore them in person, too, and from a profile view, Vance could see a crevice in the fleshy folds between his eyes, deep enough to clamp a dime. Earlier, when he'd enlarged one of Sarge's selfies, he'd noticed a pierced ear. He still wore the same hollow gold rope around his neck. It hung just below the second button of his apricot *guayabera* shirt. The attached 14-karat gold crucifix was too small for a gangbanger, but it was still tacky.

"I'd ask about the funeral, but I bet you'd rather talk about work," Sarge said, navigating the Jeep toward Coconut Grove. "So how is biz?"

"It's all right if you like prostitutes, petty thieves, and pedophiles." A sad but accurate state of affairs.

"I kind of like prostitutes. Affordable ones wearing body condoms."

Vance shook his head and chuckled. In truth, trash talk was a turn off. Sarge looked like he regretted saying it.

"Ever miss the action?" Sarge looked at him and grinned. "Police action."

"Sometimes, I guess." He shrugged. "I think maybe I just missed my calling."

"Scarier job these days, being a cop. So what is your calling?"

"That's just it. I don't know." That was the God's honest truth.

"Ah, a mid-life crisis. I had one, too. Split up with my wife."

That surprised him. "The idea of you and Maria breaking

up, I never thought that would happen." He'd envied Sarge's marriage, just never out loud.

"Yeah, well, I guess I wanted someone who acted slightly interested during lovemaking."

"You over-share, like a chick." Vance leaned away from him, resting his right shoulder against the passenger window frame.

Sarge parked behind a bicycle rental shop across from the bar. The tavern's once glossy red front door was splintered and weathered gray at the seams. The four small glass panes lining the top were grimy: outside from time and inside from exhaled carbon dioxide. It was dimly lit and smelled like a potpourri of mustard and second-hand smoke. Vance dragged a barstool over the concrete floor and sat. Sarge did the same. He ordered two beers from the bartender.

"She's hot." Sarge's eyes were glued to the tattooed bartender. "*Muy caliente.*"

Sarge was in a trance, watching her every move. Vance snapped his thumb and forefinger in his ear. The longer he stared at the barkeep, the longer it would take to find out why the impromptu meeting. *Twenty years.* He wanted to know what couldn't wait.

She scurried around the bar and returned with two cold beers, popping the caps one-handed, like a magician. "You gentlemen wanna run a tab?"

Sarge was more than happy to pay. He pulled his wallet out and handed her his credit card. She scuttled off to wait on some young men. "I can't help myself. The chance to impress pretty girls, well, it's just too much for me."

An emaciated college student folded up on the barstool next to Vance and drew hard on an E-cigarette, tilted his head back, and emitted a contrail of bluish smoke. The vapor annoyed Vance. He wanted to get down to business. He gulped his beer, trying to think of a way to jumpstart the conversation. The alcohol went straight to his brain, easing the nagging feelings of despair that had followed him from his mother's house to the bar. Being with Sarge was better than being home by himself. *Lighten up. Let Sarge have a little fun.* But Sarge was dragging it out.

"So, why are we here?" Vance asked him. "What's up that couldn't wait?"

"I wanted to pick your brain about something."

"Go ahead. Pick away."

"I wanted to get some advice about online dating."

Vance laughed so hard he grabbed his stomach with both arms. It felt good to belly laugh. "Oh, gosh." He laughed again, harder this time. *Yeah, right.*

Sarge put both hands on either side of his face, palms facing out, a thumb in each ear. "Got me." He cupped his hands and yelled, "Two more beers, gorgeous!" He turned to face him again. "I got a little update from the high security prison in Florence."

Florence. The Alcatraz of the Rockies. Supermax. There was only one reason Sarge would bring up ADX. Sarge was fishing. "Oh, yeah? What sort of update?"

"There's a rumor there's an impending hit on Chago Marino."

Chago Marino, his Uncle Tony's former partner-in-crime serving a 205-year prison sentence. "How do you know that?"

"I know people. I got connections, *gallego*."

"So what did your people say?"

"Chago's had 'round-the-clock protection since he was moved from ADX to the high security block." Sarge picked up the bottle of beer and suckled it like a baby. "Someone on the outside's been keeping his payments to the Aryan Brotherhood current. Rumor has it the payments stopped."

Chago Marino had been in the Colorado prison for fifteen

years, and dozens of high-priced lawyers had been working on a variety of strategies trying to appeal his conviction. They'd performed a miracle getting him moved from the maximum-security prison to the high-security block. They'd been hoping for another magic trick for a decade.

The bartender stopped by and asked if they wanted another round.

Sarge asked, "¿Cuánto cuesta?"

"Twelve bucks." She plucked Sarge's credit card and ticket from inside a highball glass next to the register.

"Thanks, sweetheart." He added a fat tip to the check and watched her expression. She glanced at it and stuck it in the cash drawer. Sarge looked dejected. But he snapped out of it when he stood to leave. The Friday night crowd had grown three deep at the bar. Students clamoring for somewhere to sit moved in on them like hyenas. Sarge pushed his chair to make space to stand.

"OK, babe," Ruiz yelled at him. "I hope you had fun on our date."

Vance was having the same problem, so he rammed his chair stool back into the crowd when the drunks behind him didn't respond to normal cues. "Thanks for the beers, honey. It's fun to get together every twenty years."

It was nightfall on the ride back. Sarge asked if he knew that over eighty percent of online daters posted lies about something *muy grande* on their dating profiles.

He shrugged in the passenger seat. "I'm not surprised."

Sarge took his eyes off the road and looked at him. "Are you on any dating sites?"

Sarge was so nosy. He shook his head and rolled his eyes, but didn't answer.

"Aha! Guilty! That is a great big *si!*" Sarge howled. "There goes the online dating world. So what tall tales did you tell?"

This was another conversation he did not care to have tonight. "I checked the divorced box."

"Why? Are you married or attached or something?"

"No." The reason seemed silly now.

"Then why?" Sarge looked at him with great confusion, the fissure between his eyes deepening.

"Research says women prefer losers to non-starters ten times out of ten. I read they'll pass over the older bachelors." This was sure to fire Ruiz up.

"Ya think? They might find a forty-five-year-old guy who's never been married a risky investment? The ladies are usually looking for a little experience. They figure if you did it once, you'll jump off the plank again. Divorce is better than no experience. So what sites are you on?"

"I'm not going to tell you that."

"Oh, come on. Which one?"

Sarge was in beginning-stage badgering and had a reputation for tenacity, getting confessions from the most adamant criminals. Tonight he didn't have the energy to fight him. He grimaced. "Um. MatchMeUp."

"Uh-huh. No one's on just one. What others are you fishing?" Sarge looked over again. "Come on."

He was exhausted. Sarge was going to give him a raft of shit either way. Might as well bargain. "If I tell you, will you promise to answer my question?"

"Sure."

"Fish-a-Plenty."

"You mean Pussy-a-Plenty. Jeez. There's a box on that site

that asks whether or not you have a car. A car! That's a pretty low standard, don't you think?"

He sat quietly. Sarge was queuing up for one of his pontifications. Here it came.

"Here's the thing, *gallego*: We look at the pictures. The cha-cha's, they look for the money. That's how it works. Unless you have a Warren Buffet-sized Fidelity account and post it, you better look like Brad Pitt. You got an edge on me in the looks department, I gotta admit it. But lying about being divorced? That gets you off on the wrong foot from the get-go. How long you think it takes before they figure it out?"

He listened until Sarge was done. "OK, now it's my turn." He'd moved in closer to the center console to watch Sarge's reaction. "Why do you have the picture of the murdered Mutiny girl as your Facebook profile picture?"

Sarge hardly looked ambushed. He showed no element of surprise. "So, you remember her." He fixed his eyes on the windshield. The only sound was coming from the Renegade's tires crunching the road. After a long pause, he said, "Ever have one of those cold cases you couldn't let go of?"

Vance had. "Sure. Lots of them." The Mutiny girl was one they shared. The unsolved ones, especially the ones you knew you could solve, those ate cops alive. This one was low-hanging fruit, but they'd never arrested anyone.

Sarge glanced at him, stopping at a four-way. "It should have been an easy case if there wasn't such a big conspiracy to cover it up. There was enough evidence for my dead grandmother to put it together. But the folks running the hotel were so corrupt we couldn't do a decent investigation. Add to that, that jurisdiction-wise, it was a mess since they found her body in Monroe County and she was killed in Dade County, in the hotel. Anyway, you already know that's how I think it went down. Unless you forgot."

"No. I haven't forgotten. But Dan, that was a long time ago. And not only that, you were outside your jurisdiction."

Sergeant Daniel Ruiz had been a Fort Lauderdale homicide detective. Broward County. It's how they first met. After the murder, Ruiz was snooping around the Hotel Mutiny in Miami where he had no official business. Vance was socializing with his Uncle Tony at the hotel. It seemed odd now for a cop to hang out drinking hundred-dollar champagne with his uncle, a drug lord. But the Hotel Mutiny lacked all boundaries, moral, ethical, legal, or otherwise, with kingpins at one table, FBI agents at another. It was the one stain on his police record, partying at the club with his uncle and his sociopathic partner, Chago Marino. Vance had never claimed to be a saint but this crossed the line.

They rode in silence until Sarge turned the conversation to a lighter topic. "So what's your username?"

"What?"

"No. Seriously, what's your username? Took me an entire day to come up with mine. *AngelBatista*. What do you think of that?"

He shrugged. "Should I think something?"

"Well, yeah. Angel Batista, the detective on *Dexter*. The one who wore the fedora and had the hot thing with the black lieutenant? Don't you think I look a lot like him?" Sarge pursed his lips. He couldn't hold the expression for long. He cracked up, showing his very white teeth.

His laugh was contagious. "I've never seen it."

Sarge took umbrage. "Whoa! You're kidding. The best show since *Miami Vice*, set right here in our own backyard. What's wrong with you?"

"I don't get the premium channels."

Sarge shook his head. "What's your username? Come on, I told you mine." He went in for the kill. "Why do I always get the impression you think you're better than everyone else? Like you're too good to be fishing for the ladies online with the rest of us."

He'd used this same tactic before, badgering him when he said he was quitting the department to go to law school, accusing him of being too much of a snob to stick with law enforcement. The Mutiny girl murder was a hot case at the time. But it hadn't been assigned to Vance. Ruiz wanted him to stay on, be his mole. They both suspected she was killed at the hotel, then dumped in the Upper Keys. Sarge guilt-tripped him, said Vance was duty-bound to stay on and work the case. Manipulation 101. But he'd already made his mind up and given notice. The coroner was renting refrigerated trucks to store dead bodies. Miami was a war zone, and every night there were a dozen street murders, and half the cops were dirty. "Gallego69," he finally said.

"Even you're not that cynical," Sarge said. "But you are a snob. Come on. Give it to me."

"MileMarker45. Happy now?"

"Hmm. *Muy bueno*, catchy. I like it. Nice little play on your age. And the Florida Keys, right?" Sarge nodded slowly, looking pleased with himself.

"Well, I have to trawl with decent bait, right?"

"I agree. Since you can't use *Bazillionaire*, it's good. That, and your pictures, handsome *hombre* like you."

Sarge turned the Jeep into Vance's place. The flat-topped, three-story, green stucco apartment complex looked eerie in the thick air under the flickering streetlights, like an algae-covered shipwreck. Ruiz put the Renegade in park. "*Grassy-ass* for the enchanting evening."

Vance opened the passenger door to get out. "Don't break the speed limit checking your MatchMeUp or whatever accounts on the way home."

"No worries about that." Sarge held up his phone. "Got the apps. Don't want to keep the ladies waiting."

Vance shook his head.

Sarge pushed his phone closer to Vance's face. He tapped the screen. It lit up in the dark. "Check it out. Have you seen this? Uses GPS. Shows you where the ladies are right now. If you want to get laid, you swipe this way, and if you want to work on getting your virginity back, you swipe the other way, like this."

He pushed Sarge's hand away. He wanted to get out of the car. Instead, he closed the passenger door and stayed in the air conditioning. The humidity wasn't the reason. Sarge hadn't answered his question yet. They'd made a deal.

Sarge found what he'd been looking for. He held up the phone and showed him a picture of a cute senior. "I did the wild thing with her on the first date, after she chugged a bottle of Chardonnay. She's kinda hot, don't you think?"

He grimaced and looked away, changing the subject. "So who's been taking care of Chago's payments to the Aryan Brotherhood?"

"His kid, I think, the one with the club foot. Can't remember his name." Sarge was preoccupied, trying to enlarge the picture.

"His name is Gregorio. And it's not a clubfoot. The kid was born with elephantiasis. His mom kept a shoe on it to keep it . . . contained. She bought him a new pair of Thom McAn leather lace-ups every year and made him sleep with one on. His foot is shaped like a size ten shoe. I saw it once. It has a few folds where his toes should be and there're some things growing out of it, like toenails. I still can't understand how he learned to walk on it normally."

Sarge squinted. "How do you know all that? About the kid's foot?"

"My uncle's best friend was married to his mother. There was a lot of family gossip about it, the foot."

"Wow. Nice job, way to go, playing it down. 'My uncle's childhood friend.'" Sarge rolled his eyes. "You mean your fugitive uncle's business partner who's serving a triple life sentence in a high-security prison. Who also happens to be in arrears to the Aryan Brotherhood." Sarge raised his eyebrows. "It's not like they were stealing loaves of bread to feed the poor. Los Guapos is a sin on the heart of all Miami."

Vance stepped out of the Jeep and closed the door. The passenger window whirred down. He poked his head inside with his arms folded on the frame. "Thanks again for the beers."

"*De nada*." Sarge chuckled. "Let's stay in touch, Mile-Marker45."

Vance gave Sarge a middle finger.

"What's that for?"

"Your IQ." He'd dropped to Sarge's level.

"I'd say it's for your number of Cuban parents."

"You really need to grow up, *Detective Batista*."

Sarge returned a one-finger salute and drove out of the apartment parking lot.

VANCE STOPPED AT THE CUBE, grabbed the cigar box and documents he'd stashed under the driver's seat, and jogged three flights of concrete stairs to his apartment. It didn't make sense for the Aryan Brotherhood to take Chago out; Chago Marino was the biggest cash cow the Brotherhood had ever seen.

If Sarge's sources were right, Chago's son, Greg, with the deformed foot, was the conduit to the money protecting his father on the inside at the high-security prison at Florence. All organizations, even the most despicable ones, function with a code. He understood the drill. Cash was used to bribe guards, maintenance, and medical personnel, enabling the Brotherhood to move goods and services inside. The hierarchy within the cellblock was a delicate environment best left to the inmates. His Uncle Tony should have been on the same block as Chago.

The miles of cocaine snorted up nostrils during the '80s and '90s from Studio 54 in New York to the Rainbow Bar and Grill in Hollywood had a ninety percent chance of having been imported and distributed by the Los Guapos Syndicate.

But their crime stories had different endings, Tony and Chago.

The lump in his throat returned. The funeral. Watching his mother trying her best to manage the grief. The cigar box she'd given him, filled with memories. The document he'd put on the kitchen counter in his apartment: his father's Last Will. It would predict her future. He'd have to detach emotionally while he processed it, then boil it down. He'd have to explain it to her later.

3

LATE FRIDAY NIGHT

HE'D MEANT to lie down for just a minute but must have dozed off. Nose-blind to the smells of unwashed bedding and the sour molds growing inside the walls, he wished his ears were as good at muffling the bass music coming from downstairs. It was a typical weekend late night with the same sketchy characters hanging out, listening to hip-hop in the parking lot. He stuffed a pair of waxy plugs in his ears and tried to sleep.

The pounding on the door was loud enough to wake him. Probably the wrong apartment. He staggered half-asleep and, rolling one hand over his best eye, looked through the peephole. He leaned back, blinking. Squinting, he tried to focus through the glass dot. Being friendly around here could get him nominated for a Darwin Award for sacrificing his life in an amazingly stupid way. He heard a voice. He pulled a plug from his ear and pressed his head sideways against the grimy door.

"Hey, man, open up!" The voice was low, a loud whisper.

He was still in Darwin territory. He stumbled to the couch and fumbled for his 9-millimeter Glock stuffed beneath the cushions. He popped the clip in and stuffed the gun down the back of his pants. He cracked the door with the security chain still in place.

"Come on, man, open up!" The voice was hushed, yet intense. Familiar. Raspy. Slightly accented. Suddenly they were eyeball-to-eyeball through the two-inch gap. But it was dark out.

"Who are you?"

"Come on. Hurry up! Open the door before somebody sees me!"

He pulled the gun and poked it through the crack. "Who are you?"

"Jesus—*Vance!* Open the door! It's Tony!"

He quickly unchained it and his fugitive Uncle Tony slithered inside. Craning his head out into the walkway, he looked left and right, then yanked the door shut and clicked the deadbolt.

Vance narrowed his eyes. He couldn't believe it. Before him stood a man he hadn't seen in over twenty years. His adrenaline pumped. "Damn, we all figured you were dead. What are you doing here? You're on the FBI's Ten Most Wanted List. Oh, man. Interpol, DEA and the FBI are all hunting you." He rubbed his eyes with balled fists. "And the Department of Justice would like to catch you. U.S. marshals will be back on my tail. I couldn't get a haircut for ten years after you disappeared without a Silverado in my mirrors. Shit!"

"I have nowhere else to go. I'm not planning on staying long."

"You're right about that—you're *not* staying. What are you doing here? And how the fuck did you find me?"

Twenty years was a long time to drop off the grid. He'd come to believe Tony was dead. Vance flopped down next to him, raking his fingers through his hair. He hung his head between his knees.

Tony Famosa and Chago Marino had used racing boats and private airplanes to smuggle billions of dollars of cocaine through Florida. They were looking into buying decommissioned submarines from the Russians before their operation went under.

"You can't stay here. I don't want to get caught up in whatever you got going on." What were the chances of Daniel Ruiz and Tony surfacing on the same day? That was too hard to sell to himself as a coincidence.

"How have you been?" Tony asked.

Tony lowered himself onto the sofa next to him and put his hands behind his head. He propped his feet up on the plastic crate doubling as Vance's coffee table. The bronze tone of his olive skin suggested tourist, not fugitive. But he was gaunt with sinewy biceps and forearms, practically a skeleton. There was a smattering of gray in his hair—the good kind—just in front of his ears.

Then the sordid memories washed over him like a tsunami. He was too dog-tired to keep his mouth shut. "Gunning down a federal judge in his driveway, in front of his wife and two little girls? So you guys could get a mistrial?" It was disgusting. "And then sending those pictures?" The U.S. Attorney, a rising star who went on a drinking spree, was photographed stuffing cash in the G-string of a stripper after he lost an "open and shut case" after the judge was murdered. The case ended in a mistrial. The result? Los Guapos was no longer a criminal enterprise that needed to be prosecuted. It was killing machine that needed to be put down.

"I had nothing to do with it. And you know it—"

"Bullshit, Tony." He felt another rush of adrenaline. *Had nothing to do with it?* He sucked air through his nose and exhaled slowly through his closed lips. "Your associates paid for it. With your money."

Tony refused to own it then, and now.

Prosecutors started cutting deals with anyone who'd talk and Tony got lucky. They'd made him a once-in-a-lifetime offer: a reduced sentence of twenty years in prison in exchange for testifying against his partner, Chago. At first Tony refused. Then the first domino fell when Los Guapos's banker, Ramon "Mongo" Solana, turned state's witness after the Feds threatened to charge him with money-laundering and racketeering.

"We need to talk." Tony looked exhausted.

"I don't think so. You need to leave and I need to pretend I never saw you. I could lose my law license. Or worse."

Tony dropped his arms by his sides. "OK, I'll leave. But I don't have to go far."

"Do me a solid. Go as far away as possible, like back to wherever you came from."

His uncle was oddly charming, the way he remembered him, with an infectious smile that started on the left and rolled up and out like the break of a wave. He wore his dark hair down to his shoulders. Even emaciated, he'd aged well with shallow lines fanning his eyes, but the skin beneath them was ashen, sickly. His angular cheekbones cast a flattering shadow across his face, but when his smile waned, the skin hung on his cheeks like tiny awnings. He looked drained.

Tony stood. "Fine. I'll walk home."

He's playing victim? Copping an attitude? "I hope you understand. I can't harbor a fugitive. You're staying somewhere within walking distance?"

"Yeah. I rented the place next door."

"You're kidding, right?"

"No." Tony turned around and knocked on the water-stained wall separating his studio apartment from the one next door.

"You're joking."

"No, *sobrino*."

Sobrino. Tony was playing the old family card, the nickname he'd given Vance when he was just a kid. Spanish for nephew. "Who knows you're here?"

"You do, and maybe the Syrians who made my passport. They're in Cuba now, you know, making fake documents. Thanks to Gitmo. And the Castros."

"Is that where you've been?"

"Gitmo? I wish."

"Not Gitmo. Cuba?"

"*Si.* I got an airline ticket and walked right through Customs at Miami International." His tone changed from one of flippancy to sadness. "Sorry to hear about your *popi*."

"How do you know about that?"

"I'm not dead*, sobrino.* Heard you left Miami homicide and now you're a lawyer."

"You need to leave. You being here is making me a felon." *Would this day never end?* "If someone sees you here, I could be charged with a federal offense. I could go to prison."

"This place is a dump. Handsome man like you in his prime, you should be doing better than this. I could help you." He patted Vance on the cheeks with two hands, stood up, and reached for the doorknob. "I could help us both."

"It beats ADX."

Tony turned to face him. "I just left the world's biggest prison."

Vance looked at him, perplexed.

"Cuba. I should have just done my twenty years here. It would have been easier." Tony let himself out.

Vance heard the door next to his open and clank shut.

VANCE REVIEWED HIS MEMORY. When Mongo Solana turned the banking files over to the government as part of his plea deal, he'd given the Feds plenty to indict Chago and Tony. Handwritten receipts for payments to international assassins, loans to gunrunners, and bills of sale for a pair of single-engine airplanes. Proof of purchase of Ocean Eagle, Inc., a reputable powerboat-builder. All cash deals tied to the Los Guapos drug cartel.

The government's forensic accountants made a stunning discovery. Around a hundred million in cash was missing from the bank's books. The rat-banker denied knowing anything about it.

While Tony sat in jail keeping his oath of silence to the cartel, his wife, Elina, was shot point-blank in the face leaving a Coral Gables beauty salon. Tony flipped out. The judge refused to release him to attend her funeral. He told his lawyers to cut a deal. He turned and testified against Chago.

The motorcade transporting Tony was ambushed en route to begin his twenty-year sentence. A mid-morning shootout ensued and his uncle disappeared. That was the last anyone heard from Tony. His reappearance wasn't random. He was up to something. He had to have a pipeline to information. How else did he know where Vance was living? He didn't hitchhike here.

Tony tapped out some friendly beats on the thin wall separating their adjoining apartments. The place went quiet for the first time ever. It was surreal. The maddening mariachi and booming rap music, screaming babies, street brawling, and domestic disturbances that seemed to run on a never ending loop—all of it went quiet.

———

TONY HAD MADE A VALID POINT. Vance *was* living in low-income housing. It wasn't the plan. He'd moved in as a student during law school and had every intention of moving out once he got his solo practice up and running. But then the Great Recession hit, and the place starting going downhill, and the landlord complained he couldn't afford to do even basic maintenance. A lot of people moved out, and less desirable neighbors moved in.

And Tony was right about another thing. His current situation sucked. He'd been advertising his legal services on the Internet, writing and managing the campaign himself. It wasn't the backstop he'd hoped for, and his law practice was in a freefall. He'd welcome a DUI, an uncontested divorce, even a speeding ticket. Jaywalking. Anything.

He was waiting for the economy to get back to normal. It was mental hell being far less successful than his father—and grandfather. He put it out of his mind. Things would turn around. This was America.

Tony Famosa was back in town, the fugitive co-head of Los Guapos, the most infamous drug cartel in American history. If someone had asked him earlier how his day could possibly get shittier, he wouldn't have been able to come up with anything as good as his fugitive uncle moving in next door.

4

SATURDAY MORNING

LAUREN GOLD WHISPERED in his ear, "If I'd met you first, I wouldn't have two ex-husbands." She giggled. Being able to laugh was a milestone. She sat in front of a wide-screen monitor at her home studio, waiting for a video file to upload to the Web. The progress bar estimated five minutes to upload complete.

"Too bad you're too young. Plus, you don't look like the kind of fellow who'd go for a cougar." She scratched his head. "Come on, Sinbad." She picked up the leash.

The first time she saw Captain Sinbad on the rescue site, he was advertised as a miniature poodle mix. When she went to meet him, she was shocked. The dog was a mess: shaved and covered with wounds still stitched with heavy black thread. He cowered and scratched at the visitation room door, howling for the handler to come and take him back to the metal cage.

Though there was no logic to it, she returned the next day with a doggy sweater and leash she'd bought for the occasion.

Double-checking that she could bring him back within thirty days if it didn't work out, she took him home. Within six months he was so cute he could have modeled for a pet food company. Once he came out of his shell, he was a playful, shameless love bug with personality galore.

Looking back on it, she was in about the same shape as the dog the day she adopted him.

On the days she didn't want to face the world, he'd stand on his hind legs and place two front feet on the edge of the mattress. Then he'd tuck his head between his paws and stare at her face on the pillow. Who could resist those soft brown eyes and that funny, crooked smile?

The dog had done a lot to fill the gaping void of loneliness that set in after Peter walked out. Her first divorce ended mutually and amicably. This recent one had blindsided her and turned her world upside down.

Sinbad hopped on his haunches and snuffled her fingers, then barked just once.

Time for our walk!

She scratched his mop top and clipped the leash to his collar. "Such a big bark for such a little dog." The smile on her face was so big she could feel it. They'd become the best of friends: a heartbroken woman and an abused dog. But the way Sinbad felt about other dogs, that was another matter.

"You're a lot less maintenance than those guys," she said, walking out the door of the condo, past the foyer lined with framed pictures of her jumping horses at Florida A-rated shows. Most were of a gorgeous gray horse that had turned whiter in each photo.

Her Uncle Jack had passed away four months back, and she couldn't figure out what to do with his estate. When she arrived at his Coconut Grove townhouse, the refrigerator insides smelled like week-old pads from raw chicken packaging. Jack had been dead for a couple of days before the fellow next door called the police. He was the kindly neighbor who rolled Jack's trashcan to the street and collected his mail. She was his second call, after the authorities.

Matthew gave her the key and let her in. That scene—the aftermath of Jack dying alone—was pungent and heartbreaking. Dear sweet Jack, her dad's only brother, had been her only family member living in Florida. As a closeted gay man, he'd never had a steady partner, opting for solitude over judgment. She'd spent the holidays with him since the death of both her parents and somehow assumed her relationship with Jack was that of caretaker. While there was some truth to it, why was she so devastated when he passed? Her ex would have blamed it on her uncanny ability to deny reality.

She paid for Jack's cremation and costs to ship his ashes to the family plot in Michigan. Legally speaking, she was squatting in his condo. She'd driven down from West Palm where she was living when she got the news of his passing. Weeks turned into months, and with no sign of a Last Will, she moved her things in and converted the spare bedroom downstairs into her video production studio. The timing was good. Her divorce from Peter was almost final. She'd dragged her feet on the paperwork, but now she was ready to let go.

But the mystery of Jack's estate wasn't moving forward. She riffled through boxes and drawers and files and stacks and stacks of paper trees sprouting everywhere and was no closer to figuring it out. She paid Jack's bills and hadn't heard from any angry collection agencies. She kept the landline going but mostly answered calls from solicitors and robocalls warning about cuts in Medicare and Social Security.

SINBAD WAS terrible on the leash, pulling and spinning like a hooked billfish, barking at everything that moved. She stopped at the end of the driveway as a car sped by. Hurried commuters used the residential side streets for shortcuts to avoid traffic, and the dog was oblivious to the danger. She crossed the street to the gated dog park with the colorful obstacle course and running track circling the perimeter. Sinbad's nose was in overdrive. He was debating between two trees and a hedge when her cell buzzed.

"Lauren Gold."

"Lauren?" the voice said.

"Yes, who's this?" The connection was lousy.

"Ray Dinero. Can you meet me? I know it's short notice."

Sinbad went into a barking frenzy. The dog-walker a few feet away winced. She covered the mouthpiece and shushed the dog, which did nothing to settle him down.

"Hello? Are you there?" Ray asked.

"Yes, sorry." She craned her neck and cradled the phone on her shoulder.

"Can you meet for coffee? I know it's Saturday. But it's important."

"I have a draft of the video for you to see. I'm uploading it now. I'll have it to you in ten minutes, fifteen tops."

Sinbad saw a squirrel and leapt into the air. He jerked her arm. The phone went flying. She caught it mid-air, just in time to hear Ray's response.

"That's great. Can you meet me at the Java Chalet in an hour?"

"Umm. Sure." What else could she say?

Ray was her only client. Lucky for her he'd found her online and hired her to produce a marketing video for his boatyard. She was surprised he was calling now. Even more surprised when he first called in February out of the blue. She hadn't heard from him since she'd moved to West Palm from Miami back in the '90s. Ray paid quickly and didn't dicker over price. An impromptu meeting on Saturday morning was a hassle, but she was grateful for the work.

"God works in mysterious ways," she said to the dog.

Sinbad looked up at her while peeing on a tree stump.

The dog lunged at a car while they were crossing back to the condo—at a tire, to be precise. Poor thing knew nothing of the outside world before he was taken as a cruelty case. She knew because she called the behaviorist when she had trouble house-breaking him. It was so frustrating. For the first month, they spent thirty minutes at the park twice a day where he'd sniff every square foot. As soon as they got home, he'd lift his leg on her favorite chair leg, and then squat. The behaviorist told her hoarders let their animals go potty in the house. Thank good-ness that part was over. She'd been on the verge of returning him to the shelter when he'd had a pee-pee poo-poo epiphany.

She let him off the leash and he curled up at her feet under her desk. The video file had processed and was ready. She copied the link and sent it to Ray.

She reached over and picked up two piles of mail from the credenza. Most of hers had been backed up for months with a double change of address. Her heart skipped when she saw the batch with the yellow stickers that had all arrived in yesterday's mail, all from the IRS. She thought they were Jack's. When she saw her name on them, she organized them by date and opened them slowly. The first one was a tax due notice. The next were lien warnings. The levy notice was a month old. She scanned the amount due. Her mouth fell open. *Ninety thousand dollars?* It had to be some sort of mistake.

Her fingers trembled as she logged onto her personal bank account. She had a negative balance. Three checks had bounced and another over-drafted while she watched the screen, like live

TV. She tried to swallow but her throat closed up. She got out of the chair and paced back and forth in the foyer, glancing at the horse pictures hanging on the walls. Sinbad followed but kept getting under foot. When the confused dog crossed in front of her, she stumbled, and almost fell. She stepped on his paw.

Au! Au! Au! Au!

The high-pitched yelping spiked her anxiety. "Damn it! That was your fault!" She immediately dropped to one knee to apologize. He'd picked up on her stress and was trying to be helpful, following too closely. She stroked him from head to tail and hugged him. "Sweet thing, I'm sorry. It's so not fair to be mad at you."

Arf! Apology accepted! He chased his tail in delight.

Sinbad followed her upstairs but kept a safe distance.

She picked up the mascara wand from the vanity, but her hand shook too much to paint her lashes. *Ninety thousand dollars. No way.* Lauren took a deep breath and ran her shaking fingers through her hair. She stared at her face in the mirror with her hair pulled back. *Get it together, girl.* She'd been in tight spots before. *You'll figure it out. It's got to be some sort of mistake.*

WHEN SHE'D RECONNECTED with Ray three months ago, she was following up on the bid he'd requested to make a marketing video for Bis-Cay-Bay Yacht Sales, his boatyard and yacht brokerage company. When Ray called, he sounded just like he did back when she first met him. For a native-born Cuban, he had no accent, and his vernacular was as all-American as it got. And he talked fast.

"I want our IT guys to have something they can use to help with search engine optimization, the video. Can they rename the files?" Ray rat-tat-tatted.

She kept up, saying they could.

When she first met with him about the project back in February, the young receptionist with razor-sharp black bangs and jade eyes seemed to be expecting her.

"Come with me," the woman said.

Her tone wasn't friendly but she was efficient. Lauren followed her as she marched in six-inch heels toward an office in the middle of the modern stainless aluminum-and-glass showroom. The executive office was empty but the woman walked in anyway. Maybe she was going to call Ray. Lauren had looked around and seen large-framed photos and watercolor paintings of the Ocean Eagle Racing team. The biggest photo was of the *Holly Golightly*, the powerboat Ray had always been partial to. The images of the racing boats flying in the air above the water were all dramatic. The three men in the open cockpit wearing orange helmets, looked small. Lauren snapped into the present when she heard papers rustling. The receptionist was wandering around Ray's office like she was looking for something other than Ray.

"He's not here."

Duh. She kept herself from saying something sarcastic.

"So, he's taking a break on his boat." She sneered on the word *boat*. Half her upper lip followed the upturned nostril, showing teeth so white they flashed blue. "It's at that end of the dock. Look for the *Bookoo Bucks*." She pointed the direction with a glittery blue fingernail.

Walking alone along the bulkhead holding back the brownish-green waters of the Miami River, she passed a huge corrugated metal building with piles of wet sand in front, past fifty-five-gallon, blue-brownish plastic drums stacked near a rusted front-end loader with a scooper full of soupy dredge material. At the very end, in the last slot, she spotted the *Bookoo* docked stern-first in a finger slip.

The double outriggers on the trawler were folded up against the main mast like giant macramé grasshoppers about to jump. The worn netting swayed in the salty breeze. It was a big beauty of a boat, a '50s throwback made of cypress planking. The peeling yellow paint had faded to beige with ribbons of orange rust stains dripping from corroded metal hardware. The wide-nosed bow turned up, like a Chinese junk. She could see why Ray liked it.

She spotted him sitting on a strappy lawn chair at the back of the boat sipping a diet Coke with his knees apart, enjoying the February weather. The plastic cooler next to him was one of the expensive ones she'd seen in the showroom boating shop, a white Yeti that looked out of place on the old trawler.

"Hey, there." Ray jumped up when he saw her. "You don't look a day over twenty-five."

"Still the flirt." He hadn't changed much.

His blondish hair had been thinning at forty. Now a senior, the wispiness seemed perfectly natural. He was a tick over six-foot, barrel-chested with scrawny arms and skinny, bald legs poking out of loose-fitting shorts. His face was a big moon-pie with twinkly hazel eyes that matched the muddy river water. His skin was fair, his teeth slightly yellow. And he applied lip balm compulsively—an old habit. His smile said, 'I'm at home in this skin.'

"Is this your place? The marina and yachts?"

"Yep, all mine. Bought it out of Chapter Seven way back when. Just got done paying it off last year."

"You always loved boats. How long's it been since this thing's been out on the water?"

Ray looked at her, put his hands on his hips, and smirked. "A long time. Can't remember, come to think of it."

"The name," she said. "*Bookoo Bucks*, now that's funny. A

better name for one of those yachts you're selling, not this old thing."

Ray's sparkly eyes narrowed and he grinned, his lips glistening like morning dew.

THIS TIME they were meeting off site at a coffee house, and Ray was already waiting when she arrived. She brought her laptop at the last-minute, figuring she'd make notes about a new project. Or keep track of any changes he wanted to make to the one she'd sent an hour ago. She hoped he'd watched it and liked what he'd seen.

But that's not what he wanted to talk about.

He got right to the point. "I need a favor. I need you to go on a blind date."

"What? You're joking. Right?" She pushed her shoulder-length blond hair behind one ear, and crossed her long legs at the knee and again at the ankle.

"No. You need to join MatchMeUp, the dating site."

"Jesus, Ray, I don't want to do that, online dating. The stories—"

"Come on. It's not a real date." He pulled his phone out and typed something. "He's a nice guy. I just texted you his username. You can sign up for the free trial. You're going to have to get over Peter sooner or later."

Peter? She wasn't even thinking about that. "It's creepy. And I'll have to write a profile, post pictures—"

Ray stopped her. "It's what you do for a living, Lauren. You can do it in like what? Ten minutes?"

"I guess. But why?"

"It's complicated."

"With all due respect, Ray, I need a little more than a 'it's complicated.'"

"It's a favor for an old friend."

"Jeez, Ray, that's weird." A blind date? Blindsided was more like it. A request right out of left field.

"I'll make the weirdness worth your while."

She looked at her phone. "*MileMarker45*. That's his username?"

"Yeah."

She dropped her shoulders and sighed. "He's not an ax murderer, is he?"

Ray looked at her and squinted. "You don't think I'd do that to you. Do you?"

"I don't know." She hoped not. She'd made plenty of bad choices before, all by herself.

"He's very handsome," Ray said. "Sign up and then contact him."

"I have to contact him?" She chewed on the inside of her cheek.

"How else would it work? The sooner you get it over with, the quicker you can take your profile down. Good-looking guy."

"I heard you the first time. Handsome. That's something, I guess." A date. The idea scared her. But it was a ruse, not a real date. She couldn't say no to Ray. Like Sinbad, he'd practically saved her life when he went to the trouble of finding her online and offering her a job, the one she'd just finished. It might be fun, the date. No. It wouldn't be fun. It would suck. But she owed him.

5

SATURDAY AFTERNOON

VANCE POURED wine into a coffee mug lined with reds and browns like tree rings. He tipped it back in his mouth, gulped, and refilled it. He tucked the bottle of cheap cabernet under his armpit and grabbed his iPad. He went back to bed and sprawled atop the worn comforter with his shoes on. Checking for new online dating messages would be a good distraction, a way to unwind. A way to pretend his uncle wasn't living next door.

He deleted another sales pitch from iHarmonize. He resented the company. He'd given their introductory offer a shot in the past. But when he'd gotten to the fifteenth of way-too-many questions, he'd stopped. It felt like he was filling out a tax return while getting a colonoscopy. The geniuses in the marketing department kept bombarding him with spam, as if a bout with early-onset dementia was what stopped him from completing the questionnaire.

It was like fishing, the online thing. He never knew what

might be on the other end of his screen, making it intriguing. When he signed up for his first MatchMeUp free trial, he was hopeful, borderline excited at the prospect of meeting someone suitable. But the reality was different. Almost all the women who messaged him were nonstarters.

Some posted profile pictures of themselves with their daughters. Very poor judgment.

One contender's headline read, "*Independant Woman,*" a fatal typo flaw.

There was a subset that recycled high school yearbook photos, and another group that didn't even bother with pictures, reassuring potential suitors they "*wouldn't be disappointed.*" They were right. Disappointment didn't quite sum up the disillusionment he experienced once, driving eighty miles round trip to meet a woman about the same age as his dead grandmother.

Ones that listed main activities as fine dining and shopping were out. A message from *Wares-Ur-Ink* was another memorable write-off.

Atheists and hardcore Christians scared him equally.

And so did smokers, especially the pot-bellied woman wearing a crop top, her muffin top hanging like blooming dough over the waistband of a pair of shabby cutoff jeans, a cigar clenched between bared teeth.

It wasn't like he was twenty-five and the world was full of optimistic, semi-sane women looking for a soul mate. After a few months he figured a senior dog on a rescue site had better odds of finding suitable human companionship. And tonight was no different. There was nothing in his inbox worth pursuing.

Occasionally he threw out the first line with something pithy like, "Hi—I'm Vance." He did this only if he saw a woman who interested him, and that was usually after three or four mugs of wine. Even impaired, he had a certain discipline. He saved the profiles of the ones who piqued his interest. Then waited 'til morning to cull through them. None looked nearly as good over morning coffee.

If they were passable, he waited another day. After that, he forgot about them. It would be nice to get laid, but that was tricky. The ones who looked easy didn't interest him, and the ones worth pursuing looked like too much work. Separating the real from the fabricated, the oversold from the understated, and the bright from the dull wasn't easy by just looking at a computer screen. Maybe it was because of all the lying. "Over eighty percent lie about something important," isn't that what Sarge said? He'd grown tired of the lineup of twenty-four computerized matches sent daily to his inbox.

His iPad pinged. He opened the cover.

A new MatchMeUp message lit up on the screen. Hmm. He took of swig of wine and tapped on the link. A profile picture of GroveyGirl came up. Sarge was right. The photo was the sale. She was tall and lean, and promising. He enlarged her pictures and was studying them when an instant message popped up: Hi, what's up? The IM startled him. Her Online Now green light flashed. He worked quickly, reading her profile. She'd know he was online because his green light was flashing too.

He typed, I like your profile

Like urs 2, it's my birthday, she messaged back. What's ur name?

Milemarker45.

Know that. OK, 2 can play. Where do you live?

Coral Gables. U?

Coconut Grove. Want to meet at H Mutiny bar tom?

That was forward. Ballsy. Enticing. Sure! What time?

6

See you there. Btw—Happy B-day!

Thx!

That was easy.

GroveyGirl. For Coconut Grove, maybe?

In half her pictures she was either jumping a big white horse or posing with it. He wouldn't tell her he was afraid of them.

The new pics he'd copied from Kathy's Facebook page were paying dividends. GroveyGirl did the inviting. That was refreshing. The newly remodeled, family-friendly Hotel Mutiny in the Grove was a good idea, too. Telling her he lived in Coral Gables was sort of true. So what if that was back in high school, when he still lived at home, a few decades ago. If they met in his actual neighborhood, it would have to be at the mobile taco cart or at the Valero station for week-old egg rolls served up by his buddy, Ahmed.

He was doing his part, contributing something to support the eighty-percent of online liars. The small green dot next to her photo disappeared. A sense of excitement was growing. He had a date with a good prospect. He wanted to study her profile again but didn't want to risk her seeing his green light flashing again.

Vance refilled his wine mug, energized. He picked up the cedar cigar box from the rickety nightstand. The H. UPMANN crest burned into the wooden top looked familiar. He Googled "Upmann cigars." The brothers Upmann, Carl and Hermann, were 18th century German bankers before they were makers of fine Cuban cigars. On the top of the box, the word HABANA was charred and corralled inside a crude octagon burnt into the wood.

He took the box and bottle of wine to the kitchen table where the light hanging from a bare bulb was brighter. He turned it upside down. The contents shuffled. The MADE IN HAVANA-CUBA stamp on the bottom side was the English iteration with a V. He rubbed his thumb along the seams. The tongue-and-groove woodwork was smooth as glass. He lifted the top, the brass hinges still taut. He ran his thumb across an emblem on the upper right corner on the side of the lid, a lion with the initials EMS embossed into the wood. He held the box closer under the light bulb.

THE ORDINARY PRICE OF CIGARS HEREIN CONTAINED
IS INTENDED BY THE IMPORTER TO BE MORE THAN
TWENTY CENTS EACH
NET CONTENTS 25 CIGARS
ENGLISH MARKET SELECTION

HE REMOVED the folded news clippings covering a half-dozen sepia photos. He studied the pictures first: a portrait of his dad as a boy and another as an adolescent. He looked at the picture of his parents on their wedding day. Then he smiled. The way they looked at each other, so young and so in love.

He removed the paperclip holding a World War II draft card to a photograph of a Naval destroyer. His doctor-grandfather, Harold, never talked much about the war other than the Hellcat fighter operations he'd seen on the aircraft carrier, a recall that animated him in an out-of-character way, like a child stepping off a Disney ride.

His grandfather's medical school diploma still smelled like leather. He opened it, the name of every graduate handwritten in calligraphy. He rolled his grandfather's gold wedding band between his thumb and forefinger: perhaps a more appropriate keepsake for his sister Kathy? All the *Miami-Herald* clippings he'd found inside the box were dated February and March 1933.

He studied a fuzzy portrait of his grandfather on a foxed front page of one, next to a photo of Franklin Delano Roosevelt, and beneath them a headline: FDR NARROWLY ESCAPES ASSASSINATION ATTEMPT IN MIAMI. He read another covering the death of the Chicago mayor, Anton Cermak, who'd been struck by a stray bullet. The third showed an expressionless photo of the gunman set to be executed. He studied the face of Giuseppe Zangara. He could have passed as a matinee idol with his angular cheekbones and brooding good looks. FDR was sworn into office; Mayor Cermak died from complications of the gunshot wound meant for the President-elect; and Zangara was promptly electrocuted under the penalty of transferred intent. He knew why his father kept the news clippings.

There was something at the bottom of the box—a watchcase. The brown leather veneer was fragile and peeling. He turned it over and could barely make out the faded gold lettering.

Farrell Jewelers
Serving Miami since 1910

THE OLD METAL hinges were loose and brittle. He opened it gently. The velvet lining had faded to a purplish hue, almost yellow at the seams. A speck of leather flaked off the casing, like dandruff.

Something poked out from under the insert fitted into the top. He picked at it with his fingernail. A small piece of paper chipped off. He took a dull knife from a kitchen drawer and used it to carefully pry it out. The edges of the paper were brittle, the texture of baklava pastry. Fragments drifted onto the table like confetti and sawdust. He assembled them, laying the six pieces out like a puzzle until he could read it:

State of Florida Certificate of Death.

Name of the Deceased: Giuseppe Zangara
    Date of Death: March 20, 1933
    Cause of Death: Electrocution
    Place of Death: Starke, Florida
    Date of Birth: September 7, 1900
    Place of Birth: Havana, Cuba

He'd heard the name Giuseppe Zangara lots of times. The box in his hands brought his grandfather back to life. He heard his gravelly voice, proudly retelling the story about treating the Chicago mayor, and about the night he met FDR. Dr. Harold Courage was just twenty-four years old, a young intern on call at Jackson-Memorial Hospital on the night of the shootings.

"The country was in the middle of the Great Depression, and a big crowd had shown up to hear something inspiring from the President-elect." He could smell his granddad's spicy aftershave. "FDR just came back from a fishing trip. He planned to go home the same night, to New York. He was still the governor. That's how I met FDR. He came to the hospital to check on his friend, the mayor from Chicago. Poor chap was standing on the running board of Roosevelt's car when a thirty eight-caliber bullet hit him in the stomach."

Harold left out parts of the story, parts Vance was reading now for the first time. Reports about how the mayor's doctor— Grandpa Harold—"guaranteed" a complete recovery and was "pleased to report no internal organs or arteries had been damaged."

Anton Cermak died on March 6, 1933, nineteen days after the new president was sworn into office. The reporters didn't hide their disdain for the gunman or grisly details about the execution. Zangara was strapped into the hand-carved oak electric chair at Raiford Prison in Starke, Florida, and electrocuted.

Old Harold lived to be ninety, and up until his death, never seemed tired of the story. "Boy oh boy, was the country lucky the gunman missed the President."

Naturally curious, Vance asked his granddad why someone would want to kill the President. Harold always gave the same answer: "Because Zangara was a communist, a crazy, unemployed, bricklayer from Italy who had it out for the rich capitalists in America."

He put the pieces of the death certificate back into the cedar cigar box, atop the photos, clippings, and watchcase, and set the cigar box back on the bedside table. He stretched out on the musty linens and stared up at the water-mottled popcorn ceiling. Why hadn't he seen the death certificate before now? There must have been some sort of error. Why did it list Zangara's place of birth as Havana, Cuba? Maybe his grandfather had made a mistake. Then again, he'd never mentioned he'd "guaranteed" the wrong prognosis, either. Maybe he kept the death certificate as some sort of trophy?

Vance reran the story in his head over and over. "A bricklayer from Italy who had it out for the rich Americans." He was positive that's what his granddad had said. That's what the newspaper reported, too. Strange. The death certificate said he was born in Cuba.

HE KEPT the curtains drawn out of habit. Tony knocked on the door three times and Vance ignored him. Any contact with him now would constitute a co-conspiracy. He couldn't turn him in, but he couldn't harbor an FBI Ten Most Wanted fugitive, either. Tony had been MIA for two decades. He couldn't expect Vance to just pick things up like none of it ever happened. He also couldn't avoid him forever.

6

SUNDAY

HE WOKE WITH A BANGING HEADACHE, squinting at the streaks of sun bleeding through the thin curtains. He rubbed his temples with his thumbs and rolled onto his back, picking up the iPad next to him. He held it overhead and opened the cover. A message from *GroveyGirl* flashed. He tapped the screen: `See u tonight HH at H Mutiny`. Good thing, technology. He might have forgotten he had a date tonight. He closed his eyes and pondered the meaning of HH. Bingo. Happy Hour. That meant he could bail fast if she was a dud. Nice. She'd had the idea first.

He clicked on her profile. The *online now* light next to her photo flashed green. He snapped his tablet shut. He got up and took two ibuprofen pills from a big bottle in the bathroom cabinet and swallowed them. He shoved the waxy plugs in his ears, pulled the blanket over his head, and went back to sleep.

THE HOTEL MUTINY had been purchased out of bankruptcy the last time in 1999, but not before it hit its bottom as an eyesore and a squatters' paradise. Vance looked it up online and read the recent reviews. They were all good, four and five stars. He hadn't been there since it closed down for the first time in the late '80s. The hotel web site advertised itself as "... *a great family-friendly choice and for travelers interested in nightlife.*" He recalled the original hotel and chuckled at the irony.

He found a Hotel Mutiny blog and read a few old comments. Someone wrote that the club's original disc jockey had passed away, posting a scanned 1980s Polaroid of the DJ in front of an industrial-grade turntable. Someone else asked about the gentlemanly harp player, Alberto, who looked like—and was—a choirboy. No one followed up.

Someone else posted some remarks about the initial bankruptcy, about how the first set of new owners tried to clean up the clientele—an idea that sank the Hotel Mutiny into Chapter 11. Now the hotel was owned and operated by a corporate real estate investment trust.

Vance fished a pair of khakis hanging from a hook in his closet. He pulled them on.

During Miami's days as the epicenter of the cocaine trade, the hotel's Upper and Lower Decks were private clubs, and he got in whenever he wanted to on Tony's VIP membership. During its heyday, the place was packed every night with arms dealers, FBI informants, rock stars, cocaine cowboys, CIA operatives, assassins, gold-diggers, and celebrities, all seemingly content to co-mingle over New Orleans-style barbeque shrimp and Snapper Provençal.

The hotel rooms were a fascinating display of debauchery,

designed with one over-the-top theme after another. He'd been inside the Egyptian Suite with the Roman tub, ivory columns, and mirrored ceiling. He'd seen the Jungle Room, too, decorated with the skins and tusks stripped from endangered wildlife. He'd only heard about the most sought-after room: the Bordello Suite with hardcore porn on videocassettes, a state-of-the-art VHS videotape player—and allegedly—a typed, laminated directory with home phone numbers, photos, specialties, and prices of blue chip prostitutes. Herbie Mann's flute had been stolen from the Saharan Palace Suite when the musician stayed there.

He shot the last two sprays of Paco Rabanne cologne on his shirt.

The first time he'd seen Sergeant Daniel Ruiz he'd been sitting at the Upper Deck bar nursing a beer, conducting a little unofficial police business. Vance overheard Sarge ask the bartender if he'd remembered seeing the missing waitress, Margarita, the night she was murdered. Sarge nodded at him as he'd passed by to use the restroom. Cops do that, sense each other.

Vance cut down 27th Avenue from Dixie Highway to Bayshore Drive.

A third of the Mutiny club regulars were on one half of the law, another third on the other side. Ten percent were upstanding members of the Miami community, oblivious to the underbelly of the place. The rest were hybrids, unscrupulous operators working whichever side suited them on any given day.

When hotel management got wind that Sarge was asking questions about the missing girl, they arranged for his swift departure. He was immediately kicked out when Chago complained to the hostess that Sarge looked like a cop. The head of security, a brute of a guy whose former boss was a deposed

South American dictator, ejected him. The head of security had a reputation to uphold. He'd bounced a pair of CIA operatives from the club once, blowing their cover, calling them "*fucking spooks*" loud enough in his heavy Spanish accent to cause a scene. That guy's career ended when he was gunned down in the Mutiny parking lot. Vance heard about it, but his boss at homicide didn't think the case was high priority. Operatives suspected of working with the cartels were chalked up as getting their comeuppance. That's how his boss saw it, and Vance saw no reason to disagree.

He stopped at the red light and checked himself in the rearview mirror.

A tourist discovered Margarita's body. She hadn't been in the water long. The left side of her body was dark purple where the blood settled. She hadn't drowned. Dry lungs and maroon ligature marks around her neck told the story. She'd been strangled.

The killer had the *cojones* to wrap her in a hotel blanket before he'd dumped her in the Jewfish Creek inlet. Vance had seen the Mutiny logo on Tony's membership card: the outline of a pirate's face with a patch over the right eye, headband, and an upturned mustachio. He'd seen pictures of the crime scene, the same logo embroidered into the gold merino blanket used to cover her dead body.

HE ARRIVED EARLY and parked the Cube on the other side of the street at the marina. He jogged across the grassy median to the hotel. He asked for a table overlooking the water. The view of Sailboat Bay was nostalgic. The mangrove-lined mooring field inside the small inlet opening up to Biscayne Bay was full of sailboats. Vertical masts on dozens of sailing craft jutted out of the water, bobbing like a sea of Popsicle sticks. Vance watched as the last of the Sunday city sailors finished up for the weekend.

A tall, whippet-thin blonde with a delicate nose and mouth sailed into the restaurant and stopped at the hostess stand. She looked a little like GroveyGirl, and Vance hoped she was, but he'd never been pleasantly surprised by an Internet date and had never heard of anyone being pleasantly surprised by one, either. He figured she was there to meet someone else. But no one appeared to be waiting for anyone.

After a short exchange with the hostess, she breezed over to his table. He stood. She reached out and shook his hand. He smiled at her, shaking her hand and squeezing her palm firmly.

"I'm Lauren," she said, letting go and picking up a napkin from the table. "Lauren Gold."

"Vance, nice to meet you."

She sat first.

"What would you like to drink?"

"Club soda. With lime."

"Cheap date. So how long have you been online dating?"

"I'm fairly new at it. And you?"

"Ah, a while, not that long." He was stammering. He didn't want the awkward gap to linger, but he didn't want to elaborate on his online dating, either. "Do you work?"

"I have a small video production business."

"Sounds exciting."

Lauren half-smiled. "Sort of. If you think having people tell you they want to change the color of a room you just painted over and over again while you're still watching the paint dry, then I guess you could say it's exciting. Anyone ever tell you that you look like Harry Connick, Jr.?"

"Anyone ever tell you you look like Gwyneth Paltrow?"

"Once," she said. "But I like to think I'm more likeable."

Her light blond hair was tidy. She was dressed chic yet understated in a pair of designer jeans, a light-red V-neck sweater and matching espadrilles. She got up and excused herself to use the ladies' room. He noticed people watched her as she left the table, men and women alike.

He liked what he saw. She was a hand-shaker. That was interesting, borderline intriguing. At some point he'd have to face up to the lie on his profile about being divorced. But there was no point unless he got a second date. He puffed up and arched his back against the booth when heads in the room turned again and followed her back to his table. He stood when she returned.

She slid back in, opposite him. Her lips looked shinier, like she'd applied gloss. "I used to work here."

"*Here*? Really?" His eyebrows went to full staff, inverted V-shapes.

"Yeah, just before the club closed, a couple of years before I met my first husband and moved to West Palm. My dad helped me get a summer job. He was a club member. A lot of doctors and lawyers and legit businessmen were members, too. My dad had no clue what really went on here. If he did," she paused, "he probably would have tried to get me a double-shift." She laughed. "My dad was not the overly-protective type. Do you remember this place back in its heyday?"

"Barely," Vance lied. "So what did you do here?"

"I was a Mutiny girl."

A Mutiny girl?

Mutiny girls were legendary. They waited tables in Vanna White couture. There was a lot of whispering, wishful thinking, that they were actually prostitutes. They certainly dressed the part, draped in tacky gowns covered with sequins and glittering fabrics that sparkled beneath the clubs' disco balls and candlelight. The girls had to wear hats, some with veils and plumes, and their make-up, heavy on the eyeliner, rouge, and lipstick, did little to dispel the myth they might be for *hire*.

Mutiny girls were pseudo-sommeliers, trained to uncork overpriced bottles of champagne and wine using simple flat silver corkscrews. The girls could bat their eyelashes flirtatiously while opening a thousand-dollar bottle of Château Laffite Rothschild.

"I hope I didn't cast myself in a bad light, telling you that."

"No, no. Well, the Mutiny girl thing, it did throw me a little. The place was, um, notorious."

"I sold nine thousand dollars' worth of Dom Perignon one night. We used to add a twenty percent tip on to the South Americans' tabs. Sometimes they didn't notice and they added another tip, a tip on top of the tip. But the cocaine cowboys, those guys always tipped *big*. The girls knew how to get a room temp bottle of Dom to the perfect forty-three to forty-eight degrees quickly if cases were coming in off a flight. The busboys dropped bottles in buckets of half ice, half water in the back room. Voila, in twenty minutes we were ready to pour the perfect flute."

Her frankness was making him uncomfortable. Not because he suspected she might have been a prostitute or a coke whore. He was feeling uneasy because he'd told another lie right to her face while she was being straight with him.

"I met a waiter who worked at the Jockey Club at the after-hours club, Manhattan. He laughed in my face when I told him how we chilled champagne in a jiffy. He gave me a hard time about *shocking* the champagne. It wasn't like we were putting *puppies* in buckets of ice, for heaven's sake. Plus, the drug dealers were so amped up on cocaine, they chugged hundred-dollar bottles of champagne like Kool-Aid."

She wasn't making this stuff up. He knew from Tony the

hotel management had cases of Dom Perignon flown air courier from Seattle when the Los Guapos high-rollers pulled all-nighters. On lots of occasions, they drank the hotel's entire supply of top-shelf champagnes in just hours. With mountains of illicit cash on hand, they had to find ways to spend it.

"Anyway, this place used to sell thirty thousand dollars of fine champagne on any given night. I'm pretty sure the dealers wouldn't have known Dom from André in a taste test." She laughed out of the side of her mouth. "The Jockey Club waiter, he was just jealous. The Hotel Mutiny didn't hire *boys.*"

He remembered watching the girls pushing their way through the packed, smoky rooms in their evening gowns and fancy hats, hoisting heavy trays of chateaubriand, soufflés, and Red Snapper Provençale above their heads with both arms. And they were making more money than most entry-level attorneys, and almost all of it was cash.

Vance wanted to ask Lauren if it was true that management checked their fingernails before they clocked in for work. Instead, he asked, "Would you like another club soda? Or is one your limit?"

"I'll have another. And please don't tell anyone."

"Who cares if you drink club soda?"

"No, not that, that I was a Mutiny girl. All those drug dealers and FBI agents. Rather sordid, all of it, really. I didn't know any better. I was barely old enough to drink. So what do you do, Vance?"

He pulled a business card from the top pocket of his shirt.

"Seriously?" She stared at his card. "Your last name is Courage? And you're a lawyer?"

"Yep."

"What kind of law do you practice?"

"I do a little bit of everything. I represent the plaintiffs. I handled an EPA Superfund case once. Last year I won a case against a bug extermination business that was selling fraudulent franchises. Really, it's just run-of-the-mill stuff. It's not very interesting."

"So basically you're a personal injury attorney. An ambulance-chaser."

"Yeah, well, lately it feels more like I've been chasing lawnmowers. My clientele isn't exactly upmarket."

"Riding or self-propelled?"

"Cute."

She thought so. She threw her head back and covered her mouth with two hands to keep from laughing too loudly. It was just fine with him that she thought he was joking.

"I speak about five words in Spanish. A lot of clients don't come see me because they don't speak English."

"So why don't you learn?"

"I'm stubborn." At least he was being honest about that.

"I don't speak much, either. Up in West Palm, it's not a big deal. But working here in Miami, it can be a big disadvantage."

She talked and he listened, studying each expression and gesture. He was practically in a trance when he realized she'd been asking him why she had to ask the same questions twice to get an answer. "I don't want to bore you any more with my chit-chat," she said, getting up.

He scrambled to his feet. "Can I, um, get your number?"

She set her messenger bag on the tabletop, riffled through the contents. She was digging through the bottom, turning things over like garden dirt.

"Here," she said handing him her business card.

He looked at it. "I'll call you."

"I like text better. If you don't mind." Her tone was curt.

He did mind. He hated typing sentences on a little screen. "OK. I'll text you."

He finished his beer while waiting for the waitress to bring the check. He watched her through the big picture window overlooking the bay and noted her walk was purposeful, like she was in a hurry, as she crossed the street. He'd blown the date. He didn't even think to wish her a belated happy birthday. It was his fault she'd misread him. It wasn't boredom that had pulled him away from the conversation. In fact, he was enthralled with her. There was just so much shit piling up in his life it was hard to concentrate. It wasn't her fault it didn't go well. It was his.

HE SLIPPED his key into the apartment deadbolt. The mid-May evening humidity was brutal and the door handle was slippery. Footfalls came up from behind him in the darkness. His cop instincts kicked in. He spun, drawing his gun from under his arm. Acting on reflex, he gripped the Glock with both hands, arms outstretched. A silhouette appeared. He aimed the red laser at the stranger's thigh. Not a kill shot, but something to stop whoever was stalking him on the walkway.

"Hey! Hey!" Tony stepped out of the shadows, beneath the misty yellow light. He held both hands up. "Take it easy."

"Jesus, you'll get yourself killed like that. That would make a hell of a headline, 'Lawyer Shoots his FBI Ten Most Wanted uncle at Casa del Crapbox.'"

"Sorry. I didn't mean to scare you. I've been waiting for you. Can we talk?" Tony had on the same clothes, now rumpled as though he'd slept in them. But he looked rested. Less battle-fatigued.

"I don't know why you're back, and I don't want to know."

"*Oye*, we're blood, *sobrino*. I need some help. That's what family's for, right?"

The family card again. "Isn't there another relative, or someone else's life you'd like to fuck up?"

"Doesn't look like you have much of a life. Not much to fuck up, if you ask me."

"No one asked you." Vance unlocked the door.

"Can I at least watch TV at your place?" Tony pushed his way inside. "Is it true Major League Baseball has its own channel?"

Vance used two fingers to spread the thin vinyl blinds covering the window looking out over the parking lot. "I think I'm under surveillance."

A white SUV drove slowly through the complex. It rolled to a gentle stop across the street, a few feet from the glowing streetlight. "Take a look for yourself. If I go to prison for aiding and abetting a fugitive, you're going with me. And there's a whole litany of other laws I'm breaking right now. Would you like me to lay it out from the point of view of a cop or a lawyer?"

"Is there a difference?" Tony asked.

"I know you have something up your sleeve. I wasn't interested then, and I'm not interested now." He poured red wine into the stained coffee cup.

"I could make you a very rich man. You could move out of this dump."

He didn't answer. He was in a tight spot money-wise and naturally he was intrigued. But whatever it was that could make them both rich could also land him in prison. Or worse.

Tony peeked out through the slats of the blinds covering the front room window. "How can you live in this place? In Castroland, no one has a choice. But you do. You have lots of choices."

"This one beats prison."

"Not by much."

It was worth considering. How much *did* his current situation beat prison? He handed Tony the television remote. "Do me a favor, don't look out my windows." He went into the bedroom and closed the door. He picked up his tablet and opened the cover. Three new women had "Favorited" him. He skimmed their photos and hit delete. An instant message popped up:

So when r we going out again?

Wow! He was surprised to hear from Lauren already. Maybe the date hadn't gone as badly as he thought.

He pecked out a reply: Soon.

How about tomorrow? Same place?

He thought for two seconds: What time?

7ish?

He pinged her: Looking forward to it.

He searched the legal definition of harboring a fugitive on a government website. Federal statute 18 U.S.C. § 1071 had four elements of proof.

1. Proof that a federal warrant had been issued for the fugitive's arrest. *Check.*

2. The accused had knowledge that the warrant had been issued. *Check.*

3. Proof that the accused actually harbored or concealed the fugitive. *Check.*

4. That the accused intended to prevent the fugitive's discovery or arrest. *Hmm, open to interpretation.*

But any prosecutor worth his salt would bring charges against him, especially considering his background as a cop. Add that he was a practicing lawyer. That would make his defense all but impossible.

He looked up the penalty for harboring a fugitive: one to five years in a federal penitentiary. Maybe Tony was right. Maybe his world really was on par with prison life. They'd led two very different lives up to now and ended up in the same place: his dumpy apartment in a low-class neighborhood. He might end up in prison after all, for harboring a fugitive. But there was one thing for sure. There was no way he was turning his uncle into the authorities, and if he kicked him out now, he'd be throwing him to the wolves. Tony would likely turn to Sophia, and that would pull Vance's mother into it, too.

4. That the accused intended to prevent the fugitive's discovery or arrest. *Check.*

7

MONDAY

MORNING RUSH HOUR traffic was more stop than go. He arrived at his Bird Road office a half hour late.

A squat and disheveled Hispanic woman with three barefoot children was camped out on the stoop. He politely excused himself as he waded through them.

The woman pushed her way toward the door alongside him. She had a large mole on her upper lip with a pair of curly black hairs growing from it. "I being kicked out."

He stood sideways in the doorway, making way for her and her kids, pressing his back against the frame to avoid body contact. He closed the door behind them, before more humidity could invade the small building. He glanced at the large picture window and saw a dark Mercedes sedan pulling into the drive-way. The driver backed into a spot next to the Cube.

"It America. They no can kick me out." The mother reached

into her plastic Prada purse and handed Vance a crumpled notice with a sheriff's logo on the header.

Vance looked it over. "If you don't pay your rent, the sheriff can evict you." To help make it clear, he said it another way. "The landlord can evict you after three days of non-payment."

"I only one day late."

Her youngest child, a boy who appeared to be about four years old, smiled sweetly.

"This notice is three months old." He handed it back to her. "Here you go." He opened the front door to usher her out, gesturing in a way that left nothing ambiguous about which direction he wanted her to go. "'Bye, 'bye. *Adios,* have a nice day."

"Lollipop!" the oldest child demanded, pointing at a jar of ancient, colorful blow pops.

"Sure." Vance grabbed three time-softened lollipops and handed one to him, and the little monster grabbed all three before he could pass them around to her other kids. "'Bye now, you have a lovely day."

"Miami sanctuary city!" the woman shouted from the stoop. "You no kick me out."

"Off you go." He waved them away with the backs of his fingers in an effeminate gesture.

He had his hand on the lock when the woman pushed the door back open. "Screw you, you *caca!*" She wadded up the notice and threw it onto the porch along with the taco wrappers, empty plastic drink bottles, and other piles of litter.

"Yeah," her feral pack chimed in unison, "*caca.* You *caca.*"

"Doodle-do." He stuck his thumbs under his armpits and flapped his elbows.

"Not bad improv," commented a man who'd just ambled up the walkway. He tiptoed around the trash on the doorstep grinning, carrying *The New York Times* folded between his left elbow and ribs. "Looks like you're having a fun day at the office. I made an appointment on your website. Jake Fleming." He offered his hand for a hearty shake.

He was dressed like he was about to leave for Martha's Vineyard, wearing pastel-green, pleated cotton shorts, a pale-pink-and-white-striped, button-down, long-sleeved shirt, a fabric belt with small repeating whales circling his waist, and no socks. His voice had an unnerving horror movie character tone to it.

He was about four inches taller than Vance, but they looked eye to eye because Jake was hunch-backed, like a candy cane, the kind of posture that comes from decades of sitting in front of a computer. His head was too big for his broad shoulders and hung down from his neck like a grizzly's.

"Vance Courage. How do you do, come on in." He sat down on his side of the desk, facing the doorway leading to the foyer. "You're a breath of fresh air. Have a seat."

"Your website says you practice employment law. And I believe I have a work situation."

"You should know Florida is a Right to Work state."

Jake nodded. "I know. I did a little reading. Thought I should talk to a lawyer."

"So what's going on?"

"Well, I've been selling cars at a local dealership. A while back, a woman came over from Sarasota to test drive a used BMW she saw on our website. I remember distinctly because I had to stay until ten o'clock that night, finishing up her paperwork with the finance office. Anyway, she's had all sorts of problems with the car, and we don't have a dealership in Sarasota and it's cost-prohibitive for us to service it. I've been trying really hard to help her out. The car wouldn't even start a couple of times. I finally went to see one of the sales managers and told him they need to fix the deal.

"I suggested they give the woman her money back or replace the vehicle. Since I'd been going 'round and 'round with them for weeks about it, I told my manager the deal was a tar baby, and I went back to my office. Two hours later, the sales managers, two of them, came in my office and terminated me—for a racial slur."

Vance burst out laughing. "Well, sorry to say it, but you might be the first person in history to be fired for being literate."

"Exactly. Thank you. So what are my options?"

How could Vance explain it? Shouldn't it have been obvious? He shouldn't have laughed. This new world was a tough one for white men to navigate, and he had to choose his words carefully. "You're not a protected class."

Jake leaned forward. "What exactly does that mean?"

"Well, certain classes of people are considered protected classes."

Jake furrowed his brow showing deep lines. "What? Like an endangered species?"

"That's as good an explanation as I've ever heard."

"You're saying I don't have the same equal employment protections?"

"That's right," Vance said.

"When did that happen?"

"The laws have changed over time. The Equal Employment Opportunity Commission protects the rights of workers."

"But not mine. Are you serious? Even if I was fired without cause?"

"Yes. Sorry to say." He wanted to tell Jake that he *should* have recourse, and personally, he didn't think it was fair since he believed that Jake had no ill intent. Instead, he said, "You don't have a case. Even if you did, your employer would have to insist it was a racial slur. Otherwise, they would admit wrongdoing, and that would leave them open to paying damages. That's the legal game. Are you following me?"

Nodding, Jake reached into the monogrammed pocket of his

shirt and got out his black-framed reading glasses. He read aloud from his phone screen. "'*Tar Baby. Something from which it is nearly impossible to extricate oneself.*' That's the Merriam-Webster definition." Then he tapped the screen again. "Here's something more contemporary, from Wiktionary: '*A difficult, abstract problem that worsens when one tries to handle it.*' The problem with the used BMW was not one of *abstraction*. It was a fucking electronic nightmare."

"You can get another legal opinion. I feel your pain, and I believe you meant nothing racial, but you don't have a case. Was the customer, the one who bought the car, African American, by any chance?"

"What difference does that make?"

"It shouldn't, but it does."

"Yes." Jake leaned against the chair back. He ran his fingers through his slick black hair and locked his hands behind his head. Then he crossed one bare leg over the other, resting a swollen ankle atop the opposite knee, pointing the well-worn sole of a Gucci loafer at him. Jake's front teeth were big and slightly off center. He still had the kind of boyish looks that could belie his age, but the news he'd just gotten had put a couple of dog years on his face.

"You screwed up. I get that it was an accident, but these days you have to be extra careful with the words. But let me buy you lunch. It's not every day that intelligent life walks through my door. Not that what I think what you said to the sales manager was very smart, because I don't." They probably let him go for other reasons, but Vance decided to take his own advice and keep his mouth shut.

"I certainly didn't mean to insult anyone." He had a Jack Nicholson thing going on. "I'm fifty-eight-years-old with an MBA from a top school, and I can't find a decent job."

"Off the record, a jury would not find you to be a sympathetic character. They would probably dislike you. And they would hate me, too, for representing you."

"It's hard, this aging process," Jake said. "In some ways the world is much cruder and in other ways it's much more sensitive. It's hard for a man my age to navigate. I hope you know I meant nothing derogatory. I minored in English in college."

They walked across the street to the café serving Cuban sandwiches.

Jake told him he'd been an investment banker in New York City for thirty years. Earned his MBA from a top Midwest college and was recruited right out of school to work for an energy group in Houston. He moved to San Francisco and then to New York, making it to Managing Director in eight years. Worked for Jeffries. Solomon. Goldman.

"I'm divorced from my second wife," Jake said. "She wanted me to retire after we had the kids, my second set. At one point we had a co-op in New York, a house in Greenwich, and a vacation place in the Hamptons. I always thought Greenwich had nice beaches, but I was a rat-racer. I was on board with the early retirement plan. We sold everything and moved to North Carolina with eleven million dollars in the bank. Thought I could enjoy life. My dream was to invest in real estate. I was leveraged up the wazoo when the housing bubble burst. We lost everything.

"My kids are thirteen and fifteen. They have a long road in front of them. My son from my first marriage just graduated college, so I have a pretty good idea what it's going to cost. My second wife has family here. Then oil and gas prices tanked, and I figured I wouldn't get another at-bat at big league in investment banking. It's a young man's game or an old lions' den. That's how it's turning out and why I took that two-bit job at the dealership. I'm not whining. But it's tough out there. Did you know the highest suicide rate in the nation is for white middle-aged men? I see why. And no one cares. I guess I'm just collateral damage for social justice."

He listened to Jake drowning in self-pity. It was a good reminder not to go down the same path.

"Maybe we only get called up to the big leagues once," the old lion said.

"I wouldn't know. I'm waiting to be called up to the peewees." He was trying to imagine what Jake's fall from grace and prestige must have done to the man's ego. Then again, how many people know what it's like to retire with millions in the bank and then blow it on real estate? At least he hadn't blown his brains out.

"You got any kids?" Jake asked.

"Nope. Never been married."

"I'm just trying to build up enough money to put my two kids through school." He pulled out his phone and showed him a picture of his son and daughter, the boy older than the girl. "When I first went back to work, I got a job at a small investment firm and transferred to Houston. I thought the job wasn't good enough. I was used to flying first class to Houston from New York and staying at the Four Seasons. Then right after I moved to Texas a couple of years ago, oil tanked to under thirty bucks a barrel and I was laid off. I couldn't find work so I came to Miami so I'd at least be closer to my kids and could help my ex out. Felt horrible being an absentee dad. On a positive note, I love the water. And the weather."

"The only thing I know about oil and gas is that regular is around three bucks a gallon and the cap on my car is on the passenger side. And everyone here likes cheap gasoline, but they don't want oil platforms popping up anywhere they can see them from the shoreline."

Jake picked up the paper menu and put his glasses on. "Does this place serve good mojitos?"

"I don't think so."

"Then I'll have a beer."

"The place doesn't have a liquor license."

Jake sighed.

A text message pinged on Vance's iPhone: `Meet earlier? Wrapping early. 6? Same place?`

He apologized to Jake for poor etiquette, for looking at his phone, and messaged Lauren back: `Sure—Mutiny.`

"What a pity."

"I know," Vance said. "Getting fired like that."

"No, I was talking about no liquor license. That's a pity."

Jake handed him a business card. It was engraved on fancy stock. A line had been neatly drawn through a New York address and replaced with a Miami address handwritten beneath it, a place on Brickell Avenue. "The phone number is my cell. I got a line on another car sales job. You never know when you might need a new used car."

Vance slid Jake's business card behind the one credit card in his wallet, the slot he put the ones he planned on keeping.

The busboy delivered plastic glasses filled with ice water. Jake reached across the table and picked one up. The stainless and gold Rolex swinging from Jake's wrist reminded Vance of the watchcase in the cigar box, and the odd death certificate. And Tony. When Jake walked through the door, he'd hoped his luck would change, but Jake's situation was bleaker than his.

As VANCE WALKED BACK to his office alone, his phone vibrated in his pocket. Sarge. He didn't answer. His phone pinged: `Ur VM full again - Call me.` Sarge couldn't leave a message because Vance had never deleted a message in the five years he'd had the phone. It buzzed again. This time he answered.

"So, meet any interesting women lately?"

"What's with the sudden fascination with my private life?"

"I care because I'm your friend."

"Right. I don't hear from you for a couple of decades, and all of a sudden you want details about my dating life. Some men just can't stand to be alone."

"So I'm a dog—"

"And a voyeur."

"Is that the name of a new dating app? Sounds interesting."

He crossed the street on the red light and had to jog when the approaching vehicle sped up. It looked like the white SUV, the Escalade he'd seen at the cemetery. But there were thousands just like it in Miami. The African-American woman behind the wheel wore aviators that reflected a beam of sunlight, like a laser. He squinted, temporarily blinded. "I have a date tonight," he said, shielding his eyes. "Should I call you and give you a full report later?"

"Please do."

"Not a chance." Vance ended the call.

⁓

HE LEFT the office at five-thirty to meet Lauren and parked Edgar at the marina across the street. When his phone hummed, he expected Sarge, but it was his sister, Kathy. Lauren pulled up behind him. Sticking his arm out the car window, he held up one finger, then pointed to his phone. He made a V-formation with two fingers hoping she'd know he meant he needed two minutes. She zipped into an open spot and parked.

"Hi, how are you?"

"Great." Kathy was her usual *positivity* self. "Busy with the kids. And you?"

"Same old, same old."

"That's good. Hey, I was wondering if you could help me out

with something. I hate to ask last-minute, but something came up and Larry's going out of town tomorrow. I have a doctor's appointment I can't change. Can you pick the boys up from school and drop them at Mom's? She can watch them, but it's too complicated for her to pick them up."

"Sure, yeah, text me the address and time and I'll do it." He watched Lauren cross the median.

"Mom was wondering if you had a chance to look at Dad's stuff. I don't know if you talked to her yet."

"Not yet. But I will. Is everything OK with you?"

"Oh, just some tests. I'm sure it's nothing."

"What kind of tests, Kat?"

"It's nothing really." She paused. "Just a PET scan."

"What for?"

"I don't want to scare the kids. That's why I'm asking my big brother for help. If Mom or the kids get wind of it, it'll worry everyone."

"Does Larry know?"

"Yeah, but it's a work thing. He can't get out of it."

"All right. Send me the info. I won't tell Mom, and I'll talk to her about Dad's stuff as soon as I have time to look it over."

HE SAT in the car for a couple of minutes. PET was short for *positron emission tomography*. He'd taken a case on contingency right after he went into private practice. The spokeswoman for the group, a fortyish female PhD chemist, was worried about her sister whose hair had fallen out. A lot of people living close by were getting sick too, with similar symptoms. They were living next to an EPA Superfund site but had never been told. The judge ordered the defendant, a barge-cleaning company, to pay for DNA tests. The PhD took it personally. Her sister had been diagnosed with medullary thyroid cancer, a type that's either environmental or inherited. The defense was insinuating the twenty-two plaintiffs living within a half-mile radius of one another were inbred. That made the chemist with the doctorate degree very mad.

When the DNA tests came back proving otherwise, that none of the defendants were related, the judge ordered the defense to pay for PET scans. Radioactive glucose was used as a tracer to search for cancer cells that show up as bright yellow spots on radiology reports. He was stunned when he saw bright yellow dots on the necks of ninety percent of the litigants. They all tested positive for the same medullary thyroid cancer. Groundwater tests showed high levels of benzene and vinyl chloride. It turned into a major environmental lawsuit, and a big box firm stepped in. He got an eighty thousand dollar cut when the case settled out of court. It was the rainy day fund his office was burning through just trying to keep the doors open.

He had a good idea why Kathy's doctor ordered a PET scan. But she seemed unworried, almost upbeat. *Positive*. That business about Larry not being able to accompany her was crap. Kathy's husband worked for a Fortune 100 company. All Larry had to do was ask permission to go with his wife, and if they declined or retaliated, unlike Jake's case, Larry's lawsuit would be a bonanza.

───────

"Sorry about that." He slid into the booth opposite Lauren. She'd picked a table with a panoramic view of Sailboat Bay.

"No problem. Men can't multitask. There's scientific data about it. The brain hemispheres are separated by a neurological Grand Canyon."

"Whatever that means." The conversation with his sister was

repeating in his head. A PET scan? The last thing he needed was a distraction while Lauren was giving him a second chance. He opted for some small talk. "At least they kept the views intact when they remodeled the place."

"Huh? I thought you said you barely remembered this place."

Backpedaling, he said, "I guess I didn't want to make a bad first impression."

She furrowed her brow. "Oh, so you just let *me* make the first bad impression. Gee, thanks."

"So you're divorced. For how long?"

"Which time?"

"More than once?" He was surprised.

"Twice." She said it matter of fact, not the least bit self-conscious. "And you?"

The lie on his profile was about to catch up with him. He felt the blood rush to his face.

She picked up on his discomfort. "Oh, my gosh. More than two times, that's impressive. So how many times?"

"Um." He lowered his voice to a loud whisper.

She craned her neck closer to hear him.

"I've never been married."

"Oh," she said recoiling. "Did you say you've never been married?" She leaned to the left and gave him a sideways glance, crinkling her nose.

He rolled his head slowly from side to side.

"Why not?"

"I don't know. Why have you been married twice?"

"Because they asked me."

"That's romantic, and so touching. Your profile says no kids. Why not?" He saw a white Escalade in his periphery surfing the lot across the street where they'd both parked. He wanted to look over at it, but he didn't dare break eye contact with her while she was sharing personal information.

"I'm old-fashioned. It's too easy for people to split up. My dad left when I was three. My parents had a bad divorce. Plus, I grew up in the middle of the feminist and zero population growth movements."

"Motherhood is back in."

"Why do we do what we do?" She sighed. "People get together for all kinds of reasons. I've decided ending up with someone who will tough it out for the long haul is dumb luck as much as anything. The older we get, the smaller the number of available people gets, as in good available people, which is depressing. And people get crazier too. Or maybe they just stop trying so hard to hide it."

Unable to stop himself, he peeked out the window, hoping she wouldn't notice. The Cadillac SUV driver stopped behind Edgar. If he'd had a set of binoculars, he'd have used them to see if it was the same woman who'd sped up in the crosswalk earlier, the one wearing aviators he'd seen when he was walking back to his office from lunch with Jake.

"What do you think?" she asked.

"About what?"

"Are you even listening?" There was a hint of irritation in her voice. "This is what I meant when I said men can't multitask. What are you looking at?"

"I'm sorry. I've had a rough few days. My father passed away." He folded his hands and placed them on the table. "His funeral was the same day you messaged me. I didn't want to say anything. It would have been poor form on a first date. I didn't want to spoil it."

"Gosh, I'm so sorry. I had no idea." He'd knocked her off balance. "We can get together in the future, when things are, um —better?"

"No, no. These two dates are the best thing that's happened to me in a long time. Let me put it another way. If you can—please don't end our date now. I love your company. It's helping me, not being alone. Plus, I get to look at a beautiful woman."

"OK."

"Why did you move back to Miami?"

"A couple of months ago my uncle died. We were very tight. I came back to settle his estate, but I still can't find his will."

"That's a tough break." At least his father had left one, and it reminded him that he couldn't put off looking at it forever. He abruptly changed the subject. "Did you know Chago Marino and Tony Famosa?"

"The Los Guapos kingpins? Hmmm. Never heard of them." She put an unpolished fingernail on her temple. "Seriously? Of course I knew them. Everyone knew them. Whenever they came in the club, the managers practically parted the Red Sea. They were high-rollers. They used to order expensive champagne and ask for *cups*, not glasses. We joked about it privately, in the back room, of course. Not to their faces. But can you believe that?"

He wondered how red his face was because it felt like it was on fire. "How long did you work there?"

"A year and a half. I was eighteen when they hired me. I was fired before I turned twenty. It was supposed to be a summer job but we were making so much money—"

"Fired? Why?" Talk about candor. If only he were as comfortable with the truth as she was. How was he going to be honest about his connections to the old hotel now that things just got a lot more complicated? She clearly remembered Tony.

"They never said and I never asked. But I'm pretty sure it's because I was paying the cashier on the Upper Deck under the table to get the high-roller tables. She sat in this little cubby right by the kitchen door. Nothing got by her, including over-cooked steaks sent back to the chef.

"Anyway, she hinted if I cut her in for a percentage of my tips, she'd make sure I got the best tables. She used to pretend like it wasn't going on, saying things to the other girls to make them think it was a coincidence that some girls randomly got the best tables all the time."

"So you think they fired you for gaming the system?"

"That was part of it. But there was another thing. One of the girls disappeared from the club. The hotel had a strict policy about not hiring Spanish-speaking girls. But they made an exception when the owner was in town and happened to see Margarita applying for a job. She was wearing my clothes when they found her. She borrowed a pair of white pants and a red-and-white-flowered shirt, and that's what she was wearing when they found her body. There was a lot of hush-hush talk about it at the club, that she was murdered."

"She was wearing your clothes?"

"Yes."

Something wasn't sitting well with him. A lot of coincidences were piling up, and the Hotel Mutiny was the common denominator. Now she had his full attention. "Do you know who killed her?"

"No. We all had our suspicions. But I don't know for sure. There was a big cover-up. She had just signed a modeling contract with one of the big agencies in New York. She had a six-month-old baby and was married to a regular guy who worked for the phone company. She was going to quit working at the club. One time we were in the ladies room and two customers, middle-aged women, literally stopped in their tracks in front of the mirror where she was touching up her lipstick. One of them said, 'My lord, you are beautiful, young lady.' Margarita smiled and politely thanked them. She used to stay away from the club unless she was working. She tried to get the early shifts so she could go home to take care of her baby.

"When the police and some reporters from the Herald came to the club asking questions, management was not cooperative. Since it was members only, the managers kicked the cops out. Then they held a staff meeting and told all of us if we talked to any reporters or investigators, we'd be terminated. I was glad when they fired me, if you want to know the truth. Covering up the murder of an innocent young mother. That's just wrong."

"I heard about it. Before I was a lawyer, I was a homicide detective."

She leaned back against the booth, her eyes wide. "Really? Do you remember when the Herald did an investigative report, a big spread in the Tropic section of the Sunday paper?"

He nodded.

"I showed it to my dad. He thought it was a PR stunt to get the hotel some free publicity. He didn't believe the place he liked to have Sunday brunch would conspire to cover up a murder. He pooh-poohed me when I told him it was true, that I knew the girl who was killed."

"Maybe the Herald was trying to get someone to come forward."

"Maybe. But it's still a cold case, as you detectives like to call them. If the cops interrogated the night managers, that might have led to the killer, or killers. Rumor had it a 'Mr. Green' checked into the room. It wouldn't have been that hard to figure out which room was missing a blanket."

"Mr. Green was obviously an alias."

"Obviously." She used a cocktail napkin to dab the corners of her mouth. "That's probably *way* too much information for a second date."

"At least you didn't bash your exes. That's refreshing. What's wrong with a little mystery and intrigue?" He caught the insensitivity of his remark. "Not to discount the loss of your friend."

"That was a long time ago," she said. "I was friendly with one of their pilots. The same night Margarita disappeared, the guys were stressed out about something, huddling at the table, deep in a conversation. Then I saw a story on the news about a drug bust in Clewiston—a Cessna single-engine plane was seized packed with a hundred kilos of cocaine. The pilot ditched the plane in a field and ran on foot. The next time I saw the pilot, his face and arms were scratched up pretty badly. It crossed my mind that it might be him. But then I thought, no way."

"Why did you think it wasn't him?"

"I guess I just didn't want to believe it. He was always such a nice guy."

"Do you think it *was* him?"

"I do now. I saw a documentary on NatGeo. I was channel surfing and almost tipped over. There he was, on camera, recounting his life as Los Guapos's drug pilot in an interview. The producers reenacted some of the scenes. It was like a war movie. I could barely watch it. A little birdy on my shoulder kept telling me it couldn't be true. But there was Ray on TV, telling his story. My ex says I have a PhD in denial."

He'd never heard about the documentary. Definitely he'd have watched it. But until recently he hadn't given much thought to the old days. The prosecution was cutting so many deals back then, Ray Dinero must have gotten a good one.

"Los Guapos had a banker who used to come to the club," she said. "Sometimes he paid the tab with the bank's corporate credit card. A mean-looking guy whose eyelids hung down. Not from age, just flaps of skin, and he had terrible acne scars. He used to come in with Ray. Sometimes Ray worked at Ocean Eagle, the boat-building company Tony and Chago owned. The company built the hulls for the Guapos' offshore racing boats. Their cartel already owned S and A Engineering, the powerboat engine-builder, S and A for Santiago and Antonio. Sometimes they'd bring legit Ocean Eagle clients to the club and entertain them. On those nights, it was champagne, no drugs, of course. Did you know the Los Guapos higher-ups raced powerboats?"

He glossed over her question. "You sure know a lot. Were you his girlfriend? The pilot?"

"No." Lauren looked offended, then laughed out of the side of her mouth. "He was too old for me. He paid me to run a few errands for him and he paid well. Perfectly legal odd jobs, like getting his car washed. After I got fired, I didn't see him for a really long time. Plus, he had a young girlfriend, a Florida bumpkin named Holly."

He was digging himself into a very deep hole. But he was in too deep so he kept right on digging. "Do you remember the banker's name?"

"Yeah. Ramon Solana. They called him Mongo, a stupid typical Cuban nickname. He was at the club the night she disappeared, prowling around. He was scary, like a sociopath. No, more like a psychopath. I heard on the news that he turned over Los Guapos's bank records and did time in a Club Fed somewhere. I think he's out now. So many bad things happened at this place. Maybe it wasn't such a good idea to come here." Her expression turned somber.

"No, look around. It's almost cheery. It's a shadow of its old self, a family-friendly place now." His phone pinged. "Excuse me for a sec." Shielding the screen under the table, he read a text from Sarge.

Imp. Will stop by your place in 20. Need to talk.

That wasn't happening. He answered: Not home. Where r u?

Sarge texted: Gun club—meet me in 20 mins.

Under any other circumstances he would have said no. But something strange was going on. All these people were popping up, and he was sitting in an old haunt with someone somehow connected to his past. His uncle had magically appeared on his doorstep. The woman across from him knew Tony. "Hey"—he looked up at Lauren who still appeared downcast—"I hate to be rude, but I have to cut this short." He cupped his phone in his hand and held it up. "It's a work thing. Duty calls."

He walked her to the lot across the street where they'd parked their cars.

"I'm really sorry about your dad. I'm glad you told me. The first time we went out, I thought you weren't interested in me because you seemed like you were, um, distracted. It's so easy to forget that other people have difficult things they're dealing with and not to take everything so personally. I wonder," she said, reaching into her messenger bag, "if you wouldn't mind looking these over?" She held out a short stack of envelopes banded together. "When you have time, of course."

"What are they?"

She looked at her shoes, then up at him sheepishly. "IRS notices?" Her tone went up, turning it into a question.

"You have a tax problem?"

"No. No. It's some sort of mistake."

That's what the occasional client with an IRS problem always said. It was some kind of "mistake." Usually it wasn't true, although liars were not limited to those who owed money to the government. Most clients stretched the truth. "Tax problems are not my specialty, but I'll take a look." He snapped the rubber band holding the wad together.

"I'll pay you for your time."

"I offer my clients free consultations, so you get one too. Plus, this way I'll get to see you again." He held the notices up as he turned to head toward the Cube.

"If I'd seen you driving that on our first date, I'm not sure we'd be on a second one. Is that what I think it is, on the roof?"

He grinned. "His name is Edgar. There's a story." He looked

around for the Escalade but it wasn't there. "Let me walk you to your car."

"It looks like his body was amputated at the leg." She nudged him gently with her hip and laughed. It was intentional, but he wasn't sure if it was friendly or flirtatious. "There's something I need to tell you."

"OK," he said cautiously. His lower lip jutted out, an old involuntary response when he sensed unexpected, likely unpleasant news was about to drop.

"My divorce really threw me for a loop." She lowered her shoulders and exhaled. "You're the first date I've been on because I wasn't ready to meet anyone. I just wanted you to know that. I like you, but I think my breakup took a bigger toll on me emotionally than I even realized. It was like the rug was ripped out from under me."

He reached around to open her car door. She stopped his hand with hers. For a split second he felt something exciting, like an electrical charge. It looked like she felt it too. She squeezed his hand gently before releasing it.

"I got it," she said, very businesslike, opening the car door herself.

"Thanks for telling me—about how you're doing. I'm not in a hurry, no pressure."

"A lifelong bachelor? I wouldn't expect you would be. Either way it's good that you know where I'm at, emotionally. And thanks for looking at those notices. I really appreciate it." She got into her car and backed out in a hurry.

WHEN HE GOT BACK to the Cube, he clicked on the dome light and pressed the redial button on his phone. Sarge answered on the first ring.

"Meet me at the gun range over on 142nd Street."

"I'm coming from the Grove."

"Good. Then I'll see you in thirty."

"This better be good."

"It is."

Sarge's tone was sober. Traffic was light and the drive gave Vance time to clear his head. The second date with Lauren had gone much better but the ending was a downer. While he hadn't been divorced himself, he'd heard others likening it to the death of a loved one. The loss of his father was a fresh wound, and maybe that gave them some common ground. He'd heard of people making odd connections, ones based on tragedy and bad timing. "Don't be such a selfish prick. And don't get ahead of yourself." He said it aloud to remind himself not to have expectations, because that kind of thinking always led to disappointment. She'd been direct with him and he needed to take it easy, let it play out. Having his fugitive uncle sleeping on the couch, his career in a tailspin, and the marshal following him didn't exactly make him Romeo anyway. If he understood correctly, what she said was she needed more time.

⸻

HE ARRIVED at the gun club in less than a half hour and found Sarge sitting alone on a bench outside a glass partition. A group of off-duty officers were on the other side of the glass, shooting at tin bowling pins lined up on a two-by-six wooden sawhorse. "So what's the emergency?" Vance asked.

"I didn't say it was an emergency. I said it's important." Sarge looked tired.

"OK. What's so important?"

"Chago's dead."

Vance stared at the officers wearing their protective earmuffs and eyewear, listening to the gunfire muffled by the thick transparent partition. "You said you'd heard some chatter about it, an impending hit?"

"Yeah. Seems a mob surrounded him during a routine prison movement. The guards said they couldn't tell who killed him even studying the video a frame at a time. My source tells me all they saw was a mountain of men gather quickly. After they cleared, Chago was bleeding out from over fifty stab wounds. They found a pair of surgical scissors by the body. Wiped clean. A pack kill."

"Aryan Brotherhood, like you predicted?"

"That's what I think. If he had lived another week and made his monthly phone call to his lawyer, he would have found out he was behind on his payments to the Brotherhood. Someone stopped depositing money into the accounts. You know the rules, they're not protecting a guy who's not paying."

Why had Sarge taken such an interest in old Los Guapos business? It was weird. So he asked him, "What's your angle?"

"My angle?" Sarge scratched at his budding goatee. "I don't have one. I'm telling you because the same sources are saying your uncle is back in Miami."

Panic set in, he chewed the skin on his thumb, and his muscles in his neck seized up. Sarge heard Tony was back? He craned his head back as far as it would go until his cervical vertebrae popped.

"You OK?" Sarge asked.

"Sure," he lied, running a new scenario in his head, one with others knowing Tony was back. "This is old business." He rubbed his eyebrows with the bottom of his thumbs. "It would be helpful, a big favor actually, if you told me who your sources are, where you're getting this information."

Sarge absently fingered the chain hanging from his throat. "My sources are twenty-four-karat gold. That's all I can tell you. I have every reason to believe everything I'm hearing. They're not going to investigate the murder of a piece of shit like Chago. In the prison handbook, Killing is Article 100 and carries a max penalty of two more years. Two more isn't much of a deterrent if you're never getting out, anyway."

"I gotta go." He was having trouble focusing and needed to be alone.

"Next time I'll book us some time."

"What?"

"Some shooting time. I have a membership."

"Oh. Gotcha." He stopped and faced Sarge. "One more thing." He hesitated, picking his words, "Why are you telling me this? I haven't seen my uncle in over twenty years. It seems odd, these sudden blasts from the past."

"I thought you'd want to know," Sarge said. "I would. One more thing."

It was starting to seem like Daniel always had one more thing. "What?"

"Maria left *me*. She found an old high school boyfriend on Facebook and the next thing you know, she wanted a divorce. Moved up to St. Augustine to be with him. She got half my pension and shot an arrow right through my heart." Always the drama king, Sarge closed his eyes and placed his hand on his chest.

"I'm sorry, I really am." Was social media good for anything? "I'm glad you told me. I don't have much of a track record in that department, but I know how much you loved her."

"I wasn't the perfect husband, but I keep thinking I could've done better."

HE DESPERATELY NEEDED some fresh air. The information was a

game-changer. Sarge knew Tony was back and that Chago was dead. If he and Tony got caught, they'd both be sentenced to federal prison. His uncle would likely be shipped to the Supermax at Florence. That was one scenario. Another might be that someone wanted them both dead.

8

I t was late when he got home from his impromptu meeting with Sarge. The Escalade was out front, parked beneath the misty halo of the flickering streetlight. It was a drizzly and hot Florida night, and when the weather was muggy and suffocating, he was irritable, especially when he was tired. And it had been a long day. He didn't have much energy climbing the stairs, even with the adrenaline spurt from the ominous sighting of the SUV parked again out front.

"What's all this?" he looked at stacks of neatly folded clothing on the kitchen table.

Tony was sprawled out on the sofa in a pair of shorts watching a baseball game. "Don't take it out on me if your date didn't go good. It's your laundry. Took the whole day. Did as many loads as I could 'til I ran out of laundry soap. Didn't want to put your stuff away. I hate it when I can't find things. Cleaned the kitchen too. Made a list of stuff we need."

"Thanks, but it's creepy having a dude wash my underwear."

"Yeah? You should try doing laundry in the old country. Made doing the wash pleasurable, a machine. If you wonder about life before the turn of the century, I know a great little island south of here. And I'm not talking about the new millennium, either. I'm referring to the one before indoor plumbing. Beats the hell out of a washboard and a clothesline."

Vance cupped his ear on the wall. "I hear the apartment next door calling you."

"Guess you didn't notice our friend parked out front. I can't very well leave during a stakeout. Look at our lives, *sobrino*. Me, a life of crime and you, well, you don't really have a good excuse. We got jack shit between us."

"At least I'm not facing a bright future in a Supermax cell between the Shoe Bomber and the Unabomber. That's where you'll end up if they catch you."

"You haven't called the FBI yet. A million-dollar reward would go a long way if you turned me in."

"I can't do that, Tony, and you know I can't." He was exhausted. "What do you want from me?"

"How about a *café con leche*."

Vance filled his cheeks with air and deflated them slowly, making a hissing sound. "I have red wine. And beer."

Tony filled a glass under the kitchen faucet. He held it up. "Here's to *first world* water." He took a long drink and began: "The reason I'm back—"

"Hang on, I need something a little stronger." Vance returned with an opened bottle of red wine in one hand and his favorite tree-ringed mug, now sparkling clean, in the other.

Tony began. "Chago and me, we paid our banker Mongo—"

"Sociopath."

"All right, sociopath. Anyway, Chago and me had Mongo set up cash accounts for us through his family bank."

"I believe money laundering is what they call it."

"OK, money laundering. That's where we kept most of our cash, in his bank. But we figured we might need a secret slush fund where we could stash money in case of an emergency.

Chago and me moved a couple of million dollars down to Grand Cayman in the hull of one of our powerboats. Cayman was a safe haven, you know, nice-looking teller counted and deposited the money for us, no questions asked. After I left—"

"You mean escaped in a shootout with law enforcement. On the streets of Miami."

"Left, disappeared, whatever. OK, after I escaped, I tried wiring a small amount, five hundred dollars as a test through the Cuban National Bank. But someone at Commie Credit saw the transfer. Next thing you know it's gone, my rainy day fund, all of it, two million U.S. dollars. Probably went into landscaping Fidel's oceanfront compound. Ever notice despots and dictators lead the high life?" Tony sighed and paused. "The Castro brothers stole my money, took every frigging peso. So when this diplomatic thing started, normalized relations or whatever they're calling it over here, I figured it would be a good time to leave. Then I heard from the underground that I was part of a U.S. Department of Justice prisoner swap."

Vance was so dog-tired he was having trouble keeping up with the conversation. The red wine was kicking in, too, making it harder to concentrate.

"When the Castros refused to turn over Joanne something-or-another, the Jersey cop killer, as part of the new Cuban-American diplomatic relations, the Cuban government offered me up instead. The cop killer, she's a celebrity. She walks free on the streets of Havana signing autographs. But not me, I was just a fugitive drug smuggler. The Feds agreed to the exchange so I needed to get off the island before the manhunt got underway. Luckily, it's not a very efficient place. I traded my Presidential Rolex for a Panamanian passport and an airline ticket to Miami from some guys who said they forge documents for ISIS. They make damned good papers, whoever they are."

"You're not just a fugitive drug smuggler, Tony. You're a cop killer, too. Cops, jurors, witnesses, *a judge*—a lot of people got killed because of Los Guapos."

"I never killed anyone. Ever. And you know it."

Vance poured the rest of the wine down his throat. The words were about to fly. "You may as well have pulled the trigger. You paid for it. Murder for hire, the cowardly route, the way I see it." The alcohol loosened his lips.

"You need to take that back, Vance. I never once planned a hit on anyone. That was Chago."

"So let's say you're the marketing guy for a company that sells products that kill people. Let's take it a step further." The wine was making him zealous. "Let's say the marketing guy absolutely knows that his company is responsible for those deaths. Are you saying he has no culpability?"

"It's apples and oranges. It was a long time ago. I was practically a kid. And my wife was murdered in cold blood."

They sat quietly for a minute.

Tony broke the silence. "Look, I'm sorry I dragged you into this. I really am. If I had other options, I would have gone a different route. All the family I have left is my two sisters and you. And you know I can't put them in danger. I need your help. I need you to get a message to Ray."

"Ray?" His head was about to explode. He'd heard that name too many times recently.

"Yeah, Ray. Ray Dinero. The pilot."

"Really?" His lower jaw jutted out. "How do your propose I do that? Oh, I know, I'll run downstairs and ask the marshal outside for a personal favor. I have a better idea. Why don't you go out and buy yourself a burner phone. You contact him. I like my freedom, regardlessh of how *sjack shitty* you think my life ish." The wine had definitely kicked in.

Tony held out a piece of paper folded four ways to the size of a Post-It Note. It looked old, yellowed. "Give this to Lauren Gold. Ask her to give it to Ray Dinero."

"Lauren!" He rubbed his temples until red marks appeared. "Shit. I washh shtarting to think there were too many old friends cropping up out of nowhere." Tony may as well have kicked him in the balls. This had just morphed into full-blown conspiracy, and he was right in the middle of it. His head pounded and blood pumped through his jugular. "How the fuck do yoush know about her? And how the fuck dosh you know I know her?"

"Isn't it obvious?"

His mind was racing but his tongue was slipping. Ray Dinero. He did not like being cast in Tony's puppet show without being asked. He rolled his fist in a ball and punched the drywall, then doubled over in pain. "That should have been your facesh," he said, looking at the dent in the wall. Tony looked surprised. "Is she your mule? How much are you paying her?"

"It's Ray's plan. I swear it," Tony said, putting the paper next to the cold coffee pot. "I swear to Jesus I don't know anything except the plan was for her to pass the information to Ray."

Vance sat rubbing his fist. "Tell me, ish she a patsy too? Or juss me."

"I'm leaving it next to the coffee pot. And I made a shopping list too."

Fucking A. "A shopping list. Gee, what a great idea. Thass just what I wass thinking, that I should do a little lash minute grocery shopping before we go to *prison*." He looked over where Tony sat. Two canvas duffle bags with all his worldly possessions were lined up neatly next to the crate by the sofa. Tony had washed the spare sheets and made a bed for himself on the couch. He'd moved in. Without asking.

HE COULDN'T KICK him out. He couldn't turn him in. Either way he couldn't take the chance; his life would be ruined if the authorities found out. If Sarge heard Tony was back in Miami, who else had? His thoughts were clearing. Ray Dinero must know. He lay down on the bed and closed his eyes but sat right back up to stop the room from spinning. He stumbled to the doorway separating his bedroom from the rest of the tiny apartment. He peeked into the living area. It was dark but he heard Tony snoring in fits and spurts. He closed the door between them.

He woke up two hours later at four o'clock in the morning. The window unit banged and buzzed. So did his head. The A/C unit did nothing to improve the air quality, but it helped cancel out the ambient noises coming from the parking lot. Lack of insulation let the heat and humidity invade the cramped apartment, and it was stifling. His stomach whirled and his head pounded.

Boy, had life changed for Tony. The one-time top-ranked Los Guapos kingpin who'd lived the high life was now sleeping peacefully with his whole life stuffed into a couple of travel bags at the foot of a ratty couch.

He rubbed his temples. Twenty years ago, money laundering was a much simpler affair. Couriers working for Tony and Chago smuggled gym bags into Mongo's bank vault where they filled safe deposit boxes with cash. The bank in turn loaned money to a slew of shadow companies that Tony and Chago owned but couldn't be traced to them. Cash was used to buy houses in Coral Gables, a place at the Doral Country Club, three Brickell Key penthouses, a condo in Vail, a strip mall, a few small office buildings, a Manhattan co-op, and even a ranch near Lake Okeechobee, replete with its own airstrip.

He rolled over on his back, his eyes and ears following one squeaky blade of the ceiling fan slowly grinding above the bed.

Forensic accountants working for the Feds were baffled. A hapless finance MBA from the Wharton business school assigned to oversee the investigation complained in sworn testimony before a tittering grand jury that trying to sort out the web of companies was like "trying to find a fart in a thunderstorm." The MBA said there were almost three hundred different corporate entities, created to move money around like a cup-and-ball trick on steroids.

Everything changed after Mongo Solana cut a deal with the Feds. The bankers' boxes full of Los Guapos's financial records gave the government accountants exactly what they needed to untangle the money trail.

So many things had gone wrong during prior cases brought against the Los Guapos leaders that the U.S. Attorney for Southern Florida sent an armored vehicle to pick up the bank records, ensuring they'd be delivered and entered into evidence. The prosecution worried that more dead bodies—witnesses, cartel members, jurors, and even judges—might pile up.

He covered his head with a pillow, wishing his brain had an off button.

Tony and Chago used the same legal teams Panamanian dictator Manuel Noriega and mobster John Gotti had used. In interviews, the U.S. Attorney ironically called the Los Guapos co-heads "the untouchables." For more than a decade, almost every U.S. Federal and Florida State agency had had some sort of ongoing investigation into their criminal enterprise. Tony and Chago worked their drug empire like a Fortune 100 company, developing a culture of accountability and a vision for growth. The most valued virtue, however, was silence.

What Vance valued above all else was his freedom. As inviting as it was, he'd resisted pressure and the temptation to join his uncle's drug empire. He'd left law enforcement for law school to get away from the conflict. After he graduated, he'd turned down offers from the biggest firms trying to recruit him when he figured out the partners expected him to bring the Los Guapos business with him. He had no intention of defending his uncle, or any other drug dealers, for that matter. If he'd accepted a job, the firm would have eventually fired him for refusing to bring in the family business.

He got out of bed to take a leak.

Tony and Chago went to jail multiple times, but strange things always happened, like once when the jail log was mysteriously altered. Chago was released after serving fourteen days of an eight-year prison sentence. As infuriating as it was to the prosecutors that he just walked out the door, the only repercussions were the firings of a sheriff's deputy and two jail employees. The three were later booked on suspicion of bribery. Chago's lawyers successfully argued their client had been "released."

Tony was captured for the final time in 1993 at his nine-thousand-dollar-a-month rented oceanfront mansion.

His thoughts turned to more productive ideas, like shuttering his lousy little Bird Road law practice. More like bird shit. That's what it had devolved into: a practice, hardly a profession. He'd have to break the lease. But what landlord would pursue a lawyer who could represent himself? And what would the damages be? The place would rent in thirty days.

He didn't have a single working case. With a click of a button, he could suspend his account and disable the website. If his site disappeared from the Web, he'd be out of business in less than an hour. *Adios* advertising, email, self-scheduling, free consultations, and clients with lousy cases.

In the fog of insomnia and a hangover came clarity.

He picked his tablet up from the nightstand and folded back the cover. It opened to a free porn site. He cleared the search history, cancelled his sponsored ad, selected the DELETE ALL option on his calendar, and pressed the I'M SURE prompt. He stuck a wax-hardened plug in his ear.

Fuck them.

That's how Vance felt about anyone who'd already scheduled a free legal consultation with him.

They could all go and fuck themselves.

Call 1-800-ADIOS-MF.

9

TUESDAY

WHEN HE AWOKE, he felt refreshed, like a weight had been lifted. And he smelled coffee and eggs. But the relief was short-lived when he saw Tony busy at the stove making breakfast.

"You shouldn't surf porn sites on my tablet."

"*Buenos dias* to you, too. What are you, a practicing Catholic these days?"

"It's not that. If I'm under surveillance and you're on my tablet and I'm not here, they're going to notice."

"I didn't look at any pornography."

Then he remembered how the online dating site phished him with the pretty brunette. "OK. I realize you've been living in a time warp. Surveillance is a lot more sophisticated now. The marshal is following me. They use really high tech stuff now." He peeked through the blinds. The SUV hadn't moved.

Tony challenged him. "You're saying they can track you from your computer?"

"Yeah. They can. And from my phone. You don't think they're looking for you by now? Why do you think she's still out there?"

Tony scratched his ear and crunched his forehead. "You're saying they can see inside? And the U.S. Marshal hires *mujer*? Don't you think you're being a little paranoid?"

Vance heard a light aircraft buzzing overhead. "Yeah, they hire women. Do you hear that plane? That's probably what they're doing right now. Collecting data. The U.S. Marshals have high-tech tools to track fugitives. They have an electronic device called a dirtbox. They can stick it on a single-engine aircraft, or on a drone. It mimics a cell tower and tracks mobile phones and wireless devices. If they're tracking me on my cell and I'm at work, and someone is watching TV or using my tablet, that could give them probable cause to get a warrant."

Tony looked at him blankly.

Vance was trying to be patient but patience was rapidly turning into exasperation. "You think I'm making this stuff up?"

Tony sat quietly, thinking. "I don't want to get you caught up in anything illegal. I really don't. I wish it were like the old days when I could get a hotel somewhere for cash and not drag you into it. This was the only safe place I knew I could go."

He was glad Tony said that. At least he had a clue about what the risks were. And he believed Tony when he said he didn't want to mire him in a plan that might send them both to prison. But there were powerful forces all around, and it would take luck as much as anything now to keep them out of big trouble. He could trust Tony. That was the most important thing. He just had to make him understand the far-reaching powers of the government. The FBI could get a FISA warrant for a fugitive from Cuba. There was a good chance they were already being spied on. The world had changed so dramatically since his uncle went underground. Vance didn't have the time or energy to explain it.

Tony said, "May I watch TV? When you're gone?"

"That's fine. Just don't channel surf. Pick a station and stay on it until I get back." He flopped down on the sofa and chided him. "I should just call the marshal and turn you in myself. I could use the money." Then he saw the cigar box leaning against the sofa cushion and blew up. "Don't go through my personal stuff!" He grabbed the open H. Upmann box and saw the stack of IRS notices Lauren had given him, underneath it. He hadn't had time to go through them, but apparently Tony had. "You looked through my client's personal papers too? What's wrong with you?"

Tony winced. His tone was sheepish. "I thought it was part of the family stuff, like the stuff in the box. Did you know the IRS is after her for ninety thousand dollars?"

"Give me those." He glanced at the paper on top. It was true. The IRS was after her for $90,000. Tony handed him a cup of coffee. He grabbed it, splashing some hot liquid on his wrist. His fist still hurt from punching the wall. He set the cup down and rubbed his forearm with two fingers as he skimmed through the liens and levies.

"Did you know your new girlfriend has money problems?" Tony asked.

He glared at him. "Who said anything about her being my girlfriend?"

"You've met her twice at the Hotel Mutiny. I saw messages come up on your little computer. I didn't know that place was back in business. The memories. . . ."

During a routine software update, his phone had synced to his tablet, and since he lived alone, he hadn't thought much about his privacy, until now.

"Sometimes when I look at your little computer, there are

messages from other women, like they want to meet you. They send Winks and make you a Favorite. They advertise dating sites like crazy on TV, but who knew you'd stoop to that, looking for *mujer* on a computer. Is that how you met her, on the Web?"

Tony was way out of bounds. "You need to mind your own business." Picking up the cigar box and IRS notices, he stalked into the bedroom looking through the tax documents. If he was reading it right, someone named Chris Gold had received a refund check over ten years ago. The IRS was trying to get the money back and had started adding interest and penalties beginning in 2008. He put the stuff in the dresser drawer and stuck his head through the doorway. "You can watch TV but stay off my tablet. As a matter of fact, stay out of my bedroom unless you have to use the bathroom."

"The stuff in the box, it's our family stuff." Tony raised his shoulders innocently. "We're blood, man. But OK. I respect that. I won't do it again. Here, I made a list of things we need."

When Vance returned to the kitchen, Tony tried to press the list into his palm, but Vance pushed his hand away. "You need to be very careful. You hiding here makes me a felon They'll throw the book at me. And you."

He'd started out being civil, but that plan of action obviously wasn't working. Tony had been manipulating him from the moment he knocked on the door. He was under surveillance and being followed. He didn't want to get pushed up against a wall with his hands behind his back. "How long do you think it will take for the authorities to figure out you're here? All they need now is probable cause for a search warrant. I'm not going down with you, Tony. Do you get that?"

Tony was undeterred. "You have to get this to Lauren."

His saying her name aloud again pissed him off even more. "Give me the fucking paper." Without reading it, he stuffed it in his pants pocket along with the shopping list. "I will do this one thing, Tony. But that's it. I'm not kidding. This is your mess. I have my own problems. I don't need yours. I will not break the law any more than we already have. Understood?"

Tony nodded appreciatively. "OK. Thanks. She needs to get it to Ray—"

"I heard you the first time."

He slammed the apartment door on the way out. A young mother was playing with two toddlers on the walkway. "Sorry," he said as he passed by, still mad.

There was more to the relationship between Lauren and Ray Dinero than she'd admitted when he confronted her about it. He'd suspected it, but Tony confirmed it. Feelings of betrayal were pumping stomach acid up his esophagus. *Family, my ass.* Tony was the same conniving liar he'd been before he escaped. Tony and Ray were communicating. But how? Tony hadn't left the apartment. Or had he? He didn't have a phone. Or did he? He'd been going on Tony's word, and what was that worth?

Jogging down the stairs he chewed on his thumbnail. The Escalade was gone. Seeing the giant roach leg sticking up from the roof of the Cube made him angrier. "Fuck you!" He kicked the bumper. "Ouch!" He took his shoe off and rubbed his big toe. A sawn-off, hairy roach leg was the perfect symbol for just how shitty things were going on every front.

10

He got to the office late, well after ten. Two men dressed in hoodies and loose shiny basketball shorts were waiting for him when he arrived. He let them in because they were already there, loitering in the parking lot. They'd signed up for free consultations before he'd disabled the Courage Law Firm website in the middle of the night. Paying clients generally took "No" for an answer more readily than the freeloaders. Often the non-paying clients got belligerent and confrontational like the eviction lady, and he was in no mood for conflict. It would be easier to let them in and go through the motions of listening while secretly playing solitaire on his desktop. He kept a spare .45 in the top drawer of the mahogany desk his father gave him as a graduation gift, in case anyone got too far out of line.

One was looking for a lawyer to defend him on a burglary charge and the other for driving without a license. Both yelled at him when he told them he couldn't represent them. The second one threw some angry jabs in the air, and after he was gone, Vance locked the door and started packing boxes. Around two o'clock, he left to pick up his sister's kids from school.

The bright, white cumulus clouds hanging overhead turned charcoal as he drove. The wiper blades on Edgar flapped and scraped, trying to keep up with the storm. Kathy had been texting him at two-hour intervals, reminding him to pick up the kids, but her messages had stopped around lunchtime.

Inching along in parent pick-up zone, he pinged Lauren: Enjoyed our visit — third date? Delivering the note was the last thing he was doing for his uncle.

WHEN HE ARRIVED at his mother's house, he drove past the first time without stopping, circling the block twice.

"Where are you going?" his second-oldest nephew asked.

"The scenic route. Are you guys in a hurry to get to your grandma's?"

The boys liked his humor and laughed. A black Tahoe idled on the street in front of the house across from his mom's. When he passed the third time, he rolled down the car window and waved. No response. The windows were tinted, almost black. His mother, Isabel, was standing in the driveway when he pulled up. She ambled up to his open car window.

"See, ju no come for so long, ju drive right by. I saw ju." She looked at the black SUV across the way. "Ju know her, Vance? I saw ju wave." Isabel looked up at Edgar and shook her head, then looked inside at her grandsons and smiled.

He saw the attractive fortyish woman behind the wheel of the black SUV when she rolled down her window.

"I don't think so. Do you?"

"She's in real estate. She wanted to know if I want to sell the house. I tol' her no. I thought maybe ju sent her." His mother was angry with him.

The kids bounded out of Edgar. He stayed in the car. It was

cleaner and faster to exchange pleasantries from the driver seat. It would be too hard to face her while keeping the secret that her brother was back. That Tony was still alive. She didn't mask her disappointment, standing with her arms folded against her chest.

Backing down the driveway, he watched her herd her grandsons into the house. He worried his mom's place was under surveillance too. *A realtor asking her if she wanted to sell the house.* He'd read that some agents scoured the obituaries for leads. That might be an interesting lawsuit.

The urge to turn around to give that woman a piece of his mind was interrupted when he rolled to a stop at the four-way. Kathy approached in her Subaru Outback. He pulled up alongside. The earlier downpour had morphed into a breathtaking periwinkle blue sky, bringing with it drier, fresher air.

He rolled his car window down so they could talk. "Wow, what timing. A minute later and we would have missed each other. How are you doing?"

"Good. Thanks so much for getting the boys. I hope they weren't too much trouble." Her eyes were hidden behind a pair of oversized sunglasses.

"Not at all. What about you, how are you?"

"OK."

"How did the test go?"

"OK, I think."

"When's Larry coming back?"

"Tomorrow night. Thanks again for helping me out."

"Anytime." He was genuinely glad to be helpful. "Let me know about the test results."

BACK AT THE OFFICE, packing boxes, he tried to ignore the blue-jacketed Last Will and Testament on top of his desk. But with realtors stalking his mother, he'd better start getting things in order. Resentment was building, deepening each time he saw the will. Why hadn't his father asked him, his son-the-lawyer, to do the legal work? Maybe his dad thought he was incompetent or possibly untrustworthy? Either way, it hurt. The fact remained that his dad had paid someone else to do it. Putting it off wasn't going to make him feel any better about it.

He put his feet up on the desk and leaned back in his office chair. On reading the document, it became clear why Dr. Jim Courage hadn't wanted his son preparing his Last Will. His father was dead broke. No. It was worse than that. He was in debt. He felt gut-punched. He was so riddled with anxiety that he had to get out of his office.

He parked the Nissan crap wagon a block away from his apartment and sent a text to Lauren as he approached the stairwell to the third floor leading to his unit where Tony was hiding out. She hadn't answered his earlier one, the one still on his screen: Good looks and charm can't get me a third date?

Three gray dots danced on his phone. Ping. A text popped up: Sorry. Busy day. Third date accepted.

Meet me later? He glanced from his phone screen to the street, back to his phone. He looked for the Escalade. It wasn't there.

Lauren answered: OK. Same time & place 2nite?

No. Meet me at Publix on 56th.

HE DETOURED on foot to the gas station behind the apartment building and purchased a dozen eggrolls rotating on metal rollers. The clerk plucked them from under the heat lamp and dropped them into a brown paper sack. *His dad was broke?* He filled his pants pockets with as many sweet and sour gel packets as would fit.

Tony was startled when he came through the door. He caught him red-handed with the TV remote channel surfing, switching between two baseball games.

"I told you not to do that. Do you *want* to spend your golden years in solitary confinement? I'm not kidding, Tony. It's a big deal that you're holed up here. How long do you think it will be before the FBI comes knocking? I'm being followed. You're going to wreck my life too, if you keep it up." He threw the bag of eggrolls at him.

"Sorry," Tony said, contrite. He held the bag up. "Thanks."

Vance was a caged animal. His apartment was a trap. His law practice was dead. And his mother's lovely Coral Gables residence was in the crosshairs of a greedy realtor hoping Isabel would have to sell it.

11

Lauren had pitched the new client for an entire month before landing the gig and was in the middle of the shoot when it started going downhill. "I should have pushed *harder* for it," she whispered in Dan the director's ear.

She meant she should have insisted on a teleprompter. The video crew was enduring the twentieth take.

The company CEO had written his own script but couldn't deliver the two lines with a camera staring at him. She'd recommended the teleprompter during preproduction meetings, but the marketing department, a bunch of know-it-alls, unanimously declined as part of a boss-butt-snorkeling marathon. They reassured him he'd ace it.

"I'm sorry," he said, a bona fide alpha male with unusually good manners. "I really am sorry."

What he meant was he was humiliated. It wasn't the first time she'd seen a man of power melt down in front of a camera lens. Like many things in life, it seemed a lot easier than it was. When Dan yelled, "Rolling," the CEO's word-to-mouth path short-circuited.

"Will someone please get my powder?" Lauren asked.

The lighting guy Ben trotted off and returned with her field make-up bag. She grabbed a handful of napkins from the lunch table and tucked them inside the neckline of the man's dress shirt. She prepped him, blotting perspiration and dabbing powder on his face with a makeup sponge.

This was part of the new normal. Since the advent of high definition, she doubled as a makeup artist.

While he studied his two lines, she texted Vance: Really, you want to meet at the grocery store?

Yes—Publix grocery store—where shopping is a pleasure.

She read the message and put her phone back on Airplane mode, then checked the shot in the monitor. No boogers, dandruff, or shiny forehead. "Be sure to tell your wife where the makeup came from." That wisecrack usually got a laugh. Not from this guy. He was focused on getting his pair of lines right so he could go back to his corner office.

By five o'clock, all that was left to shoot was a few cutaways and some B-roll, general video scenes she delegated to the team from a printed shot list. Lauren left the import-export business in Kendall early to allot for traffic. It would be easy to get to 56th Street from there.

She texted Vance en route: 10 minutes away.

Pushing my cart.

She called him from the parking lot. He told her what aisle to meet him on, near the rice.

VANCE WAS PUSHING the cart and reviewing Tony's shopping list, checking items off with a pencil when Lauren came up to him on aisle five. "I'm supposed to give you this." He slipped the paper from Tony into her hand.

"Well, hello to you too." She unfolded it and looked at it, clearly confused.

He'd pretended he hadn't noticed her as she approached the store. He'd watched every step she took across the parking lot. She was wearing a blue-and-white vertically striped skirt cut just above the knee. Low, blue patent leather heels supported ankles so delicate he could have wrapped his thumb and forefinger around them.

He eyeballed the shelves, looking for something. "You're supposed to give that to your friend, Ray Dinero."

"My friend, Ray Dinero? Where did you get this?"

"Ask him. I thought you said you hadn't seen him in years."

"Um, we're not exactly in touch. No, that's not true. I did a job for him recently." She unfolded it again and looked at it, perplexed. "He hired me to do a marketing video. That's what I do. After I split with my first husband, I pitched everyone I could think of for work, including Ray. He bought a boat yard a while back and recently called me out of the blue. I swear to you, I hadn't seen him in years."

He gazed past her toward the parking lot. He saw a white Escalade circling the perimeter.

Lauren followed him to the produce department. He picked up a sack of onions and dropped it in the cart. "I think I'm being followed. I think that's a U.S. Marshal." He flicked his eyes toward the big storefront window where the white SUV passed by.

"You sound a little paranoid."

"I feel a little paranoid. Why don't you ask Ray about it when you see him—ask him if he has any idea who might be following me."

"You seem upset."

He didn't answer. Her heels clattered on the tile floor. She was right behind him, heading toward the meat section. "Umm, did you have time to look at those IRS notices I gave you? I got another one in the mail yesterday."

Without turning to face her, he said, "As a matter of fact, I did." He selected a two-pound package of pink ground beef from the meat bin and gently set it on the bottom of the cart.

"And?"

"Ever heard of Chris Gold?"

"Sure, he's my first husband. First ex, I mean. What's he got to do with it?"

"Apparently the IRS sent him a refund check for a tax over-payment of over six thousand dollars by mistake. They want it back now. They've been adding interest and penalties for a while."

Lauren stomped her foot like a horse tired of being tied to a hitching post. "He cashed a refund check by mistake? That, that, that asshole," she huffed. "We've been divorced for fifteen years. I make quarterly IRS payments, and I did get a notice saying they couldn't find a payment. That was after our divorce. My accountant sent a letter to the IRS along with a copy of the canceled check. You know," she stamped the other foot, "it's not like the IRS gives out random prizes. If he cashed that check, he knew it wasn't his. Geez, it's shit like this why I divorced him to begin with. Sorry about my potty mouth. It's an occupational hazard."

"It happens a lot after filing joint tax returns."

"That's hysterical."

"What's hysterical?"

"Joint returns. He has a major weed addiction."

"Does he live on Unicorn Drive in Jupiter?"

"Why do you ask?"

"Because the IRS was sending the letters to him for years until he apparently asked them to do a change of name and address. To yours."

"That—" Lauren stopped herself, took a deep breath and closed her eyes. "He had to know it wasn't his money. He's such a dreamer. He always had enough THC in his bloodstream to convince himself of almost anything. I'm surprised he hasn't moved to Denver by now. I should have changed back to my maiden name. I should have taken my father-in-law more seriously. He dubbed Chris 'the Chemist' when he was a kid because he could turn money into shit."

"It does have a nice ring to it, Lauren Gold," he said. "But it's probably not worth what you'll end up paying for it. The IRS is going after you. Once you get sucked that far into the computer, it's tough to get it straightened out. I hate to be the bearer of less-than-good news, but with interest and penalties over ten years, it is almost ninety grand."

Lauren made a choking sound, like she might cough up her spleen. "I was hoping it was their mistake. That it could be fixed. That you could fix it." She clicked her heels and followed him down the next lane.

He checked Tony's list again and picked up a package of tortilla chips and dropped it in the cart. "They were sending him notices for years. They are known to run out of patience and lower the boom if you ignore them. I can write a letter for you, on legal letterhead. That might at least buy a little time, give you a break on the interest and penalties."

"I would appreciate that. This sucks, totally sucks. Where am I going to come up with ninety thousand dollars?" She held up the paper Vance had delivered to her. "I gotta go."

"Wait."

She started to run. He left the cart in the middle of the lane. When he caught up with her he reached out and grabbed her elbow. She jerked her arm away. Customers gawked as she sprinted toward the automatic doors. He had to let her go. Customers were staring at them like they were having a domestic dispute. He watched her peel out of the parking lot, tires chirping. Zipping across four busy lanes, she sped through the amber light at the intersection. The Escalade backed into the spot where Lauren had been parked. The daytime running lights were on. He was definitely being followed. He recognized the woman behind the wheel. She was the same one he'd seen earlier after lunch with Jake.

He had no idea how Lauren fit into this strange picture. Maybe she was trapped like him. She acted surprised when he'd mentioned Ray's name. He went back into the store to finish shopping.

_____

12

The check-out girl scanned his items robotically without making eye contact. He bagged his own groceries to hurry the process. The spot the Escalade driver parked in after Lauren left was now taken by a Buick. There was no sign of the Cadillac. It was common knowledge among law enforcement that U.S. Marshals had wide-ranging authority. For all he knew, she'd planted a tracking device on Edgar.

He stopped at the apartment to drop off the groceries. Tony wanted to talk. Vance didn't, ducking out fast and heading back to his office.

HIS SISTER CALLED while he was in the middle of boxing up more work files.

Kathy didn't sugarcoat it. "I knew there was a chance. But—well—I'm surprised." She dropped the bomb. "My—um—the tumor's malignant."

The news shocked him into a long silence.

"Are you there?" she asked.

"Yes. Uh-huh. Um—I don't know what to say. I didn't know you had a—ah—a tumor. How long have you known?"

"I've known for a while. When I saw the doctor today it was to get the test results from the PET scan. You're the only one who knows I had the test. I didn't want you to worry, either. I was going to talk to Dad, but then he. . . ." She choked up.

"I'm so sorry, sweetie." The news was surreal. He had to sound strong. And positive. "When do you start treatment?"

"I don't. I'm going into palliative care, which is a fancy way of saying they'll keep me as comfortable as possible until. . . ."

There was no delicate way of asking the next question. "What kind of cancer, Kat?"

"It's pancreatic. It's a rare kind. I can't even pronounce it."

He was taking notes on a pad of paper on his desk. He was accustomed to taking notes during telephone calls. As he looked at the words he recalled a few famous people who'd had pancreatic cancer. Patrick Swayze. Dead. Luciano Pavarotti. Dead. Michael Landon from *Little House on the Prairie* had pancreatic cancer and died way too young.

"Does Mom know?" He tugged nervously at his shirt collar.

"No. I haven't told her. I haven't told Larry, either, or the boys. The boys." She trailed off but sounded calm.

"Why aren't you getting treatment?"

"There isn't any. Well, that's not totally true. They can do a surgery to remove part of my pancreas and that will slow it down. There are some drug trials, but they're not FDA-approved."

"Are you're a candidate? For a trial?"

"I don't know. I think so, I think that's what my doctor said. My brain isn't working. I couldn't find my car in the parking garage. I felt like I was having an out-of-body experience. I walked every floor, pushing the key fob until I heard the car door beep. It's weird. I'm a little . . . confused. I brought some stuff home from the doctor's office to read. And I've been looking it over, sort of."

He was pissed off that Larry hadn't gone with her, to support her. How frightening to be alone.

"I have the same kind of cancer Steve Jobs had."

Wow. Steve Jobs had had all the resources in the world, and he was dead. "Is there anything I can do? To help out?"

"I don't know." Kathy began sounding less positive. "Maybe you could help with the legal stuff, the directives and. . . ." Her voice faded away again. "Did you talk to Mom yet, about Dad's estate, or life insurance, or whatever? Gosh, I know that sounds selfish of me."

"No, no, no, that's not selfish, Kat. I haven't had the chance to look it over yet. But I plan to." He had to lie.

"Mom is stressing over it. She's getting late notices in the mail. I think Dad had a lot of stuff set up online. Mom doesn't even have an email account."

He'd been trying to put his father's estate out of his mind. He couldn't tell his sister their dad hadn't left a penny. Not now. He'd paid for the extravagant funeral, the one his mother expected, out of what was left of his own meager savings. His plan to reimburse himself after he settled the estate wasn't happening now.

"There's a treatment center in Houston. It's some sort of hormone therapy. I think my doctor says there's good data on it, but it's not covered by insurance. And it's expensive. I think he said it's around fifteen thousand dollars a treatment. We don't have that kind of money—unless Dad left enough life insurance or retirement money to cover it. But Mom will need money."

Unlike him, his sister always put others first. "I'm so sorry you're going through this, Kat."

"It's so weird. I feel good, but I know I have a fatal disease.

My oncologist says Steve Jobs would still be alive if he hadn't tried to cure himself with a magic diet, a macro something-or-another, and spiritual advisors. He spent the first year eating weird food. He did the drug therapy later. I think that's why he lived as long as he did. Do you remember how skinny he got? Anyway, he had a liver transplant, too. My doctor says if Steve Jobs wasn't a magic thinker, he'd still be going to work every day, inventing amazing stuff."

His head was spinning. "So there's a surgical treatment?"

"I don't know. I guess. Yes."

"And then the treatment? If you can figure out how to pay for it?"

"I think so. Steve Jobs went to Switzerland. It costs a lot less than Houston, but of course you can't drive there. Switzerland is supposed to be so beautiful."

He looked again at the notes he'd been taking. "Will you need a liver transplant?"

"I don't know." Kathy sounded more upbeat but it was forced. "You don't have any idea how much money Dad left? I know Mom would do anything to help me."

"Of course she would. And so would I, sweetie. When are you going to tell Mom? About your diagnosis?"

He could hear his sister breathing into the phone. "Gosh, no, Vance. I can't tell her. She'll worry like crazy."

"Get me the information about the place in Switzerland. And Houston. I'd like to look it over."

"Are you saying Dad left enough money to pay for the treatment?"

"Maybe," he lied. "Email me the information so I can review it. I won't know until I look it over."

"Thanks for being the best big brother, even if you are a bad influence on the boys sometimes." She laughed gently. "I don't know what I'd do without you right now. I love you."

"Love you, too, Kat. Get the paperwork over to me ASAP."

WHAT A MESS. His father left his mother in debt, having dug a deep hole, including a second mortgage on their Coral Gables home that none of them knew about. There was no life insurance policy or savings. His Social Security benefits wouldn't be enough for their mother to make ends meet. That's why his dad had worked up until the day he died, well into his eighties. All along, Vance thought it was because his father loved his work.

He sat at his desk with his feet on the desk, staring at the ceiling, processing Kat's news. He'd planned to tell Kathy and Larry that Isabel would have to sell the house and his mother probably would have to move in with them. But the phone call with news about a malignant tumor changed all that.

Suddenly all hell broke loose. Something smashed into the metal framing of the picture window and ricocheted away from the building. The sharp sound stung his eardrums.

Holy shit! A gunshot!

He dove down to the floor, using his left hand to brace the fall, his right to push the top drawer of his desk open. He fumbled for the .45 in the drawer.

He was halfway under the desk, ears ringing, when the second round blew an orange-sized hole through the siding. The slug caromed off the baseboard and danced across the tiled entryway. He smelled gunpowder.

The third round hit the bull's-eye, shattering the six-by-six-foot glass picture window facing busy Bird Road. Splinters clattered off the bamboo furniture in the foyer.

Bigger shards rebounded off the drywall. The last fragments of glass rained down like glitter.

He braced himself with one hand while he used the other to

release the safety on the gun. He held the .45 out, raised his head slowly, keeping both hands clamped on the grip.

A white Cadillac Escalade sped away.

He scrambled out from his foxhole under the desk.

Two compact cars, their drivers forced to slam on the brakes to avoid colliding, spun like tops crossing the double yellow lines. Tire smoke wafted. They barely missed T-boning the white SUV.

People yelled and cursed. Drivers held up their phones. Others laid on the horns while the lookie-loos snapped pictures and recorded videos. He dialed 911 and watched the scene outside unfold while he waited for the dispatcher. It wouldn't be long until God-knows-what was posted all over social media. The two drivers were toe-to-toe, yelling at each other over the near miss. Strangers made it worse, shoving cell phones in their faces.

Miami weather poured in through the shattered window, bringing the scents of burnt rubber and gun smoke inside. There were no good Samaritans. Just chaos and mobs hoping to capture something they could post on their socials. Condensation welled up on everything.

The dispatcher finally answered. He couldn't believe it. She was noncommittal about sending a unit. She said his situation sounded "suspicious." He took it to mean she was wary about traps, set-ups to shoot cops. Luckily, she was an old-timer and remembered him when he gave his name. While his heart thumped under his shirt, she made small talk, asking him about the rumor that he'd left the force to go back to school. Joking that Courage was a name better suited for a cop than a lawyer, she told him to sit tight. She asked him if he was injured. He said he wasn't. She asked him if he was armed. He said he was.

When the buff, spiky-haired responding officers arrived, he lied and said he hadn't seen anything. He left the Escalade out of the report, suggesting the shooter was likely a disgruntled client. He explained he was closing his law practice, and someone may have been mad about a last-minute cancellation.

The cops dug a 9-millimeter slug out of the drywall and placed it in a clear plastic bag. They found two casings in plain view on the sidewalk. He talked them out of calling in the criminalist. Being a lawyer and an ex-cop—the latter carrying more weight—it was easy convincing them to wrap it up and leave. They wanted to get the hell out of there. No clear thinking cop wanted to hang around the scene of a random shooting.

He phoned the landlord who dispatched a handyman to board up the window. At least now he had a convenient excuse to break the lease when the time was right.

WHEN HE GOT HOME, Tony was in the kitchen, oven door open, checking something on the rack inside. Three pots steamed away on the stovetop.

He sniffed. "Smells good." He closed his eyes and slowly sucked enough air through his nose to fill his lungs. Held his breath for a few seconds. The mingling aromas of beef and cumin, coriander and onions, calmed his nerves.

Tony picked up a wooden spoon and turned the rice in a tall pot.

Vance sat down at the small kitchen table. Chewing the dried skin on his thumb, he asked, "What did you mean when you said you could make us both rich?"

Tony turned the flames down on all the three burners and wiped his hands on the faded hand towel draped over his shoulder. "So, you're finally tired of living the low life?"

"That's part of it." He wanted to see Tony's reaction, so he threw it out there like a grenade. "Chago's dead."

Tony turned away from him toward the stovetop and picked up the wooden spoon he'd been using. Turning up the blue flame beneath the saucepan with the *ropa vieja*, he stirred the sizzling oil, releasing a fresh burst of mouthwatering fragrances. "That doesn't surprise me."

"It doesn't surprise you? That's all you have to say? You've known him for how long?"

Tony shrugged. "My whole life, I guess."

"It seems like you should have a little more of a reaction."

"Vance, I haven't seen or talked to him for twenty years. Think about it."

He had thought about it. Tony was the perfect example when it came to thinking about people he hadn't seen for twenty years. Although he'd assumed his uncle was dead, he would have felt something if he'd gotten actual news of his death. He certainly felt something when his live body showed up at the front door. But then again, this was Chago they were talking about. More than once Vance had fantasized about killing him with his own bare hands. But he didn't want to do jail time for snuffing a piece of shit.

"If you got flank steak instead of ground beef, it would be more authentic. More *Cubano*."

"Are you kidding?" The smells were distracting, but his response was preposterous. Vance held him on topic. "Chago?"

"What about him?"

"Did you know he was dead?"

"I do now. You just told me. He was violent, man. I'm surprised he stayed in this world as long as he did. So no, I'm not surprised. Do you want to talk about my offer? About why I'm back?"

Sitting backward, straddling the chair with his arms wrapped around the straw ladder back, Vance nodded. "But first I want to know what you know about Chago. You've dragged me into something that has a good chance of landing us in front of a grand jury. But before you tell me what you're up to, I want to know who killed Chago."

It was, after all, largely Tony's fault he'd almost lost his job at Miami homicide after a run-in with Chago at the Mutiny.

"There's been a rumor going around for a while that his kid, Gregorio, was tired of spending money on his dad's prison protection. Can you imagine that? Choosing money over family?"

Vance was struck by the irony.

Tony continued. "When the Feds started investigating the Savings and Loans and holding the bank executives accountable for bad loans and money laundering as a way to indict the cartels, me and Chago knew Mongo would panic. Just like we thought he'd agreed to testify against us for a reduced sentence. When we got wind he was getting ready to squeal, we decided to withdraw what we could. For three days our couriers emptied the safe deposit boxes into duffel bags. The money was delivered to Ray Dinero for safekeeping."

"How much money?"

Tony lifted his shoulders and dropped them, then shook his head, stirring the meat mixture. "The government's guys said there was around a hundred million dollars unaccounted for. But I'm sure it's closer to seventy, maybe eighty million. Ray knows for sure."

"Wow." So that's how Ray Dinero fit into the picture. "A ten million dollar spread? What makes you so sure the money's still around?"

"¡Ya coño! This is Ray Dinero we're talking about. *El Cerebo.* The Brain. Never arrested, never snitched, leads a perfectly clean family life these days. I know Ray. I guarantee you he hasn't touched it, other than to keep it safe. He's the most careful man I've ever known. Of course it's there. Every dollar."

"Is Lauren in on it?" Since he was stuck in the middle, he had a right to know.

"Other than passing some information on to Ray?"

"Yeah." Vance folded his arms tighter across the chair back.

"I don't know. I doubt it. But I don't think she knows about the money. Ray trusts her, from way back."

"You remember her from the Mutiny?"

Tony grinned. "I remember every single *muy linda* girl from the club. I thought about them a lot over the years."

"Does anyone else know? About the money?"

"Besides Chago, who's dead? I don't know. It's hard to say. Mongo, maybe. You hungry?" Tony scooped two large portions of perfectly-cooked white rice and dropped it on mismatched plastic plates. He topped the rice with a generous ladling of the beef, tomato, onion, and bell pepper mixture and handed one dishful to him. "Eat up, *sobrino*."

Vance stabbed at the rice with his fork. "Do you think Chago's kid, Greg, knows about the money?"

"I don't know. Sorry I dragged you into this, but if you're gonna commit a crime, at least this one has a big payout. If anyone can pull it off, it's you working with Ray."

"Me working with Ray. That's a good one, Tony. You've been manipulating me. You realize this makes me a target."

"I'm in the same boat. If I didn't think we could pull it off, I wouldn't have dragged you into it. You're my sister's kid. I didn't ask you first because you would have said no."

"That's correct. I would have said no. As in hell no!" He leaned over his plate and stabbed the rice and meat with his fork. Something fell out of his hair. It clinked off the wooden tabletop.

Tony reached over and picked it up. "What's this? Looks like, ouch! Damn it!" Tony stuck his thumb in his mouth and sucked on a droplet of blood. He held it up as another bead of blood welled and rolled off. A crimson droplet splashed on the edge of his plastic plate. Holding the razor-sharp splinter of glass up under the hanging light bulb, he squinted. "OK, *sobrino*," he said, sucking his thumb. "I guess you're going to say broken glass just falls out of people's hair all the time."

———

LAUREN WAS KILLING time waiting for Ray, milling around the Java Chalet, browsing the shelves and hall trees filled with bric-a-brac for sale. When he came through the door he was his usual bubbly self. She followed him into a smallish alcove where they each sat in a worn leather club chair.

"Sorry I'm late," Ray said. "Miami traffic sucks. So, how did your date go?"

"Which one?" She watched his reaction. "I've seen him three times."

Ray arched one brow and squinted the opposite eye. "Who knew you'd fall in love? But then again—"

"—I'm not in love. Haven't you heard? If you fall in love, it sticks to your face."

"God, how I love a smart aleck." Ray tore open a pack of fake sugar and poured it into his black coffee. He used his index finger to stir it. "Did you recognize him from the old days from the Mutiny?"

"Vance?"

"Yeah, aka MileMarker45."

She cocked her head, "No. Should I?" She reached into her handbag and took out her wallet.

Ray held his hand up. "My treat." He grinned.

"I have no intention of buying your coffee." She took out the folded paper Vance had given her. "From your friend, my blind date, the ex-cop." She put the old paper down on her side of the low table separating them, just out of Ray's reach. "What's it worth?"

"That depends," Ray said.

"In my mind, it depends on what it's worth to you." She moved the paper closer to her side. Ray's eyes were glued to it. "A hundred grand." The demand was so ridiculous she laughed hard enough to rock her chair on its three best legs. Two men meeting at a corner table looked up from a shared laptop and scowled.

"All right," Ray lowered his voice. "I'll pay you a hundred thousand dollars for it. But I need you to do a few more things first."

"You're not serious." She rolled her eyes.

Ray ignored her. He was focused on his phone. "You need to install the app I'm sending you. And you need to have Prince Courage put it on his phone, too."

"Why?"

"Because we need to encrypt all our communications from here on. They automatically self-destruct depending on the settings."

"Why is this getting so Mission Impossible?"

"Did your new boyfriend mention who his uncle is?"

"He's not my boyfriend. And no, he didn't mention an uncle. What difference would that make?"

"It would make a difference, if you knew."

"OK." She licked her lips. "I'll bite."

"Tony Famosa." Ray's eyes were attached to his phone.

Lauren's eyes widened. Her phone pinged in her purse. "Is this some kind of joke?"

"Nope."

She looked at her phone. "Didn't the Paris bombers use an app like this? To plan the attacks?"

"Yeah. But it's not like we're terrorists. I just need you to be my go-between. To help me take care of some old business is all. I need someone I can trust."

Her chin dropped as much as her brow went up. "Trust, right. You set me up with Tony Famosa's ex-cop nephew, who by the way isn't my boyfriend, Ray. I should have known better. I should have asked more questions. I had a bad feeling about this. I would never, ever have gotten involved in any of this if I'd known Tony Famosa was involved. I thought he was dead."

"Calm down. You're fine. All you've done is meet me for coffee. I just thought you should know before you fall head over heels for the guy. Three dates in three days means there's something going on between the two of you. I just don't think it's a good idea to keep seeing him now. You got what I needed." Ray stared at the piece of paper on the table between them.

Lauren closed her eyes for five seconds and regained her composure. "*Is* Tony dead?"

"It's better if you don't know. I need to use the little boys' room. I'll be right back." Ray trotted off.

She wondered if Ray really needed to use the bathroom. When her ex, Peter, bailed out of their marriage, he'd accused her of having a PhD in denial. His affair with a coworker was so obvious he said even a blind person could see it. It was true. Everyone knew but her, and all the evidence was right under her nose. Peter started leaving the bedroom in the middle of the night because he couldn't sleep. She heard him on his phone, talking to someone at three in the morning. Looking back, she was so stupid. When she fell head over heels in love with him, she deluded herself into thinking their relationship was so special it would be immune to something as pedestrian as an office romance. The humiliation set her back on her heels. She went into an emotional nosedive worsened by an extended drinking spree.

Friends told her he was broadcasting their marriage was

over to friends and family. She recalled her exact feelings. *Stop saying that.* But trying to patch things up with Peter was like to trying to resuscitate a dead man.

That's what it was. A death. Except the ghost of Peter lived on through the cool responses he'd sent to the mean-spirited text bombs she'd flung at him when she was drunk out of her mind. Meeting Vance had given her a little bit of hope. It was the first time she had had any feelings since the moment Peter declared their marriage "broken." She didn't realize she was capable of feeling anything romantic until Ray warned her to stay away from him. Peter was right about one thing. She was Dr. Denial.

"Sorry about that," Ray said when he returned. "As guys get older, Mother Nature gives us less notice."

That was too much information, but she didn't want to embarrass him. "Here." She slid the paper across the table using her fingernail to push it, like it was radioactive. "Am I done now? With whatever this is? And just when I thought I was finished with therapy—"

"Did you look at it first?" Ray unfolded the old paper.

"Yes."

"And what did you see?"

Her shoulders jerked up and down and her neck twitched, the movements all out of sync. "I don't know, numbers, a whole lot of them. Like a Swiss bank account or something."

"I'll give you a hint. It's not a bank account. Meet with Vance one more time. Tell him to install the app on his phone. Send him a text to test it. Make sure it works." He handed her a white bank envelope. "Ten thousand dollars, a down payment. Use it for therapy. But don't get any lovey-dovey ideas in your head. This is a business deal."

"You don't expect me to believe you're going to pay me a hundred thousand dollars to go on a couple of dates, hand you a piece of paper with a bunch of numbers on it, and get him to download an encryption app on his phone, do you?" She grabbed the envelope out of Ray's hand.

"I might need you to do a couple more things." He put more balm on his highly conditioned lips and used his pinky finger to massage it in.

"You are annoyingly nonchalant about all this. I have a better idea. I could earn the hundred grand. I could write and produce the pilot for a new reality show. You and Tony could be judges. Vance could emcee. We could call it something catchy, like *Dancing with the Drug Czars*."

Ray Dinero grinned. His eyes twinkled. "Good one, but I can't dance. But oh how I love a woman who's fast on her feet."

13

WEDNESDAY

AT ITS ZENITH, Los Guapos grossed a million dollars a day in tax-free revenues. Tony's role was that of the debonair, masterful rainmaker. He forged new relationships and nurtured old ones. Chago was the henchman, in charge of dirty work like downsizing, making decisions about "personnel cuts," ones that tended to be permanent. But it was Ray Dinero who studied data, ran numbers, and calculated risk. If it had been a legal enterprise, Ray would have been director of operations.

Tony refreshed Vance's coffee. "You should have worked for us, *sobrino,* Chago and me. We added it up once. We thought it was funny when the government said we made around two billion dollars. It was more like six billion. We spent a fortune on lawyers. We hired the best criminal guys in New York and Boston. We *made* lawyers in Miami. But I get it. I don't know if I'd do it all over again. But you, you could have made a boatload of honest money if you'd have taken a job with one of the big law firms."

Vance laughed like a schoolboy. "A boatload. Ha! A hundred thousand dollar a year base salary is chump change compared to what you guys were taking in."

"A hundred thousand seems like a lot of money now that I've been living below the poverty level for the last twenty years. I'd take a job at a fast food joint. I'm not kidding."

"If I'd taken a job with one of the bigger firms it would have ruined me."

"How?" Tony looked truly confused.

"Like that Elliot Ness of a prosecutor. You guys ruined his life when you sent those pictures around of him drunk in a strip club." The tiny apartment was suffocating him and the memories of the past were casting a dark cloud over his mood. He couldn't help but wonder if Tony would have sold him down the river if he'd taken a job at one of the big firms. What if he'd defended Tony and Chago—and lost? Would they have killed him like they had so many others? The answer came to him immediately. If they killed Tony's wife Elina, of course they would have killed him. "Lots of innocent people died because of the drugs you smuggled. Do you ever think about the people who overdosed, the families torn apart by addiction, and the judge who was murdered?"

Tony lifted his coffee mug and wrapped both hands around it. Blowing softly on the hot liquid, he sat quietly for a moment. "My sisters were kids when they left Cuba. And I was just a baby. We had no dad around the house, and Sophia did the best she could to raise me. We were dirt poor. I was rebellious and full of hate by the time I got to high school. Selling drugs was a way out. Everyone was doing it. Chago and me, we were good at it. We dropped out of school because we were making so much money. And who told us to stop? No one."

"You were a good athlete. You could have done something different with your life."

"A four-hundred-meter hurdler? There's no future in that. Name one Olympic gold medal-winning hurdler?"

Tony was right about a lot of things, including that no one told him to stop. Vance was too fearful of his father to cut school, much less sell illegal drugs. He'd never considered the consequences of criminal behavior because he never got past what his father would do to him first. But Tony didn't have a father figure. By the time more of his relatives came to Miami during the Mariel Boatlift, Tony was under the protection of Los Guapos.

Dr. Jim Courage should have mentored Tony during his formative years. He was his wife's younger brother; that was reason enough. Instead, his dad talked about it at the dinner table when Vance was growing up, how Tony was a no-good drug dealer. His dad warned Vance that he might end up like Tony if he didn't do well in school. Vance recalled the pain in his mother's eyes when his father said those things. The irony of his and Tony's current plight was not lost on him. Maybe Tony showing up was the universe's way of leveling the playing field. Tony and Vance were in the same boat now, drifting in a sea of shit.

"When they finally arrested me for the final time," Tony said, "I had a million dollars cash and enough guns and ammo to overthrow Fidel. But you know what impressed the cops the most?"

"How fast you could run and how high you could jump?"

"You're an asshole." Tony lifted one leg and put his heel on the sofa to rub his ankle. "No. I had a gold brick. Something called a *doré*. Almost ten pounds, ninety-nine point five percent solid gold, stamped by the LBMA, the London Bullion Members Association, the refinery. It was a gift from Pablo. I was using it as a paperweight." He laughed at the recollection.

Pablo was Pablo Escobar, the brutal Medellín cartel boss gunned down in public by Colombian police in 1993. While the U.S. federal law enforcement agencies searched for ways to bring Los Guapos to justice, they strung enough information together to tie them to the Medellín cartel. The Colombians produced 80% of the world's cocaine, and Los Guapos acted as their distributor in the world's biggest market for illegal drugs: America.

"You didn't seem too upset about Chago's murder. That seems strange since the two of you have such a long history."

Tony slurped his coffee. "For a long time I dreamed of revenge."

"Revenge on Chago? Why?"

"I know he had something to do with Elina's death."

Vance had never suspected Chago was behind Tony's wife's murder. Elina was gunned down in broad daylight three days after she mailed an open letter to a small sensationalist newspaper after the *Herald* refused to publish it. The letter sung the praises of an anonymous hero, a cartel member who refused to cooperate with the authorities when he was caught delivering five hundred thousand dollars when Tony's older sister—Aunt Sophia—was kidnapped. A trusted Los Guapos lieutenant named Jaime Justo dropped the ransom money.

In the letter, Elina disparaged their banker, without naming Mongo, for turning state's witness.

"I told you back then I'd put money on one of your Ivy League lawyers writing it and instructing Elina to send that letter."

Tony hung his head down.

Elina's expensive handbag was found near her body, along with her cash and credit cards. The shooters left the gold Rolex on her wrist and a two-karat diamond on her finger. Two suspects, both aged twenty, were charged with her homicide, although no motive was ever established.

Tony bit his upper lip until it bled. He swiped at the pink liquid with his tongue. "It couldn't have gone down without Chago's OK. Killing a Los Guapos captain's wife? It would have started a war between the cartels. That's how I know he was behind it, because he never retaliated. While I was in jail keeping my mouth shut, Chago sent word accusing the Colombians of killing her. But he never said one word about why and nothing about revenge." Tony sucked air through his nostrils. "That's why I could care less he's dead. He wanted to intimidate me to keep me from testifying against him. So he killed my wife and blamed it on the Colombians. It backfired. It's why I turned on him."

Tony's rage was palpable. No, it had never occurred to Vance that Chago was behind it. That explained a lot. No wonder Tony could not care less that his childhood friend was dead.

Tony was trying to control his emotions. "When my sister Sophia was abducted, I was still, you know, *working*. She was pulled over by the cops and they kidnapped her." He tossed his head like the rattling might rid him of the thought.

Vance knew the story. Half the force was corrupt, and some had even snatched cartel family members for big ransom fees. Other dirty cops intercepted shipments of drugs and sold them. There was so much drug violence that the city had to lower its hiring practice because good guys weren't applying. They accepted recruits who failed drug tests; some even had misdemeanor convictions.

"We ended up having higher standards than the police. You were smart to get out when you did." Tony shook his head sadly at the memory. "I don't know if my sisters worried more about you or me."

Not wanting to get killed didn't require genius thinking.

Sophia made it home safely, but Jaime Justo did not. Her kidnapping wasn't just local police officers shaking Tony down for money; it was also an authentic DEA sting operation. Miami was so out of control the Feds sent undercover DEA agents posing as dirty cops to bust the police. Sophia was kidnapped in a double-sting operation. The local officers hoping to snag Tony's aunt for ransom were inadvertently working with Federal agents hoping to scrub Miami's police force of bad actors.

Jaime talked Tony out of delivering the money and insisted on dropping the ransom for him. Sophia was freed but Jaime got caught in the trap. He was the nameless person Elina referred to in the letter she'd sent, praising "ethics" and referring to people who "displayed courage" and "had a strong sense of character."

Elina had an eighth grade education, and it was obvious she didn't write the letter. Jaime's loyalty to Tony and the cartel was indisputable.

"Do you know Jaime spent eighteen years in a federal prison after you escaped? I followed the trial. He was convicted for tax evasion under the RICO statute. He was clean when they searched his home and cars. It was the ransom money they used to convict him. He refused to say where it came from."

Tony hunched his shoulders like a cat stalking its prey. "I guess I'll never know if it was out of loyalty or fear. But the fact remains. He kept his mouth shut and did the time. Do you know what the biggest predictor of future behavior is?"

"Past behavior."

"That's right." Tony fondled the television remote. "Do you know Jaime's son's an outfielder for the St. Louis Cardinals, and Jaime gets to sit over the dugout and watch his kid when the Marlins play at home?" Tony shook his head in a sort of amused skepticism. "I watched him play once. I knew a guy in Cuba who could tune in a few American stations with a pair of rabbit ears.

Jaime's come out best of all of us. He's an old man now, like me, watching his kid live the American dream."

"Flan, Crown Vics, and baseball."

Tony didn't laugh. His rage had lessened, but a cloud of darkness still hung over him. "Kid's still active. I saw him play yesterday, on TV. Did you know he was the second round pick in 2011? His salary is three and a half million dollars a year. Just turned thirty. I'm glad Jaime's life turned out like it did. I really am, *sobrino*. The universe rewards honor."

It was too late for Tony's world to turn out like Jaime Justo's. Time-worn now from being on the run, the best years had passed him by. Maybe there was a glimmer of hope, a sliver of optimism. If what Tony said was true, that seventy or eighty million dollars was really safely hidden, Tony might have one more chance at a life. And maybe Vance would, too.

"I'm interested," he said.

"In what?" Tony was lost in thought. He looked at him, vexed.

"I'm closing down my law office."

Tony looked surprised. "Why?"

"Because it doesn't make money. I've been keeping the doors open with what's left of my savings. I haven't had a receptionist or secretary for two years. My dad? He left my mom broke. And my sister, Kathy, she's just been diagnosed with pancreatic cancer."

Tony looked shocked. "Jesus, Vance. When it rains, it rains hard."

"You should know. I'm interested—in the money. We're probably fucked either way, so we might as well play double or nothing."

"I knew you'd come around, *sobrino*." He chewed on the inside of his cheek. "Pancreatic cancer. I'm really sorry, Van. Are there any treatments?"

"There are some drug trials. But it's expensive. Plus, what will my mom do? Whichever way this thing goes now, we're going to need a lot of money. For doctors and lawyers. Or we'll have to fake our deaths and leave the country."

"It would be a lot better if we won the lottery, but look at the bright side."

"Which is what?"

"We don't have to give half our dough to Uncle Sam."

That was an upside he hadn't considered. Half was a lot.

"And with that kind of cash we can get your sister the treatment she needs and set Sophia and Isabel up for life." He pressed the power button on the television remote, his mind disappearing into a game of baseball.

He hadn't given Tony enough credit for thinking it through. Turning state's witness against Chago took more guts than what Jaime Justo did. Tony wasn't just some coward who turned on his partner and fled to Cuba until he had to run from the next manhunt. He'd been betrayed by his childhood friend and trusted partner who turned out to be evil enough to kill anyone who threatened his power, even his best friend's wife.

He wasn't sure if he could trust his uncle or not. Not because Tony was bad, but because Tony could be reckless. He'd made a good point about fear. It had so many faces it could even disguise itself as loyalty. He studied Tony intently watching the game on TV and decided at that moment he was going to have to trust him.

14

Gregorio "Greg" Marino had known the twin girls Nicole and Lisa Solana since they were kids; they were practically related. His father, Chago, and their Uncle Mongo Solana had been business associates back in the day when Greg's father was a free man and needed a banker to launder millions for America's most powerful cocaine cartel.

But the girls knew about his deformed foot and treated him like a leper.

He heard it first through the grapevine that his dad's fugitive business partner, Tony Famosa, might be back in Florida. It wasn't much of a grapevine, really. His father's lawyer leaked it to him when he called to discuss the monthly payments he'd been making to the Aryan Brotherhood to protect his father at the high security federal prison in Colorado where his dad was serving multiple life sentences.

He was surprised the twins accepted his invitation. When the guard at his gated Key Biscayne condo buzzed, letting him know they'd arrived, he felt a wave of excitement. They looked gorgeous wearing skimpy black dresses. He offered them each a glass of pinot noir. He'd secretly added a pinch of Special K to their wine glasses and kept the vial in his pants' pocket in case he needed more.

He'd dreamt since puberty about a sexual encounter with them. He'd come close once, back when they were all in middle school. The first time he'd drugged them they were thirteen. He used Rohypnol, roofies. Their Uncle Mongo gave him the drug, reassuring him the girls wouldn't remember anything. He even helped Greg cut the tablets into powder, loaning him a mirror and a single-sided razor blade. Ten minutes after they sipped the iced tea he'd served them, they were out cold. Greg took off his left shoe and removed his sock. He caressed Lisa's lips with his deformed foot, sticking the corner of it where a big toe should have been, into her mouth. Then he pulled her panties down and parted her thighs. He was about to stick his grotesque foot between her legs when their single mother walked in on him. The whore tried to strangle him with her bare hands, and luckily Uncle Mongo heard his cries for help. Screw her. Only sluts were unwed mothers.

The Ketamine he scored on the street acted even faster.

"Uncle Mongo says he's going to make ussss richhhhh," Nicole slurred.

"How?" He shook Nicole like a vending machine. "HOW!" No information came out.

Her eyes rolled back in their sockets, and she slumped sideways, her torso crumpling on top of her unconscious sister. Nicole's long legs spread open. Her short skirt rolled up around her waist like a belt. If there ever was a sign from the gods, this was it. He pulled her panties off and spread her legs open. "Damn it! I was going to save you for last, but then you had to go and ruin it by not finishing your story. Now I'll have to save my strength."

He'd heard talk about tens of millions of dollars his dad and Tony Famosa had stashed somewhere but figured it was just that, talk. But if it were true, it was his inheritance, his fucking birthright. As the only son of one of the most notorious drug lords in U.S. history, it rightfully belonged to him. His sister, Bella, was entitled to nothing. She was a girl.

Before Chago went to prison, he'd left a lump sum to Greg's grandfather so his son could go to school, learn how to do something. But Greg wasn't interested in school or work. His father and grandfather didn't approve of his lack of ambition, dubbing him *perzoso.* Lazy. His grandfather scolded him, told him his father would be disappointed, that although his dad was a criminal, he was an industrious one.

Nothing he'd ever done his entire life was good enough. He started a social media page for his father and for three years updated it with posts, adding pictures he'd scanned. He'd worked to get a special dispensation from the Federal Bureau of Prisons to have a family Christmas portrait done at Florence's high security block. Chago's extended family had gathered in Colorado that summer. Greg had even accompanied his elderly, widowed grandmother on the flight from Miami. Bella had turned it into a family vacation, driving from Miami with her husband and kids.

It was the first time he'd been to the prison, and he hated seeing his dad locked up. At least he'd been moved from the Supermax block where Ted Kaczynski and a bunch of Middle Eastern terrorists were housed after his lawyers sued the federal government and won. His father wore a shapeless blue cotton jumpsuit and orange plastic clogs for the portrait Greg had worked so hard to organize. He looked so much older when he saw him late last summer, now bald with a gray beard.

When Chago laid eyes on his only son, his eyes lit up from behind his bifocals. It was the first time his father looked happy to see him.

"Is it true you hid money before the raid on the bank?" Greg had asked when they were alone for a moment. Instead of helping him, his dad told him to learn how to make his own way in life.

His resentment blossomed when Bella showed up. Chago's eyes had welled up when he saw his beloved daughter. He even knelt to meet his young grandchildren for the first time.

Fuck the universe. She didn't have a birth defect inside her shoe. He wished he hadn't bothered making the visit possible, going as far as threatening his father's lawyers with non-payment if it didn't happen. How did his father show his appreciation? By fawning over Bella, the child he'd always loved more.

Greg rolled Nicole off the sofa. She landed ass first with a thump on the throw rug. He knelt behind her and slid his forearms beneath her armpits, pushing her up into a sitting position. Her head slumped forward, her chin against her chest. Dragging her to the top stair he rotated her so her legs hung over the top two steps. Crouching, he dragged her down the stairs by her ankles, her head pounding each carpeted stair. His black cat, Pedro, couldn't resist the streamers of black hair and swiped her arms with open claws. He laughed.

He cared even less about Lisa, pushing her down the stairwell with the heel of his foot. Her body stopped on the third stair so he gave her a hard kick to the small of her back to get her going again. She rolled the rest of the way down.

All his experience handling dead weight didn't make moving the twins any easier. He'd been drugging and raping women all over Miami for years. At bars and health clubs, behind coffee shops, in cars, and on the beach. Online dating made it easy to stalk and catch his prey. Tap the screen. Meet somewhere. Knock them out with a dash of powder. Sexually assault them, then disappear, careful not to leave evidence.

Sitting on the bottom stair, he spoke to the unconscious pile-up of Nicole and Lisa. "Those whores were looking for hookups.

Only *putas* put their pictures out there like rescue dogs. More like putting a pussy up for adoption."

He stole photos of better-looking men from the Internet, posting them on his dating profile as lures, changing the pictures and usernames after each assault. Being a nondescript Latin man was convenient. No marks or scars, no tattoos or piercings. He kept his gruesome foot covered in a shoe. Average height. Dark hair. Greg was always cautious. He used condoms, even wrapping the deformed foot in cellophane. It wasn't fair. The elephantiasis. If he didn't have a grotesque foot, he could've led a normal life. His father would have loved him.

The crime scene investigation classes he'd taken at the community college taught him about transfer evidence, about how not to leave DNA behind in semen or on a glass or a napkin. Growing up with an absent father serving a multiple-lifetimes prison sentence halfway across the continent taught him the importance of being careful.

He was panting by the time he got the first body up on the mattress. He was exhausted by the time he got the second girl up on the bed.

"What a waste." He sat on the edge of the bed, stroking Nicole's long black hair. He unbuttoned her shirt and flicked her nipple. No response.

Stalking up the stairs, he returned wearing a rubber chemical weapons mask. Sitting cross-legged on the floor at the foot of Nicole's bed, he stuffed a wad of sticky weed into the brass bowl jutting out from the blue glass pipe fitted into the mask. He lit it and inhaled deeply, peering out from the big plastic oval eyes.

When the THC mixed with Greg's natural brain chemistry, it unleashed something primitive. The twins snored softly. Greg pushed a set of ear buds in. He dropped his pants and pulled his underwear down around his ankles.

He bucked and grunted, bringing himself to the edge of orgasm, and stopped. Dragging it out until he couldn't hold it, he exploded. His semen erupted with such force that a glop hit the eight-foot ceiling and hung there. He rolled onto his stomach, on the floor, between the twin beds and dozed off.

———

THE GIRLS MUST HAVE SMELLED *café con leche* brewing in his fifteen-hundred-dollar coffee machine. It lured them up to the kitchen.

"What happened?" Lisa rubbed her temple. She and her sister wore the clothes they'd slept in. She pulled out a barstool and sat.

Nicole stuck a paper towel under the kitchen faucet and wiped dried blood from her arm. The long scratch mark looked like it came from a cat. She massaged her scalp with her thumbs, "God, my head hurts."

Pedro rubbed against Greg's hairy ankle and meowed while he spooned shredded food from a can into the cat's dish.

Gagging on the smell of processed chicken, Nicole ran to the powder room off the kitchen, barely making it to the toilet.

He listened to her heaving and gagging, slurping his morning coffee, feeling refreshed. "You have a hangover." He handed her a cup of coffee.

Lisa glared at him. "How could I have a hangover from a half a glass of wine?" She massaged the small of her back with her fingers and twisted at the waist. "What's that smell? Weed?"

He laughed. "You don't remember anything?"

"Uh. No. Not really. How long did we sleep?"

"Ten hours. Straight." He held the silver coffee pot over her cup. "More?"

She caught a distorted reflection of herself as he filled her cup. She wet the corner of a napkin with her mouth to wipe at the smeared mascara and eyeliner that gave her panda eyes.

Nicole returned, looking even worse. She took the purse slung over her shoulder and put it on her knees. She stopped riffling through it. "Where's my phone?"

"Over there." He cracked his neck toward a pair of bling-skinned phones resting upright in a charging dock next to a vegetable juicer on the black granite countertop.

If the spy app he'd installed while they were out cold worked as advertised, he'd be able to read all their received, sent, and even deleted messages. It would give him the ability to monitor them remotely from his laptop. The bitches deserved what was coming. They weren't getting rich. He was.

15

WEDNESDAY

MIDNIGHT, 1.5 MILES OFF HOBE SOUND SHORE

OTHER THAN A STRIPE OF MOONLIGHT, the sea was black and the surface smooth as polished obsidian. The threesome drifted up quietly behind the sixty-two-foot Sunseeker Predator yacht. A masked man carrying a waterproof rucksack, and a pair of accomplices all clad in black wetsuits, tied the thirteen-foot inflatable Zodiac to the transom of the *Sea Food*. They stepped onto the teak swim platform, careful not to rock the boat anchored a half a mile offshore from the mansions of Hobe Sound, thirty-five miles north of Palm Beach.

Mongo crept up on the sleeping captain, leaving him helpless to warn his employers that pirates had boarded the ship. He held a six-inch-long black aluminum silencer to George Peak's head, forced him to his knees, and ordered him to crawl to the toilet mounted near the foot of the bed in the captain's quarters.

He cinched his hands behind his back with a Kevlar bicycle lock.

"I need some light," Mongo barked.

One of his accomplices pointed her phone flashlight at him.

"Not in my eyes, you moron! On my backpack."

She tilted the beam on the knapsack, using it like a follow spotlight.

It might have been a bad decision to bring them on the mission. Then he remembered why he had. He had plans for them. Mongo fished a roll of duct tape from his backpack, tore off a strip, and slapped it over George's mouth. "Be a good boy." Mongo patted the wide-eyed captain on the head.

He moved quietly toward the forward cabin, his two accomplices following closely behind. When he reached the room where the owners slept, Mongo lowered the backpack and laid it down on the floor just outside the stateroom. Holding one finger up to his lips, he tried the doorknob. The room was unlocked. He charged into the room, felt for the light switch, and flicked it on.

Charles Pierce awoke with night blindness, staring cross-eyed at a red laser. An imposing man who'd played college rugby, Charles leapt from the bed naked and lunged toward Mongo. The commotion woke the woman next to him.

The first gunshot hit the yacht owner in the right bicep. Mongo's accomplices held the man's terrified wife down on the bed.

"Motherfucker!" Charles looked at exposed muscles and tendons and felt a hole under his ribs.

Mongo put the gun to the big man's forehead and squeezed the trigger. The hollow point entered just above his right eyebrow.

The twins were trying to hold Betty Pierce down on the bed. "Shoot her!" Mongo yelled at them.

"We can't kill her!"

"You girls are nothing but pussies," he said.

"Charles, Charles!" The dead man's wife was panicking.

Mongo punched Betty in the face. The blow shut her up and disoriented her long enough for him to stick the aluminum silencer on her Botoxed forehead. The hollow point bullet mushroomed the instant it entered her skull, ripping a hole the size of a donut.

"She was looking right at you, Uncle Mongo," one girl said.

"Jesus! You killed them both!" The other one sounded stunned.

"Shut the fuck up," Mongo the rat-banker said. "What did you think we were doing tonight, delivering groceries?"

Covering the mouth of the knitted facemask with her hand, Nicole retched a half dozen dry heaves.

"Quit bitching and start helping me."

The girls pulled the black masks from their heads and shook their long black hair. The stateroom was surreal, like a Christmas snow globe. But in this perverted version, the confetti was blood splatter and bone fragments. Red droplets spattered the white leather headboard. Irregular blotches soaked the comforter and bed skirt like a bloody Rorschach test. More had pooled on the light-oak flooring. An expression of horror and surprise was stuck on the couples' faces, as if stunned they were dead.

Blood-speckled reading glasses rested atop a paperback book spread open, facedown on the nightstand. Droplets of blood dispersed like octopus ink in the half empty glass of water next to it.

Mongo planted his massive forearms on the mattress and leapt over Charles's torso like a chimpanzee. Straddling him, he covered the naked body with the top bed sheet. He dug his heels into the mattress and rolled the carcass to the edge of the bed, then booted it onto the floor. The late Charles Pierce landed with a thud, rocking the boat. He hopped across the bed and jerked the bottom fitted sheet out from the corners and rolled Betty in it. He nudged her off the mattress. She landed on top of her dead husband with a dull thump. Mongo wiped his hands on the linens like a butcher, unzipped the wetsuit, and tied the arms around his waist.

He glared at the horrified girls. "What do you think this is, a fucking movie? Get over here and help me. Grab a leg."

The trio hauled the two hundred and eighty pound man by his legs, six inches at a yank, to the stern of the yacht. They propped him against the bulkhead leading to the transom stairs.

"Uncle Ramon, you never said anything about *killing anyone*," Nicole whined.

"I said I'd make you rich. What did you think? That I'd share a winning Powerball ticket with you?" He pulled off the mask, his yellow snake eyes glinting. "Let's get busy."

He dragged Charles by the ankles face down to the opening to four white fiberglass stairs leading to the swim deck. Mongo grunted and groaned. The dead man's head pounded each tread like a bowling ball, leaving teeth marks and streamers of blood in the wake. He left the nude and battered body of the renowned restaurateur in a heap at the base of the bottom stair. Using his muscular forearms, Mongo pulled Charles to the edge of the wooden deck and heaved the man's corpse into the warm Atlantic water.

Covered in blood, he stalked back up the stairs and scooped Betty's limp body off the oak bedroom floor. The girls watched as he crabbed out of the room and headed to the transom. The sheet he'd wrapped around her had fallen loose. The blood-soaked linen floated like a tie-dyed kaftan, the moonlight reflecting off Betty's pale skin. He tried cradling her with one arm to cover her glassy green eyes staring up at him. But the bloody bed sheet wrapped around his foot causing him to stumble.

"Goddamn it!" he yelled, grabbing the stair railing just in time to keep from tumbling.

He'd used her body to brace against the fall and the impact caused blood to spurt from her head wound. Mongo sat on the top stair with her body curled in his lap, wiping the spatter from his face with the back of his forearm. Resting for half a minute to catch his breath, he stood holding Betty and walked to the edge of the stern. Kneeling, he gently dropped her into the sea. She floated away in the current, the moon overhead illuminating the blood-mottled cloth until it drifted out of sight.

The girls were standing on the top stair and had watched silently.

When he saw them, he said, "Jesus, you two have more brains splattered on your tits than you have up in your heads."

Moonbeams cast a flattering light over the exhausted, twins, accentuating their silky black hair and narrow eyelids. They stripped out of the wetsuits they'd worn to protect them from the ocean spray to identical black bikinis. Sitting on the swim platform they dipped their bloody feet and hands into the warm salt water. They stood, bent their knees, and dove elegantly off the edge like a pair of synchronized swimmers, making barely a splash.

Mongo headed back to the stateroom. He took the silencer off the pistol and stuffed it in his knapsack. Clomping across the sticky oak floor, he riffled through a rack of clothing neatly arranged on hangers in the master closet.

The twins surfaced from the black water and gripped the stainless boat ladder. Mongo held up the Pierce's matching his-and-hers monogrammed terrycloth robes he'd fished from hooks on either side of the headboard. "Put these on." He draped the robes over the steel railing. Then Mongo took a running start, jumped in the air, grabbed his knees, and cannon-balled into the calm Atlantic water.

THURSDAY MORNING

VANCE WAS late and Lauren frowned at him when he arrived. He had a bad habit of being tardy, and now that his intentions were no longer tied to getting laid, he was being himself. Late. And underdressed, donning frayed, camo knee-length shorts, hillbilly Crocs, and a faded T-shirt he'd gotten for free at a gun show.

He ordered a cup of black coffee and dropped onto the Chesterfield sofa opposite her. The Java Chalet looked like a life-sized dollhouse. The tiny rooms were loaded with pastel hutches crammed with gifts for sale, all sorts of useless stuff, some of it humorous, all of it certainly destined for yard sales. The upholstery was grandmotherly, mostly plaids and floral patterns with ruffles. But it had a sense of intimacy, unlike the chain coffee houses.

"So what's up that couldn't wait, and why do you look so annoyed?" he asked.

"I met with Ray. I gave him the note, the one with all the numbers on it. So when were you going to tell me?" Her tone was snippy.

"Tell you what?"

"That you're Tony Famosa's nephew."

"Ray told you that?"

"Yes."

He was caught completely off guard. Why in the world would Ray tell her that? "I was going to tell you. Really, I was." In truth, the thought of telling her Tony was his uncle *never* crossed his mind.

"I think you might have gotten me involved in something illegal. Those numbers I gave to Ray look like bank accounts. But Ray says they're not."

"I don't know." He was careful not to make eye contact. "I was just passing it along."

"Do you expect me to believe that?"

"You can believe whatever you want, but I don't know what those numbers are for and I don't want to know. I've learned to compartmentalize."

"Spare me. Men don't need to *learn* how to compartmentalize. Right now I wish I could pigeonhole my IRS problem into a mental man drawer." Lauren sighed and pursed her lips. "This is not where I envisioned my life going. Getting a divorce at my age is so cliché. Getting dumped for a younger version. It's not like I let myself go. It seems like all the things I've worried about my entire life didn't happen, and things I never thought about are happening."

Lauren was doing something on her phone, under the low maple coffee table.

"If there's any advice I'd give the younger generation, it's this," she said, "select a mate and accept it won't be perfect, that on some days you'll want to kill the person. Then grow old together. Don't go shopping for love when you have high mileage. You might be able to find a newer model, but don't kid yourself. It won't be worth it."

"Don't you think you're being a little rude?"

"What? Did you take what I said about high mileage personally because you're a lifelong bachelor?"

"That's not what I meant. I was talking about texting under the table." His phone blipped. He plucked his out of his shorts pocket and looked at the screen. It was from her.

"It's an app. Ray said to tell you to download it on your phone. It's encrypted, for texting. He said it's how we should communicate from here on out. Go into the settings and familiarize yourself. It's easy to figure out. You can set it to destroy messages at intervals—"

Great, he could add another co-conspirator to possible criminal charges. "We need to encrypt our communications?"

"I set mine so it deletes messages right after I read them. It works just like regular texts."

"Did you ask Ray why a U.S. Marshal is surveilling me?"

"No. I didn't think I needed to. Don't you think it might have something to do with Tony? Gosh, you're good. *'I barely remember the place.'* Ray asked me if I recall seeing you at the Mutiny."

"Ray told you that too?" He reached over Lauren's shoulder and lifted a corner of the pink-and-white gingham curtain behind her. The white Escalade was in the parking lot across the street with its running lights on. "So Ray's paying you? To be a messenger girl or something?"

Lauren cocked her head, her pale complexion turned scarlet. "I prefer liaison."

"And when were you going to tell me your little secret?" he tit-for-tatted.

"My little secret?" She furrowed her brow.

"About who sent you?"

"About who sent me? You mean here, for coffee? Obviously Ray did."

"The online dating thing. Who put you up to it?"

"Very good." Lauren smiled wickedly. "Very intuitive. Most men can't detach from their egos long enough to figure out it wasn't all about them. It makes men too easy sometimes. Anyway, Ray did. He gave me your username and told me to contact you. I guess he did it to get those numbers." Lauren sank deeper in the Chesterfield. "I really wish I didn't need money as desperately as I do, but I do. As you know."

He checked his phone. He told her the app had finished downloading.

Lauren typed fast, with her thumbs, like a teenager.

His phone pinged: `I'm breaking up with u in a text.` He read it and laughed out loud. "I knew it. I knew you were that kind of girl the moment we met."

She glared at him. "Whatever you got me involved in, Ray says we need to stop communicating with each other. I can't believe I confided in you about not being ready to get involved in a relationship."

"I don't think I got us involved in anything. I think you did." She didn't deny it.

"Text Ray. He wants you to test the app."

She got up and left without saying goodbye.

He stayed and sent a test message to Ray who answered in less than ten seconds. Ray told him to stay put. It wasn't like he had anything more important to do.

Though they'd never officially met, Vance recognized him. Ray sat down in a hurry and skipped coffee because he said he already had the jitters from too much caffeine. Ray squeezed some creamy lip balm from a metal tube and worked it into his lips with his pinky finger while tapping the rubber sole of one flip-flop on the wooden floor. "Your uncle wasn't sure if you'd help us or not, but I'm glad you decided to."

Help? "I didn't exactly decide to help. It's more like Tony and you mired me in something that I don't fully understand."

"Did he talk to you about money?"

"More or less."

"The faster we get it, the less chance we'll have of getting caught. We need to start moving."

"Where is it?" Vance asked.

"Offshore."

"Grand Cayman?"

"No, offshore as in the hull of sunken powerboat. I don't know if you remember or not, but back in the day Tony and Chago owned Ocean Eagle, the hull manufacturer. It was my idea to buy the company. We retrofitted our fleet with secret compartments. When Mongo cut a deal with the Feds, I was in charge of moving as much cash out of the bank's safe deposit boxes as I could before it was raided. I filled waterproof transport cases and loaded them into the hull of one of our racing boats. Then I sank it offshore, where it's been ever since."

"Is it really seventy-five million dollars?"

"Close estimate."

"How much of this does Lauren know?"

"Nothing. I used her to get to you. I paid her to do it, to meet you on that dating site. She makes bad choices when it comes to men anyway, and from what I've heard, you make no choices when it comes to women. Seemed like a perfect match."

Paid her to do it? She makes bad choices? I make no choices? Ouch, on all counts. Damn.

"I'm just kidding, Vance. Don't take it so personally. She likes you."

He sat silently licking his ego.

Ray looked sympathetic. "I guess I'd feel the same way. I didn't know you two would hit it off, and I wouldn't have guessed you'd get your feelings hurt."

"Who said anything about hurt feelings?" He was grumpy.

"It's sort of obvious."

"Yeah, well, just so you know, I haven't formally agreed to anything. I can't kick Tony out on the street. But not turning him in, like the Unabomber's brother did, is a crime. I'm pretty sure I have a U.S. Marshal tail on me. Everywhere I go there's a white Escalade in my mirrors, parked outside my apartment, at my office, even at my dad's funeral." Ray had to know all this. He was the one who set the trap.

"Oh, I meant to say this first. Sorry about your dad."

"Thanks. Do you know if I'm being followed?"

Ray ducked the question. "Just be careful. Tony needs to lay low, and you need to go about business as usual."

"With all due respect, Ray, I know more about the law than you do. As for business as usual, forget that. I'm closing down my law practice. There was a drive-by shooting there yesterday. This sounds crazy, but a white Escalade fled the scene, like the one that's been following me."

"A shooting? Is that why you're closing your business?"

"I'm closing it for the same reason I'm still sitting here. Business has been going downhill for a long time, and I'm not cut out to work at a big firm. I need money."

"We need to add someone to our team, someone new from the outside. You're a—were a—personal injury attorney, right?"

Vance nodded.

"We need to recruit someone, and I'm guessing you can find a good candidate. Someone smart, discreet, and professional."

"Why not one of your clients? I heard you bought a big yacht brokerage on the river."

Ray spoke quickly. "What we're up to isn't exactly on the up and up. I need someone desperate, and desperate people aren't out shopping for million-dollar yachts. Desperate people, they're the ones recovering from illness, divorce, accidents, unemployment, custody crap, DUIs, you know, the bad stuff, and they all eventually go see a lawyer. A lawyer like you."

He wished they were coming to see a lawyer like him.

"We need a smart guy with big balls. No young guns, either. Someone mature, with life experience to join our team," Ray said.

Since when had he become part of the team? He hadn't agreed to anything yet. "Before I start headhunting, I need more information. Like what exactly am I signing up for, and what do you plan to pay me?"

"Do you know anyone who fits the bill?"

"Maybe." He wasn't playing any cards until he had more details. Who was he kidding? He had no cards to play. Paid her to do it? She makes bad choices? I make no choices?

"What did he come to see you about?" Ray asked.

He fixed his eyes on Ray, watching for facial cues. "He's not going to work for peanuts, that I can tell you. And it will depend on what you want him to do."

Ray leaned forward and twisted his torso, like his back was out of place. "What sort of problem did this guy have?" Rotating his upper body in the other direction, his vertebrae made a series of pops, like the last few kernels in a bag of microwavable popcorn.

"He came to me about an employment situation. He didn't have a good case so I took him to lunch instead. Very bright guy with a couple of young kids still living at home. He's a geezer dad, like you. MBA. Top school. He was a Wall Street investment banker for over twenty years, or maybe he said thirty. Retired early and lost his life savings in real estate during the housing bubble. Tragic situation, really."

Ray rolled his shoulders and leaned back. He cracked his neck. "Got young kids, huh. What's his name?"

"Jake Fleming."

"What's he doing now?"

"Selling used cars, I think."

"Give old Jake a call. Ask him if he wants to work for a big bonus."

"How much are we talking about? He's going to ask."

"Tell him ten million, minimum, and the same for you, if we pull it off. If he agrees, set up a meeting for the three of us. Use the new texting app. And there's one more thing. This one is non-negotiable. Stay away from Lauren Gold."

Ten million dollars and *stay away from Lauren Gold*? A cold sweat broke under his shirt. He hadn't expected an offer that generous. Lauren had already told the other news.

"I'll do it. I'll contact Jake." His paused. "Are you sure? About the amount?"

Ray stood. "The money?"

"Yeah."

"Barring anything unforeseen, yeah."

"And Lauren doesn't know about it? The money."

"No. That's why I need you to stop seeing her. She's smart. She already knows we're up to something."

"Thanks to you and your loose lips."

Ray sat and lowered his voice. "What do you mean by that?"

"You told her Tony's my uncle."

"Oh, that. Like I said before, I didn't think you two would hit it off. She went through an ugly break-up last year. I thought she'd sworn off men for a while. I gotta go. The Memorial holiday is going to be busy at the boatyard."

He stayed after Ray left and played it back in his head. The date was a setup. He hadn't suspected anything. A piece was missing. Then it dawned on him. Sarge kept busting his chops about his online dating username. *Milemarker45.* That's how Sarge fit into the puzzle. But what was his angle? For all the years he'd investigated con men and criminals, and defended people who'd been victimized by their deeds, this was the first time he was the patsy. And it felt like shit. The betrayal.

Ten million. That was a lot of money. He needed it to pay for Kathy's experimental cancer treatment. His mother could lose her home. Some vulturine realtor might be sitting in her living room now, pressuring her to sell the house. He wanted to tear open his wallet and call Jake. But the impulse had to wait.

WHEN HE GOT BACK to his cramped apartment, Tony was dozing in front of the TV. He sneaked past without waking him and went into the bathroom, closed the lid on the toilet, and sat. He removed the American Express card from his billfold and retrieved the card he'd tucked behind it.

Jake Fleming
Managing Director

He searched *managing director investment bank* on his smart-phone. A website called mergersandaccusations.tv came up.

A video played. A snarky metrosexual in his early thirties standing in front of a plain white wall had recorded himself on a cell phone.

"So you want to be a Managing Director at an investment bank. First, let's talk about what you don't do. You don't actually loan money. Your world is a jungle and you are the alpha at the top of the food chain.

"Ninety percent of your hundred-hour work week is spent kissing ass, otherwise called taking meetings. It helps to dress British and think Yiddish. When you're not working—"

He stopped the video and dialed the phone number Jake had handwritten on the business card.

Jake answered on the first ring, "So are you in the market for a used car?"

"Not exactly." He picked his words as though the world was listening. "I thought we could catch up. How's the job search going?"

Jake laughed his Freddy Krueger laugh. "I'm selling vehicles at one of those no-name lots in Little Havana. Place self-finances at twenty-five percent interest. Of course, we're really in the tow truck business. Turns out it's easier than selling Beamers. Now I just sign poor people up. They drive off in an old beater. Can't make the second payment after putting every *peso* in a car with bald tires. And then Guido-the-repo man puts the car on a hook, brings it back to here, and we sell it to another undocumented worker. See? I've learned to be PC. This job sucks, exponentially. But my people skills have improved."

He was refreshingly sarcastic. "I have a business idea I would like to discuss. Can you meet me for a drink?"

"I'd love to. But I'm stuck on the lot until eight tonight. You could probably get me to rob a bank at this point. You know what amazes me? How poor people prey on poorer people."

"That's human nature. Each man for himself."

"So, can I interest you a low-mileage PT Cruiser? It's almost as ugly as your roach coach."

"Funny. Eight-thirty, Tavern in the Grove? It's not Tavern on the Green, but the beer's cheap."

"Sounds more my speed. See you there."

Vance's phone buzzed. Sergeant Daniel Ruiz. *That asshole.* He hit the red Dismiss button. He didn't feel like talking to him. On second thought, he had a better idea. He tapped Redial. It was a chance to test the waters.

Sarge answered instantly. "*Oye, flaco, ¿Que pasa?* I was just about to send you a text."

"What do you want?"

"It's hard leading the bachelor life on a retirement account. The ladies expect me to pay all the time."

The dating banter was getting tiresome. "You sound like a dirty old *señor.* You could sell that gold brick, the *doré.* You'd get twenty grand easy for it. That would finance a lot of dates."

"I don't know what you're talking about."

Hmm. Sarge was lying about it.

"These fucking normalized relations. Thanks to *diplomacy,* I'll be sleeping on my floor pretty soon. Couch is stacked three high."

"What are you talking about?"

"Every relative remotely related to me is coming over on visas courtesy of Uncle Sam. It's worse than the Mariel Boatlift. I have six raft monkeys sleeping at my apartment. And how long do you think they'll be staying? For-fucking-ever."

"So I guess this puts a damper on your online dating." He enjoyed poking the dating bear.

"You think? I may as well go back to work because the U.S. government just fucked up my retirement plans. How's the hot blonde horsey chick?"

"I didn't tell you anything about a horse chick."

"Yeah, you did. Early dementia. Happens to me all the time. We're at that age, you know."

"Maybe you are, but I'm not." He was positive he hadn't so much as breathed a word about Lauren Gold to him. He knew because Sarge would do what he was doing now, torturing him. He'd seen a rare gold *doré* brick just like the one Tony described at Sarge's house back when they were still active duty. His then-wife Maria had invited Vance to dinner. He'd opened a drawer in the kitchen and was poking around for a bottle opener when Sarge had practically jumped him, slamming the drawer shut on his thumb. His nail fell off a week later. Sarge tried to convince him it was a fake. Now he was trying to make it seem like a hallucination.

"You should post a picture of yourself with that gold brick on your dating profile. That would be the chick magnet to beat all chick magnets."

"I don't know what you're talking about."

"Early dementia. Happens to *you* all the time. *You're* at the age now, you know. Did you call me for a reason or have you forgotten why already?"

"Never mind." Sarge was pissed and ended the call.

The gold brick he'd seen was leverage in case he needed it.

How Daniel Ruiz had ended up with the gift Pablo Escobar gave to Tony remained a mystery. Better friend than foe. That's how he'd always felt about Sarge. He dressed hurriedly to meet Jake.

TAVERN in the Grove was crowded, loud, and smelled foul as usual. Jake listened, squeezing the lower part of his jaw with his hand, molding his mouth into fish lips.

"*How* much cash?" Jake's cheeks and lips slowly returned to their natural jowly sag when he let go of his face. He ran his fingernails through his slick black hair.

Vance repeated it. "Ten million."

"You can guarantee that?"

"No, not exactly. All I can tell you is that the information comes from a reliable source."

"As an attorney, I'm sure you've heard the expression 'due diligence.'"

Vance volleyed back. "As a guy sitting across the table from me, I'm sure you've heard the expression 'take it or leave it.' I'm pretty confident you're not in a position to leave it."

"No. I'm not. And that's not a good place to be, especially at my age. I had other ideas about what I'd be doing for the third act. I figured I could always work ahead of my financial needs. Turns out that's not true so far."

That's what Vance's dad must have thought too.

Jake tilted the bottle of beer into his mouth and gulped. "Is what we're doing legal?"

"Legal is open to interpretation. You'll just have to trust me."

"Trust you? You're a lawyer for chrissake. I'm intrigued, and interested. That much cash, well, first of all, it's unbelievable. But if it's true, it's going to be this side of impossible to hide." Jake's brain was supercomputing. "With the industry down to just a few big banks, it's going to take some thinking to keep that much cash off the government regulators' radar screens. You picked me because you know I'm down on my luck."

"Well, there's that. And there's your fashion sense too. Not many criminals dress in the same colors as a frozen yogurt stand."

"Ones outside the New York financial district, you mean."

"Good point. If that's how the one-percenters dress, then I guess being a ninety-nine-percenter has its advantages. So what do you think—are you interested?"

Jake didn't have to think. "Of course I'm interested. I have nothing to lose. I'm definitely in. Maybe I can catch up on my retirement plan. I'm pretty sure this is my last chance."

"My business associate wants to meet you."

"Let me know when. This sounds too good to be true, and you know what they say about that." Jake slammed the empty bottle down on the bar and called out for another round.

16

WEEK TWO
FRIDAY

VANCE PICKED the coffee place to introduce Jake Fleming to Ray Dinero. Ray sized him up immediately. It was as if Jake was standing in a spray-on tanning booth and Ray's eyes were the nozzles—up, down, turn around, up, down, side-to-side —repeat.

"This place is precious." Jake dropped two quarters on the counter and reached into a glass barrel filled with pink licorice. He pulled out a string of candy and bit off one end. He studied the hall trees and armoires jam-packed with shiny stuff made in China.

The frumpy owner recognized Vance. "You're here early. Not with your girlfriend today?" She handed him a black coffee.

"No, not today."

The small side room with the low sofa was unoccupied. Vance and Jake sat on the Chesterfield. Vance sat near the edge of the cushions, leaning slightly forward to keep the 9-millimeter Glock from digging into his lower back. Ray sat opposite them on a floral wingback chair. All three wore shorts and looked like they were in a man-spreading competition.

"I'm a business guy." Jake lowered his voice when speaking to Ray. "If what Vance says is true, seventy-five million is going to present some challenges."

"I know." Ray swiped his lips with balm.

Today's fragrance reminded Vance of a dental office.

"Is the money in an offshore account?" Jake asked.

"You could say that," Ray said.

"Cayman? Zurich?" Jake looked puzzled.

"No. It's offshore, as in *on* the ocean floor."

Jake furrowed his brow, clamped his hand on the armrest, and leaned farther forward, listening.

"It's packed in the hull of an old power boat, the *Holly Golightly*," Ray said.

Jake looked at Ray suspiciously, with narrowed eyes.

VANCE REMEMBERED the *Holly* as the winningest offshore power-boat in the Los Guapos racing fleet. Ray copiloted her to dozens of victories in the '90s, acting as the navigator for Tony and Chago.

"How do you know for sure it's still there?" Jake asked. "The money. Or the boat."

"The same way I know today is Friday. Better question, how do you like selling used cars? That's what you're doing, right?" Ray lifted his hips and reached into both front pockets of his shorts and extracted a pair of smartphones. A small stack of business cards was fastened around each with a rubber band. Ray handed one to Jake and the other to Vance. "Burners.

Download the texting app. Use these from here on out." He looked at Jake. "Use it to contact Lauren Gold—"

"Who's Lauren Gold?" Jake looked confused.

"Vance will get you up to speed, and he'll send you the link to the app. We need you to pose as a prospective client."

This was the first Vance had heard about this plan.

Jake plucked one of the business cards banded to his new phone and read aloud,

Jake Fleming
Director of Special Projects & Strategic Marketing
Cormorant Cases, Inc.

"Is this a real company, Cormorant?" Jake flicked the corner of the card with his fingernail.

"Yeah. We're borrowing their logo." Ray gave Jake a photocopy of Lauren's business card. "Call her and tell her you're working on a confidential project for Cormorant. Ask her if she knows of any underwater cameramen with experience and equipment."

"Then what?" Jake asked.

"You're going to hire her to produce a top secret marketing video that the Cormorant company hopes will go viral. Use me as a reference. She's done some video production work for my boatyard. She's not in on this part of the plan."

Vance didn't know anything about this part. Sure, Lauren lied to him and bruised his ego big time, but it sounded like Ray was putting her in harm's way.

Jake dabbed at a droplet of coffee he'd dribbled onto his pastel-green Bermuda shorts. "So you want me to lie to her?"

"I don't think this will be the first time you've lied to a woman. Here, I know you need some operating cash." Ray slipped an envelope into Jake's palm. "It's fifteen thousand.

You're going to have to pay her something up front, enough to cover her and her guy. Ten thousand for her, three grand for her guy, and the rest is for you to use as petty cash. You should probably keep selling cars for now. You need to keep a low profile."

"And what exactly is the strategic marketing plan?" Jake asked.

Ray talked fast. "Tell her your company sank their waterproof cases offshore back in the nineties as a time capsule. Tell her you're contacting her because the company wants to make a video of the salvage operation. Emphasize that Cormorant needs total confidentiality from her, that they want to use it for social media. If the cases are tampered with or any information leaks out, tell her it'll kill the deal. Vance is going to draft the Non-Disclosure Agreements."

"I am?" Vance cocked his head. Ray was dumping a lot of new information on him right in front of Jake.

"What's to keep her or whoever she subcontracts from opening the cases?" Jake asked.

"Tell her she won't get the balance of the money. Tell her that if she so much as thinks about opening those cases, the deal's dead. And we'll sue her. Put it in the NDA, Vance. Remind her that the point of the video is to open the cases in front of a live Web audience. No manufacturer has ever done anything like this. But if they touch the latches, it's over. Vance will get the agreements to you, Jake. Have her sign one. Her guy will have to sign one, too."

"How do you know who she'll hire?" Jake asked.

"Because I asked her if she knew a cameraman who's a certified underwater diver and cameraman when I hired her to make the video for my place. She does great work. Don't forget to tell her I referred you. She's worked with the same camera guy for a long time."

"So you think she'll go for it?" Jake snapped the corner of the business card again.

Ray tapped his toe on the old cherry-wood plank floor. "His name is Davis Frost. I guarantee she'll hire him."

"I don't know much about making viral videos, but I'm pretty sure I can pretend to be a marketing executive. That can't be too hard," Jake snickered.

"Just stick to the script. Call her and set up a meeting. Tell her what the budget is and give her ten thousand now. Tell her she'll get the other half after you get the video files and cases. Tell her it's very important not to discuss it with anyone. When she brings up Davis Frost, tell her you have to meet with him first, one-on-one, that he'll have to sign an NDA, too. Tell her you'll pay him a deposit when he signs the agreement. We don't need a naval minesweeper anchoring out there."

Ray looked at Vance. "That paper you passed to me? It's not a bank account. It's the coordinates to the wreck. You're going to pass as Cormorant's in-house counsel. Give Davis one of those business cards when you meet. I want you to be there, too, when Jake meets him. Give Davis the coordinates." Ray handed Vance a photocopy of the paper from Tony with the numbers on it.

Jake rubbed his jaw. "Where did the seventy-five million come from?"

"As your lawyer, I'm telling you it's better if you don't know."

"Very funny. *Now* you're my lawyer, after I practically groveled."

"One more thing. And this is very important," Ray said. "There are two sets of cases down there packed in the hull. Yellow ones and black ones. Tell her we want the yellow ones and to leave the black ones behind."

Jake repeated it. "I'll tell Lauren to have her guy recover the yellow cases and leave the black ones in the hull. What if she wants to know why?"

"Between the two of you, you'll think of something," Ray said.

"Is she good-looking? My new video producer?" Jake asked.

Ray said, "Definitely."

"That's good. Wouldn't matter if she were butt-ugly. For a nice chunk of a seventy-five million dollar pie, I'd do just about anything."

A bad feeling swept over Vance. He felt a pit in his stomach. There were many things he wouldn't do for money. He'd already proved it. He'd turned stuff down his entire life. While most cops stole cash from dealers and skimmed drugs from big busts to sell on the side, he'd turned every cent and gram into the evidence room. By the time he was thirty, he'd turned down enough bribes to retire comfortably in the Turks and Caicos. Tony tried to give him cash and drugs as gifts, but he'd refused him too. Now he pondered the wisdom of bringing Jake to the deal.

Ray pushed a two-inch-thick bank envelope into Vance's hand. "Your retainer."

He took the money and stuffed the wad in his pants pocket. After a lifetime of judgments and flaunting a holier-than-thou attitude, the minute he took the money he crossed over to the other side, the dark one. He slid his hand in his pocket and felt the envelope. There was no lightning strike or burning bush. No guilt. No attack of morality.

What had he been thinking? He'd turned down insane salaries at multiple law firms pursuing him right out of law school because they wanted him to defend drug dealers. When he was a detective, no one wanted to partner with him because the cops shook down dealers for drugs and money, and no one wanted a choirboy getting in their way. He refused bribes ranging from cash and drugs to jewelry. He never accepted one single thing under the table. Never even entertained the idea of breaking the law. He'd tried not to mix legal or police business with Tony.

He counted to ten in his head, waiting for an attack of virtue or at least some anxiety. It didn't come. Maybe he'd have a delayed response. But right now the dark side didn't feel bad at all. It was a relief. He reached into his pocket and patted the envelope. It was exciting. Who had he been kidding? He'd been depriving himself all this time.

FRIDAY AFTERNOON

SINBAD HAULED LAUREN around the dog park, and her impatience was growing. He had his own communication system, and if she worried if she hurried him he might revert to doing his business in the house, dropping encrypted doggy messages she'd been unable decipher.

Her cell buzzed. A 212 area code came up. A lot of New Yorkers came to Florida for film and video work, though May was the end of the season. It was too tempting to let the call go.

"Lauren Gold."

"Is this Gold Productions?" The voice sounded distorted.

It annoyed her. She didn't respond, a tactic she used to get rid of solicitors.

"My name's Jake Fleming. I was referred to you by Ray Dinero."

She turned cheery. "Of course, Ray Dinero, yes. How can I help you?"

Jake poured it on thick. "I'm with the Cormorant Case Company, and we have an upcoming *special* project I would like to discuss with you. It requires discretion. We've known Mr. Dinero for a long time and have done business with his boat yard. We need to hire a video crew with knowledge of underwater work for a salvage project. Is this something you'd be interested in?"

"Absolutely," she said, trotting behind the dog, trying not to pant. "I am. Very interested."

"Before I can give you any details, the company attorneys are requiring vendors to sign Non-Disclosure Agreements first. Do you have a problem with that?"

"No. No. Not a problem," Lauren was out of breath and loosened her grip on the leash, hoping Jake couldn't tell she was walking her dog at two in the afternoon on a Friday.

"Let's meet."

"Sounds good. You said it's an underwater shoot. Do you know the depth?"

"You need to sign the NDA before I can give you any more specifics."

"Understood."

"I'll call you later today to set up a meeting tomorrow. Is tomorrow OK? To meet?"

"Yes. No problem." Tomorrow was Saturday, but in her profession people worked nights and weekends.

"I'll have the NDA ready, and I'll bring it with me tomorrow."

SHE'D DONE some work for Motorola in Boca Raton back when they were testing robotics. It was a secret project and the company made her sign an NDA. They were using robots to make pagers. It sounded silly now, but pagers were big back then. She could keep her mouth shut.

She jogged across the street and let Sinbad off his leash inside the townhouse. She scrolled through her cell phone contact list while the dog sniffed around. She pressed the little telephone icon next to Davis Frost's contact information.

DAVIS WAS LYING AROUND, taking life in like a beached whale, depressed, soaking in a sea of self-pity. For Davis, taking it in was a visual activity, and the visuals of his Plantation Key apartment were abysmal. The once-white vinyl kitchen floor was peeling and yellow. The avocado green shag rug smelled like four-tenants-ago. Everything metal inside was pitted or rusted, the side effects of living in salt air. But saltwater was the whole point of the place.

Davis had met Lauren through her ex, the reefer-of-madness, daydreaming, tax-refund-check-cashing director of photography still living up north in Jupiter. The real world had put Davis in a tough spot. He had exceptional taste in everything, especially women, but he had not been graced with anything to attract the women he desired. No power, no good looks, no enviable wit, nor charm or money. Even his youth was gone.

After decades of irrational crushes and quasi-stalking, followed by days of rejection-induced blackout drinking, it occurred to Davis he might have to settle for reality. Settling meant sharing a bed with someone his visual equal. Another version of settling meant going back to the deep freeze, Minneapolis, where he'd met Lauren's ex when they worked together as news cameramen for the local NBC affiliate. He decided to give up unattainable women and commit to the Florida Keys instead.

Davis's big, friendly Saint Bernard head sprouted wisps of white hair. His clear, icy-blue eyes were set too close together, but they complemented his fair Norwegian complexion that was never going to tan. No matter how much time he spent in the sun and surf, Davis always turned shades of pink and red. He was built like a Viking seafarer with giant hands, huge thighs, and wide shoulders. A massive gut covered by a tangled web of red stretch marks hung from his abdomen. Even as a young man he'd always worn an unkempt beard, now gray but for a ring of wiry orange whiskers growing around his lips. It gave him the look of a surprised clown, even from a short distance. He always looked like he was on the cusp of grinning.

Lauren Gold's ringtone snapped him out of his funk. "Hey dere, Lauren."

"Long time. How are you?"

"Good," Davis lied, unconvincingly.

Lauren got to the point. "Do you still have your ROV?"

She was referring to his submersible, remotely-operated vehicle.

"Yeah." His attitude perked up. "What do you have up your sleeve?"

"I might have a dive gig for you. What's your day rate?"

"Rate card is eight hundred a day. And that's just for me, the basic camera kit, lights, and the ROV. What kind of project?"

"It's confidential, so I can't tell you much. I need your word that you won't discuss it with anyone other than me."

"Can you give me a clue?" Davis asked.

"I'm still getting the details myself. But you know the drill. I have to run the numbers."

"How many days of work do you think?" He fondled the lucky gold coin hanging from his neck, a souvenir from a salvage dive of a Spanish galleon that went down off the coast in the 1600s.

"I don't know. Figure three to five for now. Do you have a GoPro?"

"Yeah. I could rent a housing and shoot anything from an Arriflex to an iPhone. It depends on the video format and the look they want, and the water depth. And it depends on the budget of course. There's lighting, too. That drives costs up. How deep? Do you know?"

"Not yet."

"I want to work on this project." Davis sounded almost desperate. "And you know I'll work with you on the rate. If it's deep, I can mount a camera on my ROV. If it's shallow enough, a hundred feet or less, I can tank dive it. We should give the client options."

"I love options," Lauren said. "Plus, you're always fair."

"This video business is killing me. The kids living at home with Mommy and Daddy are happy to work for peanuts. I've been filling in as the relief DJ for a little Internet-based radio station down here. Doing their IT work, too. If I'd known it was going to be like this, I probably would have stayed at the station and waited for my union retirement. Is this a corporate gig?"

"I don't want to jinx the deal. But yeah, it's a corporate client, and just know that if I get it, you're in."

"Hallelujah. I've had my fill of assholes and deadbeats. Not to say corporate clients can't be assholes. But they usually pay."

JAKE PHONED her that night as promised, and they set a meeting for six o'clock the next morning at Black Point Park and Marina, a public park with a boat ramp off SW 87th. It made sense to meet at dawn on a Saturday; it was a good way to be discreet.

SATURDAY MORNING

LAUREN ARRIVED AT FIVE-FORTY. It was pitch-black and the park was closed. At fifteen minutes after six, a black Mercedes diesel pulled up. She watched the silhouette ambling her way.

Jake called her on her cell as he walked over and opened her car door with his phone still stuck to his ear. She caught a light whiff of cigar smoke on his clothes.

"Jake Fleming." He held onto the upper frame above the car window and dropped clumsily into the seat. He was hunched over, his upper body curved like a gaffer hook.

She twisted her torso in the driver's seat and contorted her right shoulder to shake his hand. Jake pulled the Non-Disclosure from the inside pocket of his blue blazer and handed it to her. Without reading it, she thumbed to the last page and signed it under the dome light of her car. He exchanged it for a business card, one for the Cormorant Case Company.

"Here's the deal. The manufacturer sank their military-grade waterproof cases about sixteen miles offshore, near Biscayne National Park."

"How long ago?"

"Nineteen ninety-four. The cases are time capsules. The marketing team thinks if we make a video of the salvage and open the cases live during a webcast, it will be a marketing bonanza. We want to show that the contents are still dry."

"Wow. What a great opportunity." She wished she could see Jake's face, but there wasn't enough available light.

"They're hoping for a big Web audience. Today's marketing, I guess I don't have to tell you how everything's video now."

"That's for sure. I have the perfect guy for the project. But a search operation like this can take time."

"I have the coordinates," Jake said. "For the wreck."

"That will make it easier."

"We think your guy should launch from here, at Black Point. There's a public boat ramp."

"Did you mention a boat?" Jake was still mostly a silhouette, and his natural voice sounded strange.

"Is that a problem? Does your guy have access to a boat?"

"He has one, I think. At least he used to, an older sport fisher. It depends on the size of the load. We'll need to know more details—dimension and weight for starters. I know I asked you on the phone, but do you know the depth?"

"Around fifty feet."

"That makes it easier."

"The load weighs over a thousand pounds, but it's broken up into smaller increments in transport cases. Your guy, what's his name?"

"Davis Frost."

"We think he should base the operation out of Boca Chita Key, the island."

"The place with the lighthouse?"

"That's it. It has campsites, a bulkhead with dock space, and restroom facilities. He'd fit in as an enthusiast out diving, shooting video."

"It's a public park—that might work. What's down there, in the cases? That's a lot of weight."

"I don't know. Old phone books, CEO's rock collection. All I know is that they want the cases recovered unopened. That's the catch and the hook. The contents have stayed dry for over twenty years. That's what the marketing team is going to promote to build a social media audience. That's why you and your guy can't tamper with the latches."

She was sure Jake hadn't said anything about a boat during the first call. "Let me talk to him. A thousand pounds, that's your best guess?"

"Ballpark. But the company wants me to deal directly with him. We're not going around you. I promise you that. They just want me to meet him in person, get a feel for him. Keep things confidential." He reached inside the breast pocket of his navy sport coat and removed an envelope. "Here's a ten thousand dollar deposit. Enough to get you started. Ten more when we get the cases and the video files. We budgeted six for him but understand it could be more. I need his contact information. The in-house lawyers want me to meet with him to get the agreement signed. I'll give him three thousand after he signs the NDA."

Lauren looked inside the envelope and rolled her thumb across the bills. "Cash. This is a little unconventional, but OK." She pulled up Davis's contact information and sent it to the mobile number on Jake's business card. "This is a different number. It's a Miami area code. You called me on a 212 number."

"That was my personal phone." Jake's burner pinged. He looked at it. "I can't see without my readers. Is that his contact information?"

She glanced at the screen. "Yes."

The rising sun glowed and streamers of light bounced from the brass buttons on Jake's jacket to the Rolex hanging from his wrist. There was no wedding ring on his finger. She looked at his business card again.

"Tell Davis I'll be calling him direct." Jake grunted as he struggled to get out of her car.

She watched him walk to his black Mercedes. It wasn't black in the morning light. Rather it was a very deep, almost metallic purplish color. "What man of power drives a Barney mobile?" she mumbled under her breath, watching Jake drive off.

17

Face-to-face, Davis was not what Vance expected. He was morbidly obese and emitted an unpleasant odor. Vance introduced himself as the company lawyer and Jake as the marketing boss from the Cormorant Case Company. He opened his briefcase and handed Davis two copies of the NDA.

Davis scanned the document stopping on page three. "It says I can't communicate with anyone, even Lauren Gold?"

He was sharper than Vance had anticipated. "That's right. I'm sure she told you that this is a highly confidential project. I'll summarize. First, you have to go completely off the grid."

Davis nodded his big, friendly, Saint Bernard head. Vance handed him a paper folded in half. Davis opened it.

"Those are the coordinates."

Davis stared at the numbers stuffing a glazed donut topped with sprinkles in his mouth. "OK. This is very helpful. I'm pretty good with the ROV. It takes good hand-eye coordination."

"Don't put the information in your GPS until you're heading out to the site. I know it sounds like overkill, but that's what we lawyers get paid to do."

Davis was still chewing when he pushed the signed agreement across the table. "Lauren said the stuff's been down there since the nineties. There have been some pretty big storms since then. A smaller craft moves with the currents." He paused to swallow. "How do you know for sure it's still there?"

"We're confident it's there," Jake said. "In about fifty feet of water."

"Some of those cases float if there's any air inside."

Vance was again impressed with Davis's knowledge. "They're packed tightly in the hull."

"We're authorized to pay you an additional two-fifty a day for your boat," Jake said. "The company wants you to salvage the yellow cases. There are black ones down there, too. But just bring up the yellow ones."

"The boat is the *Holly Golightly*." Vance said. "You might be able to make out the name. She was an offshore racing boat in her day. There's a compartment located under her bow."

Jake reached into the breast pocket of his coat and took out a bank envelope of money. He put it on the table. "Three thousand to start. Three more when the job's done. Plus boat rental." Jake handed Davis a business card. "When the mission's complete, don't call me, call him. He'll arrange for pickup and payment."

Vance gave Davis his fake card. "Call me when it's done."

"Jeez, you guys seem pretty serious about this." Davis put the last piece of the donut back down on the table. "Do you know the overall weight? I'll need to see if my old boat is, uh, up to it."

"I'm sure it'll be fine. Ever see how many Haitians can pile onto a homemade raft?"

Vance glared at Jake. "He's joking around. They're plastic transport cases loaded with ballast. A little more than a thousand pounds total."

"Just to reiterate, I'm salvaging the yellow cases and leaving the black ones behind," Davis said.

Jake looked up from the paper napkin he'd been doodling on. "Yeah, our marketing team thinks the yellow will look more dramatic on video. Black is pretty boring."

Vance shrugged. "They're the marketing guys. I'm just the lawyer."

"I don't care if they're purple—I just want to have it straight. A lot of television remote trucks transport gear in those kinds of cases. They're pretty big and bulky."

Vance's burner blipped. Using his hands to cup the screen, he sneaked a peek under the table. A message from Ray: Offer him 5K bonus if job is done in 72 hrs.

The waitress pulled a notebook from her apron pocket and a pencil from behind her ear. She totaled up the bill in her head and dropped the ticket on the table without speaking.

Vance waited until she was out of earshot. "The load probably weighs closer to fifteen hundred pounds, rough guess."

Davis rubbed his beard. "Fifteen hundred? I thought you just said a little more than a thousand. There's a big difference between a thousand pounds and fifteen hundred. I have a twenty-three-foot sport fisher with a single outboard."

"I know, but we just don't have the exact weight." Vance slipped a twenty under the tab. "As an incentive, we're offering you a five thousand dollar bonus if you can get the job done in seventy-two hours."

Jake jabbed Vance in the ribs with his elbow. Davis was too excited to notice.

"Wow. When does the clock start?"

"Tomorrow, at noon." Vance was making it up as he went.

"All righty, then," Davis said, sliding out of the booth, hoisting his burly body to his feet. "I need to start prepping."

Jake confronted Vance in the parking lot. "Where did the bonus come from?"

"Ray." He could tell Jake was annoyed, and he loved the look of exasperation on his face.

"Why didn't I know?"

He didn't know the answer. "Just do your part, Jake."

VANCE WAS home for less than a minute when someone knocked on the door. He looked through the peephole and gestured to Tony to hide in the bedroom.

Sarge pushed his way inside. "Went by your office first. *Nada* person or car in sight—you retire or something? Or does being here instead of there have something to do with the boarded-up window?"

"Come on in. Make yourself at home."

"Tried calling. Can't leave a voicemail. And you weren't answering my texts, either."

"What's the emergency this time?"

Sarge sniffed. The air inside the apartment was moist and strong with the aroma of home cooking. "She officially your girlfriend now, the horsey chick? She cooks for you, huh? Nice. That's what I miss most about married life. The home-cooked food." Sarge looked at Tony's duffel bags next to the sofa made up as a bed. "You got company?"

"Daniel, why are you here? And please, cut to the chase."

Sarge sat where Tony had been sitting a minute earlier. "I have some information I thought might interest you. Remember the couple that disappeared from Palm Beach? The ones that own those fancy restaurants on Worth Avenue?"

Vance shook his head no.

"I don't see how you haven't heard it, it's big news."

With all that was going on, he didn't know anything about a missing couple and hadn't checked the news in days.

"Anyway, they went on an overnight boating trip and never came back. No sign of them for a couple of days. No distress signal. No mayday, no *nada*. Sixty-something-foot yacht, the *Sea Food*, poof, missing. Nothing from the boat captain, either."

"And?"

"And a fisherman up in Delray saw something bobbing in the water. Scared the daylights outta him. Turns out it's the missing husband, Charles Pierce. The old guy was naked, shot twice. There's a rumor going around that might interest you."

"Oh yeah?"

"*Si.* The first bullet tore half his bicep off, like a defensive wound. The one to the head killed him. But get this, the slug that hit him in the arm lodged in his chest." Sarge used his thumb and forefinger to turn the diamond post in his right ear. "Ballistics matched it to an unsolved murder that might be of particular interest to you."

Sarge had his attention. "Which one?"

"Matches the forty-five used to shoot the federal judge, the one murdered during the Los Guapos trial. But you didn't hear it from me. And you're not going to hear it anywhere else, either. The Palm Beach DA has a gag order on the report. The shooter was a dummy. The body was in good shape, nice and fresh. Easy ID from the prints. The shooter should have done something to weight it down."

Sarge was right. The pH of salt water usually made ocean forensics very difficult. It could take months for a body to wash up. But this year the warm El Niño currents kept surface temperatures off the coast of South Florida tepid, and while warm water could speed up decomposition, it could also keep a body floating on the surface. "The killer probably figured there wouldn't be any fragment evidence," he said. "And I agree with you, a shot to the arm suggests some sort of struggle. You said he was shot in the head too?"

"Yeah. Face and head are a fucking mess. Big cranial exit wound. The slug the coroner pulled from his chest, the one that passed through his bicep, looked like a starfish. Medical Examiner says it hit a rib. Slowed it down. ME told my source it looked like a train derailed inside the poor guy. But the body was in good enough shape to ID him."

A hollow point was not intended to slow down the target. It was designed to stop it in its tracks. It was a smart choice for a boat shooting. Blowing a big hole in the hull would have been a bad idea.

"There's something else too." Sarge rubbed his hands together. "I made a call when I saw your office window. You filed a police report, a drive-by. There's video on YouTube of something that looks like a getaway scene right in front of your office. Turns out some overly enthusiastic criminalist took it upon him or herself to run ballistics on that scene too. Care to guess?"

"Geez, Sarge. What is this, NCIS Miami or Columbo? Don't you have better things to do, like take the grandkids to the zoo?"

"I take offense to the Columbo comparison. I like to think of myself more as *Señor* Kojak. Anyway, turns out the ballistics report from your office shooting is tied to someone we both know. Wanna guess?" He rubbed his head. "Tick tock, tick tock. Last chance."

"I give up."

"Matches one tied to you."

His heart pounded under his shirt. "So? I've bought and sold lots of guns. And not all of them have been with the paperwork. But they were all honest transactions between people I know, law-abiding citizens."

"This wouldn't be one you bought or sold. The 9-millimeter slug and two spent cartridges match an old Glock."

He felt a rush of adrenaline. Trying to stay calm, he said,

"That's not exactly a spoiler alert. I prefer Glocks to other guns. So what?"

"Really? Do you want me to use hand puppets and flash cards? The Glock, it's police-issue. It's a match for the one you reported stolen back when you were still active duty. Don't you think that's a little weird? Two ballistics matches in less than twenty-four hours that can be linked to you, from two different guns, both off the grid for more than twenty years? One loosely tied to you personally? And the other tied to you from a professional point of view? Or did you forget about your unpaid leave of absence?"

Hell no, he hadn't forgotten. He was equally stunned by both stories. He felt gut-punched. He was a common denominator in both shootings. So was Tony.

"OK," Sarge said, letting himself out. "Seems like this is all news to you. If I hear anything new, I'll be in touch."

Sarge had his own agenda. That was obvious. But his motive was a mystery.

HE KNEW EXACTLY what year he'd reported his police Glock stolen: his rookie year, 1992, and it had almost upended his career. He told Internal Affairs he'd left the gun in his unmarked unit while he was running an errand. There was no way he could tell the truth, that he'd been at the Hotel Mutiny hanging out with his Uncle Tony Famosa. He'd gone to the men's room, and Chago and one of his goons overpowered him while he was taking a leak in front of the urinal. They surrounded him, shoved him up against the wall, and ripped the holstered gun from under his left arm. They laughed and ran out the door, disappearing into the dark, crowded club.

TONY CAME out of the bedroom. "I heard that. So the glass that just happened to fall out of your hair, it's from a drive-by shooting at your office?" Tony seemed worried. "The cops are going to be all over that missing yacht if they think it has anything to do with the murdered federal judge."

Vance dropped onto the sofa like a rag doll. "I need this shit like a hole in the head."

Tony nodded sympathetically. "You know it started out as a joke, right? When Chago decided to play hide-and-seek with your gun?"

"Yeah. That was really funny." The memory made him angry.

"He was so fucked up on coke. You shouldn't have let him take it."

"*Let* him take it! Are you joking? He was out of his mind. I got suspended. That was the biggest humiliation of my entire career. And now the gun's surfaced and it's tied to a drive-by, aimed at me?"

"I shouldn't have kept bugging you to come to the club. You were practically a kid. I didn't think Chago would do that."

"He killed people. Why wouldn't he humiliate me in front of you?" It was a long time ago. And Tony was right, that he'd been young and impressionable. But still, he should have known better. He was a first year cop, for chrissake.

"I saw the story about the missing couple from Palm Beach. It's all over the news," Tony said.

"Something strange is going on. If the same gun used to kill that judge was used to kill the yacht owners, what are the odds?" These were not random events or people surfacing from the past. They were somehow connected.

"And someone used the Glock that Chago stole from—"

"Shut up, Tony. I ask you nicely not to bring that up again. Ever."

WHAT CHOICE DID he have after Chago refused to give him his gun back other than to lie to Internal Affairs? Two weeks without pay. Six months on probation. He'd have never been up for promotion. Telling the investigators he'd left his patrol unit unlocked went into his permanent record. All the inside jokes, *Hey, Dick Courage, don't forget to lock your vehicle.* If he'd stayed, it would've turned his career at Miami PD into the road to nowhere. If Sarge's story about Chago being killed in prison was true, then that piece of crap got to find out what it's like to be surrounded and overpowered. Still, the timing was strange. How and why did his stolen police weapon show up now, and who'd had it all this time?

The Coast Guard had probably been searching for the missing yacht. That meant Homeland Security was involved.

CAPTAIN PEAK DOZED during the night like a prey animal: in spurts. He couldn't sleep sitting with his knees up to his chest, and his wrists and neck anchored to the handicap bar fastened to the cabin wall. His hip and shoulder joints ached.

The morning sea remained calm, and that was good. But a flat ocean meant no wind, and no wind meant it was stifling hot. He had a delicate constitution for a boat captain. Peak wore a prescription anti-nausea patch behind his ear, hidden beneath his sun-bleached straw hair. During the night, he'd used his tongue to work at the duct tape. It wouldn't budge but his tongue ached from the muscle spasms. It was the last day to change the anti-puke patch, but that didn't seem like it was going to happen. With his lips glued together he worried he might choke on his own vomit if the wind picked up enough to churn the sea.

Mongo startled him, appearing with a bottle of cold water in one hand and a Heckler & Koch HK 45 caliber semi-automatic pistol in the other. His captor knelt, pointing the gun at his head. The twins watched from the doorway. Mongo released the chain shackling George's neck to the handrail.

"Take the gag off him," Mongo barked.

Nicole trotted over and picked at the duct tape. "It's hard to, with my nails. I don't want to break one."

"Get out of the way." Mongo pushed Nicole aside and ripped the tape from George's mouth, exposing a horizontal red rash. He picked up the water bottle and tilted it. George closed his eyes and opened his mouth like a baby bird, swiveling his head and neck until the cold water met his aching tongue. The whites of his turquoise eyes were mottled with red lines from despair and sleep deprivation.

"I'm gonna unlock your hands," Mongo hissed. "You do anything funny you'll end up like your former employers. Understood?"

He nodded. The ex-con banker held the gun firmly on George's temple, rotating his snake eyes from the lock to his hostage and back as he turned the key. The bike chain dropped and he was freed.

"Get up," Mongo motioned with the gun. "Slowly."

He couldn't make a fast move even if he wanted to. His joints had rusted overnight. He turned his right wrist clockwise, slowly, then his left. "They were nice folks—"

"Shut the fuck up." Mongo whacked him across the head with the barrel of the HK.

George fell forward onto his knees, covering his injured ear with his hand.

"Get up," Mongo said, "or I'll smack your other earhole."

George grimaced, using his sore arms to push himself to a sitting position.

"Don't hurt him." Lisa's eyes were fixed on George's shapely buttocks. "He didn't do anything wrong."

Mongo swung the gun around toward Lisa and held it on her. She cowered. He pointed it back at George and frisked him with his free hand. He had nothing on him. "Where's your cell?"

"On the bridge." He kept his hands above his head without being asked. Mongo stuck the nose of his gun on the back of his skull and herded George to the bow. He sidestepped past the streaks and sticky drying pools of blood lining the path to the helm.

Four cell phones resting in a universal charger sat in front of a console of flashing electronics and computer screens. Mongo tossed the lot overboard, then dug through the drawers. He found a pink, snub-nosed .38 Special Ruger, the one George was supposed to keep under his pillow. In the event, Charles had warned him, that something like *this* might happen.

"That's so cute," Nicole said. "Can I have it?"

Mongo stuffed the pink gun down the front of his saggy pants.

"Boca Chita Key," Mongo barked at George. "That's where we're going. Set a heading. Nothing funny." He banged the .45 into George's forehead again, hard enough to leave a red ring. "You get on that radio and you're a dead man. You'll be feeding the fucking crabs."

George nodded, dropping into the captain's chair in front of the controls. He raised the electronic anchor and punched a heading into the ship's GPS system. The sixty-two-foot yacht turned southeast, toward the island. "The ship drafts just over five feet. Might be too shallow if there's a low tide at Boca Chita," George said.

Mongo took the bike chain he'd draped around his own neck and bullwhipped George between the shoulders. The captain tried swallowing the pain but yowled instead.

"I thought you understood English," Mongo said. "I told you to *shut the fuck up*."

18

WEEK TWO
SUNDAY

MID-MORNING TRAFFIC WAS light heading north on the Overseas Highway toward Miami, making hauling the old twenty-three-foot sport fishing boat easier. Davis Frost ran the mental checklist obsessively. Remote operated vehicle, three kinds of batteries, a terabyte of media storage, fins, mask, snorkel, tanks, regulator, dive knife, salt water scissors, weights, tent, chargers, mosquito fogger, toothpaste, toothbrush, extra fuel, five hundred cash, GoPro, underwater housing, underwater light, underwear, toilet paper, towels, MREs, spear gun, sleeping bag, extra blankets for padding, pillow.

He paid fifteen dollars cash to the attendant at Black Point Marina and backed the trailer down the ramp. Launching the loaded boat alone was easy; it floated up off the aluminum trailer. He walked through the thigh-high water, pulling the *Leaky Witch* like he was leading a horse through a pasture, and tied it off to a dock piling. He parked the rented Toyota SUV and trailer in the public lot, stuffed the rental agreement under the visor, and hid the key fob atop the passenger-side front tire.

The Yamaha two-fifty horsepower engine could be downright recalcitrant on a cold start. After two tries, the motor puffed and huffed, then roared to life. He pushed a pair of neon orange, reflective Wayfarers on, slathered sunblock on his flabby thighs, and typed the coordinates to Boca Chita Key into his phone. Within the hour he had the landmark lighthouse within sight.

Boca Chita was nearly desolate. The upcoming Memorial weekend would be a different story, especially if the weather was nice. Then it would be a zoo. Boaters who couldn't find bulkhead space would ignore the warning signs and throw anchor in the shallow water. When he arrived, there were only three boats docked at the horseshoe-shaped marina. Two were late-model sport fishing craft. The third one was pure nautical eye-candy, an impressive yacht, the *Sea*-something-or-other. He couldn't make out the full name because a black rubber raft tied to the swim deck blocked his view.

Something big and unexpected was brewing over the skyline, off to the west. The ominous thunderhead coming from the south wasn't in the forecast, either. He'd seen lots of weather systems coming from the south and west collide off the southeast peninsula and he knew the results could be unpredictable, so he hurried to get himself settled. He staked the red dome pop-up tent into the sandy soil and unloaded the essentials.

By early evening, the wind was howling. Inside the tent it sounded like the middle of a drive-through car wash. He poked his head out of the waterproof canvas tent. The waning full moon was shrouded by storm clouds, and the wind-driven rain stung his cheeks. He'd picked a spot beneath a wide-brimmed palm tree to pitch the tent, which did nothing to stop buckets of rainwater from pooling and seeping inside. Then it began to pour.

Davis clutched the neck of a of half gallon of spiced rum and swigged it until passed out between lightning strikes.

WEEK TWO
MONDAY

Davis awoke to the stench of rum vapors he'd exhaled during the night. He unzipped the tent and stuck his aching head out. It was still dark, and he heard the zinging sounds of insects. He shined his flashlight around. A black cloud of mosquitos awaited him.

He slathered repellent on his arms and legs and shot clouds of mosquito fogger from a can of insecticide. He slung the dive bag over his shoulder, counted to ten, and made a run for the boat. He waddled as fast as he could, smashing dozens of stinging bugs on his arms and legs, slapping himself on the face, and splattering tiny pockets of his own blood. The insides of his thighs burned from chemicals. If he weren't so excited he'd have felt the hangover more.

Everything he needed for the trip was stowed down below, in the cuddy. He'd have slept in the boat but there was no room. The Yamaha turned over on the first try. He entered 25 58150 - 80 146550 into his GPS and opened the throttle, cutting a wake before sunrise, leaving the cloud of mosquitos behind.

"THE BLOB BOUGHT THE STORY," Jake said at the debrief Ray set up. "Davis definitely thinks I'm the double-oh-seven marketing guy. So did she."

Jake was such a jerk, but Vance had only himself to blame

for bringing him to the deal. One the other hand, he was perfect for the role of faux master marketer.

"Did you make it clear to those two they need to stay off the grid?" Ray asked.

"Yeah, we made it very clear. Here are the signed NDAs." He handed Ray the legal documents he'd prepared.

"Davis knows staying off the grid means no contact with Lauren either, right?"

"Yeah, we told him. I wrote it into his agreement. He seemed fine with it," Vance said.

"If I need to talk to her, I'll use the burner," Jake said.

"Why would you need to talk to Lauren?" Vance cocked his head and waited for Jake to explain. He looked to Ray to referee, but Ray said nothing. "Ray," he said, "why would Jake need to talk to Lauren? I thought you said we weren't supposed to contact her. Neither one of us, right?"

"What if she calls or texts me?" Jake asked.

Vance drummed his fingers on the side table. "When Ray said we're not supposed to communicate with her, I took it to mean that we don't answer calls or texts from her either. Ray?"

"You guys make me glad I'm married. Gee whiz, sounds like you're sparring over a woman. But I get it. I chased her myself twenty years ago." Ray sighed. "She wouldn't even let me take her to dinner." Ray looked at Jake. "What did you tell her?"

"I told her that she's not supposed to communicate with Davis. I said the company wanted the lawyer and me to deal with Davis directly. I didn't tell her she couldn't talk to me. I'm the client."

"Jesus, Jake." He'd managed to annoy Ray too. "You're the pretend-client. I specifically told you that I don't want either of you talking to her. Not until we get those cases salvaged. You should have made that clear to her."

What part of *stay away from Lauren* did Jake not get?

The deposed Wall Street banker looked at his watch like he needed to be somewhere. He stood. "If this shit blows up, look for me in Carmen del Playa. And tell my kids and my ex-wife I'm sorry I fucked up. Again."

LAUREN WAS UPLOADING a four-gigabyte video file, drone footage for a stevedoring outfit based out of the Port of Miami. It would take about five minutes: a perfect window to walk Sinbad. When he heard her pick up the leash, he raced toward the door and jumped in the air, twirling and making it hard to fasten the leash to his collar. She'd researched and printed out the doggie boot camp information like the behaviorist at the shelter suggested, but she hadn't made an appointment yet. Soon she would have the time. And money.

Sinbad lunged forward when she opened the townhouse gate to cross the street to the dog park. Suddenly the leash broke from the collar, and the dog took off at a dead run. She'd accidentally clipped it to a flimsy pet ID ring that broke when the dog lurched forward. Panicking, she yelled his name, but the dog gleefully ignored her, dashing into the street. A Volvo swerved to avoid hitting him, locking up the ABS brakes, chirping, and leaving stitches of fresh rubber on the pavement.

Her heart pumped. Sinbad sat on the opposite side of the street on a patch of grass in front of the dog park fence facing the road. He watched her wide-eyed with his cute crooked smile and pink tongue hanging out, panting with excitement, oblivious to the danger.

An old pickup truck hauling a rickety trailer overloaded with landscaping equipment sped from the opposite direction, from Virginia Avenue. Sinbad had no fear of cars, bolting across the street toward Lauren, his tail at full staff.

"No!" Lauren screamed. "No! No! No!"

Then he saw a squirrel run up a tree trunk and did a U-turn, galloping toward the grassy side. At least he was heading toward the park where she'd have a better chance of coaxing him to come to her. She walked calmly toward him, and when she got close, reached her hand out slowly. He thought it was a game, getting down on his forepaws, planting his head in the damp grass, and barking. Her heart raced. *Stay cool.* The old truck rolled through the stop sign at the intersection. *Don't spook him. Go slow.* She reached her hand out again. "Here, boy."

Arf. Arf! I'm free!

"Sinbad, come here." She smooched to entice him.

He was happy to be free. He spun and chased his tail.

The truck full of landscaper materials sped up, and her dog was still off his leash.

"Hey, slow down!"

His window was open but the driver ignored her. Or didn't understand her. He was going over forty in a twenty. The equipment clattered in the trailer and the wheels squeaked. The tires were low on air and thumped the asphalt as the truck raced toward the park.

She tried to swallow but her throat closed. "Hey, boy," she said softly.

Arf!

"Sit!"

That was the one command he knew. He sat on the grass by the chain link fence, panting with excitement. She tiptoed toward him. She needed to grab him by the neck. She lowered her hand. Her fingers were an inch from his collar. She slipped one finger under the leather, but he leapt backward, escaping her grasp and bolted back across the street toward the condo. She couldn't breathe. She saw the speeding truck and galloping dog. The gap was closing fast. He didn't have time to make it across. She froze. And prayed that the dog would stop. He paused. Thank God.

Then Sinbad changed his mind again and reversed course, scrambling back toward the house. The front left tire of the truck rolled over the top of him. Then two more sets of trailer tires rolled over his back and neck. Lauren screamed. The driver didn't slow down. He just kept going.

Sinbad howled. *Au! Au! Au! Au!*

The driver stuck his head out the window and looked back at the scene. He shrugged his shoulders and frowned. Lauren froze, staring blankly at the truck as the driver made a lazy left at the intersection and disappeared.

She ran to the whimpering dog lying in the road, motionless. Blood oozed from his eyes and mouth. "No!" She fell to her knees. She tore the skin on the backs of her fingers shoveling her hands beneath his body, scooping him, to carry him to safety. He convulsed in her arms, and his neck twitched uncontrollably. When the seizure stopped, he looked at her with his soft, brown eyes, helpless and confused. A crowd formed around her. They'd run from the park, many with their dogs. They covered their mouths, too horrified to help. Sinbad was dying.

She did what she'd learned from the horsemen that taught her to ride. She pulled her shirt over her head and held it tightly over Sinbad's nose and mouth. Tears spilled down her face.

They'd roughhoused every day, and the little dog was strong from chasing balls, playing tug-of-war and lunging at cars, and rushing at other dogs on their leashes. He thrashed his neck left and right and arched his back as he struggled for air. She was suffocating him with her hands, tightening the cloth over his nose and mouth, a river flowing down her cheeks. He looked up with wide, curious eyes.

"I'm sorry," she sobbed. "I'm so sorry!"

She hung her head and shut her eyes, keeping her hands

tight around his snout. When his body went limp, she stood and ran, cradling the dog in her arms until she reached the walkway leading to the condo. Clutching his warm body against her chest, waves of grief shot from her throat to her stomach. She rocked the lifeless dog in her arms and wept, then dropped to her knees and shivering, screamed.

She tilted her head up and saw a man standing over her. He dropped to one knee. Her world was spinning; she felt lightheaded.

"Oh my God, are you OK?" he asked. "My name is Daniel Ruiz. I saw the whole thing—"

People were coming from different directions and hovering over her, asking questions like reporters talking over one another. She felt like she was going to suffocate. The last thing she remembered was a shiny gold cross hanging from his neck, swaying like a pendulum. Then she passed out.

AFTER RAY and Jake left the coffeehouse, Vance stayed and composed a text to Lauren on his personal phone. Maybe she'd heard something from Davis. That was bullshit. He wanted to keep the hook in her mouth. Contacting her was breaking the rules, but what choice did he have? He wasn't playing by the rules anymore. He was about to send it when his phone buzzed. Sarge. Vance was taking his calls now.

"Hey."

Sarge's voice cracked. "Something bad just happened to your girlfriend's dog."

"I don't have a girlfriend."

Sarge sniffled. "Her dog was run over. Figured you'd know by now."

"What are you talking about?"

"Lauren's dog was hit by a truck. I saw it. It happened in front of her condo."

"You saw it? Like you just happened to be passing by, and you saw it?" He didn't even know she had a dog. "Is the dog OK?"

"No. I've seen a lot of stuff in my day, and this just broke my heart," Sarge said. "And she's a mess."

"How do you know where she lives? And why were you near her place?"

"In case you haven't noticed, there's a detail on you. I was checking to see if she's being followed too."

"You're joking. You were stalking her?"

"You don't get it. She's torn up about the dog. She passed out in front of me, hugging the dead dog. There was blood all over her—"

"Jesus, I didn't even know she had a dog," he said darting through traffic.

"Anyone ever tell you you're an asshole? A cold-hearted asshole."

"Maybe I am. But why are you in my business?"

Sarge didn't respond.

"I told you. I didn't know she had a dog." Still nothing. He looked at the screen. Sarge was gone.

He deleted the text he'd been writing to Lauren and composed a new one: Sorry about your dog. His finger hovered over the green button. He called on every ounce of discipline he could muster to keep his finger off the Send button. He pushed the Cancel button instead.

He suspected Sarge might have had something to do with setting them up on the date, practically interrogating him on the trip back from the Tavern until he told him his user ID. Mile-Marker45. Now he was convinced Sarge was somehow involved.

19

Davis Frost killed the outboard and dropped anchor in about sixty feet of water, then turned his phone off to conserve the battery. He opened a Brisket Entrée Meal-Ready-to-Eat sealed in a tan plastic bag. He added water to the dotted line to start the chemical heating process. He smeared a biscuit with peanut butter and bit into it, chasing it with water. The main course was ready in ten minutes. Davis scarfed the shredded cat-food-looking entrée. He stowed the chewing gum, toilet paper, and moist towelette in the *Witch's* center console doubling as the boat's junk drawer.

He assembled the ROV and unfurled the loops of cabling wound around the base. He checked battery power and inserted a media card into the onboard video monitor and lowered the submersible over the gunwale of the Dusky. When it reached the ocean floor, the cable slackened. Visibility was bad. Using the joystick to test-drive it, he turned it left and right, but the water was too murky to see much of anything. He pulled the equipment topside and plopped overboard to rinse off and commune with nature. He snorkeled around the bottom of the boat with the GoPro camera strapped to his forehead.

When he was back in the boat he pulled up the Boca Chita website on his phone. He couldn't locate shore power when he'd landed the night before because of the storm. This morning, the mosquitos had forced him to make a run for the *Witch*. Plus, it was still dark out when he left the island. Crap! Written in red, all caps: BOCA CHITA DOES NOT HAVE SHORE POWER. How had he missed it when prepping for the trip? This was going to be a big problem since his gear ran on batteries. He motored around until midday and checked the water again. Visibility was still awful, so he headed back to the island.

The tide had run out while Davis was inspecting the dive site. When he returned, he saw the *Sea Food* aground, listing at an angle, her hull grinding against the concrete bulkhead. He backed off engine power and coasted slowly to gawk. A female voice called down to him from the ship.

"Hey there, young man, are you hungry?"

Davis looked up and saw a leggy brunette posing in a black bikini, leaning over the bow railing. She bent one knee to compensate for the angle of the yacht.

He tilted his head back and flashed a goofy grin. "Did you ask if I'm hungry?" he yelled over the idling of the Yamaha outboard.

"We have food!"

Davis cut the engine and coasted closer. Lisa appeared and stood next to her twin sister, Nicole.

Holy mother of God, I think I'm hallucinating. Tell me I'm not seeing things.

"Come over when you're finished up. We have lots of yummy food to eat," Nicole said.

The insects descended on him. "Uh, OK, thanks!" He swatted at mosquitos and no-see-ums. "My name's Davis!"

Lisa cupped her hands like a megaphone. "Hi, Davis!"

"Let me clean up and I'll be over! Thanks! Do you have power?"

"I think so! Do you have a cell phone?"

"Yeah! And it needs a charge!"

Lisa funneled her hands over her mouth. "We have electricity!" She held her phone out like an offering. "Give me your cell number! That way if we need to be rescued, we know who to call!"

Davis hollered out the numbers.

Nicole typed them into her phone.

Davis's phone buzzed in his hand.

"That's my number! My name's Nicole."

"And I'm Lisa!"

"OK, Nicole and Lisa!" He plopped back in the seat. He held up his phone. "Got it!" Pressing the microphone icon he activated the voice recognition and said: My name is Davis Frost. He pushed the send button. A second later the twins each held a thumb up.

―――――――――

DAVIS BOARDED the *Sea Food* carrying a dive bag full of dead and dying batteries. He steadied himself against the listing bow railing and held up a tangle of battery chargers. "Do you mind if I plug these in?"

An ugly man came up from below. "Go ahead. Take all the juice you need. Outlets are in the galley."

Davis plugged the chargers in and inserted the batteries. They slid off the countertops and hung over the edge, their charging lights flashing. His mouth watered at the scent of garlic and meat. Nicole offered him a cold beer.

"Will you ladies join me?"

"*We do not drink.*" Nicole sounded defensive.

Lisa toned it down. "We don't mean to be rude, we just *don't drink alcohol.*" The twins looked at each other in solidarity.

Davis turned the palm of his free hand toward them. "Whatever. Didn't mean to upset anyone, eh."

The meal was fancy: lobster, steak, asparagus, and risotto with saffron. He skipped the asparagus. He went to the galley fridge and to help himself to another beer. A six-pack was tucked behind packages of professionally prepared foods. He moved the containers to get to the beer. The meals were from a fancy Palm Beach restaurant.

Mongo came up from behind.

Davis pulled his head out of the refrigerator, closed the door and jumped. The man wore a pair of ill-fitting khakis wadded up at the cuffs and cinched at the waist. He did not look like any yachtsman Davis had ever seen.

"What are you doing? Snooping around?"

"That's our uncle," Lisa stood behind Mongo.

"I was just getting a beer. This is a beautiful boat," Davis said. "She's run aground pretty deep."

Mongo snarled, his upper lip curling and quivering, but he said nothing.

"How do you plan to sail her?" Seemed like a logical question.

"Why don't you shut the fuck up?" Mongo said.

"Golly, I was just trying to be friendly. And I wondered if maybe I could help."

"You understand English about as good as those two." Mongo snapped his head toward the twins. "Whenever I tell them to shut the fuck up, they just keep on talking."

Uncle Mongo and his twin nieces appeared unbothered that the million-dollar ship's hull was digging deeper into the sandy bottom, her fiberglass body groaning against the concrete docking, like she was dying. Davis did not ask any more questions. When his belly was full of food and his batteries full of electricity, he collected his things, stuffed them into a small duffle bag, and politely excused himself, waddling down the stairs to the swim platform.

He held on to the stainless steel railing and hopped onto the dock with the bag over his shoulder, making a run for the tent, waving his free arm, trying to break up a black cloud of mosquitos. Thank God he'd found juice for his batteries. Without power, the whole video salvage operation hung in the balance. From the looks of things, he could freeload electricity and maybe even gourmet meals for a couple more days. The *Sea Food* wasn't sailing any time soon.

GEORGE WAS PREPARED to die when Mongo appeared in the stateroom.

He was belly chained to a built-in bedpost connected to the blood-soaked mattress. The squall last night had rocked the *Sea Food* like a carnival ride, giving him a bad case of the dry heaves. The ship listed on a steep angle, and the chain around his waist anchored George to one leg of the bed, keeping him from sliding across the stateroom floor. Incessant scraping sounds coming from the hull rocking back and forth against the concrete bulkhead were unbearable, like the sound of fingernails dragging across a chalkboard. Under normal circumstances, he'd be performing heroic deeds to save the ship. But he was a prisoner, and he was too sick to care.

His reflection in the full-length mirror on the back door of the master bath was that of a stranger. He was barefoot, sitting cross-legged, wearing a *Keep the Keys Weird* blue tank top draped over a pair of Daisy Duke-fringed cutoff jeans. His face bloomed hunter green and he had two black eyes. Not from a pummeling, but from heaving his guts out.

Now that the sea had calmed, his brain had begun processing random logical thoughts. The Coast Guard would be looking for the Pierces' missing yacht by now. George's girlfriend would be worried too. She got testy when an hour went by and he didn't answer her texts. On the other hand, sometimes the Pierces liked to go on impromptu trips to West End, Bahamas, or even as far as Great Abaco, and cell service could be spotty. It had been an awful storm, the kind of monster that swallows ships as big as the *Sea Food*. And with no Mayday calls, it was possible the authorities assumed they'd capsized.

Nicole arrived with a plate of food. He looked at the risotto with saffron and started to heave.

"Oh, God," she said. "He looks like he's going to die."

"Shoot me," George said. "Please. Put me out of my misery."

TONY GOT up from the sofa and peeked out between mini blinds. The apartment was sticky from the big rainstorm that had passed during the night.

"The marshal's still out there," Tony said. "In Cuba, they track you the old-fashioned way, with government men in military vehicles."

"They do here, too." Vance looked through a set of binoculars. "But they don't drive World War II Army Jeeps."

"I'll just keep cooking and cleaning. Just happy to have air conditioning and cow meat. I can hang here, no *problema*. Man cannot live happily on rice and beans alone. I know. I tried."

"Where will you go? If we get the money?"

"I have a Panamanian passport."

"Your buddy, Manuel Noriega, is dead. Died in prison not too long ago."

"That guy was so, what's the word?" Tony searched his brain for it.

Vance helped him. "Corrupt."

"Yeah, corrupt. We paid him at least ten million dollars in the eighties to move blow through Panama. He was working for the CIA and us."

"Typical dictator."

"He was a sock puppet for sale to the highest bidder." Tony turned his hands into finger puppets and made them box each other and laughed.

Vance chewed his cuticle. He would have laughed, but at the moment nothing was funny.

BEING STUCK in the small apartment with the shades and curtains drawn was getting to him. Tony was better-natured. He'd been stuck inside for over a week. Vance couldn't figure out how he stayed upbeat. "It would do you good to get out and walk, breathe some fresh air." But then he remembered Tony couldn't leave the apartment.

"I had enough of that," Tony said. "Beef and air conditioning, that's like paradise. I'm perfectly happy right here. How old is your sister now?" he asked.

"Thirty-five. I think." He was terrible with dates and ages.

"So young to get sick." Tony shook his head sadly.

"Do you remember her?"

"Not really," Tony said. "Your father was very protective. He didn't like me being around her."

"You can't blame him for that."

"No. If I had a daughter, I wouldn't let her hang around me, either. Especially back then."

———

TONY NEVER SPOKE about the mother he never knew. He sensed Tony's fear when Vance told him Kathy had been diagnosed with cancer. It was their bond—both their lives were connected to it. Tony's mother had died of ovarian cancer when he was an infant. Vance's dad was the doctor who saved people but rejected Tony like a bastard child, as if it was his fault his mother got sick and died.

Vance's father had rejected him, too, his own son, shutting him out of his personal life and keeping his financial situation a secret. If he had known, maybe he would have taken a job with one of the big firms. But he didn't know. His father cared more about keeping up appearances.

He broke the silence. "There are some experimental treatments. My father didn't leave my mother in a good place. Financially."

"*Oye*, I would never have guessed that, your father the doctor? My father, the peasant, yes. A man of little means, he left our family with nothing because he had nothing. But your dad, the big shot doctor?"

"My dad was a shitty businessman."

"We have more in common now, *sobrino*. And we both have more to gain than we have to lose." Tony smoothed the smattering of gray hair at his temples with his fingers. "We are more alike than you think."

Vance scratched his ear. "I hope it turns out better this time around, for both of us. I don't feel like faking my death. Or sharing a wall with you at ADX."

"No shit. Keep telling us that. I need to believe it too, *sobrino*."

TUESDAY

DAVIS FIGURED out women could be confusing back when he was a young gun shooting TV news in the Twin Cities. At twenty-five, he was already fat and had a body odor so foul that some reporters refused to work with him. It didn't take long to figure out why girls who otherwise never gave him the time of day were interested in him. It was the thirty-pound broadcast camera on his shoulder and the chance at being on the local news. The Nicole-Lisa duet had reactivated the stupid chip in his head.

As he motored out on day two, the twins leaned provocatively over the bow railing of the *Sea Food*. He was on task. But then one of them waved.

"Morning!" Lisa hollered, taking pictures of him with her smartphone.

"Hey, dere! Morning to you, too!" He put the *Witch* in neutral.

"You're up and at it early!" Nicole stood on the bow in her bikini, smiling, shifting her hips in titillating waves like she was working the paparazzi on the red carpet somewhere.

He could hardly believe it when he saw them. The temptation to stop and chat was too great. Even on deadline with the five-thousand-dollar bonus the lawyer and marketing guy promised. What difference would five extra minutes make? He swung the boat around by the stern and pulled up alongside, giving Nicole a view straight down into the *Leaky Witch*. He looked up at the girls, using his hand to shield the light, but shards of morning sunlight bounced off the water, blinding him.

Lisa studied the screen on her phone and spread her thumb and forefinger, zooming in on Davis who was standing with his legs apart. He used the center console to brace himself. Lisa leaned off to one side to level the camera with the horizon and clicked a dozen photos in rapid succession.

"So where are you going?"

He couldn't tell which one of them asked. He sat in the seat under the partial shade of the faded pale blue Bimini canvas top with his fat, sunburned thighs spread wide like he was airing something out. Lisa zoomed in and saw a softball-sized pink testicle sagging down from his shorts. She giggled and took a picture of it.

"Going for a dive!" he said.

"Are you like a photographer or something?" Nicole asked while Lisa clicked more photos.

"You could say that!"

"Uncle Ramon says this is a national park and we can't even fish here," Nicole said, all pouty. "Are you allowed to dive here?"

"No! I'm going farther out, east of the boundary!"

Lisa lowered her sunglasses to the tip of her nose and slung her slinky, long, black hair over her shoulder. He saw it in slow motion. "What are you looking for out there with all that equipment?"

"A wreck."

Mongo appeared on the tilting bow. It was too late to fish the words back out of the air.

"A wreck, you say! What wreck?"

Davis shrugged his blubbery shoulders one at a time. "Supposed to be some good wreck diving up near Stiltsville." He throttled the outboard.

Mongo pushed Lisa aside. "Stiltsville. Huh. I doubt that!" He looked down into Davis's boat. "That gear you got, it doesn't look like recreational stuff to me. Looks like professional stuff. I bet you got to put a giant weight belt on to sink that fat ass of yours!"

Davis revved the outboard louder. He spun the Dusky

around. The teak-handled spear gun he'd brought along almost
went over the side. He grabbed it midair, laid it down, and sped
out of the horseshoe marina.

———

"THAT, LIKE, WASN'T VERY NICE." Nicole put her hands on her
hips and stared at her ugly uncle.

"What the fuck are you two morons doing?" He struck like a
cobra, snatching Lisa's phone from her hand. He squinted,
studying the top of the screen. The progress bar was creeping
along, four out of five pictures had already been sent. He
banged his forefinger on the red X Cancel button. "I told you to
stay off these fucking things!" He flung his hand behind his ear
like he was about to pass a football and aimed the phone at
the water.

Lisa lunged at him, snatching the phone back. "I was just
sending pictures of our new friend to my sister."

Nicole's phone pinged.

Uncle Mongo grabbed Nicole's phone and saw (__!__) and
said, "What the fuck is that?"

Nicole bit her upper lip so she wouldn't laugh.

"It's a fat ass emoticon. You know, for our new friend,"
Lisa said.

Mongo looked like a chimp studying an Etch-A-Sketch
screen. "What the fuck is an emoty-kon?"

Nicole held two fingers up in a L-formation behind Uncle
Mongo's head. Loser.

Her phone pinged again, another message from Lisa. (!)
Code for Uncle Ramon, the tight ass.

Mongo looked at the (!) on the screen. "What the fuck is
this?" He looked at Lisa since she was the one who sent it.

"Nothing," she said.

Nicole snatched the phone back. Mongo went back inside the cabin of the tilting yacht. Lisa sent a :(to her sister.

———

On day two when Davis lowered the submersible vehicle into sixty feet, the water was glassy. He drove it as far as the tether would go, two hundred feet in each direction. He watched the live video feed on the waterproof monitor topside, scouring the sandy bottom in a grid search. His heart rate jumped when a hull-shaped reef appeared on the screen. Davis maneuvered the ROV closer, then backed it off to get a wide shot. The outline looked a lot like an offshore racing boat. He drove the submersible closer. On a tight shot, he saw that sea life had taken root all over the hull, and a community of small tropical fish darted in and out of the coral. He motored the *Witch* closer to the wreck and dropped anchor.

He pulled the ROV onto the deck and wound the tether into a pile. He heard a ping and searched for his phone stowed with the junk in the center console. A text message from his cell phone carrier had popped up in a bright green bubble. His bill was overdue and the company texted the option of paying from his mobile. Davis pressed "1" to "Pay Now" and the message disappeared. He tossed the phone back into the junk drawer.

He stretched the rubber dive mask strap around his head and adjusted the GoPro headband on his brow, centering it. He shoved his feet into the long rubber fins, placed the mask over his eyes, stuck the snorkel in his mouth, and rolled backward over the side, making a wave big enough to rock the boat.

Davis snorkeled until he spotted the outline of the wreck from the waterline through the window of his mask. It appeared tiny in the refracted light, like a toy boat. It took him two tries to wrangle himself back into the Dusky. He dressed for a tank dive. He put one arm through the wraparound buoyancy control vest and slung it over his shoulder, bending at the knees. The jacket weighed thirty pounds with the extra ballast built in. He put his free arm through the opposite opening and shook his shoulders to settle the tank on his back. He fastened the heavy nylon groin and gut strap extenders. Bending over, he wrapped five-pound weights around each ankle.

He stuck the regulator mouthpiece between his teeth, checked the gauges, grabbed the spear gun, gloves, and flashlight, and rolled backward off the edge of the gunwale. Gravity and ballast did the rest, pulling Davis down slowly.

When he landed on the bottom, he bounced gently like an astronaut. He felt for the Record button on the GoPro strapped to his forehead and pushed it. Using his fins the way a whale uses its flukes, he swam toward the wreck. Davis zeroed in on a lionfish hunting in the coral nursery. He went into a controlled rage, pulverizing the spiky brown-and-white-striped venomous fish against the seabed with the butt of his spear gun until it looked like it had been through a food processor.

Davis switched gears, watching contently as the pretty damsels and angelfish nibbled at bits of it. Rumor had it someone in Fort Lauderdale had dumped an aquarium of lionfish during Hurricane Andrew, releasing the first ones into the wild. They flourished, traveling as far as Australia, wreaking havoc, preying upon juvenile fish growing in the coral nurseries. All good reef stewards killed them on sight.

His regulator gurgled rhythmically, sending streamers of bubbles to the surface. The powerboat listed at an angle, stern down and nose up. It hadn't moved much with the currents because it was chained to a massive concrete pillar like the ones the Department of Transportation used to hold up the elevated Interstate-95 interchanges. He put the 1200 lumens flashlight under his left armpit, and using gloved hands pulled himself around to the inspect the sides of the hull.

A school of small scavenger fish followed him, nibbling at the hairs on his arms and legs. The hull was covered in a thin matt of sea life. Davis gently ran a gloved hand along the fiberglass in long, sweeping arcs, searching for a fabricated door, but he couldn't see or feel anything like a secret hatch.

He rolled over onto his back and floated beneath the raised part of the bow in the fetal position with his fins pressed against the hull bottom. He softly hammered at the thicker layers of coral and mollusks with the butt of the spear gun. His ass bounced against the seabed, disturbing thousands of specks of calcified material until he turned the ocean into a blizzard.

WHAM!

Something big blindsided him, slamming his shoulder hard enough to knock the regulator from his mouth. He held his breath and used his eyes and hands to hunt for the mouthpiece. His heart pounded. He shoved the breather back in. The second strike was faster, pummeling his ribcage. He doubled over in pain, inhaling a teaspoon of seawater, and coughed. The visibility was so bad it was like looking through three layers of cheesecloth. Whatever it was, it was coming back. Fast.

CLANG!

His air tank crashed into the hull. Davis held his breath. He saw it coming this time—a seven-foot shark. He grasped for the spear gun leaning against the wreck, but in his panic knocked it over, out of reach. The tall wooden gun rotated down through the haze to the sandy bottom in slow motion. He dove for it. The shark circled him. It arched its back. Its eyes were big and black and as expressionless as the glass on the bottoms of old-fashioned Coca-Cola bottles.

It was a bull shark, and he knew how they hunted their prey. It was a game of bump and run. If he hadn't muddied the water, it wouldn't have bothered him. But bull sharks liked hunting in low visibility. It was their specialty. The apex predator took another run at him, ramming its blunt nose into his exposed thigh. Its pectoral fin caught the bottom front of his billowing T-shirt and spun him around. The water cleared enough for him to see the spear gun. He used the tip of his long fin to work it in close enough to reach it. He froze as the bull approached. It slowed down before passing by, sizing him up, turning its jagged teeth toward him. He shined his flashlight into its vacant eye.

The shark shimmied away, buffeting his body in short powerful waves. He dove down onto the sand, landing on his exercise-ball gut. He grabbed the five-foot-long spear gun, and bounced back up, kicking more sediment. The shark appeared out of nowhere and rushed him, baring its meat-grinding teeth. Davis swung the spear gun overhead like a javelin-thrower and aimed for the shark's eye. The metal tip tore the skin where an eyelid might have been.

The bull shark retreated out of sight. Davis waited, breathing in—out, in—out, *one-two, one-two, one-two, one-two*, until his heart rate slowed. His gauges showed he was almost out of air. He swam to the surface to regroup.

Running on adrenaline, he practically walked on water getting back in the boat. He dropped the regulator from his mouth and sucked in a gallon of air. He wobbled to the captain's chair, using the spear gun as a walking stick, and plopped down. He rested his head facedown on the steering wheel, under the shaded canvas top.

When he looked up, he cocked his head at something in the distance. He fished his binoculars from under the seat and spotted a barge, the kind the city hired for its annual fireworks display, a featureless rectangle floating on the horizon. He could make out *BoatTowAmerica* painted on the arm of the crane. It was a commercial salvage vessel. The lettering was old and faded, but the name was still visible: *The Waterhog*.

The last thing he needed right now was company. Was it here to recover the *Sea Food*? The yacht had burrowed so deeply into the sand bar that a high tide probably wouldn't be enough to right the ship. He saw a half dozen men milling about the deck. But the vessel wasn't moving. It appeared to be anchored. Boca Chita would be easy to find if that was their destination. The sun was dipping in the western sky, a sign to call it a day. First he saved the exact coordinates on his phone.

20

J ake couldn't help himself. He left the used car lot and
went to the public library at lunch. He typed the coordinates into Google Earth, the numbers he'd secretly
copied onto a napkin at the donut shop. Being able to
read upside down was practically a prerequisite in the world of
investment banking. He'd written quickly and stuffed the
napkin in his pocket. He studied the underwater geography on
the map, moving the cursor over Boca Chita Key. Zooming into
the screen, the lighthouse came into view. He texted Lauren
while gazing at the No Cell Phones sign posted on the wall:
`Meet at JC—9 PM tonite?`

She answered: `Coffee place?`

`Yes.`

`OK.`

LAUREN WAS ALREADY THERE when Jake arrived, folded up on the
Chesterfield with her arms wrapped around her knees. He sat
next to her on the low sofa.

"What's wrong with you? You look like you lost your best friend or something."

Her eyes were red and swollen. Tears welled and her lip quivered. She dropped her head, buried her face in her knees, and began to sob. Jake put his right arm across her back and squeezed her shoulder with his giant hand.

She looked up at him and hiccupped the words one by one. "My—dog—was—run—over."

"Is she all right? Your dog?"

She shook her head, plucked a napkin from the tabletop dispenser, and dabbed the tears rolling down her cheeks. She blew her nose into another napkin and placed it in her lap.

The frumpy Java Chalet owner stopped by the table. "If you want something later, just let me know. We close at ten o'clock."

Jake nodded and waved her off.

Lauren composed herself, taking in deep breaths until she calmed down. It was not professional to cry in front of a client, but she couldn't help it.

"I'm sorry about your dog. I've been there—they're such great companions," Jake said.

She nodded.

"Have you heard anything from your guy Davis?"

"No. Was I—supposed to? I don't remember."

"No. I guess I'm micromanaging. Just curious. Let's get out of here and get something a little stronger. Take your mind off things."

"OK," she said, "but coffee is my limit for mind-altering substances."

"Well, *I* need a drink."

"Where do you want to go?"

"My place. Come with me." He grabbed her hand.

SHE FOLLOWED him on a five-minute drive to his Brickell Avenue apartment. He showed her where to park her car in the visitor section of the garage. The condo was just off the tenth floor with a view of the financial district. She would never have guessed his decorating taste in a trillion years. An ornate, round-backed corner chair with an olive green velvet seat took up half the foyer. Past the entryway, the shelves of a tall bookcase were jam-packed with hardcover books. Two mismatched black and gold-leafed ladder-backed chairs with cane seats were tucked under a piecrust tabletop. Vintage white-on-blue jasperware Wedge-wood china filled the antique oak hutch. Needlepoint pillows were strewn on the cozy floral sofa and a large oil painting of a foxhunting scene set in a baroque gold frame hung above it.

Jake poured himself a goblet of red wine and delivered sparkling water she'd asked for, served in a stemmed glass.

Jake sat down next to her on the sofa, lifted her hand gently, and held it in his. She leaned into his shoulder and sobbed.

"You should lie down."

Her mind was foggy.

He led her by the hand into his bedroom and helped her onto the white chenille bedspread. He removed her shoes and rubbed her feet. He left and returned with a glass of water and an extra pillow. He'd refilled his wine goblet.

He gently brushed the hair from her face and dabbed the tears from her cheeks, wiping his wet thumbs on his shirt. He sat on the edge of the bed and stroked her arm, and kneeling over her, put his mouth on hers. She didn't resist. Jake turned out the light. He caressed the inside of her thigh and removed her panties. Lauren arched her back. Jake gathered her hair into his hand, making a ponytail. "Are you OK?"

She nodded.

He tried wrestling with her naked body under his Egyptian sheets, but she wasn't feisty like he'd expected. He'd stalked and caught his prey. Going in for the kill, he entered her. Grunting and pumping his body on top of hers, he bellowed loud enough for the neighbors to hear. When he finished, he rolled away into the fetal position, with his back facing her. Lauren rolled closer to him, wrapping her arms around his shoulders. He was done.

SHE WASN'T LOOKING for fireworks. She was looking for comfort. Wincing at the memory of Sinbad—his sweet brown eyes trusting her right up to the moment she suffocated him with her bare hands—Jake was exactly the distraction she needed. She wanted something different to take away the pain.

She'd bargained with the universe, desperate for relief. Jake said nothing when he was finished, groaning like an animal. She felt the tears and rolled away from him, hugging herself. He drifted off to sleep and started to snore. Remorse set in, followed by humiliation. She couldn't sleep but didn't want to wake him, didn't want to face him. She hated him. She hated herself more. When he asked her to meet him for coffee she felt obliged. He was a big, new client.

She hadn't met a man that had made her think about moving past her breakup with Peter, until Vance. And she'd catfished him as a ruse, working for Ray.

Ray sensed her interest in Vance and had forbidden her to talk to him until after the Cormorant job was finished. What was she supposed to do? Suffer alone? She thought about calling her best friends Susan and Liz. But Susan had just discovered her own husband's infidelity and, like Lauren, was the last to figure it out. And Liz was on an exotic cruise somewhere in the world with her ka-zillion-aire husband.

Now Lauren had broken her own rules by sleeping with a client. Not just any client, but the VP of marketing for the biggest manufacturer of watertight cases. Worse, the job was a referral from Ray Dinero. What if Jake bragged to Ray about it? And somehow Vance found out? In the best-case scenario, she'd have to keep it secret from Vance. Or maybe even lie about it if the boys gossiped. Maybe she'd wrecked any chance at a future with him.

Her first instinct had been to call Vance, but she couldn't afford to blow the deal and not get paid. If she violated the NDA, that would void the contract for the video gig she desperately needed. Now the longing to call him and tell him how stupid she'd been for sleeping with Jake was gnawing at her. But that was a no-go; it would put a wrecking ball on any future they might have.

Why didn't that fucking landscaper slow down! Then none of this would have happened. If her ex Chris hadn't stolen her tax money, she wouldn't be in a financial disaster. Why was her man-picker so broken?

She wanted to message Vance, see him, have him comfort her, wrap his arms around her. She wanted to tell him what happened. Instead, she'd sat on her hands, waiting for the impulse to pass.

It wasn't like Jake forced her to go to his place. She followed him, driving her own car, for crying out loud. She heard Peter's words in her head: *You have a PhD in denial.* She could easily have done a U-turn and gone home, but she didn't want to be alone. If the speeding landscaper had slowed his vehicle, or swerved, or if she'd clipped the leash on Sinbad's collar properly, she wouldn't be at Jake's place right now. She'd be home in bed with her beloved dog sleeping at her feet. Her entire body shook and suddenly she was chilled to the bone. She had to get up. She tiptoed into Jake's bathroom and closed the door.

Sᴀʀɢᴇ ʜᴀᴅɴ'ᴛ ᴘʟᴀɴɴᴇᴅ on spending the night behind the wheel of his Jeep at Jake's condo parking garage. He'd followed Lauren to the coffee shop where she met Jake, and then from the coffee shop to Jake's place where Sarge dozed off around midnight. He awakened when he heard the elevator coming down. Sarge rolled his neck from side to side until it popped back into place. He ran his tongue over his teeth, grimacing at the taste and texture.

He saw Lauren striding toward her black Audi parked four cars from his in the covered garage. He lay across the center console, resting his head on the passenger seat. His neck cracked and popped back out of place.

———

"Jᴇsᴜs, *gordo*, do you know what time it is?"

Sarge didn't like being fat-shamed, but that never stopped Ray from calling him *gordo*.

"I have an update you'll be interested in."

"Hang on," Ray whispered. He walked into the master bathroom and closed the door. "My wife and daughters are asleep. What's up?"

"She spent the night at Jake's place." He was parked outside of a gas station drinking yellow coffee from a paper cup.

"*Que?*"

"The video chick, Lauren. She spent the night with Vance's guy, the New York guy."

Ray repeated Sarge's words as if he couldn't believe it. "*Oye,* how do you know that? It is too early for weird news."

"I've been following her like you asked." He sipped the coffee, picking grounds from his tongue and flicking them out the window of the Renegade. "I thought you told him to stay away from her."

"I did. But Jesus, a guy's pecker has a mind of its own. I'll talk to our mutual friend. This is all we need, a dick in the middle of the deal. I didn't have a good feeling about him."

WEDNESDAY

TONY WAS in a deep sleep on the sofa. A soccer game flashed on the flat screen. Unlike every other Cuban in the history of the island nation, Tony had no interest in soccer. He'd fallen asleep during the ninth inning of a Dodgers game and awoke to the smell of java and the sounds of soccer.

"*Buenos días,*" Tony said when he saw Vance up and at it. "Sorry. Good morning." He rubbed his eyes. What time is it?"

"Early," Vance said.

"What are you doing up? I thought you quit work."

"My sister's surgery is this morning. I would have told you, but I know how you feel about it. And it's not like you can go with me."

"I wish I could. And I wish you told me she was going to the hospital today. Maybe it would help, you know, make you feel better, talking about it."

He handed a full mug to Tony. "I don't think so."

"You don't look so good."

"Stress and lack of sleep. I keep thinking about what will happen if we get caught. My sister and my mom, they're in a tough spot, both of them." He blew his cheeks up fully and held his breath.

"That's what you used to do when you were a kid. When you got nervous, you used to hold your breath."

"You remember that?"

"I'll pray for her," Tony said, pulling the blanket over his shoulders.

"You pray? Seriously?"

"I do. How do you think I survived twenty years in Cuba?" He put his palms together, hands pointing up and closed his eyes.

He didn't think of Tony as a man of God.

"I keep my thoughts to myself. I've been spared from many things—dodged a lot of bullets, literally—so I thank God when I remember to. It's the only thing I can do now to help. Because when you think about it, Vance, we're pretty helpless."

He hated the mantle of helplessness. He had enough self-awareness to know the more something pissed him off, the truer it was. They *were* helpless.

"You should try it," Tony said. "Praying."

Tony evangelizing was not helping because talk about God activated his stubborn side, the part of him that had to believe he was in control. He changed the topic. "Do you know Sergeant Daniel Ruiz?" He watched his uncle's expression, but there was no reaction. He just looked half asleep.

"Should I? More coffee, *por favor.*" He held his cup out.

He grabbed the pot from the counter and topped it off. Tony clung to the cup with two hands. He watched him blow on the coffee like they were somewhere freezing cold.

"Maybe." Vance stuck a plain, black ball cap on his head to cover his hair.

Tony asked, "As in police officer *sergeant*?"

"Retired."

"I might. I knew a lot of cops in my day."

"Get up."

"What for?"

"Just get up for a second." Vance used both hands and made a scooping gesture.

Tony stood with the blanket draped over his back like a cape.

Vance squatted and stuck his hand under the cushions, up to his armpit. He dug out a 32 caliber Walther PPK double-action semiautomatic. He handed the classic black handgun to Tony. "Hold on to this. You might need it."

"Nice. Looks like something out of a James Bond movie."

"I am deeply sentimental about that gun." He slung the holstered Glock over his shoulder. "This is my best gun. But that one's my favorite."

Tony rubbed his eyes with rolled fists. "Think you'll need a gun at the hospital, *sobrino*?"

"It's kind of like a seat belt. It works best if you do it all the time."

"Good point." Tony stroked the metal nose of the Walther. "Where do you keep spare ammo?"

He pointed to the sofa. "Under the cushion. There's another clip, too. And a box of ammo."

HE HEADED toward Jackson Memorial Hospital feeling better leaving Tony in a position to defend himself if he needed to. The idea of Tony praying had come out of the blue. Did he get down on bended knee and clasp his hands? He'd never seen him doing it. "You'll never find any atheists in foxholes." His granddad told him that once, and it stuck with him. He and Tony were sharing a foxhole now.

He glanced at the rearview mirror. The white Cadillac SUV appeared from a side street and fell in behind Edgar and followed him for about a half mile, then disappeared.

When he pulled into the visitors' parking garage, the machine spit out a ticket and the gate lifted, letting him through. Jackson Memorial Hospital reminded him of his granddad,

Harold Courage. It's where he treated the Chicago mayor. "I met the future president of the United States," his grandfather boasted for as far back as he could remember. "That was the greatest moment of my life, when I shook the hand of the future President." As Harold aged and his mind grew weary, he told the story more often. "Tried to shoot FDR and killed that damned Chicago mayor instead."

Where did his grandfather get the death certificate for the gunman? And if it was a trophy or a souvenir, why didn't his father or grandfather show it to him while they were still alive?

When he reached the automatic glass doors on the ground level at Jackson Memorial Hospital, a strange feeling came over him. He turned around. The white Escalade was across the street, idling in the *No Loading* zone.

21

On the morning of the third day of the salvage, dark clouds twirled in from the south, and Davis's stomach gurgled from hunger. The clock was ticking on the five thousand dollar bonus, but he had to stop to eat to keep working. He prepped an MRE, dropped the ROV in the water, and watched the monitor while he wolfed the food, checking for any signs of yesterday's shark. The fisheye lens showed something he hadn't seen before: an indentation on the hull near the bow, barely discernable up close, but unmistakable from the camera's wide shot.

The sun was at full staff and beating down on him. He squinted over the horizon. The muddle of gray clouds offshore to the south had cleared enough to see that the barge was still anchored in the same spot. Leaning over the gunwale and cupping his hands, he rinsed his face and chest with salt water. After dressing for a tank dive, he rolled backward off the *Witch,* making a whale of a splash.

Using the tip of the spear gun, Davis carefully chipped and chiseled chunks of coral reef growing on the fiberglass under the bow of the *Holly*. He picked at the edges and crevices like a dental hygienist, wiping debris with his gloved thumbs. He excavated a thin gap, digging with the sharp end of the spear along the seam of the secret hull where a rubber gasket must have been. When he tapped the metal hinges, they disintegrated like glitter. The heavy door crunched open under its own weight and sagged at a slight angle. He grabbed the top and hung from it with his arms, but it didn't break away from the boat.

Davis threw his bruised shoulder at the partially open door, wincing. He pulled on the hatch with his big arms, but the door clung stubbornly to one side of the hull. He wrangled it side-to-side, frenzied, twisting the hatch like a madman trying to straighten a picture frame. The door broke free and floated lazily toward the bottom like a notebook page on a soft breeze. He pushed off and did a somersault beneath the bow, straightening his fins and gracefully intercepting the sinking hatch as big as a horse's stall door just before it hit bottom. He turned it over and laid it gently on the seabed, living-side up. A school of red squirrelfish hurried into the waving coral and hid.

Davis swam to the opening of the hull. It was a dark hole. He propped his flashlight in the sand at an angle, illuminating the cavity. His heart sped up when he saw a load of plastic transport cases tightly packed inside. He removed the GoPro strapped to his forehead and looked at it. The red recording light was flashing.

He pulled one Cormorant case from the hull, a black one. Covered in algae, it slipped from his grip. He swam to it and guided it onto the sandy bottom, careful not to kick up debris that might attract a shark, and returned to the opening. A greenish yellow case was visible behind the space where he'd removed the black one. He pulled it out and, hugging it, kicked his way topside. The slippery case was much heavier at the surface, one hundred fifty pounds at least. He tried side mounting the Dusky like a horse, slinging one fat leg over, using his free hand to hang onto the case at the waterline. He was so out of shape that his arms and legs already ached. He changed body contortions, trying to get the rest of his body in the *Witch*, but he couldn't get enough traction or the right angle to get his other leg into the boat. The Dusky swiveled on the anchor line, turning him into a sumo wrestler trying to land a billfish from a lily pad.

He released the waist buckle of his vest and shrugged the dive jacket off his back, tossing the aluminum air tank into the boat while treading water. Free of the extra weight, he dropped back into the water and used one hand to hang on to the boat and the other to hold onto the yellow case. He rested for a minute, recharging.

In one continuous powerful motion, he dropped feet first into the water, sinking until his head was under the heavy case. Using his fins like a dolphin, he exploded up out of the water, rocketing the heavy container up and over, into the boat, where it slid across the deck. He flew backwards, floating with his eyes closed inside the dive mask, panting and shooting water from his mouth like a blowhole. There was no way he could do that nine more times.

He pulled himself back inside the boat and opened the hatch where he stowed a spare seventy-five-foot anchor line. He flung his dive vest back on, stuck the respirator in his mouth, threw the coiled rope over his shoulder, and toppled backward into the water.

He worked quickly, carefully unloading the remaining yellow cases from the *Holly*'s hull, arranging them a few feet apart on the ocean floor. He threaded the rope through the handles, stringing them together like pearls on a necklace, and swam to the surface carrying one end of the rope. He stripped his dive gear, hoisted himself into the *Witch* with the rope between his teeth, and tied the end of the line to a metal cleat at the stern.

The air was stifling. Working under the blazing sun, Davis grunted and slung, swatted and scratched, wrestled and stumbled, cursed and rested, until the last yellow case was aboard the boat. He splashed fresh bottled water on his face and sat under the shady canvas top until a pack of mosquitos arrived. Rushing about, he distributed the weight the best he could. He packed the ROV and camera gear, and pulled the anchor. Waddling barefoot between the stacks of slimy cases, he held his arms out to balance himself as he made his way to the center console. The engine turned over on the second try. He scoped out the barge through his binoculars. It still hadn't moved.

He opened the throttle gently. The *Witch* lurched forward clumsily, like a lumbering elephant. Davis headed toward Boca Chita. What if *The Waterhog* headed to the island to rescue the *Sea Food* and saw him packing up? Or the twins wanted to know what the cargo was? Going back for the tent and a few supplies wasn't worth the risk. Plus, he was dog-tired. He changed course and pointed the Dusky toward Plantation Key. He'd go straight to the storage unit, instead. There was no wind and the ocean was flat. Still the Yamaha outboard gasped and sputtered under the heavy load. He motored slowly between the red-and-green channel marker flags.

A powerful blast, like an underwater sonic boom shook Davis to his core. He turned to look back to the island. His eyes stung. He blinked, holding the wheel. A strange powerful pulse passed through his body, and a massive wave snaked beneath the boat. The fifteen-hundred-pound load shifted from side-to-side, sloshing gallons of water up and over the gunwales.

He wiped his eyes on his wet shirt and turned to look again.

A massive orange mushroom cap of fire and black smoke bloomed against a pale blue sky. The still-growing fireball at Boca Chita was at least ten stories high. He couldn't hear the *Witch*'s outboard. He stuck a finger in his ear and twisted it. A wave of intense dry heat blew over him. The air seared his nostrils and singed the hair on the back of his neck.

"Oh God, please don't blow," he prayed aloud to the five-gallon red plastic containers onboard filled with fuel. "Stay cool, man. Keep your heading. Don't look back." He kept repeating it over and over and over again.

THE WATERHOG BARGE motored and anchored directly above the submerged *Holly Golightly*. Four frogmen dressed in blue camo wetsuits dropped into the water. The fat diver who had just left had done all the hard work. It took them less than a minute to organize a human chain to raise and load the black cases onto the barge.

The barge crew had staked out Davis for a day and a half, taking turns watching him. Nick, the towboat company owner, had personally assembled the team and supervised the operation because his valued customer, Ray Dinero, had asked him for the favor. As soon as the ten black cases were loaded onto the deck of the barge, a sleek, red, forty-foot Donzi, the Ferrari of powerboats, appeared from the horizon and rendezvoused with the *Hog*. Even idling, the Donzi's 1200 horsepower engines growled ferociously, drowning out their voices as the frogmen on the *Hog* slung the black transport cases to the crew manning the speedboat. They worked quickly, like airport baggage handlers facing a too-tight connection. The Donzi sped off to the northwest with the load, the wake from her powerful outboards rocking the salvage vessel, the echoing of her engines thundering like a storm in the distance, until she was gone from sight.

The blast that followed tossed the *Hog* around like a bath toy, knocking her crew down to the deck. The men clung to what they could to stay aboard, some hanging to whatever they could with their fingertips.

The crane broke free from its restraints, sweeping over the deck like a pendulum of death.

"Stay down!" Nick yelled at his crew.

He wanted to get the hell out of there, but first he had to secure the crane to ensure his men were safe. The guys ducked and wove until the swaying slowed enough to use the winch to lower the arm of the crane onto the decking. They were pulling anchor when a black Zodiac raft approached from the west. It carried two girls and a stocky, shirtless man in chinos. Nick told his crew to cut the engines and dropped the emergency ladder to help them aboard.

"You OK?" he asked coughing and covering his eyes. A massive plume of black smoke spewed from the island. "What the heck happened?"

Mongo pulled the 45 caliber HK from the waistband of his pants and rushed Nick, who'd turned to run. Nicole stuck her leg out and Nick belly-flopped onto the deck. He slid headfirst into a metal cleat, cracking his head open. Mongo dove on top of him, wrapping his thick forearm around his neck.

"Get up," Mongo ordered.

Nick gasped for air. Mongo pressed the nose of the gun in Nick's right ear. "It'll be fucking loud if I put a fucking bullet in your fucking ear!"

The crew watched, helplessly.

Lisa waved Charles Pierce's pink thirty-eight caliber snub nose at the crew with the accuracy of a child holding an open umbrella on a windy day.

Mongo ordered Nick to his feet, swinging the gun randomly, pointing it at the divers. "Get off the boat! Move! Move! Move!" Mongo bashed Nick's forehead with the nose of the HK. Blood dripped into Nick's eyes.

"Go!" Nick said, blinking and choking. "Go now!"

Four frogmen dropped fins-first from the barge into open water.

"Ray's place!" Mongo ordered Nick. "Or I'll make your brains look like last night's spaghetti."

"Thanks for letting me push the button," Nicole said. The girls giggled. "That was like making an action movie."

IT HADN'T TAKEN MUCH TRI-CYCLIC acetone peroxide to blow the *Sea Food* into bite-sized pieces. Mongo had brought the Mother of Satan aboard the Pierces' yacht the night they overtook the vessel. Before the trip, he'd fashioned a wireless cell phone detonator using a soldering gun and eight Double-A batteries while watching a YouTube bomb-making video. He'd siphoned diesel fuel from the *Sea Food* to use as an accelerant. The explosion was impressive, way bigger than he thought it would be.

Nick squinted into the sun. He snapped his head back to the burning island. "Is that your handiwork?"

"Shut the fuck up! How *many times* do I have to repeat myself?"

THE FIRST TO ARRIVE WAS THE Coast Guard. The fire raged on the water. There was nothing recognizable about the Pierces' luxury yacht.

"Looks like a terrorist attack," Lieutenant William Goodpaster said. He stood on the bow of the orange-lipped, forty-five-foot response boat, spotting the charred remains of a torso in cutoff blue jeans bobbing in the water. "Move back!" he yelled. The skipper reversed the engines and backed away from the searing heat. The cutter had been dispatched from the USCG station in Miami Beach signaling Homeland Security was in the loop.

The explosion ripped a pair of sport-fishing boats from their slips; they were taking on water. The fishermen radioed for help. A thirty-three-foot USCG Special Purpose Craft arrived and pulled all five to safety.

Goodpaster looked up at the news choppers thumping overhead. He got on the radio. "We need to clear the airspace. They're transmitting live shots."

Dispatched from the Naval Air Station in Key West, a pair of F/A-18 Super Hornet fighter jets screamed overhead, shutting down the airspace around Boca Chita.

<hr>

"BIS-CAY-BAY YACHT SALES." Mongo jammed the .45 into Nick's temple again. Nick winced. "That's where we're going. Get this pig moving!"

Nick nodded. "I can't imagine where else we'd be going."

Mongo whacked the back of Nick's skull with the butt of the gun. "How many times do I have to tell everyone to *shut the fuck up?*"

Nick ground his teeth. He called upon the intestinal fortitude taught during his Army Ranger training, waiting for pain to morph into endorphins. He turned the wheel and pointed the barge toward the Miami River, en route to Ray's boat yard.

When they reached the river, he spotted the speedboat crew, the one that had taken the black cases they'd salvaged after

Davis left the site. The muscular, metallic red Donzi was docked in a wet slip at Blue Cove Marina, just down river from Ray's place. The crew chugged beers under an awning watching news of the explosion on a big-screen TV. He hoped one of them would turn around and notice the *Hog* crawling past upriver, but none did. The crazy gunman sat on the ledge beneath the crane pointing the .45 at him.

The Donzi crew had been instructed to deliver the cases to Ray Dinero's boatyard and to wait for Nick at the Blue Cove bar.

———

VANCE HAD BEEN SITTING in the surgical waiting area for hours. He'd taken breaks, walked the hallways, chatted with the harried nurses and receptionists, taken the elevator to the first floor coffee shop three times. As the leading trauma center for Miami-Fort Lauderdale, Jackson Memorial Hospital was a bustling and chaotic place. The personnel was edgy, a familiar vibe from his days as a homicide detective. He'd been sitting alone in a corner, thumbing through old magazines, unable to ignore his brother-in-law's fidgety clock-watching. It wasn't long before Larry left, promising to return to drive his mother-in-law home, but Vance wasn't holding his breath. He moved over to where Larry had been sitting with Isabel. They blended in with the other families and friends huddled in the big waiting area. Some were pensive. Others emotional. Some looked bored stiff.

Beneath the urgency, there was a steady rhythm to the place. Surgeons in scrubs came through the double doors and checked with the desk. They'd be directed to the family; the doctors would introduce themselves and debrief next of kin, or whoever was waiting. How they had the patience to answer so many questions was beyond him. When they finished, the doctors jogged back through the double doors, ready to work on the next patient. Twice he saw loved ones herded into a small ante-room, followed by the surgeon. The room with the thick-paned window was where they delivered the bad news. He could tell by watching their body language, and the boxes of tissues passed around. What if he and his mother were called to the side room?

Both his father and grandfather had done their medical residencies at Jackson. His mother had been thinking about it, too. He could tell by the lost look on her face.

"The time goes so slow here," she said.

"I know, Mom. It's a complicated surgery. Plus, it's a busy place."

Isabel nodded. "Thank ju for being here, for staying."

It would have been nice if Larry had waited until Kat was in recovery, but he always bailed when things got tough. The company Larry worked for was self-insured, and the HR department had approved his sister's surgery. Thank God for that. They couldn't pay for the experimental treatments because they weren't FDA-approved. But they were paying for the surgery, and that was a good first step that needed to be done before she could start therapy.

In a few hours the seventy-two-hour clock would end on Davis's bonus. Vance had been checking his phone obsessively.

"He's a good man," Isabel said, reading his thoughts. "Some men have too many feelings. They can't show them."

"Like Dad?"

"Jes, like jur father. He didn't show it much, but he loved ju kids, more than the world."

"Larry Weaver." The woman running the post-op desk scanned the room. "Is Kathy Weaver's family here?" The doctor was standing by, waiting to be connected to the family.

Vance jogged up to the desk. "I'm her brother. Her husband had to leave. My mother is with me."

Double-checking the paperwork, her doctor came into the waiting room. "She's your daughter?"

Isabel nodded.

"I'm her brother."

The doctor looked at his clipboard again. "Any relation to Dr. Jim Courage?"

"I'm his son. Kathy is his daughter. This is my mom, Isabel Courage."

"I heard he passed away recently. We were all sad to hear the news," the physician said.

"Thank ju. My daughter? How is she?"

"She's in recovery. She did great. You can see her in about an hour. I see here she'll be following up with her oncologist. We'll send the samples to the lab for biopsy. It looks like we're keeping her here overnight."

Isabel hung on every word. "When can I see her?"

The doctor looked over their shoulders up at the banks of televisions on the walls behind them. "What the heck is that? A terrorist attack?"

Every monitor filled with talking heads and aerial images of a blast. Vance walked up to the TV and stood on his toes, and turned up the volume. The people in the waiting room moved in closer. Some of them gasped.

"Oh my gosh!" Isabel said.

A lower third graphic came up on the screen. BREAKING NEWS. TERRORIST ATTACK AT BOCA CHITA.

Holy cow! "Mom, I gotta go! I'll text Larry and remind him to come and get you. If not, Mom, take a taxi."

Isabel stared at the scenes of the smoking inferno, with pieces of what the reporters said was once a luxury yacht, bobbing in the waters around the horseshoe marina.

"Mom! Did you hear me? I gotta go. Call a taxi if Larry can't come and I can't get back in time."

"OK, Vance, I heard ju. But why do ju have to go?"

He kissed the top of her head. "I'll explain later. I love you, Mom. Tell Kathy I love her, too."

HE SHOVED the parking ticket and credit card into the parking machine and the gate lifted. A Level I trauma chopper was dipping down onto the rooftop helipad. He took a left on NW 12th Avenue just in time, watching the police shut down the perimeter from his rearview mirror.

Traffic on the Palmetto Expressway had ground to a halt. Emergency vehicles blared as response vehicles crawled along the shoulder. He messaged Larry, letting him know Kathy was out of surgery, reminding him to pick Isabel up from the hospital. Jackson-Memorial would be a zoo if there were victims. What were the chances of a terrorist attack on the island while Davis was there working on the salvage? What if Davis was dead? The money lost in the chaos? He'd promised his mother and sister he'd take care of Kat, that he could pay for the experimental treatment. He lied. He'd told them his father left enough life insurance money.

He felt a strange vibration pass through his spine. He'd heard about the low frequency siren, a high-tech emergency alert system that used sound waves intended to alert the deaf. The Hazmat team stuck in traffic behind him deployed it. Drivers listening to loud music through ear buds and others in soundproof luxury vehicles couldn't hear the sirens. He watched a fireman in full regalia dismount the truck and jog to a vehicle. He pounded on the window and ordered the driver to get out of the way.

Vance spun through the English-speaking AM news stations. Miami was elevated to Force Protection Condition, FPCON, code red. People were being told to go home and shelter in. The news announcers suggested the offshore explosion might be part of a bigger plot, like the coordinated terrorist attacks in Paris that left more than a hundred and thirty dead.

Traffic was at a standstill.

His burner pinged. He pulled it from under his right thigh. He raised his eyebrows.

`Sarge here. Meet me. Urgent.` Followed by: `Bring sidearm.`

`Call me.`

`Can't talk. Meet behind Casablanca SF ASAP`

He reached under the driver seat and felt for the Glock. He'd planned to go to the apartment; surely Tony would know something. He changed course, driving on the shoulder until he reached the first exit. He swung the Nissan around and headed north, toward the river. SF stood for seafood. Casablanca Seafood was another old haunt, a hangout for Miami and Fort Lauderdale cops. How the hell did Daniel get the number to his burner? It was proof he knew more than he'd been letting on.

TONY WAS ANNOYED. ESPN interrupted the telecast again. Now that he could watch baseball in HD on four channels whenever he wanted, they were constantly disrupting the games. A few days ago, full screen weather alerts came up for the first three innings. Silver alerts. Amber alerts. He was waiting for a Green alert announcing Martians. Now there was a terrorist alert. Except this one wasn't a warning. It was an attack. The timing was horrible. Jaime Justo's kid was on deck, a full count with bases loaded.

Vance's tablet pinged just as the station went to a Network News bulletin. The reporter said there had been a bomb attack sixteen miles offshore at Biscayne National Park. Holy crap! Vance's tablet was off-limits, but this was an emergency. He read the text Vance sent to Larry, Kathy's husband. Thank God Kathy was out of surgery and doing OK. More warnings popped up on the screen. He looked through the blinds. The streets were desolate.

DAVIS WAS IN INFORMATIONAL DARKNESS. Blast deafness cancelled out the grunts of the overtaxed outboard, now rattling. But the sounds coming from the naval F/A-18s sweeping overhead jangled his tired bones. His destination, a storage unit on Plantation Key, was located a hundred yards or so from a deserted bulkhead. It would be easier to unload the *Witch* there and drag the yellow cases on foot. Davis had completed a reconnaissance run before the trip. After the lawyer gave him the address and combination to the lock, he'd tested it. He'd entered the numbers in the Notes app on his iPhone backward as a precaution.

EVERY SHORTCUT, back road, and escape route Vance knew of was clogged. A military convoy of a half dozen hardened vehicles passed by, heading the opposite direction from Casablanca Seafood.

Another text from the same number: Where the F are U?

30 min—best I can do.

Daniel messaged back: K.

He pressed his foot on the accelerator, but the Cube reacted more like a sewing machine than a muscle car.

RAY STARED at the fifty-ton marine maintenance lift he'd prepped himself. Two days ago, he'd driven the hulking thing over to one of the open slips cut perpendicular into the bulkhead. He'd hired Nick's boat salvage company to raise the *Holly* and needed a place to put her. The lift looked like an earthmover welded onto an Airbus landing gear with slings wide enough to hold a humpback whale. It was where Ray planned to put the retired thirty-foot racing boat until she'd dripped dry. He wanted the old girl for old times' sake.

It was after shift and his employees were gone for the day. The working part of the Miami River was quiet: partially because of the hour, but mostly because of the offshore explosion. Ray had been alone since the speedboat crew unloaded the black cases into the maintenance building. He sat on the lawn chair perched on the back of the *Bookoo* sipping Diet Coke and swatting mosquitos, doing his best to keep calm.

He'd texted and called Nick several times, and when Nick stopped answering, Ray called the BoatTowAmerica office. The woman who'd answered the phone was worried. She'd been trying to reach Nick, too.

VANCE BACKED Edgar into a space next to the Jeep at Casablanca Seafood and rolled the window down. The smell of shellfish and saltwater burned his nose.

"*Oye, gallego*, glad you could make it. Shut that appliance down and get in *pronto*, and bring your weapon."

He climbed in. "Like to share what's going on?"

Daniel looked over his shoulder, backing out.

Vance stared straight ahead at a cartoonish hand-painted

shark sticking its head through a yellow life preserver. The mural had been on the restaurant wall forever. "This better be good."

"We're going to pay Ray Dinero a visit." He looked at Vance. He jammed his foot on the gas pedal. Unlike Edgar, the Renegade responded, tires spinning as he reversed out of the spot.

22

L auren paused at the four-way stop. She stuck her arm out the window and drained a half empty bottle of water that had been left in the cup holder of the rental van. She drove through a maze of Plantation Key residential streets until she arrived at the rundown storage facility at the end of a gravel road not far from an abandoned marina. She looked for a place to park and picked a spot behind a grove of Buccaneer palms shrouding the U-Kan Store-It facility. It made a good lookout point. The day laborers she'd hired sat quietly in the back seat. She closed her eyes, hoping her passengers weren't wanted felons who'd put a knife to her throat.

SHE'D SEEN the documents folded beneath a twenty-four-pack of Cialis, something that should have been tucked away in Jake's underwear drawer. It was the middle of the night when she'd had a panic attack at Jake's and couldn't sleep. She'd locked the bathroom door after she discovered the paperwork. A copy of Davis's confidentiality agreement was folded in half, over hers.

She put her hand over her mouth and gasped when she got to the part of Davis's deal where he agreed to "cut contact with Lauren Gold." She read all of it, including details about delivering the cases to a storage unit in Plantation Key. And the extra five thousand dollar bonus they offered Davis. What a bunch of double-dealers.

Earlier that night she'd taken Jake up on his offer to charge her cell in his bathroom. She snapped pictures of the agreement before riffling through the pockets of his blue blazer hanging from a hook on the back of the door. She laid the business cards she'd found inside the left breast pocket on the vanity counter. She didn't know if she'd just had sex with a marketing executive, an ex-Wall Street banker, or a *used car salesman*. In the other pocket, she found a rumpled napkin, the chintzy kind from a fast food joint. On one side was a bunch of numbers. There were handwritten notes on the other:

$1 million cash = 22lb. Total load = $75 mil = approx. 1,650 lbs. RD says cut 4 ways (VC, RD, VC-unc, & me)—guarantee min $10M ea.

It wasn't too hard to figure out VC was Vance Courage; RD, Ray Dinero; and VC-unc—Vance's uncle, Tony Famosa. That made the "me" Jake Fleming. Vance and Ray were screwing her, too. She'd wanted to wake Jake up. With an air horn on his ear!

A whopping hundred thousand dollar cut? What's that? Like less than one percent? Even a messenger deserves more. And Davis? Six grand, eleven tops? Jake was making ten million bucks for impersonating a marketer with a bullshit story about a viral video?

She stole the receipt for the Plantation Key storage unit and the sticky note with the combination to the lock. She hid the paperwork inside her panties, tiptoed to the bedroom and dressed quietly. Before she left, she hid Jake's box of Cialis under the sink behind the toilet brush, just to be a bitch. She snuck out without waking him.

—————

SHE RENTED the cargo van from a ma-and-pa place in South Miami, agreeing to leave a thousand dollars in cash as a deposit after the owners promised not to run the credit card she'd left for assurance. Highway traffic heading south was light. She stopped in Homestead, and surfed the parking lot of a big box home improvement store. Two Hispanic day laborers sat beneath a tree waiting for contractor work. She flashed four one hundred dollars bills at them. The pair jogged to the van and climbed in.

—————

MINUTES AFTER THE STAKEOUT BEGAN, Davis emerged on foot from the thicket of mangroves, hauling one of the salvaged cases. He looked terrible: beat-up, sunburned, and hunched over, swatting mosquitos. She watched him load the cases into the storage unit. When he finished, he pulled down the rusted overhead door. He slipped the padlock through the latch and was about to click the lock when he hesitated, yanked the door back up, and snapped a cell phone picture of the double stacks of yellow cases piled on the cement floor. Panting, he sat down for a minute, then locked the unit and staggered back to the *Witch*. She heard the outboard start and waited until the plume of gray smoke dissipated.

Backing the van out of the hiding spot, she parked it parallel to the overhead door. She took the sticky note from her purse and hopped out of the van. After she turned the combination lock dial left, then right and back, and clockwise once again, it dropped open. Gesturing with her hands and arms, she signaled to both workers to load the yellowish Cormorant cases into the van. They'd been quiet the entire time, not speaking a single word, even to one another. In less than five minutes, they were back on the road heading north, her nose stinging from the fishy fumes wafting from the slimy cargo.

She backed the van into the driveway of her condo and flung the back doors open. Spinning her right hand like a wheel, she mimed a message to the men to hurry. They followed her cue, hauling the cases through the tiled entryway, past the foyer, to the walled outdoor courtyard to the right, just off the living room. The wet transport cases smelled salty, and the acidic odor lingered inside the house.

"Come on, come on." She spun her wrist and hand again to hurry them. When they were finished, the two men jogged to the van and crawled into the backseat. The ride to Homestead was uneventful but for the irritating mechanical squeaks and groans of the old panel truck and the stench of dying sea life.

She wasn't sure what her next move would be, but now she had leverage. She had the money. *You have a PhD in denial.* Peter's voice was in her head again. How could she have been such a sucker?

The sun was dipping to the west over the huge strip mall where she'd found the workers. Most of the others had gone already. One of the guys tapped her on the shoulder from behind. She jumped in her seat and swiveled at the waist to look. He used his hands to calm her, patting the air like an invisible dog.

His co-worker handed her a postcard with a pen attached to it. When she reached for it, he pointed to the fresh wounds on the backs of her knuckles, from scooping Sinbad's body off the asphalt. He turned his own over and showed her deeps cuts, now scarred over.

She read the card: WE ARE DEAF. YOUR DONATION WILL HELP.

"Oh my God!" She covered her mouth. Her eyes widened. "You're deaf!" She placed the roller pen in her purse and opened her wallet. She handed them five hundred dollars each.

They shook their heads and tried to return all but the two hundred she'd promised to each of them.

"NO." She shook her head more insistently. Clasping her hands together as if in prayer she closed her eyes, and tilted her head back, facing the roof of the van.

"TANK U," one said.

They nodded, each placing a palm on their shirts, patting their hearts.

They held their hands together like church steeples and looked at her. The scars on their hands extended to their wrists and forearms, past their elbows, all the way to their biceps. There was no way to know the story of the wounds, long since healed over.

"Thank you," she said.

They nodded and hopped out of the van, turning and waving to her, holding back wide grins to hide their rotten teeth. Watching from the window, she stayed for a few extra minutes and observed them as they trotted toward the alley behind the big building. They had a spring in their step she hadn't seen earlier. She hoped the extra money would ripple their universe in some positive way, though she'd never know.

She stayed until they were out of sight. Picking up one of the WE ARE DEAF pens, she rolled it between her injured fingers and closed her eyes. Who had she become?

RAY LAUGHED ALOUD at the old Maine Coon cat rubbing its fur

on his leg. He watched the sky darken sitting in his strappy lawn chair on the stern of the *Bookoo,* waiting for Nick to arrive. A series of alerts blew up on his phone, news of an explosion at Boca Chita. It was hard to imagine it wasn't connected to the salvage.

He stroked the cat's head. "Looking for fish scraps, old boy?"

The Coon leaned harder against his leg, arched and curved its back, then looked up at him curiously.

"Would you believe I was the ace smuggler pilot for the old Los Guapos cartel?" He took a tube of lip balm from his pocket, painted his lips, and smacked them. The cat meowed. "I'm not going to lie to you, it was exciting."

The familiar melodies of the river—the humming of work-boats, the clinking of metal, and swishing of torn nets and trot-lines hanging from the outriggers, low flying jets heading in and out of Miami International—had stopped. Less familiar sounds took their place, a cacophony of sirens, cell phone alerts, and chopper blades.

The disagreeable noises would have been harder for another man to ignore, but Ray was cool under fire. "I named the *Holly Golightly* after my old girlfriend. She was best offshore racing boat in the Los Guapos fleet."

The cat looked up at him, bored.

He jumped to his feet when he saw *The Waterhog* ambling up river. There was no sign of the salvaged powerboat hanging from her deck crane. Nick waved to Ray and then saluted with his right elbow up and his hand flat above his left eyebrow, cutting through the air. Ray's heart skipped a beat. That salute was a warning signal, the one the two had agreed upon if there was trouble.

The shadowy figure behind Nick held something to his head, but he couldn't make it out in the backlight. A last glimmer of sun setting in the west glinted off a pistol stuck in

Nick's ear, blinding Ray like a laser. As the barge drifted quietly toward the dock, he heard a splash, like a body going overboard.

A northwest wind suddenly picked up and pushed the barge faster toward the wooden pilings near the wet slips. The worn car tires strung around the hull like holiday lights cushioned the impact when the *Hog* slammed into the bulkhead. A man and two women jumped from the barge as it collided with the dock, landing and falling hard on the concrete.

Ray leapt from the trawler and ran toward the maintenance building. When he passed through the doors, the automatic overhead lights clicked on.

He flipped the motion sensor to the off position, and sprinted past the pile of black plastic cases the speedboat crew had delivered less than an hour ago, stacked and draining on the middle of the cement floor.

He climbed a twelve-foot ladder leading to a thirty-foot catamaran hanging from a dry dock hoist. He crouched down on the deck of the boat. *I've been waiting for you.*

Mongo rushed into the building. "Come out, come out wherever you are!"

"Yeah," Nicole and Lisa sang in unison. "Come out, come out wherever you are."

Mongo pointed the .45 over his head and fired a round, tearing a hole through the metal roof. The blast was deafening, like a cannon.

"Well, well. What have we got here?" Mongo squinted, kicking at the black plastic cases.

Ray peeked out from over the side of the hanging catamaran. He was surprised to see the lithe doppelgangers with silky black hair. He didn't know them. He held his breath as Mongo walked around the base of maintenance lift, surveying it. As the snitch banker took a step closer to the ladder, the interior fluorescents went dark. The only light coming in now was a dim streak from the jagged hole Mongo had shot out of the metal roof. In minutes, the sun would be done for the day.

"I'll fucking kill you!" Mongo said, fumbling around in the dark.

Ray was balled up on the deck of the boat, motionless as a mannequin. His middle-aged bones ached. He'd set a trap and caught his prey, plus two.

"Get your phone. Get me some light," Mongo barked to the twins. He paced, the cuffs of Charles Pierce's khakis dragging, the soles of his shoes slapping the concrete.

Lisa felt inside her shirt and fished her phone out of her bra. She turned the flashlight on.

"Don't point that at me! Find the fucking door and open it!"

"Like, where is it?" Nicole asked.

"*Like* that red exit sign is a big hint!" Mongo flung his hand toward it. "Get over there. Open the door! And find the light switch."

Ray's ears were trained on the audio cues. Lisa inched toward the illuminated sign. She bumped into a metal toolbox on wheels. A wrench fell and clattered on the concrete, the noise echoing off the corrugated metal walls. Ray twitched in the hanging cocoon.

Lisa shone the light on the doorknob. Nicole tried turning it left, and then right. Mongo screamed at her, "Open the door!"

"I'm like trying! As hard as I can." It sounded as if she was throwing her body against it. "We're locked inside. I can't open it."

"I knew my sister was stupid," Mongo said, heading to the door, following the cell phone light, "but your sperm donor must have been a fucking retard!"

"That's not very nice," Nicole said.

Ray peeked over the gunwale. Mongo shoved the girl aside. She fell to her knees. He grabbed the doorknob with his left hand and twisted it with his powerful palm. He couldn't turn it, either. He shoved the gun down the front of his pants, and covering his left hand with his right, used both to twist it harder.

"It's not locked, you idiot!" Mongo said. "Someone's holding it from the other side!"

VANCE AND SARGE saw the salvage barge approaching from the southeast. They were crouched behind the Jeep. Ray Dinero hustled off the deck of the shrimper and made a run for the maintenance building.

Vance heard a splash. "What was that?" he whispered.

"Don't know," Sarge said quietly, looking around.

A Latin man and pair of tall, dark-haired girls jumped from the bow of *The Waterhog* when it smashed into the dock, then fell to their knees. The barge knocked two telephone-pole-sized pilings off kilter, then the unmanned *Hog* caromed off the concrete and floated away, its middeck crane jutting out.

"I think that's Mongo—Ramon Solana," Vance said.

"That's right," Sarge said. "Come on, let's go. Ray's gonna need our help."

"Wait a minute. What's Mongo doing here? What are we doing here?" Vance felt for the Glock holstered under his left arm.

"He's here to rip you off. Ray knew he would, so he set a trap."

"Jesus. Where's Lauren?"

"I don't know. She's not here, if that's what you mean. We don't have time to chitchat. Let's move."

Adrenaline pumped. Vance swallowed hard.

They stooped, advancing toward the huge metal building. It was dusk and the last of the orange sun was dipping fast.

Sarge scanned the perimeter, hands wrapped around the pistol grip. He used his belly to steady his elbows, swinging the gun like a searchlight. "Mongo's inside, and he's armed."

"I thought the money was with Davis. That was the deal."

"The black cases inside are a decoy. Ray's idea, to keep you and Tony safe."

"How do you know that?"

"I'll explain later. Come on." Daniel snapped his neck toward the building. "Let's go. The missing yacht, the one I told you about?"

Vance nodded.

"That's what the explosion was. It's in pieces, shrapnel, floating out there in the water. Mongo blew it up," Sarge said.

Vance tripped over a broken chunk of concrete and almost went down.

"I have a buddy with the Coast Guard," Daniel said. "Mongo is dangerous. He's killed for a lot less."

"OK." Vance took a deep breath. "Let's do this."

They rushed the door to the maintenance building. Just as Vance put his hand on the handle, someone grabbed it from the inside. Using his eyes, he gestured to Sarge to look at the knob. There was just enough light coming from a pole outside.

It twitched in Vance's hand.

Sarge nodded.

They'd have to strike fast. Vance increased the torque on the handle. If the snitch banker was on the other side, he'd try to shoot them at close range. They'd heard the blast of a big caliber gun tearing through the metal roof earlier. Sarge put his ear on the door and nodded. Suddenly he felt a more powerful hand grab hold from the inside. "I'm not going to be able to hold this for long," he whispered.

"On my count of three, one, two, three—"

He let go of the handle. The knob turned from the inside.

Vance and Sarge rammed their shoulders against the metal door. It flung open, casting a flash of light from the outdoor fluorescent lighting the dock. Mongo turned and ran, plowing shins-first into the pile of black transport cases. He flew four feet into the air before landing on the concrete, splaying out on his belly with a dull splat. The HK .45 skidded away.

Sarge ran for Mongo's gun.

Vance felt for the panel and switched on the banks of overheads. Lisa was standing there, pointing the Pierces' pink snubbed-nosed pistol at them. "Gimme that!"

She handed him the gun.

"Hey," Ray rasped from above. "Boy, am I glad to see you guys." He flung both legs over the bow railing and dropped down to his feet. He landed thwacking his flip-flops on the hard floor. He stood spread-eagle over Mongo with his arms folded under the Bis-Cay-Bay Yacht Sales logo embroidered on his shirt.

"What the fuck?" Mongo sneered, looking up at him. "You getting ready for a little Cossack dance? How you been, Vladimir?"

"Get up, asshole," Ray said.

Mongo didn't move. Ray kicked him in the ribs. Ramon Solana groaned.

"Get up," Sarge said, holding Mongo's HK on him. The same red dot that marked the point of entry on Charles Pierce's head now danced on Mongo's jugular.

Sarge held the same gun that killed the federal judge all those years ago. Vance backed away two steps and stared at the rat. "We've all wanted to put you out of your misery for a long time, you murdering, double-crossing piece of crap. Get up before we draw straws to see who gets the honors."

Mongo rose slowly, holding Charles Pierce's khakis up with one hand, putting the other hand in the air.

"Put them both up," Vance said.

Mongo stuck the other arm in the air. His pants dropped around his ankles. Sarge looked at Mongo. Vance looked at Sarge. And Ray looked at Vance. They all looked at Mongo's paunch hanging over his dingy tighty-whities.

"Not much going on there," Sarge said, eliciting rousing group laughter.

"Open one." Vance gestured toward the stack of black cases. "It's what you came for, right?"

Ray kicked at one of the cases. "Go ahead. Listen to the man. Open it!"

Mongo pulled his pants up and fell to one knee. He lunged at the case closest to him. The padlock was brittle from corrosion and broke like a dried macaroni noodle. He tried lifting the cover. It wouldn't budge. It was cemented shut with calcium build-up and decayed sea life.

"Get out of the way," Vance said, "you worthless parasite." He took the HK from Sarge and used the barrel of Mongo's prized gun to chip and chisel at the sediment. When it was loose enough, Vance turned to Mongo. "Go ahead. It's all yours."

Mongo scrambled at it, like a rabid dog.

The twins cowered by the ladder, watching in a hypnotic trance. Sarge kept his Glock pointed at them. Their expressions changed from fear to pleasure. They were enjoying watching their uncle in a state of submission.

Mongo yanked on the top half of the case, but it wouldn't open.

"Try harder," Vance said.

Using his massive forearms, Mongo twisted the lid from side to side, grunting and groaning. Picking it up a few inches off the floor, he slammed it down. It cracked open at one seam. Sand spilled through the side.

The ex con looked confused. "Sand?" he asked, childlike. He

pulled the top open and dug into the case like a dog looking for a bone, sand flying. "Nothing, but—sand?" Mongo rocked back on his heels and sat.

"Yeah," Ray said. "Twenty-two pounds of carefully measured sand. You thought I wouldn't be one step ahead of you? Then? Or now? Hey, Sarge," he said, "think you can recruit him as a full-time informant?"

Vance couldn't help himself. "The cops have standards, and this asshole doesn't qualify."

"As you know," Ray said, "an important part of Los Guapos' business was weights and measures. Plus I have a reputation to uphold. Get up, Ramon. Did you really think you could do an end-run around me?"

Mongo rose. Ray kicked him in the ass with a flip-flopped foot. Mongo toppled forward onto the cement floor, planting his face into a pile of sand. Ray rubbed his ankle, then his hip. "I'm too old for this shit." Ray turned to Sarge. "You got what you wanted."

Sarge pulled a police-issue cable tie from his pants' pocket. "Stand up and turn around," he said. Mongo obeyed. Sarge bound Mongo's hands behind his back with the flex cuff and yanked it tight.

"He *like* stole that big boat and killed the owners," Nicole said.

Lisa chimed in. "He made the bomb, too. The one that blew it up."

"No one was supposed to get killed!" Ray walked away to cool off.

"Let's see. A convicted felon jacks a yacht, kills two people, and detonates a bomb in a national park on federal land. What would you call that?" Vance stroked his chin with his thumb and forefinger. "Hmm. I'd call it homicide and terrorism."

"The whole city is in a panic," Sarge said. "Heck, the whole country is. I'd like to make the call sooner rather than later." Sarge turned to Vance. "You and Ray need to get out of here. And take those smokin' hotties with you. Take them somewhere, anywhere. Tell them to keep their mouths shut."

"We can hear you, you know," Lisa said.

Nicole chimed in, "Yeah. Like, we have ears."

Vance said, "Then, *like* use them to listen very carefully and use your little brains to keep your big mouths shut. Say goodbye to your uncle now."

"Goodbye, Uncle Mongo." Nicole blew kisses his way.

"What about the money?" Lisa asked, pouting. "Uncle Mongo promised to make us rich."

"Feel free to take as much as you want," Vance said, kicking at the dunes on the floor. "There's more where that came from. A lot more."

"Come on," Sarge said, "let's get out of here. I'll take this piece of shit down the road and call it in. No sense involving you or Ray in any of this. It won't be good for the boating business. Plus, I got what I want." Sarge flicked a finger in Mongo's ear hole.

"He killed the other man, too," Nicole said. "The one that was driving the big boat. He was still on it when it blew up." She made a sad face. "That was like the nicest boat I've ever seen."

"He was handsome, too," Lisa said, picking at a chip of blue nail polish on her index finger.

"Three murders. Hmm, thinking like a lawyer *and* a cop, I'm thinking death penalty." Vance gave Mongo one final look. "Geez, it smells like red tide in here." The burner in his pants' pocket vibrated. He looked at it. "I got to go," he said, jogging outside to talk. "Are you all right?"

"Yeah," Davis said.

"Status report?"

"Done. Delivered and locked up."

"As described?"

"Exactly as described. Safe and sound."

"Does anyone else know?"

"Nope. Haven't talked to anyone. Just you, like you said."

"You haven't by any chance heard anything from Lauren, have you?"

"You made me swear I wouldn't. Is she OK?"

"I hope so."

"What do you mean?"

"Nothing." He shouldn't have agreed to cut contact with her. What if she needed his help now? "Meet me tomorrow morning, nine o'clock, at the storage place. I'll need a hand. Plus, I'll have something for you."

"OK. I'll bring the video files too."

Oh yeah, the video files. He ended the call. Of course the money wasn't in the maintenance building at Ray's boatyard. That was a red herring, classic Ray Dinero. More than smart, clever. Ray, the Los Guapos mastermind, moved billions of dollars of product up through Central and South America only to have Tony and Chago screw it up with their reckless behavior. Ray had always been smarter. He hurried back inside where they were waiting for him.

"That smell you mentioned," Ray said. "Might be Mongo." He wriggled his nose like a cartoon mouse sniffing a block of cheese. "Kind of smells like a dead rat, don't you think?"

Everyone laughed, everyone except that piece of shit-rat-banker, Ramon Solana.

"Get their phones," Vance said to Sarge.

"How will we find our way home, without them?" Lisa asked.

"You don't know where you live?" Vance asked.

"They are dumb mutha—"

"Shut the fuck up, Uncle Mongo." Lisa licked her painted lips.

"Well, yeah, but we don't know where we are right now," Nicole said.

"Hmm. Let's see here." Vance held his phone up, mocking Nicole. "Well, *like*, yeah, I have GPS on my phone. So you girls tell us where you live and we'll drive you home."

"You guys go," Sarge said. "I'll take care of the rat."

Vance tossed two phones into the river, the ones belonging to the girls. "I'm going to keep this one." He was holding Ramon Solana's phone.

23

D avis Frost was happy to be home despite being in the throes of gastric distress from eating a month-old enchilada he found in the fridge. His legs bothered him, too. The bug bites covering them oozed a yellowish fluid. They weren't healing because he'd scratched them into a bloody mess.

The third thing Davis did after he got home from loading the storage unit yesterday was shower until the hot water ran lukewarm. After he unloaded his equipment, he took a nap. He'd tied the *Leaky Witch* off to a pair of pilings behind the rundown duplex. He awoke at sundown. He'd meant to call Vance Courage earlier, to tell him "Mission accomplished." But he'd passed out. Luckily, the lawyer wasn't pissed at him. Vance was measured and kept the convo cryptic, instructing Davis to meet him at the storage place in the morning.

Later, Davis connected his GoPro camera to his laptop and copied the video files onto a portable drive. He grabbed a cold beer and gulped it while the files transferred.

He opened the folder and looked at the thumbnails laid out like a storyboard. Thank God. The files were all there. Davis had just completed a one-man act on an episode of Wicked Salvage Operation: shark wrestler, captain, diver, photographer, navigator, data wrangler, and full-time fat guy. It was a high-wire act. Especially on a job like this one where a do-over wasn't an option. He scrolled through the footage. The 1200 lumen light gave the video surprising detail.

Davis watched himself smash the lionfish to smithereens. His heart pounded all over again watching the picture shake as the bull shark rammed him, the GoPro recording the whole thing in Hi- Def.

Frost ran his hand over the back of his neck. A thin scab was crusting from the burns. Tired and too exhausted to sleep, he flipped on the late news. WSVN was reporting that the explosion at Boca Chita was a terrorist attack. He surfed the channels. The 24-hour news outlets were all regurgitating the same story. According to reports, the only eyewitnesses, the fishermen he'd seen there, had been detained. The authorities told the media the men would not be available for comment.

Davis clicked off the TV.

He went into the bathroom and slathered aloe vera cream over the red spots on his legs. He leaned over to rub his ankles. The corner of the beach towel popped open and dropped to the floor. He looked at himself in the full-length mirror. His body was a landscape of ugly cleavages. He covered himself up to his armpits and lifted the coin hanging around his neck, dabbing gel on his sunburned chest.

He flopped back on the sofa, beat-to-shitsville, and turned the local news back on.

"The yacht blown up at Boca Chita has been identified as one owned by murdered Palm Beach couple, Charles and Betty Pierce, reported missing three days ago . . . ."

Davis flipped to a cable network news channel and turned up the volume.

"An eyewitness reports spotting the Sea Food, their sixty-foot yacht docked at Boca Chita on Wednesday. Other unconfirmed reports suggest the boat may have been grounded at low tide. A fisherman discovered a man's body near Palm Beach, thought to be the yacht owner. The coroner has determined the cause of death was from a single gunshot wound to the head. Another body was found floating today in the debris field near the explosion. The authorities believe it's the body of the couple's missing boat captain. His name is being withheld pending family notification. Homeland Security has not issued additional information. The last terrorist attack on a U.S.-flagged vessel was the USS Cole in Yemen in 2000, but this is the first in American waters. We'll be right back."

Davis stared at the 800-number crawling across the lower third of the television screen while the reporter encouraged anyone with information about the attack to call in immediately. No way, there was no way Davis Frost was getting caught up in a terrorist plot. He'd narrowly escaped. Volunteering any information was out of the question. He turned off the television.

JAKE'S BOSS at the car lot made his employees work long hours six days a week. He'd worked ridiculous hours as an investment banker, first as analyst and later as an associate. But the Wall Street hours were a rite of passage to multi-million dollar bonuses. His current job was the road to hangovers, swollen ankles, and ibuprofen abuse.

Jake was slowly catching on that Lauren was unhappy about something. She hadn't returned his flirtatious Up for round 2? message.

Jake passed through the metal detector at the public library minutes before closing time.

The gal at the desk said, "You're becoming a regular."

"Hardly. Heard about that bomb?"

"Who hasn't," she said, eyes back on her flat-screen monitor. She used a hand-held scanner to log in a pile of returned books. "Here to use the computer again?"

"Yep."

"Need some help?" She removed her tortoise-rimmed reading glasses from her make-up free face and twirled them in her hand.

"Do I look like I need help?" Jake aimed his off-center grin at her.

"Sort of."

"Being a geezer dad has its advantages. But if I do, I'll let you know. By the way, nice to see someone under forty without a phone glued to her nose."

"I'm weird. I prefer books." The scanner bleeped as she swept another book beneath it.

Jake had decided not to take any chances using his laptop at home. If the National Security Agency was competent, which was doubtful given his experience with the Securities and Exchange Commission in New York, he didn't want to take any chances that might put him on their radar screen.

He logged onto the library computer as a guest and searched *Bomb blast news Miami*. Dozens of hits filled the screen. He clicked on the top link and watched aerial footage of the aftermath. He'd already seen the ruins of the landmark lighthouse at Boca Chita on his phone. He hit PAUSE several times and enlarged the scenes. There was no sign of a boat carrying a load of yellow cases.

Jake was living and working in New York on 9/11 and knew a half dozen people working at Cantor-Fitzgerald when the towers fell. He'd seen firsthand how fast chaos could erupt and how slowly investigations could go. And how inaccurate the media could be as they scrambled to be first. The online aerial news footage of the debris field showed pieces of a mangled yacht and fire burning on the water. It looked like a plane crash.

"Wow," the librarian said, looking over his shoulder. "That's awful."

She startled him. Jake closed the video window.

A homeless man came toward the front door. "Goodness," the librarian said, "I have to go."

"Me, too, sweet cheeks."

"Sweet cheeks? Wow," she said. "Just wow."

He watched her persuade the unkempt man not to come in, prodding the three vagrants sitting inside near the front door to leave. What a terrible predicament for a book lover, dealing with the library's unspoken function, as that of a daytime homeless shelter. He texted Lauren. Maybe a more businesslike approach might work: Anything new on the project?

VANCE TOOK off the black ball cap he'd had on since he left for the hospital that morning. He told Tony everything. His uncle didn't seem surprised. "I hope he rots in prison this time."

"You're not worried about the money? I'm scared we're not getting out of this. We're involved in the lead story on the news."

"Sure. But like I told you from the beginning, this is Ray's specialty. I haven't been holding out on you. I haven't been able to talk to him. He didn't want to take the chance. Ray knew someday we would be back for the money. With Chago out of the picture, I had to choose new partners."

"Choose? It feels more like I've been trapped, and betrayed."

Tony nodded. "You can take care of your family. Thank God for that."

"You're not scared?"

"Of course I'm scared. They'll send me to the catacombs at Supermax. I could get the death penalty. Hell, yeah, I'm scared. All we can do now is press on. You said you're meeting with the guy who has our money in the morning?"

Vance slumped on the sofa next to Tony, exhausted. He picked up his personal phone and checked it. He'd sent six messages to Lauren. No response. "See if the Escalade is back out there."

Tony made a slit in the blinds. "No. I think every law enforcement agency is busy, including the marshal."

ESPN *Desportes* was back to broadcasting baseball.

Vance reached for the remote.

Tony snatched it from his reach. "Can you at least mute it?"

"Why?"

"So we can talk."

Tony shut it off.

"You said you didn't know Sergeant Daniel Ruiz. I don't believe you. He knew Mongo was going to rip Ray off before it happened. That's why we were there, before Mongo showed up. Sarge called me on a burner phone he wasn't supposed to know about. We met at a place on the river, near Ray's boatyard. Mongo couldn't rip us off because the money wasn't in the cases. The ones at Ray's were full of sand. I got a call from Davis and he has the money—"

"Who?"

"Davis Frost. The video guy, the diver, the one Lauren knows."

"I don't know anything about a Davis Frost."

"Did you know Mongo killed that couple?"

"What couple?" Tony turned toward him. He wore a blank stare.

"The couple that owned the yacht."

"The ones on the news? The missing Palm Beach couple?"

"Yeah. He killed them, dumped their bodies and blew up their boat."

Tony finally looked surprised about something. "The one on the news? Mongo blew it up? You're saying Ray and Mongo have something to do with that bomb, the terrorist attack?"

He could read Tony's expressions like an old map and knew he was being truthful.

"Ray had nothing to do with the bomb. So you really don't know where it is."

"Where what is?"

"The money."

Tony launched into a diatribe. "How would I know? I've been living in the dark ages. Looks like you all talk, using gadgets, or whatever. I've never, how do you say, even *surfed* the Internet. I saw it once in a café in Havana. The Castros made it all propaganda, and expensive, so no one wanted it. That's how you kill something in the marketplace. Make it shitty and cost too much in a place where people can't buy food.

"Most people would rather watch mold grow on the walls than pay to listen to how great the Cuban government is. Someone showed me a story in an American newspaper saying how happy the Cuban people are. Yeah, I believe they were happy, happy to see an American. Some Americans don't get it. They think the Cuban people are happy living in a theme park that looks like America in the 1950s.

"I didn't make a telephone call in over a year. In Cuba, I walked everywhere and talked to people. Now I see things on the baseball games, on the TV, Twitter and Facepage. 'Sam from Fort Worth wrote this, that, or the other.' I don't know what they're talking about, Facepage. Or Twitter."

"Facebook. Supposedly the cash is in a storage locker in Plantation Key. Jake rented a place and told Davis Frost to drop it there."

"Who is Jay?"

"No, Jake. He's, ah, he's helping us move the cash. He's been working with Lauren Gold. She was a Mutiny girl."

"Lauren Gold, I remember her," Tony said. "She worked on the Upper Deck and was friendly with Ray."

"That's right. She's in the video business now. Ray made up this thing, a video project, so Lauren would think it's for a marketing campaign, for YouTube."

"What kind of tube?"

"Never mind. I keep forgetting. You're stuck in 1994, or 1950. Anyway, we made something up so she'd hire a diver to salvage the cases and make a video of it. Ray told me the cash was stashed in a boat offshore, and this was the way we could get it. The other guy working with us, Jake Fleming, he used to be an investment banker."

"Why do we need an investment banker?"

"We don't. Well, not exactly. We needed a front man to pose as the client to get her to fall for the plan, and the guy just happens to be a retired investment banker." He paused and put his head in his hands. "What a mess. I wonder if we'll ever see it. The money. It's not like I had a choice, getting dragged into this thing."

"Sure you did. You could have called some of your friends at the Department of Justice and had me arrested. You could have earned a million dollar reward. I'm on the FBI's Ten Most Wanted List. You said it yourself."

"I couldn't do that."

"Sure you could, *sobrino*. You could have made a call from anywhere. From the palm of your hand."

"I couldn't do it." This had to be the longest day of his life. He ran his hand over the top of his head. "How could I do that, Tony? Turn you in? Maybe you would have done it to me, stabbed me in the back for the money."

"Come on, enough of the doom and gloom already. There's plenty of money to go around. And Ray's fair. So what were you saying?" Tony sounded amused now. "That Ray's working with a banker and a diver?"

"A diver, a video producer, a washed-up investment banker, an ex-cop turned lawyer, a retired cop, and a fugitive. What an ensemble, huh?"

"Yeah. All soon to be millionaires."

"I was thinking of another scenario. That we could all go to prison. Homeland Security is all over that explosion."

Tony turned his focus to the TV. A baseball game was in progress. "It's a better time to get rich. I got rich as a kid and look what it did. It ruined my life and a lot of others too. Hey, look, Justo's kid is playing outfield." Tony turned up the volume. "His life worked out, but he paid his dues and kept his mouth shut."

"You call that working out? He spent eighteen years in a federal penitentiary. Missed out on his kid's entire childhood."

"Yeah, but he was loyal and kept quiet and the universe rewarded him."

Vance shook his head solemnly. "Is that what you think? That his kid is a professional baseball player because Justo wouldn't testify against you, against Los Guapos?"

"I don't know." Tony shrugged. "Ray kept his mouth shut too. At least they had some kind of code they stuck to, and life turned out a lot better for them than us. There's bending the rules and then there's bending God's rules."

"You mean like killing people? Like murdering witnesses and a federal judge?"

Tony shook his head from side to side. He looked full of regret. "That was Chago. I never killed anyone."

"No. Not directly. You just paid other people to do it. Some things never change."

"What's that supposed to mean?"

"You're still paying people to do your dirty work. Three more dead bodies have piled up, and you haven't left my apartment."

"You got your hand out now. Just like everyone else. You're chasing the money just as hard as me."

"It's not for me, it's for my family."

"Why do you think I did it?" Tony yelled. "You think you're so different from me, that because you're more educated than me, that because you look like your father, you're different, better? You just had it *easier* than me." Tony wasn't finished but his tone turned calmer. "It's why I like baseball, *sobrino.* It comes down to small events. They start piling up, changing the course of things. A home run with bases loaded, a grand slam. Your mother marries your dad. A batter gets hit in the head by a ninety-mile-an-hour fastball. I became a drug smuggler. The high school pitcher is hit in the hand with the ball he just threw, and his career is over before it starts. My mother dies when I'm just a baby. Baseball is like life. It boils down to a series of single events. When I watch baseball, I see *life.*"

"Yeah, and Mark McGuire used steroids and Pete Rose's legacy was wrecked by gambling."

"You see? That's exactly my point, Vance, that's life. And that's the game."

"We should stick to business, you and I." Vance was too tired to listen to more metaphorical talk about life and baseball. "Where did you get the coordinates for the wreck—on the paper, the one I gave Lauren to give to Ray?"

"I'm getting tired of being stuck in this apartment," Tony said. "Not that I don't appreciate the air conditioning, I do. It's like the Beatles song." Tony sang, *"You don't know what you got 'til it's gone."*

"Joni Mitchell. That's a Joni Mitchell song."

"That's weird. I can hear Paul McCartney in my head. This waiting around is getting to me."

All the stress plus being cooped up with Tony was making him crazy too. "Who else knows about the money?"

"You asked me before. Only three people knew anything about it. Chago, me and Ray, like I told you before."

"You mean four."

"*Que?*"

"Mongo Solana, that makes four people."

"He was already in federal custody when Ray started moving the money out of his bank. Ray probably figured Mongo had someone watching. After the government accountants went through all the boxes of bank records, they wanted to know where the missing money went.

"The Feds suspected Mongo and Mongo suspected us. But they couldn't find any proof. Believe me, they tried. They got search warrants. Ray cooperated. They tore up his place. Tore up my place, tore up my sister Sophia's place, too. In the end, I think the Feds thought Mongo was lying, that he stole the money before he cut his deal. Or that it was all total bullshit or bad bookkeeping. But Mongo, he probably knew Ray was moving money."

Vance rubbed the day-old bristle on his chin. "I'm beginning to see your point."

"About?"

"Baseball, about how it comes down to the little things. I get why Ray stashed two sets of cases in the hull before he sank it. But I'd like to know how Ray knew which ones Mongo would follow. Why did that piece of crap banker follow the salvage ship to Ray's boat yard instead of following Davis Frost?"

"I don't know. Why does one ball fly fair and another foul?"

"Physics. The speed and rotation of pitch, the angle, and the power of the hitter."

"And luck," Tony said.

"I'm starting to think this whole money thing might be bullshit. I'm supposed to meet Davis Frost in the morning and throw him some peanuts." He pulled the bank envelope from his pocket and showed it to Tony. "He could have been killed or picked up by the Feds. He has no clue he's sitting on seventy-five million dollars."

"But he wasn't hurt. Your man was lucky. Hey, check it out." ESPN cut to a live shot. Tony cranked up the volume, "Is that—Mongo?"

"Jesus." Vance's eyes widened. Mongo was shirtless, wearing a pair of chinos, cuffs rolled unevenly, held up with a leather belt tied into a knot around his waist. The snitch banker shuffled in front of the camera barefoot, in baby steps, like a geisha girl, his feet and hands shackled with nickel cuffs tied to a belly chain. As Mongo tried to turn away, the officers escorting him rotated his torso by his shoulders and pushed his face toward the scrum of cameras and reporters.

Red, orange, and blue spinning lights bounced off the high-rises of unsightly freight containers in the background.

Mongo glared into the lenses, his hair glistening. His face looked like the surface of a full moon, camera lights accenting the pocks and craters. His eyelids draped like wind-worn awnings, and the irises of his eyes flashed yellow, like a raptor's.

Tony spun through the channels. They all broadcasted the same live shot with their own reporters breathlessly regurgitating the same story:

". . . the terrorist you're looking at is a Cuban national and convicted felon who was released. . . ."

Click.

" . . . a one-time bank executive convicted of racketeering and money laundering in 1994. . . ."

Click.

". . . reports are coming in that the suspect was radicalized in Cuba. . . ."

Click.

". . . the suspected terrorist was caught by a retired police officer who. . . ."

Click.

" . . . since the attack occurred in federal waters inside Biscayne National Park, the Coast Guard is on the scene. For those of you who don't know, the Coast Guard was transferred to the Department of Homeland Security under the Bush administration. . . ."

Mute.

Click.

Tony went back to the game. "If you're meeting David tomorrow morning—"

"Davis," Vance corrected.

"David, Davis. Either way, you need your beauty sleep. The circus will be town for a while."

"Thanks for the advice, Dr. Phil."

"Doctor who?"

"Never mind," Vance said, going to his bedroom and closing the door between them.

24

WEEK TWO
THURSDAY MORNING

CHECKING THE SAFETY, Gregorio Marino tucked the Kimber 1911 Ultra Carry II .45 handgun under his right thigh. He needed it close by, but there was no sense in shooting his nuts off. At thirty, he figured some day he might want to use them to start a family. Especially when he was rich enough to get himself a hot trophy wife willing to pop out some puppies. He pushed his deformed foot on the gas pedal of the stolen Toyota speeding south on the Overseas Highway toward the Upper Keys, past the turnoff to Jewfish Creek.

He'd jacked the car earlier that morning from the parking lot of a daycare center while a dipshit young mother ran inside to drop her child off. He'd targeted her because a white Camry was ubiquitous and because she made it easy, leaving the car running with the keys in the ignition. Cruising suburban Kendall, it didn't take long to find the same make, model, and color parked on the street in front of a big apartment complex. Using a screwdriver, he removed the license plates from both cars and swapped them.

He parked the Camry down the street from Davis's ugly rental. The heels on his cowboy boots chewed the coral driveway dotted with aluminum cans and plastic soda bottles, taco wrappers, and bottle caps. He kicked an empty vodka bottle out of the way, surveying the space behind Davis's shit box where he could hide and ambush the fat turd.

The spy app he'd secretly installed on the girls' phones was the best investment he'd ever made. He'd been tracking Davis since he saw his message to Lisa pop up on her phone while the twins and that fucker, Uncle Mongo, tracked Davis at Boca Chita. They thought they were so smart, believing they were going to cheat him out of the millions his father had hidden. When he sent the fake text message, Davis fell for it. The dummy pressed 1 to Pay Now. Davis's text went straight to Greg's laptop, enabling the spy app. From that moment forward, he had a mirror image of all three of their phones on his computer screen.

It took him about ten seconds to find Davis's Facebook page. It was filled with old pictures of him working as a salvage diver, posing in one old, faded photo cradling an armful of silver ingots in a plastic bucket. Davis wore an ancient gold coin around his neck and posted a close-up of it with a caption: *A memento from my days with Mel*, the famous sunken treasure hunter, Mel Fisher. He saw Davis on LinkedIn, too, hawking his video services. He wasn't sure who'd hired Davis, but he knew from spying on him what he was up to, and he had to get to the money before Mongo did.

Greg signed up for a free trial to a reverse phone number look-up service and got Davis's address in Plantation Key. Whoever hired the fat piece of crap thought they were going to steal his inheritance. How convenient. He let them do all the hard work. Some people, like Ray Dinero, thought they were so smart. He'd show them. He was the late Chago Marino's son. He was going to get some long-overdue respect.

***

VANCE THREW on a pair of jeans and holstered the Glock under his left arm.

"We got company," Tony said, peeking through the blinds. The Escalade was out in front of the building in the usual spot, beneath a street lamp.

"I'm going out back," Vance said.

He stood on the toilet, pulled himself through the small bathroom window leading to the back stairs, and dropped onto the walkway. Jogging down the stairwell, he flicked his eyes and scanned the perimeter before crossing the street to the gas station with the pay phone on the corner. He woke two comatose vagrants sleeping against the aluminum frame. As he tried to pass, they groped him like zombies, their hands outstretched. He took two five-dollar bills from his billfold and held them out. They snatched the money and let him pass. He tried to close the cracked door, but it stopped halfway. Thank God. The stench of urine was nauseating. He dropped a quarter in the coin slot.

A few minutes later, a yellow Dodge mini-van with large, blue handicap-accessible stickers on both sides arrived. He held his hand up.

He opened the sliding door and hopped into the back.

The driver, a young woman with intricately tattooed sleeves and thinning magenta hair turned around in her seat. "Where to?"

"Rent-A-Reck on Seventh."

"Where you going after you rent the wreck?"

"Plantation Key."

"How long you staying?"

"An hour, maybe two."

"Why not just pay me? Two-fifty round trip, plus gas, and I'm yours. What do you say?" She waited for his answer, and for the light to change.

He weighed the pros and cons. There were risks, no doubt, but going to the rental place was dicey in its own way. He needed to size her up. Fast.

"What's your name?"

The van was big enough to handle the cases. Having someone else drive would allow him to scope out surveillance. That's what he was doing now, looking around for the Escalade, a police chopper, an ambush.

"Patty," she said, without breaking her stare from the rearview mirror.

"I'm picking up a load of stuff and bringing it back. Is that a problem?"

"Why would it be? You should see what the snowbirds bring when they fly in for the winter. I drove a dude who flew in with a therapy goat."

He laughed. "I heard about that somewhere. A senior?"

"Nah, some guy from Ohio going on vacation to Key West. The Uber driver wouldn't take him." She chuckled. "I did, but it was pretty messy."

Patty was a winner. "Does the wheelchair lift work?"

"Yeah. Why?"

"Some of the stuff is heavy."

DAVIS WOKE and checked the time on his phone. He had an hour before he had to leave to meet the Cormorant lawyer, Vance Courage, at U-Kan Store-It. He treated himself to Publix brand Rocky Road ice cream for breakfast. Afterward, he started a hot shower. It would be a good place to be when the sugar crash hit.

Dressed and ready, he had a few minutes to kill. He rested on a rickety, built-in bench on the grayed cedar decking backing up to the canal and sniffed the crisp salt air. He hoped the Cormorant guys would pay him the five thousand dollar bonus. He planned to argue that the explosion was an extenuating circumstance, and maybe even negotiate for more.

An osprey dropped from its nest atop a telephone pole and plunged talons-first into the water, making barely a splash. There was a lot of nature to see from the deck outside his dumpy place: dolphins, blue herons, bonefish, and his favorite, a tarpon that expected to be fed. The osprey whooshed back up to the nest with a blue-green parrotfish thrashing in its claws.

His eyes and ears were sharp from working in television, and his hearing had recovered from yesterday's blast. When he heard a shoe crunch the gravel and saw someone crouch behind his old Porsche 914, he yelled out a friendly, "Howdy!" It wasn't unusual to see tourists or locals wandering around back. He assumed it was just another lookie-loo contemplating the risk of trespassing against getting up close to the aquarium of tropical fish hanging around the pilings.

Greg sprang up and ran toward him, pointing a gun.

"Hey, hey, hey, wait a minute!" Davis stammered holding his hands up in the air.

"Where's the money?"

"What money?"

"That your piece of crap?" Greg gestured to the Dusky tied to the dock.

"Uh, yeah."

"I came for my money."

The guy was obviously at the wrong address. "I don't have your money." Then he remembered the three thousand Jake gave him, down to twenty-six hundred now. "My wallet's inside." He cocked his head toward the duplex.

"Not that money, you fucking fat moron. The millions you stole from me." Greg rushed him, jamming the .45 in his chest, groping his shorts' pockets, taking his phone. He clicked on the Photo icon. The most recent one was of a stack of cases in a poorly lit building. He swiped the screen on Davis's phone.

"You *got* my money," Greg said, shoving the phone and the picture of the twins under his nose. "I am the rightful heir to all of it."

"Money?" He crossed his eyes looking at the screen. "I thought—"

"I don't give a shit what you thought, you stupid retard. Turn around." Greg pushed the sharp nose of the Kimber into his lower spine. Greg's eyes flicked like a rodent. "Get in."

Davis climbed into the Camry, squeezing behind the wheel.

"Drive," Greg said, shoving the sharp nose of the gun into his fatty hip, to the bone. He held the picture in his face, the one he'd taken at the last minute of the yellow cases stacked in the unit. "That's my fucking money."

Davis's hands trembled on the steering wheel. He'd have to find the storage place by memory. The years he'd spent working in live television had taught him to keep cool under pressure, but nothing had prepared him for this. He'd shot an interview with Minnesota's only serial killer back in his TV news days, and the guy in the passenger seat had the same unforgettable look.

Vance called Sarge from the back seat of Patty's snowbird taxi.

Sarge had his happy voice on. "*¿Que bola?*"

"You busy?"

"Depends on how you define busy."

"I'm on my way down to Plantation Key to meet a friend. Can you meet me there?"

"Your police skills suck. Turn around and look out the back window."

He saw Sarge's Jeep Renegade about a hundred feet off Patty's back bumper. Sarge flashed his lights and waved.

The junction to Florida City lay ahead. They caravanned past the signs for the Miami-Homestead Speedway and Leisure City before merging onto the Overseas Highway, heading south toward Key Largo.

DAVIS SLOWED and turned down a short dead-end side street. An old hand-painted sign was staked out front: U-KAN STORE-IT. He parked the Camry parallel to the metal door.

Waving the gun in his face, Greg leaned across the driver's seat and yanked the key from the ignition. "Get out, you fat fuck, and open it."

Davis's hands and voice trembled. He hoisted himself out and cowering, walked to the pull-down door. He held the combination lock in his fingers. "The numbers are on my phone."

Greg fished the phone from his pants pocket. "Where?"

"In Notes. The yellow and white icon." His voice vibrated.

"Do I look stupid to you?" He pushed the screen toward Davis's face until it touched the tip of his nose.

Davis had piloted drones for Major League Baseball. He'd run cameras on wires for the NFL and RoboCams for NASCAR. The steadiness of his handheld camera work was the stuff of legend. But now his hands vibrated. He closed one eye and focused on the screen. He breathed deeply, turning the dial to the first set of numbers.

Greg kicked him in the back of his thigh with the sharp toe of his boot. Davis's tailbone tucked under, and he buckled at the knees, falling on all fours. "Geez! What was that for!"

"That's not the first number!"

"Yes, it is. I reversed them on my phone, just in case."

Greg backed away. Davis struggled to his feet. Barely keeping a full-blown panic attack at bay, he dialed the numbers on the lock until it clicked open.

"Pull it up." Greg rammed the metal gun deep into his drooping love handles until it hit a rib.

Davis squatted, heels together like a sumo wrestler, and pulled up on the metal door. It clattered and squeaked.

"Higher," Greg said.

It was dim inside and smelled like rotting fish.

"Turn on the light."

He reached up, waving his blistering arm above his head until he felt the chain. The yellow bug bulb cast sickly shadows. The cases were gone. Rectangular chalk lines of dried saltwater left a pattern on the concrete floor. A few strands of sea grass floated in the evaporating pools of water. Greg stuck his finger in it and sniffed.

Greg glared at him. "Where's the money?"

"I don't know anything about any money," he said, eyebrows arched.

Greg rushed him.

He cowered. "I dropped a load of cases here yesterday. They were here when I left. I swear to God on my mother's grave." He crossed his heart. "They were here." His voice cracked.

"Cases? What kind of cases?"

"Yellow ones, big transports. For a video." He bent forward

and held his hands out, palms up, submissively. "They're supposed to have some kind of unveiling or something."

"Unveiling? What for?" Greg snapped.

"I'm not supposed to say. I signed a—"

Gregorio swung the flat side of the Kimber across Davis's left temple. "I didn't pay the Brotherhood to kill my own father so a fat piece of shit like you could rip me off. Who you working for?"

Pain followed the strange sensation dripping down one cheek. "Uh," he stuttered, "a lawyer and—a marketing guy. From the company." He wiped his face and looked at his hand. Crimson blood.

"Don't fuck with me!" Greg racked the slide on the Kimber, dropping a slug into the chamber.

"Cormorant," he said, "they make waterproof cases. I was working for Lauren Gold."

"Is that so, you stupid patsy. I never heard of any of those people. Do you know who I am?"

He had no idea. He shook his head no.

"You lying sack of shit!"

The stranger took a wide swing, one that started halfway around the world. Davis covered his face with two hands as the madman smashed the gun into his jaw. He heard a crack and tasted blood. Oh God! The pain! A twelve on the scale of one to ten. He coughed up something sharp, a tooth. He gagged. He ran his fingers across his mouth. It was covered with blood. He saw the barrel of the .45 in his peripheral vision. It looked like a freaking canon. Jerking his head to the left, he took a step backward. The man tackled him. They went down in a pile. The metal sight of the Kimber caught his other cheek, tearing open flesh and smashing his glasses. He coughed a red mist. The skin around his eyes inflated like balloons. He saw two of everything and then four. Then his world faded to black.

When he came to, the psychopath was pressing the gun into

the fatty dent between his swollen eyes. The facial fracture made him sound like he had a mouth full of marbles. "It wazz 'ere when I weft yezzterday."

"You think I had my own dad offed so you could steal my inheritance!"

His tongue still worked. He lapped at the red streamers around his lips. Then his bladder let loose. Davis put his head down on the cool concrete floor and sucked in the smell of a rotting ocean.

Greg stuck the nose of the .45 on the top of Davis Frost's skull. *Game over.*

The assailant pulled the trigger.

Click?

No boom. Nothing. Silence.

"Piece *barato de mierda!*"

Cheap piece of shit.

The cartridge jammed in the chamber. The silver slide rod was stuck outside the barrel. Greg beat the gun on the concrete floor in a rage. Davis heard a vehicle pull into the driveway.

Greg yanked the chain and killed the overhead light. A rusty, old, blue van clattered up. Fresh cigarette smoke overpowered the smell of fish. A skinny fellow with bird legs stepped out. The woman with him had thick ankles. They removed a plastic folding table from the back and bickered about what to put where on the tabletop, and how much to charge.

"Trailer trash," Greg snarled. He went back to raging, clanging the Kimber on the concrete like a madman.

Davis heard the second vehicle and could barely make out the bottom of a bright yellow mini-van.

"Who takes a taxi to a fucking flea market?" Greg growled, banging the gun harder.

Then a third vehicle arrived. His eyes were swelling shut. Footfalls were getting closer and closer. He heard voices. The overhead metal door screeched open. He kept his head down on the cool cement floor.

VANCE POINTED his 9-millimeter at the gunman. "Freeze. Drop it. On your stomach! Now!" He kicked lightly at Davis's thigh. "You. Hands where I can see them. Slowly."

Davis lifted his busted head and looked at him through slivered eyes. He mumbled something no one could understand.

"You stay put," Vance said to Davis, planting his foot on Greg's back and holding the nose of his Glock on the back of Greg's head. Sarge jogged to the Renegade and returned with a foot-long zip cuff. Davis's assailant grunted when Vance drove the sharp edge of his heel deeper into his shoulder blades and leaned into it. Greg cried out.

Using Greg's buttocks as knee cushions, Sarge cinched the plastic tie around his wrists and pulled it taut.

Vance and Sarge each took an arm and helped Davis into a sitting position.

"Where's the stuff?" Vance asked him.

Davis shrugged and shook his head.

Sarge said, "I think his jaw's broken."

"Tink is roowken," Davis said. Tears spouted from his blackened eyes. Blood dripped down his face.

Vance looked at the chalky outline. "Where's the stuff, Davis?"

"Vas gon aweady."

"What!" Vance asked.

"Someone ripped you off before you could steal from me," Greg growled out of the side of his mouth, lying face down.

"From you?" Vance kicked him in the throat. "No one took anything that belongs to you. Who is this piece of shit?"

Sarge straddled their collar. "Chago's kid."

"Funky Foot?" Vance squatted and looked at his face. "I'll be damned. What's he doing here?"

"What do you think he's doing? He's here to jack the cash."

Vance sniffed and looked down. "Shit!"

"Help me get him to his feet," Vance said to Sarge, standing over Davis.

Sarge grabbed one elbow and Vance took the other. Sarge said, "Easy, big guy."

Davis groaned, struggling to his feet.

"Let's go," Vance said.

"No, no, no, no—" Patty yelled when she saw them helping Davis to her van. She jumped out and ran to the passenger side to stop them, but it was too late. Davis was already sprawled across the back seat, leaking bodily fluids.

"Take him to the closest hospital," Vance said. "Tell them you're a Good Samaritan. That's why you got this thing, right? To transport the infirmed?"

She held her hand out. "This is going to cost you."

He peeled off five one-hundred-dollar bills and handed them to her.

"I've seen plenty of crazy shit where I'm from in New Orleans," Patty said, "but this takes the cake."

"I'm sure it's not the first time someone with wet pants sat in your back seat, honey," Sarge said. "You young people. So careful with the words, so careless with the skin and hair."

Patty glared at him.

Vance moseyed over to the couple sitting on lawn chairs behind the folding table. They passed a cigarette between them. The squat woman exhaled a thin plume of smoke. "Excitement usually starts after noon around here. The flea market is just an excuse for folks to get all liquored up and bicker."

"I'll give you two hundred for the stuffed bear," Vance said.

"Why?" the husband asked.

"I need you to call the Monroe County Sheriff's Department. Tell them the guy in that unit was there when you got here." He snapped his head in the direction of the locker where Greg was on his stomach with his hands bound. "There's a gun on the floor. Leave it."

"Three hundred," the woman said.

"Fine." He handed her three one hundreds. "Go about your business. Best if he doesn't see you. You never saw us."

The woman took the money and nodded.

Vance ducked inside and kicked the Kimber closer to Greg. He'd wiped the prints from the door handle using his shirttail. He'd already taken Greg's wallet and two cell phones. He found a chain with an unusual gold coin and stuffed it in his pocket.

"Come on," Vance said to Sarge. "Let's get out of here." The place was so rundown there was no chance it had working cameras.

"Hang on a sec." Sarge jogged over to the Jeep and returned with an evidence bag. He left it just out of Greg's reach. "Kid's a serial rapist. Wait 'til they run his DNA. Let's get out of here."

"Jesus," Vance said. "What's in the bag?"

"I'll explain later."

VANCE CLIMBED INTO THE JEEP. "So you've been knee-deep in this thing all along," he said. "If it wasn't for you, I wouldn't be up to my eyeballs in shit!"

Sarge backed down the drive and headed toward the highway.

Vance broke the rules and called Lauren. He needed to warn her that they were being played. The whole thing was a set-up. She didn't answer. He left a voicemail. "Please call me. You're in grave danger. Uh, um, forget about the deal. Call me. As soon as possible." He followed the voicemail with a text: `Davis is in the hospital`, and he pushed the send button. "Do you know if she's OK? Lauren?"

Sarge shrugged. "I think so."

"What the hell is going on and where's the money?"

"I don't know," Sarge said. "That's the God's honest truth."

God's honest truth. That was rich. His life as a free man fast-forwarded in his head. Several Monroe County Sheriffs' vehicles sped by going the opposite direction, doing at least ninety.

"Guess they got the call," Sarge said. "That slime ball isn't nearly as clever as his father."

When they reached the turnoff to Jewfish Creek, Sarge took it.

"Where are we going?" Vance asked.

"Gilbert's Resort. There's something I want to show you."

He'd seen enough recently to last a lifetime. But he was not the one who was driving.

25

The interior of the Audi was searing hot when Lauren got back from her walk on Bayshore Drive. She'd left her phone in the center console on purpose, to keep from obsessively checking for messages. Better to let those suckers sweat for a while after they found the storage locker emptied.

She picked up her phone and dropped it like a hot potato. *Ouch!* A warning message flashed on the screen; the phone was too hot and shut itself down. By the time she got home, it had cooled off and messages began popping up. There was a voice-mail from Vance.

The first text was another from Jake: Update?

The second from Vance: Where r u?

The third, from Jake again: Anything new on the project?

The fourth from Ray: Check in please

Good. I got their attention.

There was a voicemail from Vance.

The last text was from Vance. Davis is in the hospital.

Oh my God! Oh my God! What happened? She listened to the voicemail from Vance and pressed Redial.

A THICK LINE had formed in front of Gilbert's Restaurant when Vance's phone buzzed. He told Sarge to go ahead and get a table. He jogged to a more private spot under a palm, away from the pack of people waiting to be seated.

"Jesus! You're OK! Where are you?"

"Is Davis all right?"

"He'll live. I was really worried about you, Lauren."

"What happened?"

"Someone tried to rip him off. He got beat up pretty badly, but he'll be OK. Look, I'm really sorry about all this. I haven't been honest with you. I need to see you. I want to explain. I'm really, really sorry that I got you mixed up in this. Let's meet at your place. I can explain everything. We're stopping for lunch, then we'll drive straight to your place."

"You're not coming alone?"

"No, but I'd rather tell you in person."

"I'll text you the address."

"I have it, from your business card." Plus Sarge knew how to get there.

"When will you be here?"

He looked at his watch. "Two hours."

"All right. I'll see you at my place."

At one minute after eleven, the restaurant at Gilbert's had begun to fill with locals, guests, and tourists clamoring for tables. The hostess pointed to where Sarge was seated, outside at a table under a thatched umbrella of palm fronds, near the dock.

An orange and green neon-striped Scarab catamaran speedboat was tied off to the dock. The thunderous rumbling of horsepower drew a small crowd, mostly men, to check out the boat and the bikini-clad girls leaning against the bow railing. An equally ostentatious powerboat docked behind it. The boaters seemed to know each other. But it could have just been the usual pleasantries people exchanged on water, the sort that could spark road rage in street traffic.

Vance sat on a plastic chair and chased a fly with his hand.

Sarge twisted the shiny stud in his earlobe. "Do you think people who reconcile after a divorce are nuts? I've heard of it, but I always think it's like sour milk. If you put it back in the fridge and get it out a few weeks later, it's still going to be sour."

"I don't know," Vance said. Something had come over Sarge, something akin to remorse or maybe it was just uncertainty. "I'd be about the last person on earth to give advice on that front."

The waitress arrived, a welcome interruption. He and Sarge both ordered the same thing: conch fritters and fries. After she left, Sarge's tone turned woeful. "She was found in the mangroves, over there." He pointed across the channel where a trim, thirty-foot sailboat motored slowly on diesel power. "She was wrapped in the blanket."

He cocked his head. "Who are you talking about?"

"Margarita, the Mutiny girl. They found her body over there"—he raised his chin—"floating in the water, wrapped in a Hotel Mutiny blanket."

"The dead waitress?"

"Yeah." Sarge reached into his pocket and set his billfold on the table. He took his license from the front flap and pinched the leather together behind the clear plastic, removing a wallet-sized photo. He handed it to Vance.

He recognized the picture of the beautiful young woman from Daniel's Facebook profile. Smooth skin; dimples; shiny, wavy, black hair; flared nostrils; cleft chin; big, brown eyes;

sharp cheekbones; and a sweet smile that made him smile back at the picture. He'd heard some cops went to their graves unable to let go of a cold case, but this was beyond that. "More beautiful than I remembered, if that's possible," he said, handing the picture back to him.

Grief washed over Sarge. With a deep sadness in his voice, he said her name: "Margarita."

There was more to this than an unsolved murder. Why hadn't he detected it before, back then? It wasn't Sarge's case; it didn't happen in his jurisdiction.

Putting the photo back in his wallet, he said, "Did your friend GroveyGirl tell you they were working together the night Margarita was killed?"

"How do you know that?" He sensed more was coming. How could he have been so dumb? These people were all connected. Lauren. Sarge. Margarita. Mongo. Ray. Greg. Chago. And he was the common denominator connecting them in a labyrinth he didn't understand.

"Lauren told me. She was the only one who would talk to me when I was doing my own investigation. Told me the manager made the girls take bottles of champagne up to one of the rooms that night. Threatened to fire them if they said no.

"Lauren left to get more champagne, and when she came back, there was no answer at the room. She told the night manager, and he told her to mind her own business, not to worry about it. Then Margarita didn't show up for work the next night. Her husband filed a missing person report. A reporter from the *Herald* started an investigation, but the hotel management threatened any employee who talked to the media or the police. Being a private club, they could kick out anybody they wanted to. That's what happened to me. I was banned.

"You have to remember what it was like back then. The Hotel Mutiny was ground zero for the biggest drug traffickers.

And the Feds didn't care about a missing girl when there were CIA spies, rogue FBI agents, and gunrunners to chase. It was the beginning of the War on Drugs. If she was someone important, it might have been a different story." Sarge poked at his food but he didn't eat. "That evidence bag?"

"What about it?"

"The blanket's in it, the one from the Hotel Mutiny. The one she was wrapped in when they found her body."

"How did you get it?"

"I had a contact, a Monroe County Sheriff's deputy. He gave it to me."

"That's a pretty big piece of evidence to go missing."

"Yeah, well, the case went cold. They were never going to open it back up and investigate it. He gave it to me as a personal favor."

"Personal?"

"Very."

"How is it personal? And why did you leave it there?"

Sarge turned the post in his earlobe. "I didn't want to keep it anymore." One shoulder popped up, then dropped. "Maybe someone will run the DNA. Maybe it will prove who killed her."

He just listened. Who was he to judge? He'd learned a lot about wrong-headed judgments recently.

"Go ahead and say it. You think I've been obsessing over this case for way too long."

"Well. . . ." It was true—that was precisely what he'd been thinking. His meddling was helpful yesterday. *But if he keeps it up, he's going to screw things up.* "Why don't you just let it go? If you think Mongo and his kid were involved in her murder, get word to Monroe's crime lab, tip them off, get someone to run a DNA test on it. Then hope they don't come up with yours." He'd been being reminded every day for over a week how things had a strange way of backfiring, karma being the bitch she was.

"They'll probably find my DNA."

That was a weird thing for Sarge to say.

Sarge turned inappropriately nonchalant, nibbling on a chunk of rubbery conch meat. "I've been keeping something a secret from you for a long time." He threw a half-eaten fritter to the gulls. They mewled and fought over it.

Vance braced himself for the uncertain.

"The dead waitress?"

"Uh-huh." Something dramatic was heading Vance's way.

"She was my little sister."

"Your *sister?*" A neural grenade exploded in his head. *Margarita? His sister?* "Jesus! All these years. Why didn't you tell me?"

"I don't know. I didn't see what good it would do." Sarge tossed a French fry to a begging gull. "Maybe I was scared. Maybe I didn't want to wake up dead myself. The Los Guapos guys were running scared. Lots of people were getting killed, for a lot less. Then there were a lot of dirty cops, too. I figured it would be better if I kept it to myself."

If he wasn't so self-absorbed, he might have thought to ask more questions back then. But he was trying to cover his own skin, too. "Did Chago kill her?" Vance asked.

"Mongo and Chago. They sent her to the room that night. She left a nine-month-old baby behind. My brother-in-law packed up the kid and moved back to Ohio. Never wanted to have another thing to do with this godforsaken city." Sarge threw a cold fritter on the splintered dock for the gulls to fight over. "That gold brick you thought I stole from your uncle?"

"I never accused you of that." Not out loud.

"You never said it. But you thought it. Tony gave it to me. He told me to sell it and use the money to prove who killed her."

He was even more confused, seeing for the first time an even more complex maze. Los Guapos. His police Glock, stolen two decades ago, used in the drive-by shooting at his office. Lauren, aka GroveyGirl. Ray Dinero. Jake Fleming. The yacht blown to smithereens, three dead bodies, two of them killed with the same gun used to kill a federal judge all those years ago. And Margarita: The man sitting across from him was not just some cop haunted by an old cold case murder.

His mind wasn't reliable now. He couldn't roll with any more emotional jabs.

A text came up on his phone. His sister Kathy: Mom wants you to come for dinner. He turned his phone over. He couldn't look at it.

"There's more," Sarge said.

How could that be possible?

"Your girlfriend, Lauren Gold?"

"Yeah?" His throat closed up. He didn't have the energy to deny she was his girlfriend.

"She's the one who stole the money from the storage place."

He felt gut-punched, like he was going to throw up. "How do you know that?" *Then what the hell were they doing sitting here?*

"The same way I know her dog was run over. I saw her. Ray had me following her. I was supposed to make sure she was safe. And keep an eye on Davis Frost, too. For the same reason."

Vance poured the entire beer down his gullet without taking a breath and, muffling a burp, worried he might get sick at the table. He stared blankly at a pair of white gulls bitching midair while more watched from the tops of the pilings. The ones spectating from the poles balanced on one leg, waiting for customers to leave so they could scrap over the leftovers. A teenage boy wearing a red, white, and blue floral shirt, a reminder that Memorial Day was just around the corner, kayaked by. Children giggled, racing along the dock, a barking yellow Labrador in friendly pursuit. The kids and dog headed toward the hotel beach that was really just a sliver of dredged sand.

The rest of the world was moving along at a normal pace, getting ready for the long weekend. Then a light went on in his head. Sarge was never in it for the money. His name had never come up because his angle was different. This was about avenging his sister's murder: all these years, a cop knowing who was responsible for her death, but unable to prove it or make them pay. Until now.

"Let's go pay GroveyGirl a visit," Vance said, getting up from the table. "She's expecting us."

Along the way, Daniel's mood brightened. "Guess who called me last night?"

He was afraid to ask, and that's what Vance told him.

Daniel smiled for the first time in days. "Maria, she called to see if I was OK, after the big news here with the terrorist thing. She saw the news and recognized Ramon Solana's name. She wants to come home, Vance. She said her fling is over, and she wants to come home."

If Sergeant Daniel Ruiz hadn't been driving, he'd have crawled over the center console and bear-hugged him. "That's great news."

Daniel's eyes glistened behind thick-framed glasses and his voice cracked slightly when he said, "When you find that special someone, cherish her. No matter what." He pushed down on the accelerator. "But first, let's go get your money."

26

Homeland Security had downgraded the terrorist threat from orange to yellow more than twenty-four hours ago, after a Cuban-born citizen had been apprehended for the bomb blast at Boca Chita. Jake was seriously considering sticking needles in his eyes to counter the mental anguish. Lauren's radio silence was killing him, too. Ray and Vance weren't answering, either. Not even Davis Frost. It was Thursday and his cohorts were still off the grid. Where did they get off ignoring him like this? Jake told his boss he had a family emergency and left the car lot early. The way he saw it, the possibility of losing millions of dollars constituted a *major* family emergency. Traffic was lighter than he expected, and he figured he'd get to the boatyard around opening time.

He'd been thinking about what to say when he confronted Ray. It might not be the best idea, just showing up, but what other option did he have? He hadn't heard a word from anyone since he woke up alone. That was Tuesday night, and Lauren had slipped out without so much as a note.

Just past the intersection at SW Second Avenue, an awful thumping came from the left side of the Mercedes. *A goddamn flat tire.* The car rolled to a stop in the middle of the crosswalk. Jake flung the door open.

He popped the trunk and lifted the felt-covered flap where the spare tire was stowed. He stared blankly at the empty space. How did his world as a one-time Master of the Universe, Big Swinging Dick, King of the Jungle, Managing Director at multiple major New York investment banks, come down to this? Did he ever, in any scenario during his entire life, envision himself in ninety-percent humidity, pushing a vehicle because he had no spare tire or roadside assistance plan? Did anyone stop to help him? Would he have stopped to help someone else? No, no, and no. In an inexplicable turn of events, the universe had turned on him and had Jake in its crosshairs.

His phone buzzed. Lauren: No update.

Thank God she'd surfaced. I have one. Got a flat tire—no spare. Pick me up?

Where r u?

He gave her the address to the gun and ammo shop across the street. Maybe the flat tire was a blessing. He still hadn't figured out what he was going to say to Ray. The guy at the gun store had kicked him out, accusing him of acting suspicious. Damn, it was hot out. He leaned against the car, mopping his brow with a handkerchief. Thank God she was coming. He desperately needed a status report. And he needed to cool off.

"WHY DIDN'T you answer my texts or calls?" he asked when he got in her car. "I didn't know you expected a marriage proposal after one roll in the hay."

"Is that what you think? That this is personal?"

"Kind of."

Lauren stared straight ahead. "I know men can compartmentalize, but I think your brain is, um, balkanized."

"Balkan Brain, good one."

"Davis Frost is in the hospital."

What? He straightened up in the seat. "Hurt in the bomb blast?"

"Nope."

"Don't leave me in suspense."

"I don't know, either. Not yet. All I know is that someone tried to rip him off. At the storage unit."

"Did they?"

She looked at him. "I just said, that's all I know."

"That stuff that's been all over the news? Don't you think it's hard to believe it's all a coincidence? The Cormorant folks are pretty upset, especially when I told them you went off the grid."

Her dagger eyes said it all. "Seriously? You can drop the act, Jake. I called the company. They never heard of you."

Crap. What could he say to justify his actions?

"Who are you? I couldn't tell from all your business cards."

He exhaled, making a whistling sound. "Just a guy trying to make a buck, I guess." It sounded lame, but it was as close to the truth as anything he'd told her so far.

"Do you actually know anything about this deal?"

"I thought I did." He shrugged. "What's to know, other than I hired you to make a video?"

"Ever heard of Los Guapos?"

"Los what? Los Guavas?"

"Guapos. G-U-A-P-O-S. Guapos. Google it. I think you'll find it very interesting. Especially since you're more or less working for them."

He wiped his brow with the cuff of his shirt, then put on his black-rimmed reading glasses. "You regret coming to my place?

You left without saying goodbye." He was waiting for *Los Guapos* to load in the search engine.

"You don't look interested in an honest answer."

"Holy shit!" A shiver ran down his spine. "Are you telling me *I'm involved in the biggest cocaine conspiracy in U.S. history*?"

"Gangsters, banksters like you, is there a difference?" Lauren kept her eyes on the road. "You must be working for Ray Dinero. I guess you didn't know he was their pilot. He flew tons of cocaine in from Colombia. But that's old news. You have a bigger problem now."

He was sweating harder in the air conditioning than he did leaning against the Merc. "It's hard to imagine what could be bigger." The news sucked the last little bit of life out of him and he sighed. He removed the nerd glasses, put them in his shirt pocket, and slumped forward in the seat like a little boy.

"Taking me for an idiot, well, that just pisses me off."

She seemed to be waiting for him to say something, but he wasn't listening. His mind was consuming the newest reality, that he'd be stuck in his current life forever, if he lived to tell the story. He'd been doing nothing for days but looking at his watch, counting down the seventy-two hours they'd given Davis Frost to earn a five-thousand-dollar bonus. The plan had gone to shit. It seemed too good to be true, too easy. Now he was sitting next to the woman he'd double-crossed. *You know what? I deserve this. Maybe I'll have a heart attack and die right now.*

"Earth to Jake."

He looked over glumly.

"*I* have the money. All of it." She had the upper hand and seemed to be enjoying it.

He straightened up in the seat. "What?" He sat on his hands to cover the tremors. "You have it? How can that be?"

"I'm on to your bullshit." Her eyes narrowed to slits. "I saw the stuff in your bathroom. Ray and Vance are going to be pissed when they find out how I knew where the money was. The handwritten notes on the napkin, how you're splitting seventy-five million? That was some classic shit. Wow."

It now was making sense why she'd sneaked out and why she'd been giving him the cold shoulder. He didn't blame her for being angry. "For what it's worth, you know more than I do."

"Really?" Her tone was caustic. "Where did you think all that money came from?"

"Your friend, the lawyer, when I asked, he said it was better if I didn't know."

"That was good advice."

He looked at her, cowering a little. "Where are we going?"

"Not to get a spare tire." She reached into her purse and showed him the paperwork she'd taken from his bathroom. "Thank you," she said. "It led me straight to the money."

He didn't even know it was missing. When he saw the multiple business cards neatly stapled to the top of Davis's NDA, his face burned red. "You can be so mysterious and fierce. I find it exciting." He was lying. He was scared shitless.

"Do you take anything seriously or are you just a full-time jerkoff?"

She planted her foot on the gas, throwing him against the seat back.

———

She parked in the spot reserved for her at the townhouse.

"Where are we? Is this your place?"

"Uh-huh," she said, stepping out of the car.

Someone grabbed her from behind, pinning her hands to her chest.

"*Hey!*" Her heart jumped into her throat. She arched her back. "*What the—?*"

"Easy does it," a male voice said softly. A pair of gorilla-sized arms clamped her torso.

Lauren could hardly breathe. She got one arm loose and jammed her elbow back into a belly of fat. It was like punching a pillow. He laughed at her.

"Help! Jake, *help!*" She contorted and convulsed, trying to get free. "Help me!" *Where the hell are you, Jake?*

Her attacker grabbed the crook of her elbow and bent it. "Calm down, GroveyGirl."

How does he know that?

"I don't want to hurt you. Vance and I just want to talk to you."

Vance?

The aggressor relaxed his hands the same way she loosened the reins on her mare when the horse was too fresh, little by little. When she stopped fighting, he relaxed his grip. But he kept his hairy arms around her, encircling her like she was a barrel, poised to clamp them around her again if she made a fast move or screamed.

Turning her head slowly, she squinted at his face. Cocking her head to one side, she asked, "Why do you look familiar?" She tried to place him. Then she recognized the gold chain hanging from his neck, the one with the garish, gold cross. The first time she'd seen him, she'd thought an angel had sent him.

"I helped you that day," Sarge said, "with your dog."

"I know." She furrowed her forehead and looked over his shoulder.

Vance had jumped out of a Jeep parked illegally in front of the dog park across the street and jogged over.

Jake, who'd offered nothing in the way of valor to help, got out of her car. She glared at him, then she turned to Vance. "Will you please tell me what's going on? You all know each other?"

"I only know the lawyer," Jake said. "I don't know the other guy."

"Everyone, meet Daniel Ruiz, retired sergeant, Fort Lauderdale PD. We know you have two have the cash," Vance said.

"If I had the money," Jake said, "I would be in the British Virgin Islands by now. On a fifty-foot sailboat, with a nice bottle of cabernet."

Vance turned to face her. "If you ripped us off, it's time to come clean."

She was hot, hot, *hot!* "Rip you *off*? Rip *you* off! You have nerve! You guys were ripping me off! And you"—she glared at Sarge—"you stalked me. How else would you have seen my dog and me that day? I'm sure your grandmothers told you boys what happens after you tell the first lie. I put my friend Davis in harm's way because you guys lied to me. And now he's in the hospital."

"He's fine," Vance said. "He's going to be OK."

"A broken jaw is all," Sarge said.

"Fine? OK? A 'broken jaw is all'? You think that's something to be glib about?"

Vance pulled the Glock holstered under his arm, grabbed her firmly by the shoulder and turned her gently toward the front door of the condo. He pushed the metal muzzle into the small of her back.

"Ouch!" She didn't have enough body fat and the Glock hit a vertebrae.

Vance motioned for Jake to fall in ahead of her. "I hate to do it like this. But lead the way."

Jake trotted ahead of her.

"You're joking," she said, sidestepping awkwardly toward the ornamental gate leading to the landscaped walkway.

"I didn't need a gun to get her to do what I wanted," Jake said.

She kicked him in the calf muscle.

"What was that for?"

Inside, immediately to the left, Vance saw a guest bedroom she was using as her studio, and ahead a living room filled with minimalist furniture, connecting two separate courtyards, one to the right and another straight ahead.

He rushed in front of Jake and Lauren and held his hand up to stop them from taking another step. He and Sarge swept the room with their weapons, knees slack, guns leading the way.

Jake said, "Is this a Starsky and Hutch audition?"

She looked guilty as shit. Vance followed her eyes to the yellow cases strewn around the courtyard.

He shook his head and placed the gun back in the holster. "Did you really think you could pull this off? Without getting yourself killed?"

Sarge twisted the post in his earlobe. "What have we got here, Ms. GroveyGirl?"

"Who else knows about this?" Vance asked her.

She massaged her hands. "No one. No one that I know of."

Vance ordered her to get a screwdriver.

"Don't you think it's a little early to start drinking?" Like most of the things that came out of his mouth, Jake's joke fell flat.

Vance squatted, working the flathead of the tool around the seams of a transport case. Decades of dried sediment—salt, minerals, and ocean organisms—sealed it like mortar to brick. Using the palm of his hand, he pounded on the handle, chiseling and digging along the joins. Fragments, chips, and powder dropped on the patio bricks. He wiped gummy algae from the tip of the driver on the stalk of a potted palm. He jammed the flat end between the sealed seams and twisted it back and forth, loosening it an inch at a time until it finally broke free.

He held his breath. The carotid artery under his collar

pulsed like it was going to explode. Carefully he lifted the lid. The anticipation. What would seventy-five million dollars cash look like?

Sand?

"Sand?" Lauren squinted, looking over his shoulder.

Jake opened the sliding glass door and stepped out on the patio, looking perplexed.

"Is that sand?" Sarge asked.

"This is just what I need," Vance said. "More sand."

"Will someone please tell me what's going on?" Jake asked. "That looks like sand."

Vance went into a rage, beating the open case until the contents spewed and covered the corner of the walled courtyard like beachfront property. After his outburst was over, a calm came over him and he folded his arms across his chest. He remained quiet for a moment.

"Come on," he said. "Let's go pay Ray Dinero a personal visit."

"YOU'D NEVER GUESS the city was on lockdown two days ago," Sarge said when the foursome arrived at Ray's boatyard. He complained there was nowhere to park after surfing the lot waiting for a space to open up.

"It's Memorial Day week," Jake said. "Biggest boat-buying holiday of the year."

Much as she'd rather not look at him, Lauren turned from the front seat and asked, "How would you know?"

"I don't know for a fact, but it's the day I bought mine."

Vance was in the back next to him. "What kind of boat?"

"Fifty-eight-foot Maritimo," Jake said.

The light banter was helping to take the edge off. "That's not a boat, that's a yacht," Vance said.

Jake put his glasses on and pulled up a picture on his phone. He passed it around.

"Impressive," Lauren said. "Where is it now?"

"Two happiest days are now behind me. Sold it to a yacht dealer in Rhode Island. That was my old life." He changed course. "Does anyone know what we're going to say to Ray?" He wasn't sure himself. How would they open the conversation? Why are we so dumb and you're so clever?

"Let me worry about that," Vance said.

"Look." Lauren pointed to the doorway leading to the showroom floor. Two plainclothes, a man and a woman, were escorting Ray's receptionist out. Handcuffed and teetering in her stilettos, she wriggled. It looked like she was mouthing off to the officers. "She works for Ray."

"Let me do the talking," Vance said. "I know everyone is angry, but it's better if we show a united front."

The plainclothes loaded the woman into the back of an unmarked sedan, pushing her down by the head as she arched her back and struggled to get away.

Sarge pulled up close to the police car and put his blinker on. "That one's a wildcat."

Lauren wouldn't have been as gracious. The woman with the razor-cut baby bangs and blue nails pointed at her threateningly, glaring through the vehicle glass when she recognized her. Lauren shuddered.

A well-dressed salesman held the door open for them as they filed through the steel-and-glass entryway leading to the showroom. He wore his longish white hair slicked back with neat rake marks from a wide-tooth comb. His style was too young for his age—shirttail out, thin black tie, skinny black slacks—but he did pull it off.

"He's not here," Lauren said, looking at Ray's empty office.

"Can I help you?" the salesman asked.

"We're here to see Ray Dinero," Vance said.

"He's out there. At the end of the dock, on his personal boat, you can't miss it," the salesman said.

"I know where it is." Lauren saw the Jeep Renegade out of the corner of her eye. "Is Sarge leaving?"

Vance looked out the window and saw the Jeep leaving the lot. "Yep."

RAY STOOD on the bulkhead near the *Bookoo Bucks*, away from the bustling showroom. He looked relaxed when he saw them marching toward him in lockstep.

Jake might be right about one thing: Memorial week could be the busiest boat-buying time of the year. If there weren't so many witnesses milling around all over the place, Vance would have taken a run like at him like angry bull and knocked Ray down on the dock where they could have settled it the old fashioned way, *mano-a-mano*, blood and all. Instead, he watched Ray cheerfully flick cherry-flavored balm across his lips.

"Hi, guys." Ray's raspy voice had no hint of anxiety.

What balls, so cavalier. The urge to punch him intensified.

"I've been expecting you." His knees and thighs were sunburned and the tip of his nose was red too from where his ball cap missed shading it. He opened his arms wide as they jogged toward him, not to embrace them, but to stop them. "Hey, hey, slow down."

Like they had no reason to be upset with him? Three dead bodies, one in the hospital. And a shitload of cases full of sand. "We want to know what's going on." Vance's tone was curt.

"All right. I understand you're all angry. I get it. But everything's OK. Why don't you and Lauren wait for me on my boat. Cool down. I'd like to finish up with Jake. The three of us, we'll have more to talk about."

That was the understatement to beat all understatements.

"We'd—I'd—like to know what's going on first," Lauren said, her tone bordering on anger.

"Come on," Vance said to her. "Let's wait on his boat. Unless you want to go with them."

She looked at him like he was crazy. "No, I'd rather go with you."

Ray and Jake left to talk, and Lauren followed him to the old trawler.

It was the first time they'd been alone since their third date at the Mutiny. "What a crazy few days," she said, climbing aboard the *Bookoo*, sitting on the bow and hanging her long legs over the river water, swinging them.

"Yeah. I guess I should apologize for sticking a gun in your back."

"I'm still pissed off about that." She looked over at him.

There was a long, awkward pause.

She broke the silence. "I'm the one who tricked you into going on the first date with me."

"And to think I thought it was because I put new pictures on my profile."

"Cute." She grinned. "Truth is, I would have gone out with you if we'd met under normal circumstances. Jesus, Ray is clever."

"Don't beat yourself up. He would have found another angle to get to me."

Lauren tilted her head back and looked up at the turquoise sky. "I guess I thought I was entitled to an equal share of the money. It was Davis who took the biggest risk, and he gets paid peanuts."

It was true. She and Davis contributed as much—no, they'd taken *way* more risk than he had. "Life's not fair." He shrugged. It's the best he could come up with. "On the other hand, you and Davis aren't facing felony charges if this thing goes wrong now. However it ends, being cooped up with my fugitive uncle is making me crazy."

"So Tony Famosa is alive and well. And he's been hiding out at your place the whole time." She stared at the water.

This thing wasn't over yet. He'd be in a lot of trouble for aiding and abetting an FBI Ten Most Wanted Fugitive. It was too late to do anything but wait for Ray.

"REALLY, A YACHT?" Jake said, stunned. "Although I probably would have preferred the sailboat." Considering he'd thought all was lost earlier, a canoe would have been a gift.

Ray nodded, leading the way to salesman's office, the sharply dressed man who'd held the door for them. He formally introduced them. "Tommy, this is Jake Fleming."

"Mr. Fleming. Mr. Fleming," the salesman gushed. "Beautiful boat, come sit down. Everything's ready for you. Sit, sit." He pulled a chair out and gestured to it.

Tommy scanned the fancy embossed brochure before handing the paperwork to Jake. "Congratulations."

Jake opened it with Ray leaning over his shoulder. The nine hundred-fifty thousand dollar invoice was stamped Paid In Full. Sold to him using his invalid New York address. He looked up at Ray. "Thanks."

"You ready to take a look at your new luxury cruiser?"

Jake jumped from the chair and stuck his hand out. He pumped Ray's arm up and down. "Wow," he said, shaking his head in amazement. "I thought for sure this deal went south."

His face lit up as they approached the *Arm & A Leg*. The sleek, lavish, sixty-foot yacht tied off to the pier and pilings had just enough slack in the lines to keep her off the bulkhead. He climbed aboard and sat on the plush leather captain's chair. The natural light spilling in from the surrounding windows bounced off the oak floor and cabinetry.

"The rest of your cut is down below, in dive bags with the life jackets. Thirteen-and-a-half less nine-fifty for the yacht, less out-of-pocket expenses, and I gave you a discount on my commission. Five-way cut," Ray said, reaching into his pocket for the tube of lip balm. "There's ten thousand dollars in small bills under the seat where I'm sitting. That ought to be enough to get you where you're going."

A text popped up on Jake's phone: `Daddy—want to sign up 4 school ski trip this winter, mom says to ask u 4 $`

"From my kid," he said. He pecked out a quick response: `OK sweetie—I will talk to your mom.`

A smiling emoji with two red hearts for eyes pinged on his phone. He held it up for Ray to see. His eyes welled; he was embarrassed and wiped them quickly with his shirt cuff.

Ray took a few steps back to give him a little space.

"Sorry about that." Jake blinked and sniffled. "I've got kids. They're still at home."

"Me, too," Ray said. "Mine are barely out of diapers."

"Nice to meet a fellow geezer-dad. What do you have?"

"Two little girls." Ray pulled out his phone and showed him a picture of two precious toddlers barely a year apart sitting together in pale blue ruffled dresses.

Jake pulled up a photo of himself standing between two kids, a boy and girl on the brink of puberty.

"Nice family," Ray said. "Kids, they sure complicate things, don't they? I wanted to give you this." He handed him a business card. "Guy is a good captain if you need one."

He looked at it.

Davis Frost
Director of Photography
Certified Diver and Boat Captain
Generally in Charge of Everything

"I HEARD he got banged up pretty good. I just might call him," Jake said putting the card in his wallet.

"If you do, don't say too much. He doesn't know what really happened here."

"Agreed." He hadn't been so certain about anything in a long time. He'd have no trouble keeping his mouth shut.

Ray stuck his hand out. "See ya around, Jake."

27

They'd been sitting without speaking for a few minutes. The last thing Lauren said to Vance before Ray showed up was, "You know what I've learned? The more virtuous you think you are, the closer you need to look in the mirror."

It rang so true it left him without a comeback. The Miami River was busy again, the workforce comprised mostly of noisy diesel-powered cranes, workboats, and tugs. The air and noise pollution matched Vance's mood. His private time with Lauren officially ended when he heard Ray whistling.

The shrimper dipped slightly to one side as Ray climbed aboard in his usual happy-go-lucky demeanor. "Thanks for waiting." Ray stepped over spare boat parts, rusty lobster pots, mounds of torn netting, and other junk scattered on the deck and sat on a splintered slat of wood connected to the rickety old wheelhouse. "Sit," he said. "I have a lot to explain."

He and Lauren followed, choosing a pair of fraying aluminum lawn chairs.

"I gotta go way back," Ray said, "so bear with me. Sarge came to see me back around the time Chago was indicted. I remembered seeing him hanging around at the Hotel Mutiny, and I knew he was a cop. In my old line of work, sensing certain stuff was important." Ray's eyes moved to Vance's. "He wanted to know who killed the girl, the waitress. Not every smuggler was a friend of Los Guapos, you know. A rival, a Colombian cartel leader, sent word Margarita was murdered by one of our big customers. I told Tony and Chago it was the kind of thing that could not happen." He paused and took a deep breath. "The rise of the cocaine cowboys happened because the Colombians didn't know how to do business in America.

"The Cuban-Americans who grew up here understood the culture. They needed us to handle their business in the U.S. The Mutiny was like our international distribution headquarters, being a private club and all. Some of the Colombians, they were crazy. They demanded expensive champagne, girls, cigars, lobsters, boys, filet mignon, you name it, and they expected us, their distributors, to supply it.

"I warned the guys we were crossing red lines all over the place. But mine was a lonely voice. The hotel management was happy to purvey whatever, as long as they got paid. We were making tons of cash. And Chago and Tony got caught up in it. They flaunted their money. Rolexes. Ferraris and Lamborghinis. Custom Italian suits. They started doing cocaine, snorting it right off the tabletops in the club, out in the open. They hired hookers. Ran up ten thousand dollar tabs for dinner and champagne. All cash."

Ray looked at Vance again. "What you'd call conspicuous consumption. I warned them they couldn't keep taunting law enforcement. Me? I didn't go to the club much." Ray paused.

"My uncle says you were never even arrested. He uncle calls you *El Cerebo*. The Brain."

"Is that so?" Ray's eyebrows went up. "I'd like to think I have a little better karma, too. Even criminals need standards. It's a bad habit to keep lowering the bar."

Lauren leaned closer to Ray to listen.

"They were a bunch of kids trying to impress everyone. But the powerboats, the Ocean Eagle Racing Team? That was my idea. We ran drugs right under the noses of the NBC Sports helicopters and cameras. The hulls were fabricated with secret hatches and filled with kilos of cocaine. We would have won every race without all that ballast." Ray shook his head. "Who looks at what's right beneath them, right?

"But all that changed when the girl was killed. It was like the ocean tides changed direction, or the earth's magnetic poles went off kilter. She was a Cuban, one of us. It doesn't matter when or where people live, we all need a code, something to glue us together. Don't get me wrong," he turned to Lauren, "if any of you girls got killed by someone associated with us, it would have been a problem. But murdering that beautiful, innocent Cuban girl, one of us—a young mother? That changed everything."

Ray stood and moved debris scattered on the worn deck, revealing metal grates resembling sewer drain tops. "Those go down to the holds." He tapped one flip-flop on the rusting cap. It made a dull thud. He ambled to a timeworn wooden door separating the wheelhouse from the lower deck and opened it. "Come with me," he said, stepping aside.

Vance and Lauren walked ahead of Ray.

Behind the old door with the filthy glass was a ladder leading to the lower deck. The smells of mold and dead shellfish stung Vance's nostrils. He ducked under cables crisscrossing the dim cabin, strung for a shortwave or maybe a ham radio. Spokes were broken off the cracked, wooden steering wheel. He leaned against the well-preserved teak counter holding an antique monitor, the white plastic aged to a mellow yellow, and a classic compass as round and tall as a crockpot. A skinny metal pipe jutted up near the center console.

"What's that?" he asked.

Ray grabbed hold of the T-bar attached to it. "It's the transmission. Haven't run the engines in, oh, I don't know how long. Maybe never, come to think of it."

The black vinyl bucket seats were split at the seams. Flakes of foam stuffing went airborne as Ray brushed against one. Reaching up, he unlatched the wooden drawing board built into the oak ceiling. It dropped down and opened like an easel. "The old chart room," he said. Tightly rolled paper maps were tucked up inside. He removed one. "This is how the oceans were navigated for hundreds of years using that trusty old thing." Ray pointed to the crockpot compass.

He tucked a rolled map under his arm, pushed the drawing board back up, and latched it. He moved the big compass on the console to make room for the chart and unfurled it. He and Lauren peered over his shoulders. Faded red ink-marks dotted the map, and inside it, Ray took out the little piece of paper Tony had given Vance to hand off to Lauren to deliver to Ray. He held it up. "The coordinates."

"Yeah, a lot of good those were. A map to a bunch of empty plastic cases," Vance said.

"You mean sand," Lauren said. "All that for nothing."

"Not exactly for nothing," Ray said. "Mongo thought they were the coordinates. He had a friend take a picture of it. I left it in my office, on the desk. The gal who worked at the reception desk—"

Lauren cut in, "The one with the black bangs? We saw her being escorted out. In handcuffs."

"Yeah. She was Mongo's mole. We do a background check on everyone who comes for a job. I had Sarge check her out. He followed her, and after he saw her meeting with Mongo after applying for the job, I hired her. I found her in my office a couple of times snooping around my desk. She'd hang around outside my door and listen to my calls. I'd leave my phone on the desk with fake text messages. She took a picture of this. I knew she'd show it to Mongo." He held up the paper with the numbers. "When she got friendly with Mrs. Pierce after I sold her and her husband the *Sea Food*, I figured she was just using her as a way to poke around my desk or meet a rich guy. I had no idea she was setting them up for Mongo. I'm just sick about what happened to them." He shook his head from side to side. "What a shame."

Vance had never met them, but the Pierces were collateral damage, like so many others. Nice folks unwittingly mired into a deadly hunt for money. There was no way *El Cerebo* could have predicted that.

Ray pointed to the bulkhead separating the lower cabin from the holds, the place beneath the metal caps where shrimpers stored the catch until it was sold or too rotten to sell. Ray kicked the wall with the rubbery bottom of his flip-flop. It was solid, like iron. "Money was right here the whole time," he said.

"You mean you were sitting on it? The whole time?" Lauren said with a look of disbelief.

Ray grinned and conditioned his lips with a swipe of scented balm. "Yep."

Amazing. But weren't the simplest plans always the best ones? Boy, was Ray disciplined. "Right under everyone's noses."

"*Si, señor.*" He reached into his pocket, opened his wallet and handed another paper to Vance. "Keep this in your wallet," he said.

He looked at the four squares of paper, the death certificate for Giuseppe Zangara, tucked inside a protective clear plastic sleeve. "How did you get this?"

"What is it?" Lauren asked.

He glanced from Ray to Lauren. "A family heirloom."

"Oh, it must have something to do with your uncle," she said.

"Keep it in your wallet," Ray repeated. "It's very important you do that."

"All right. I heard you. I'll keep it in my wallet."

"It looks old," Lauren said. "May I see it?"

He handed it to her. "It belonged to my grandfather. It's a long story."

Ray changed the subject while Lauren studied it. He touched her shoulder. "I have something for you, too."

"I'm starting to feel like Dorothy. Let's see. You have a brain," she said to Ray. "I thought Jake had a heart. And you?" She was looking at Vance. "I haven't figured it out yet."

Ray crouched in the cramped lower cabin and fished a shoebox from a cubby and held it toward her.

She handed the plastic pouch back to Vance and took the cardboard box from Ray. It was old and moldy, and the top was pliable from years of exposure to the brackish river air. She lifted the lid and gasped. "Oh my God!" She covered her mouth with her hand. "These are the clothes I loaned her the night she was killed."

Her face flushed white and a tremor crept into her fingers. She held up the short-sleeved button-down shirt with red and white flowers. She set the shirt down and held up a pair of grayish skinny jeans mottled with mildew stains. "These were white. I loaned her my clothes because she had to work late that night. Margarita didn't want to work late, and she didn't want to drive home in sunup traffic dressed in an evening gown and a hat. She said we looked like prostitutes. She knew I always had a change of clothes because I always changed before I left the club." She shook the empty box. A layer of sand and sediment rustled in the bottom like a snake's rattler. "Where did you get these?"

"From her brother," Ray said.

"You know her brother?" Lauren looked confused.

"Yes, the ex-cop you met, the one who helped you with your dog?" Ray said.

"Sarge? He's her brother? That's why he was helping you?" She bent at the waist, clutching the wad of clothes to her breast like a newborn. She rocked forward and back and began to cry.

The cacophony of the river went quiet in that ethereal way it does sometimes, as if Mother Nature called time out. Vance nodded at Ray and shut his eyes. The only sounds came from the caterwauling of the seagulls, the tinkling of the netting, and the cadence of the water lapping at the hull. The two men sat quietly, giving her a chance to regain her balance.

"I'm sorry. I had no idea," she said. "I thought he was an angel when he showed up to help me with my dog." She wiped her tears on the red and white shirt. "Her brother. Wow. I remember him now from the club. He was there. I remember everything now. He was the one asking me all those questions."

"He's wanted justice for his sister all these years. And Vance's uncle and I promised to help him," Ray said.

"I didn't know any of this, either," Vance said, "until a few hours ago."

"I have something else for you," Ray said.

THEY FOLLOWED him until they came to the metal maintenance building. Inside, Ray walked to a small aluminum trailer and pulled the cover off a sparkly purple wave runner. The sporty little craft seated two and was nicer than the ones she'd seen for rent at any of the touristy beaches.

Lauren looked at the stack of black cases and piles of sand spilled on the floor and said, "Hmm."

"A few more horsepower than you're used to," Ray said, alluding to her love of riding horseback.

"Mine?"

Ray nodded.

Lauren ran her hand along the side of it as though she were petting it. "Cute. Purple. Prince would have loved it."

"It's what's in it," he said. "Money's in the hull."

"The hundred K you promised me?"

"That plus one fifth, an even share, just over thirteen mil."

"What are you talking about?"

"You didn't think I wouldn't take care of you, did you?" Ray asked with a twinkle in his eye.

Ray always seemed to know the right thing to do. It's how Ray had navigated his way through the dangerous days of Los Guapos. Maybe he was right about karma, too. There was plenty of money to go around; they could all afford to give her one fifth. But Lauren wasn't happy. Both men looked at her, confused.

Ray said, "Take care of your friend, Davis Frost. Tell him whatever you want, but don't tell him the truth."

"God forbid anyone around here would tell the truth," Lauren said, stroking the wave runner. Her face felt flushed.

"Are you OK?" Vance asked.

Suddenly she had clarity. She put her hands on her hips. "I don't want it."

"What do you mean you don't want it?" Ray asked.

"The money," she said. "I don't want it." *Was she crazy? Maybe.* But still, she didn't want it.

"Are you out of your mind?" Vance asked.

"It's blood money. I don't want it. I need the hundred thousand, so I would appreciate it if you would give me that so I can pay my tax bill and go on my way."

Ray said, "You can't be thinking clearly. You're just mad at us. You need time. To think about it."

"No, I don't. I'm done thinking about it. Please give me my hundred thousand. Oh, a hundred-eighteen thousand: the ten more you owe me for my video production services, and eight more for Davis. That includes his five-thousand-dollar bonus for getting the job done within seventy-two hours. Oh, and I'll pay him for his boat rental out of my share."

"You're out of your mind," Vance said.

"All right," Ray stood. "Hold tight. Let me get the cash from my office and I'll be right back."

They were alone again.

"I don't think you should walk away from the money," Vance said. "Give it to charity. Rescue some dogs and horses, but don't leave it on the table."

"It's just money," she said.

He looked at her like she was nuts. "I don't understand."

"I don't expect you to."

Ray appeared with a manila envelope. "Here you go."

"Thank you. And thank you for understanding," she said.

Then it occurred to her that Ray actually did understand. To him *it was* also *just money*, too.

She moved closer to Ray and opened her arms. They embraced like long-lost friends. "It's too late to go out with me," Ray said. "I had to go off and marry someone else because you always turned me down, even for dinner."

She laughed a happy laugh.

"I'm going to give Vance a tour of his new luxury sailboat," Ray said. "You wanna come with us?"

"No, I think I'm going to sit here for a few minutes, if that's OK with you."

"Suit yourself," Ray said.

Vance looked like he was still trying to comprehend how she could turn it down. "I'll call you," he said to her.

She nodded. But her mind was a million miles away.

AFTER THEY LEFT, she mounted the wave runner with the $13M hidden inside and sat on the cushy seat, closing her eyes. What a ride the last two weeks had been. And that was putting it mildly. She'd worked hard to put the painful memories of the Hotel Mutiny behind her, but they'd been exhumed. She was embarrassed she'd cried in front of Vance and Ray. But when Ray handed her the box of clothes, it took her back to the night her friend Margarita disappeared. How strange. To feel tears rolling down her cheeks before despair set in—that wasn't in the right order. She worried what the last couple of weeks had done to her.

The events spun through her head. Uncle Jack's sudden death, the IRS notices, the call from Ray, her messaging Vance on the dating site. The call from Jake, the meeting at Black Point Marina to sign the NDA—all part of a fancy plan to get her and Davis to go get their millions. *The company hopes the video will go viral.* Had she changed? Had her heart hardened, explaining the emotionless tears?

Then she remembered her beloved Sinbad, followed by a more familiar pain. A tightening in her throat, a whirling void in her stomach, as despair turned to agony. Then the tears flowed freely. *Breathe, Lauren, breathe.* She put her head down in her hands, and for the first time in months, felt something besides fear and sadness. And it wasn't Peter's voice in her head, either, admonishing her for her denial. Why should she have allowed him to belittle her *for trusting him*?

Clarity was coming in waves, followed by a tiny bit of serenity. That's all she really wanted. Not love from a man to validate her. Not money. Those desires would only bring more trouble.

———

VANCE AND RAY walked past the rusty corrugated buildings, past the shiny yachts in wide slips, and slings with smaller vessels in various states of repair. Past the rundown fueling station, beyond a field of bluish-brown, fifty-five-gallon plastic barrels circling a mountain of river dredge. A gaggle of gulls howled and dive-bombed the dredge pile, picking at the dead and dying sea life.

Ray stopped at the stern of the shrimp boat. Her outriggers stuck out like dried tree branches, a maze of tangled lines draping downward. The metal bits clinked like wind chimes in the light breeze coming off the river.

"Wait a second," Ray said.

A minute later he returned with a glossy brochure and handed it to him. For all its refinement, the gull-winged sailing vessel on the cover looked menacing. Vance liked almost all the other ships at the boatyard more than this one.

"So what do you think of her?" Ray asked, stopping at the bow of the *Second Wind.*

"It's great," he said, knowing it was great as long as he didn't have to sail her. He didn't know enough about the sport to handle a rented Hobie Cat on Lake Okeechobee. "I could live on it."

He stepped onto the deck and leaned against the gunwale, tilting his head up to scan the top of the tall main halyard mast. It sprouted loose ropes fanning out from a crow's nest. It looked complicated. He tagged behind Ray as they jaunted to the fly bridge.

The main sail was neatly packaged inside a blue canvas

cover attached to the long, horizontal boom. Ray leaned with his back on it. "It's a Lagoon. Like the manufacturer says, 'the lap of luxury and the leading edge of technology.' Your cut is down below, stowed in dive bags wrapped in the jib sail. Thirteen and a half, less expenses, including this baby."

"What about Lauren's cut?" There was no way he could do what she did, refusing the money. He didn't want it, but he wanted to know what Ray planned to do with it.

"I'll keep it for her. I'll be the bank."

Ordinarily he'd have scoffed at such a promise. Instead, he nodded slowly. The guarantee was Ray's, and that made the promise surer than one from any financial institution. "Do you know anyone who could teach me how to sail this thing?"

IT WAS early evening when he headed home. Thunderheads resembling the after-billow of smoke from refinery stacks hung low. He was part cow, instinctively knowing it was going to rain. Vance drove around the block twice, looking for the Escalade, but there was no sign of the white SUV. He jogged over to the gas station and bought a sixteen-ounce can of beer, asked the cashier for a brown paper bag, and drank the beer as he walked home. It went straight to his head on an empty stomach, just the way he'd hoped. If he was going to be arrested, he might as well be medicated.

There were no signs of law enforcement at the complex. All the usual suspects were hanging in the parking lot, talking shit and shooting baskets into a net hung on an angle from the second story railing. A few big raindrops hit him on the head.

"Hey, Tony," he said, walking into the tiny apartment. A Cubs-Indians baseball game played on the television in the living room. But Tony didn't answer.

He checked the bedroom. No Tony. He looked inside the bedroom closet. Not there, either. The bathroom door was closed. He knocked. No answer. He tried the knob; it was unlocked. He opened the door and felt the humid air wafting in from the open window. The old floral curtains floated in and out; the screen leaned up against the grimy wall. He pulled the window shut as the drops turned into a heavy rainstorm.

Tony's bags were gone.

Vance sat on the bed, dog-tired, and picked up the old cigar box. The watchcase and photos were still stuffed inside. He removed his wallet from his pants pocket and set it on the nightstand. The old document, the death certificate, poked out between the leather folds where he kept his cash.

Keep it in your wallet.

Who was he to question Ray Dinero?

He was too exhausted to question anything. He needed sleep. It was over. Tony was gone. He crawled into bed and passed out.

28

ONE MONTH LATER

JAIME JUSTO STOOD on the stoop in front of his suburban Kendall home and tightened the belt on his terrycloth robe. As he bent to pick up the *Miami-Herald*, he looked around to see where the annoying buzzing sound was coming from. A drone carrying a box whirred overhead. Jaime ducked and ran into his house. He watched from the window as it descended and hovered a couple of feet above his porch before dropping a cardboard box on the walkway, like an osprey releasing its prey. The drone rose and sped up, up and away.

"Holy moly!" Jaime said to his wife, looking inside the box. It would take him all day to count the bundles of hundreds, and when he finished, it would add up to just over million bucks. Jaime's wife read the enclosed card, a note from Antonio Famosa thanking Justo for his loyalty, reminding him his son wouldn't be playing in the majors forever, and telling him to dispense some of the money to Tony's older sister, Sophia, anonymously.

"Make sure she has what she needs," Jaime's wife told him.

Two blocks away, Ray Dinero landed the drone with a joystick. He picked it up and jogged to his truck, smiling like a kid on Christmas morning.

VANCE ARRIVED at his mother's house early, in time for coffee.

"Ju no look so good," Isabel said, opening the door. "Too much goes on. First jur poppy's heart and now Kathy has cancer."

Kathy dropped her pink-and-purple paisley travel bag by the front door.

"The treatment has very good results, Mom. Steve Jobs—"

"Mr. McIntosh Apple is dead." Isabel put her hands on her hips, "Why ju have to go all the way to Switzerland?"

"Mom, he would probably be alive if he had the treatment earlier," Kathy said. "You should show more *positivity*."

"Oh, Vance, only Jesus can help her now. If the treatment is so good, why not have it here, in America?"

He and Kathy did not answer.

THE DASSAULT FALCON 7X long-range jet was waiting on the tarmac at Benchmark Aviation at Miami International when he and Kathy arrived. He'd purchased discount seats from a charter service. It was nice: no customs, no TSA, no bag check, no nothing.

Shit! He saw the marshal——the Escalade-driver, the African-American woman who'd shadowed him for days in May. His heart pounded when she stepped out of the SUV, between him and Kathy. He was about to be arrested, right in front of his sister. This is how it went. He knew from his days as a cop. Just when the bad guys thought they'd gotten away with it, the authorities showed up. They'd build their cases while the criminals decompressed.

The woman was tall, more than six foot, big enough to tackle and overpower him. He thought about running, but how far could he get on foot with no getaway vehicle?

"Sorry about shooting out your office window. Didn't mean to scare you," she said. She had something in her hands, something wrapped in a white towel. She offered it to him with outstretched arms.

He took it from her, peeking at what was under the cloth. He recognized it. His old stolen police-issue Glock, the same one Chago wrested from him in front of the urinal at the Hotel Mutiny more than twenty years ago. He remembered the Escalade leaving his office the day of the drive-by shooting, cutting across traffic, and the smell of gunpowder and tire smoke. He'd almost forgotten about the mystery of the spent casings found at his office being a match for his stolen Miami PD sidearm.

"Where did you get this?" he asked.

She held her hand out to shake his. "Kristal Ball, nice to meet you."

"You're joking, the name?"

"You're one to talk, Mr. *Courage*. The gun's a gift from Ray Dinero. I guess he's re-gifting it, actually. He's been safekeeping it. He said to tell you he's sorry. About the window."

He looked at her sideways, "You're not with the marshal's office?"

Kathy turned back when she realized he'd stopped. He waved her on. "Be right there!"

"Afraid not," Kristal said. "In the employ of Mr. Ray Dinero. I was protecting you. And Tony."

"I thought you were going to arrest me." He laughed nervously. He held the Glock up, still swaddled in the towel. "You shot my damn window out? Why?"

"Ray thought it would be a good distraction, keep you on your toes."

"He was right about that."

"Have a safe trip, Mr. Courage. Good thing they didn't catch your uncle. He'd make the Marshals 'Fugitive of the Decade' list." Kristal shook her head, amused, and jogged back to the Escalade.

VANCE SAW the pilots talking in the cockpit. A perky flight attendant with bright red lipstick greeted them at the base of the stairs where Kathy waited. One of them, a clean-cut guy, jaunted down the stairway and loaded their bags into the side compartment of the charter jet.

"Good morning," the pilot said. "Welcome aboard." He led the way. "We have one of us dead-heading today, a pilot. Hopefully, he won't bother you too much. Enjoy the ride."

His mouth watered when he looked at the wicker basket filled pastries and a tray of fresh-cut fruit on a table between rows of comfortable leather seats. "There are bagels and cream cheese, too. I'm Stacy. Would you like a mimosa?"

"I'm Vance Courage, and this is my sister, Kathy. No thanks. I'll have coffee."

"Nice name," Stacy said, smiling. "There's a fully-stocked bar, too, if you prefer something stronger."

"Thanks, but I think I'll get some sleep."

He leaned back in the oversized seat across from his sister, listening to the whine of the starboard engine firing, and then the other. The Dassault taxied toward the runway. The pilots waited behind a Gulfstream IV ahead of them.

This was the first time he felt like he could let down his guard down since that fateful day in May when Tony appeared at his door. He'd been running on adrenaline. Each time one more piece of the puzzle fell into place another muscle in his body relaxed. He'd all but forgotten about the drive-by shooting. Ray must have known how reckless it was for Chago to steal a detective's weapon. Tony probably told Ray that he'd reported it stolen. Ray would have been angry if he'd known Chago and his goons ambushed him mid-piss in the men's room, high out of their minds high on cocaine. How Ray navigated through all the insanity and recklessness was a greater mystery. By the time the Falcon was airborne, he was asleep and dreaming.

He heard Kathy's voice. "Vance. Vance." She was shaking him by the shoulder.

"What, what, what's wrong?"

"One of the pilots wants to talk to you."

Stacy handed him a hot coffee. "Here, drink this," she said. "Follow me—you look exhausted."

Who could want to talk to him badly enough for his sister to wake him from the best sleep he'd had in weeks? He pushed himself out of the seat and took the hot coffee from Stacy. He turned toward the cockpit.

"No, not those pilots. The one in the back, the one deadheading."

Stacy gestured to a man in a pilot's cap facing away from him. As he approached him the man swiveled in his chair.

"*Hola, sobrino.*"

His heart hammered. "Jesus, Tony. What are you doing here?"

"Sit down. Sorry for the surprise. Can we have some privacy?"

"Yes, of course." Stacy pulled the heavy blue dividing curtain and left.

"You have something for me," Tony said. "Ray said he gave it to you."

His brain was still thawing out. "You could have left a note or something." He rubbed his temples with his fingers, but this was Tony Famosa, one half of the most notorious smuggling cartel in American history. He shouldn't have been surprised about a second ambush. "I don't know, Tony. Do you think it would be good to give it to you now?" He'd have to fish the gun out of his bag and there was no way to do that without Kathy or Stacy noticing. "If my sister sees the gun—"

"Gun? I don't know what you're talking about. Ray was supposed to give you a paper, a death certificate."

"Oh." He shook his head to clear it. *Keep this with you all the time.* "Did you know that the marshal was working for Ray?" he asked, reaching into his pocket, removing his billfold.

"Yes."

A part of him wanted to rearrange Tony's face, but he was too thankful that he wasn't handcuffed in the back of Kristal Ball's Escalade en route to the county jail.

"The old geezer captaining this plane, he worked for Chago and me back in the day. The other pilot, he's too young, thinks South Beach has always been the hot spot in Miami. We employed a lot of people, and a lot of them are doing OK."

Lots of people tangled in the same web as Vance came out far worse than he had. "And a lot of them are still in prison. And a bunch of them are dead, too," Vance said.

"So that's your little sister, Kathy, sitting up there."

As usual, Tony dodged the topic of the carnage left in the wake of Los Guapos. "She's not so little anymore."

Tony stared out the oval window. He took the pilot's cap off and placed it in his lap. When he turned back to face him, he swallowed hard, and Vance thought he heard his uncle's voice crack. "It won't be easy, not seeing them again. My family. I haven't seen Sophia or Isabel for twenty years."

Tony needed a minute, and he understood exactly how his uncle felt. Vance sat quietly, giving him the time he needed.

"I changed the flight plan," Tony finally said. "Last stop for me, I hope."

"Where you headed?"

"Panama. A little out of the way."

Vance sighed. "You come and go approximately the same way."

"It was better if you didn't know the details about old business. I got you in deep enough. But I hope it was worth it." Tony pointed out the window. "Look."

He leaned over his uncle and looked out the porthole.

"The Motherland," Tony said.

The island nation of Cuba looked like a paradise from high above. He had no desire to go there. Ever. Seeing it from the sky was close enough. "So why Panama?"

"It's not like I have a lot of options. I'm still on the FBI's Ten Most Wanted list and there's a million-dollar bounty on me. I have to go somewhere. Panama's beautiful and it's tropical. I like that." Tony sighed. "Bureaucracies, they're just as crooked as the criminals. It's always about the money with them."

"And power."

"Yeah, money and power," Tony agreed.

"Speaking of Chago—"

Tony interrupted. "You know, I never hurt anyone. I never killed anyone, never threatened a witness. I never got revenge, ever. Sure, I schmoozed the smugglers who brought drugs into Miami, but I'm not a violent guy."

The denial, Tony believed what he was saying. It was easier

to leave it like this, not to argue. It wasn't as if his uncle could go back and change the past.

"Chago, he's the one with all the blood on his hands."

Vance just listened while Tony rationalized the past.

"And then his own son had him killed."

"What?" *What sort of man kills his own father?*

"His kid told the lawyers to stop paying the Brotherhood to protect his dad. Used the money to buy a hit instead. He was going after the cash. Ray knew he would."

"I guess I'm not shocked." It was true. He was beyond being surprised.

Tony's mood brightened and his face lit up. "Latin women are the most beautiful women on earth."

"Yeah, and at your age it's a good thing there's Viagra."

They needed a laugh.

"They sure do advertise the hell out of that stuff during baseball games, especially in the daytime. In Cuba, you just get old and have to quit the last little bit of happiness."

Vance changed the subject. "Did you know Margarita was Sergeant Ruiz's sister?"

Tony nodded, then shook his head slowly from side to side and lowered his eyes. The sadness returned. "I was in love with her—did he tell you that?"

Vance was mistaken about being beyond surprised. This was a shocker.

"I was married. She was married with a baby. Married to a *gringo*. I didn't know her brother was a cop until he came to the club trying to find out what happened to her. I promised him we would make it right one day. I gave him a solid gold brick, but that's all I could do to help. Told him to sell it and use the money to find the killers. I never wanted to involve you in any of this. It's my mess. When the chance to leave Cuba came, I left. There was no time to plan anything. There was no safe way to contact you.

Every communication is monitored. I took the chance. And it's worked out, for all of us. Do something good with your life. Marry that horse girl and move away."

Wow. Tony had so many secrets.

"Can I have it?"

Tony was referring to the death certificate. "Sure, but why do you want it? It's part of my family, the Courage family."

"Not entirely."

The hits just kept on coming. *How could that be?* "It belonged to my grandfather, Harold."

"Sophia put it in with your dad's things."

"Now you're talking crazy."

"Just give it to me."

His billfold was in his lap, but he wasn't handing the document over until he got an explanation. "After you tell me what you're talking about."

"I don't think you know the whole story," Tony said. "You take a lot for granted."

The whole story? Wasn't there already enough?

29

"I figured my granddad kept it as some sort of a trophy. From the night—"

Tony interrupted him. "Your father had it."

"Why didn't I see it?" Why didn't his dad show it to him? After all the years listening to his Grandfather Harold blustering about meeting FDR, treating the Chicago mayor for his gunshot wound. . . .

"Where to begin." Tony sighed, then paused for an entire minute. "What do you know about Cuba's history?"

Vance shrugged. "The basics. Bay of Pigs, Cuban Missile Crisis, Fidel Castro, Gitmo, Fidel's death, the horrors of Communism. And these new normalized relations."

"Ever heard of Cristóbal Colón?" Tony asked.

"Should I?"

"Since you're half Cuban, *si,* yes, you should know." Tony shook his head, disappointed. "You have much to learn. Cristóbal Colón is Spanish for Christopher Columbus."

The Dassault reached its cruising altitude, and they had just over an hour before the jet was scheduled to touch down in Panama.

Tony sighed audibly. "Do you know how your parents met?" He didn't.

"At the FDR Library in Washington, DC. Your mother was wearing a straw hat with a scarf tied to it, like a tourist. There's a display there with a bullet from the assassination attempt. The family of one of the victims, one of FDR's bodyguards, I think, donated it back in the 1940s. Your mother was on school field trip and was looking at the slug while the teacher was telling the story about what happened at Bayfront Park.

"Your mother's scarf caught your father's eye. It was one of those touristy things with oranges and palm trees on it. He introduced himself. He told her he was from Miami and a story about your Grandfather Courage being at the hospital when Roosevelt came to see the mayor of Chicago. She thought he was lying, trying to impress her. They stayed in touch, but your father waited 'til she turned eighteen to ask her out."

He searched his memory but had no recollection of this family folklore.

"When your father found a copy of the death certificate for sale at a fundraiser in the basement at Jackson Hospital, he bought it. He gave it to your mother as a gift after they were married. A souvenir, sort of, to remember how they met. Your mother was fascinated with the story. That's what your father told everyone."

Everyone but me. A souvenir? "Is this going somewhere?"

Tony nodded. "In 1965, when I was nine, I had an appendicitis attack. Your father took care of me. Isabel and Sophia donated blood. Your dad told them it would be best to give their blood, you know, to keep in the blood bank, in case I needed it. But they weren't a match."

"What are you saying?"

"That I can't be your uncle." Tony chewed on his lower lip.

"Who are you, then?" His stomach did a flip. "And what do you mean they weren't a match?"

"It's like eye color. Two brown-eyed people can have a blue-eyed kid, but two blue-eyed people can't have brown-eyed child. I carry two recessive blood genes. I'm not a match for Sophia or Isabel. Your dad, he's the one who figured it out."

"I don't get it. What are you saying? That you have a different dad?"

"Ah," Tony said, half-smiling. "I wish it was that simple. Your mother and aunt, they're not my sisters."

Vance cocked his head. His gut told him he needed a break, time to prepare for this new and strange information. "I'll be right back. I'm going to check on my sister." He walked to the forward section where Kathy sat reading.

She looked up from her *O Magazine*. "You look, um, worried. Is everything all right?"

"Turns out I know one of the pilots."

"You know one of them? The one you've been talking to?" Kathy asked.

"Yeah. We knew each other, back when I was a police officer." It was sort of true.

She twisted the ends of her hair. "I was scared something might be wrong."

"No, no, everything's fine. He's hitchhiking. We're going to drop him off."

"Oh." She furrowed her brow. "Where is he going?"

"Panama."

She smiled. "Far be it from me to complain. I just want to tell you how much I appreciate you being there for me, and figuring all this out. I love you." She held her hand out.

His eyes welled.

She jumped up, concerned. "Oh, my gosh. Is everything *really* all right? Are you OK?"

He hugged her, fighting the tears. "Everything is going to be fine." Tony was right. He took too much for granted. His precious sister had a heart of gold. He thought of Sarge and Margarita and how Daniel's sister's death had haunted him.

Kathy sat and resumed thumbing through the pages of the magazine. When he lingered, she looked up. "Go talk to him. That's so weird, bumping into someone you know, up here. I won't feel neglected."

He walked to the back of the plane where Tony gazed out the porthole at a cloudless sky. The plane bounced hard and the jolt unbalanced Vance. He grabbed the back of the seat to keep from falling.

"We just hit the wake of another plane," Tony said. "Did you tell your sister about our detour?"

"I did. She's very sweet; she's so thankful, really."

Without any prompting, Tony went on a roll. "In the late 1800s, the American newspapers were fascinated by the Cuban freedom fighters. They were in the news practically every day. Sophia told me it reminded lots of Americans about their own fight for independence from England."

"What does this have to do with the death certificate?"

"I'm getting to that. What do you know about the Spanish-American War?"

He thought it had something to do with California and Mexico.

Tony laughed aloud. "Wrong ocean, *idioto*. The Spanish-American War was over Cuba, Guam, and Puerto Rico. The Cubans wanted the Americans to invade the island to free them and end Spanish colonial rule. Did you know Thomas Jefferson thought Cuba was important, geopolitically?"

He wanted Tony to cut to the chase. "*Reader's Digest* version, please."

"I'm trying to keep it simple," Tony said. "After the war was over, Cuba wanted independence. The Cuban people didn't want to be part of the United States. So it left a vacuum."

"What a concept. Look at Iraq."

"Don't get me wrong, *El Bobo*. I love the USA. But our family went from two centuries of wealth to *campesinos*." Tony pointed his thumb up then rolled it inward and down in a large arc, flapping his lips and making a brrrrring noise, like the sound of a plane in a tailspin. "Under Spanish rule, big areas of land were passed down within families for generations. It couldn't be subdivided or sold unless all the owners agreed to sell."

"They can't even agree on where to park in front of my mom's house."

"*Exacto.* During Teddy Roosevelt's presidency, the U.S. stuck its nose in Cuban foreign policy and changed the laws. Thanks to American policies, Cuban family farmers could divide up the land. They sold pieces of it. American sugar corporations came in and bought it up for two bucks an acre. They burned the forests. They modernized the mills. The banks stopped loaning money to locals, and there was no way to compete.

"Isabel and Sophia's father joined the Cuban Revolution in 1953. His family had owned land and farmed sugar and tobacco for generations. But when the Americans backed President Batista, it started the revolution." Tony took a deep breath. "You know, it's hard enough going from being poor to being rich, but it's much harder going the other way."

He stopped Tony to remind him that he still hadn't told him why he needed the death certificate.

"I'm getting there. Your Cuban grandfather was captured during one of the first Castro-led attacks on a military installation. He disappeared, never to be seen again, assumed killed by the Batista regime. Two years later, your grandmother was picked up and detained by the government."

Vance was trying to run the timeline through the fog of adrenaline, but his brain wouldn't cooperate.

"When they came for your grandmother, they arrested her on suspicion of conspiring against the government. Anyone having anything to do with the revolutionaries was hunted and punished. When their mother was taken away, Sophia was, uh, uh, attacked, by guards, soldiers, who knows what side they were fighting on. It's strange, but it doesn't make any difference." He paused, and then clarified something important to Vance. "Isabel, she was hiding and didn't see what happened to Sophia. She only knew their mother had been taken."

He felt gut-punched. Like he might vomit. Sophia was *attacked*. "My grandmother didn't die of cancer?"

Tony shook his head. "Take it easy, *sobrino*. We're all good here."

It wasn't *all good*. Far from it. The thought of Sophia being assaulted made him sick. He dropped his chin into his hand and covered his mouth, reaching for the airsickness bag in the seat pouch. After a moment, his stomach settled.

"My mother knew all this?" Vance finally asked.

"Not in the beginning. Your father demanded an explanation after the thing with the blood. Sophia was the only one who knew what happened. She told him, and he told your mother. Later, they told me."

"But the timeline, you were born in 1959, it wouldn't have been possible—"

Tony cut him off. "We don't question the things our families tell us. Not until we have to."

Oh God. What was he saying? Vance rubbed his forehead until it hurt. Tony couldn't be his uncle. Tony couldn't be Isabel or Sophia's brother, either. The timeline didn't work.

"So now you know," Tony said.

But did he? He ran different scenarios and none of them

squared. And then it dawned on him. Sophia wasn't Tony's sister. She was Tony's *mother*. The assault was a rape. And Tony was the forbidden fruit, grown from the most rotten core of human nature. An avalanche of emotions exploded inside him. His lip quivered.

Calmly, Tony said, "The Zangara death certificate wasn't a trophy. It was an innocent gift. From your father to your mother, *primo*."

Primo. Cousin.

"A gift," Vance whispered, "from my father to my mother."

"My mother put it in that box so you would take it home. I couldn't take the chance of you getting rid of it, so I took it from the cigar box and gave it to Kristal and—"

"And she gave it to Ray." It made sense now. It would have been simple. Tony was in on it; he knew Kristal was working for Ray all along.

The timeline was still spinning in his head. His father hadn't snubbed Sophia and Tony. The belief that his uncle would have had a better life if Vance's father had taken him under his wing was misguided. Dr. Jim Courage had protected them. Tony was as far from having a father figure as it got. That's a big thing for a boy to miss. His dad, fostering a boy who was the product of an unspeakable act was a burden he doubted he himself could have carried.

He looked at Tony. "Do you ever wonder what would have happened if he'd been successful, the gunman? How it would have changed history if he'd killed FDR?"

"*Pienso en ello mucho. Si*, I've thought about it a lot. I wonder what would have happened if McKinley wasn't assassinated. Then Teddy Roosevelt would never have been president, and our homeland wouldn't have been sold to the highest bidders."

He paused. "You still haven't told me why you need it." Vance held up the death certificate.

Tony smiled. Even during all the days they were cooped up in the cramped apartment Tony been patient and pleasant.

Stacy opened the curtain with a whoosh. "Can I get you gentlemen something to eat or drink?"

"I'll have some water," Tony said.

Vance didn't want anything.

He saw the narrow mountainous landmass linking the Americas. The plane was making a slow descent off to the southwest. "You should be retired, Tony, sitting on a porch somewhere waiting for your grandkids to show up and work on your computer. Why do you need it now? The Zangara death certificate?" Vance handed it to him.

"There was no postal service between Cuba and the U.S. for fifty years. I stayed in touch with my mother by sending letters to a relative in Panama. He would mail them to a post office box in Miami. It took months to get the mail. My mother made arrangements for him to take me in, if I could get there. Not everyone who fled Cuba before Castro made it to Miami." Tony eyed the old document in the clear plastic cover. "It's how I can prove who I am. Taking me in is a big risk. There's a million-dollar bounty, and I'm on watch lists around the world. It could be a trap, Interpol or something. My mother made the plan a long time ago, when I first went on the run. The death certificate will prove who I am."

Another chill ran down his spine. Life was boiling down to the things he'd never known. "So you knew all along that Giuseppe Zangara was a Cuban national."

"The story in the American papers? All propaganda. They didn't want people to know U.S. intervention led to corruption and poverty. Even President Kennedy said it was a failed policy, sticking a nose in another country's affairs. So they made up a lie, for the media. Zangara was getting even with the Americans by trying to kill FDR. He was a Roosevelt."

Tony had spent twenty years as a fugitive during the prime of his life. And all this time he'd judged Tony as an outlier, a criminal, and a pariah. While it was true, there was another reality. We all have stories in our heads, ones we rely on to define ourselves. How do you define your life from a story that starts like Tony's did?

Vance's throat closed up. He couldn't swallow. They sat quietly, side-by-side, these newly discovered cousins, the soothing whine of the jet engines padding what might have otherwise been a suffocating silence. "Did they know you were back, in Miami? The *mothers*?"

He nodded. "They've always known where I was. But I couldn't take the chance seeing them, putting them in danger. They didn't know about the money. They thought I came back for the Zangara death certificate."

The way Sophia looked at Vance, with those imploring eyes. Not the longing looks of a sister, but those of a mother, who'd lost her only child. Tony was safe now.

Vance's mood lifted. He smiled at Tony. "Sophia was adamant I take that damn cigar box with me."

He played it back, Sophia leaning on her cane, looking up at him, her gnarled fingers, lovingly pinching the skin on his cheek. *Ju take it with ju when ju leave, no? I'll remind ju. When ju leave, I make sure ju take the box with ju.*

Tony's voice brought him back to the present. "It had the coordinates for the *Holly* in it, too. I gave it to her to keep, Ray's idea, and *my mother* put it in with your dad's things. All these years I believed that piece of paper held the secret to the money. I appreciate Ray's talents more now than when he worked for us. Always twenty moves ahead of everyone else. *El Cerebo.*"

The Brain.

Tony pulled up on the emotional altimeter. "We're almost there."

Vance rubbed the back of his neck. "You're full of surprises. And most of them aren't going to look good on Ancestry.com."

"On what?"

"You need something to do other than watch baseball twenty-four/seven."

"Twenty-four/seven?"

"Maybe you'll meet a young Panamanian lady who can bring you into the twenty-first century."

"That would be nice," Tony said, "for many reasons."

The Dassault Falcon 7X descended slowly, crossing over land from the Caribbean side, heading southeasterly.

Stacy came back to pick up the empties. "There's the Panama Canal," she said, leaning over, dropping the trash into a shiny white plastic bag. "We'll be on the ground in a few minutes."

He could see it from his seat, the fifty-mile long manmade waterway beneath them, cutting through the land, joining two oceans. The Falcon passed over a smattering of islands and buzzed the narrow tropical isthmus connecting the two Americas. The pilot made a thrifty right-hand loop over the Pacific side and lined the jet up with a charcoal gray strip. The jet crunched down on the tarmac; the freshly painted yellow lines clicked by the plane's windows. The airport, really nothing more than an airstrip, looked out of place nestled amid a rainforest of soft-topped green mountains with lush tropical trees. The Falcon rolled to a stop next to a rundown aluminum hangar with an orange roof.

The place had the unremarkable look of a sleepy banana republic regional airport, just sleepier. There were no gates or activity. No planes, no people, no ground crew, no nothing, just a stack of bright orange traffic cones sitting out front of an empty one-story white building that he guessed was the terminal.

"Well, this is my final destination," Tony said.

"Looks like a ghost town."

"Panamá Pacífico International Airport," Tony said. "The old Howard U.S. Air Base."

The younger of the two pilots, the one who'd packed the cargo hold in Miami, popped out from the cockpit. He opened the airplane door. "We're here. Welcome to the Redneck Riviera."

He pushed a button and the stairwell began unfurling from the fuselage. A gunmetal-gray Suburban approached and parked adjacent the baggage hold near the back of the aircraft. The hatch popped up and a passenger jumped out, a wiry fellow with a goatee and a hurried step. The pilot and SUV driver slung Tony's duffel bags into the back of the Chevy.

He followed Tony toward the front exit. A blanket of warm wet air filled the cabin. Tony stopped in front of Kathy and turned toward her. "I appreciate your patience on the detour."

"This is my friend," Vance said, "Tony."

Kathy stood and held her hand out. "It's nice to meet you." She grasped Tony's palm with two hands. "I don't believe in coincidence. We're all supposed to be right where we are, right this minute. You seem familiar." She crinkled her nose. When neither man responded, she said, "Have a nice trip. It looks beautiful."

"Well, I hope you're right, that we're right where we're supposed to be." Tony smiled warmly at her. "And good luck with your treatment."

Vance grabbed Tony by the shoulders and walked closely behind him until they reached the stairwell. They hugged. Tony pushed him back, facing him. "Take care of yourself, and your family," he said, then he trotted down the stairwell.

"I hope you find what you're looking for," Vance called out.

"I already have," Tony yelled as the electric motor began to pull the stairway back into the gut of the aircraft.

"Hey, wait a minute!" Vance ran down the aisle and grabbed

his old police-issue Glock from his carry-on stowed under his seat, the one Chago took off him all those years ago. Still swaddled in the white towel Kristal returned it to him in, he dropped it from the airplane door. "You might need this."

"Hey!" he yelled, catching the bundle.

"What?"

"*I'm free!*" He ran in circles, like a puppy chasing its tail. "*I'm free! I'm free! I'm free!*"

Vance wasn't sure if he'd ever felt more joy than he did at that moment watching Tony celebrating on the tarmac.

HE WATCHED from the window as Tony climbed into the back seat of the SUV and rolled the heavily tinted window down, waving a final goodbye. A carbon copy of the lead vehicle carrying Tony appeared from behind one of the buildings and fell in behind, caravanning out of sight.

"We'll refuel in New York," the pilot said. "That wasn't too bad, just a little two-thousand-three-hundred-mile detour. But I want to get out of here."

"Would you like me to convert the cabin for sleeping?" Stacy asked.

"I'd like to read," Kathy said.

"Sleep?" Vance said. "Yes, please." That would be a Godsend.

He rolled onto on his side and pulled the blanket up over shoulders. Tony was free, at last. He'd gotten out safely with the cash. He'd made sacrifices Vance wondered if he'd been capable of making. People were good at different things, and his uncle was good at running: a four-hundred-meter hurdler, after all. Did that make Tony a coward or did it make him smart? He didn't have the answer before, and he didn't have it now. Tony said it best. Life is like the game of baseball, it comes down to a series of single events, pivotal moments that might be meaningless on their own. But added up, they can change the outcome of very big things, even the spent slug of a would-be assassin's gun on display in a museum a thousand miles away. That moment was defining him now, the way it did Isabel and Jim all those years ago. On that, he drifted into a deep slumber.

30

TWO WEEKS LATER

WHEN RAY DINERO offered to move the *Second Wind*, Vance gladly accepted, and she was moored at Sailboat Bay across from the all-suites, family-friendly Hotel Mutiny. He took private sailing lessons from a salty, foul-mouthed Cockney named Tucker who gave "drunken sailor" a whole new meaning.

Ray warned him that the sailor's short stint as an instructor at the club lasted for two days when management fired him for yelling "for fuckssake" at underage students and for calling their parents "fuckeen stupeed." Now Tucker had his own unlicensed underground operation consisting of a twenty-one-foot V-hull sloop he, too, called home. Ray said Tucker might show up drunk, if at all. He liked the idea of an unmotivated, unreliable teacher who looked the part. If he guessed right, Tucker hadn't shaved in six months or bathed on land since he arrived from the wrong side of London.

"For fuckssake," Tucker said when he met him at the *Second*

Wind for his first lesson. "Why does a fuckeen stupeed bloke like you need a beauty of a boat like this?"

After three lessons, Vance abandoned the idea of learning to sail a ship as complex as the Lagoon and moved aboard. He left the contents of his apartment on the street, paid the penalty for the broken lease on his office, and cut all services except his cell phone. His mother didn't know about the offshore blind trust he'd set up, and she never knew she had the debts he'd cleared. More importantly, he visited her more often, and now that Sophia had moved in, the two old women were sharing the idyllic sisterhood denied them in their youth. They were happy.

He carried the dark family secret now, too, something that bonded the four of them, the occasional questioning glance serving as a sporadic reminder. Especially from Sophia, through those clouded old eyes, her thoughts as clear to him as the shallow waters lapping at the shores of Jewfish Creek.

They never discussed Tony or the strange contents of his father's old cigar box. Maybe someday they'd talk about it, maybe he'd buy airline tickets for all three of them to visit Tony in Panama. But not yet, not until enough time had passed and he was certain they were in the clear.

He'd wired money into a Swiss account, prepaying Kathy's treatments before cutting what turned out to be the most difficult deal: parking Edgar full time at the sailing club. The harbormaster deemed the car an eyesore and would not have approved it had he not brought a million-dollar sailing yacht to close the deal.

STANDING on the bow of the *Second Wind*, he stared across Sailboat Bay, studying the lit outline of the faded green awning hanging over the entrance to the Hotel Mutiny. He pushed the button sounding the air horn they'd given him when he signed the mooring lease to summon the water taxi. It shrieked over the gentle sounds of bay water lapping at the hulls, slack sails buffeting lightly in the evening quiet. In minutes, a young man appeared in a flat-bottom boat, and standing, the kid looped a line over the cleat of the sailboat. Climbing over the bow railing and stepping onto the water taxi, Vance unbalanced it momentarily.

"I haven't seen you before," the young man said, steadying the skiff before swinging it around, heading for land. The little outboard rat-tat-tatted as they motored toward shore. "Nice boat. Is it yours?"

"Yep. First night aboard," he said.

When they reached the shore, the kid draped the skiff's noose over a stumpy piling and docked in a space between a dozen rental paddleboats chained together for the night.

Low streetlights illuminated both sides of Bayshore Drive as he sprinted across the grassy median, dodging light traffic. It was August, the most brutal month for heat and humidity.

Back in the '80s and '90s, the side entrance to the club was the gateway to the epicenter of the world's cocaine trade. It was gone now, boarded up and refaced during the corporate remodel. He jogged past the portable sign for Valet Parking and climbed four wide concrete stairs leading to the lobby.

The aura of intrigue had been replaced with bright indoor lights throwing pastel swashes over a pair of oversized faux-finished indoor columns. Flimsy art-deco light fixtures dangled above the blond wicker furniture covered with orange-and-white-striped cushions.

A middle-aged woman at the front desk looked up at him from a computer monitor, indifferently. "Can I help you?"

"I'd like to have dinner."

"Take the elevator to the second floor." She gestured toward a narrow corridor painted seafoam green.

He picked up a shiny brochure from the front desk and read it while he waited for the elevator.

LONG BEFORE SOUTH BEACH, Coconut Grove was the "in" place for partying in the 1980s and 1990s. Originally a private club for members only, The Upper and Lower Decks were a favorite hangout for the international jet set, including Hollywood celebrities, rock stars, and sports legends. If walls could talk, ours would tell a larger-than-life tale. After first opening in 1969, the Hotel Mutiny closed its doors in 1995. Uncertain what the future held, the hotel was purchased by a group of investors. After an extensive remodel, the hotel has been consistently voted as a Top Twenty Miami destination.

NO MENTION of the nude interpretive dancers and their sexually choreographed show, the high-rollers dangling hundred dollar bills like confetti at the hostess stand to get tables next to the dance floor. Not so much as a blurb about Los Guapos and their entourage of assassins, pilots, bankers, and attorneys. Not a peep about the Sandinista rebels, Nicaraguan gunrunners, or ex-CIA-trained Cuban operatives-turned-drug runners who dined regularly with FBI agents. Not even an honorable mention about the Mutiny girls. That was like leaving the Bunnies out of the history of the Playboy Club.

Memories, many bad, had been erased during the hotel revamp. Like the Central American dictator gunned down in the parking lot alongside his bodyguard. The Ferraris, Porsches, Bentleys, and Rolls-Royces driven by a group of first generation Cuban-American high school dropouts. Rocks of cocaine passed around in folded hundred dollar bills. And there was nothing about the beautiful Cuban girl whose strangled body had been wrapped in a hotel blanket and dumped in the unspoiled waters of Jewfish Creek.

Instead, it looked like some designer from Brooklyn had just finished a Miami Vice reruns binge and decided the retro Sonny Crockett look might brighten the place up a bit.

The hostess appeared, finally. "One for dinner?"

"I'm meeting someone."

"A young lady?"

"I'm not sure how young she is."

"I heard that."

"Sorry I'm late."

"Traffic, right?" Lauren laughed. "Follow me—I bribed the hostess for the best seats in the house."

He looked around. There were only four other people in the restaurant on a Thursday night at seven. There was no sign of The Horn Room in the far back of the defunct Upper Deck, named for the tables made from the tusks of endangered animals. The wooden parquet dance floor was tiled over, the dance pole long gone. No trace of the heavy cigarette and cigar smoke that once colored the air.

No carpet domes of crystallized liquors made by the table-side coffee showmen whose poorly aimed blue streams of liquid fire missed their targets. No scent of the chocolate soufflés ordered before appetizers. No aroma of the New Orleans-style barbeque shrimp or Carolina She-Crab soup served with a pony of sherry.

No hint of temperamental Chef Roy known to throw plates of cooling food.

No trace of the decadence.

The nightclub.

The cabaret.

The forgotten Hotel Mutiny.

He didn't care for this new extended-stay place.

A waitress appeared. "Is this your first time here?"

He said, "Sort of."

They ordered their food from the corner table overlooking Sailboat Bay where Tony and Chago negotiated cargo holds of cocaine. The same table where Manuel Noriega's bodyguard ate his last meal before being gunned down at the valet stand. The one Margarita served her last customers, before her bruised body was found in the shallow waters near Gilbert's Resort.

He looked out the window across the dark-blue water at the lights coming from the cabins of dozens of boats. Light glittered from the windows of the *Second Wind*. She held steady, tethered to her buoy, the cash hidden inside her gullet, wrapped in the jib sail, the way Ray had packed it.

"What will you do now?" he asked.

"I don't know. I'd planned to get my tax problem straightened out. But then I got a notice from the IRS acknowledging receipt of my money order. And then the bank sent me the title to my uncle's townhouse. You wouldn't know anything about that, would you?"

He shrugged. He and Ray went halves on her tax levy and bought her uncle's condo from the estate, gifting it back to her anonymously. "What will you do now?"

"I've never had a hundred thousand dollars in the bank and a house with no mortgage. Keep working, I guess. I'd like to get my horse out of the pasture and fit to show." She lit up at that idea. "What about you?"

"Jake says real estate is a good place to invest, says Texas is the place to buy now. Says he knows the market and with the oil prices recovering, there's money to be made there. I'm leaning that way. Did you have a thing with him?"

Lauren's face seized up. "I don't know if I would call it *a thing*."

"What would you call it then?"

"Hmmm. A mistake?"

"Did you know he was an energy banker? He has a lot of contacts in Houston."

"I guess he told me that, and he was in Miami for his kids. I think that's what he said."

He'd told Vance the same thing. His love of his kids and devotion as a father redeemed him. "He's in rehab. I guess we'll have wait to find out if he's a drunk asshole or a pop-up asshole."

She laughed. "In my experience, the only growth assholes experience is in circumference and diameter."

"That's pretty cynical." He liked this new version of her even better. Spunky. "We have twenty-eight days to think about Jake's real estate offer; that's how long he'll be in rehab. All that cash, it makes me nervous." He glanced at the lights sparkling on the water.

"We? Speak for yourself. I turned the money down, in case you forgot."

He hadn't forgotten. He and Ray were sure she'd change her mind over time; in their minds the money was still hers. He stared at the silhouettes of boats rocking in their moorings. He felt her staring at him, studying him in profile.

"Did you know the old guy that owned this place is still alive? Old Bernard?" she asked.

"How do you know that?"

"Internet search. And get this, he sells self-help books and DVDs to cure cancer and treat addiction. He advertises a cure for cocaine addiction."

"OK, that's funny, in an ironic way." He was surprised the old man was still alive.

"He's eighty-five. He uses his age to market his products. By the way, how's your sister doing?"

"Good. Thanks for asking. Her doctors say the early diagnosis was a miracle. The drug therapy is working."

As for old Bernard's cancer-curing DVDs, he'd give those a pass.

"I talked to Davis," she said. "Jake hired him to captain his yacht to Texas. I Googled it—it's a God-awful place: Freeport, with oil refineries and chemical plants all over the place. Jake said it's low-key, and there's a marina run by a family that's used to big yachts coming and going. Looks pretty rundown."

"Sounds perfect. Oh, that reminds me." He lifted one hip up off the booth and pulled something out of his jeans' pocket. He reached across the table and dropped it into her hand.

"Oh my God! This is Davis's gold coin! He never took it off."

"Yeah, well, he didn't exactly take it off. I found it in the storage unit, after he got beat up. I thought you could give it back to him when you see him."

"You realize you're getting another chance now. I hope you don't mess it up. All that cash," Lauren said. "I wouldn't want to be responsible for it, toting it to Texas. Poor Davis, he'll be in harm's way again. I hope Jake's paying him good money this time around. Who knows who'll be out there following them?"

That was a valid point and one he'd spent a ot of time pondering. "The money is probably safer on open water than in a bank or a mutual fund. I'm sure Ray will be one step ahead of everyone." He picked up the hotel brochure and skimmed it. "Did you see this? '*If walls could talk*. . . .'"

"Yeah, I picked one up on our first date."

That reminded him of their first meeting. "I liked you the moment we met. I thought we were on a real date. Who knew you were scamming me? I would have asked you out again. Maybe even to Joe's for stone crab."

"Now that you're a rich guy, I might go out with you," she said. "By the way, it wasn't totally an act, I liked you, too," she said, locking her eyes with his, then gazing down at the tabletop. "You've never been married, and I'm not up for training a novice." She shrugged. "Maybe I'll make an exception. And, you're right, the owners of this place better hope the walls never start talking."

He looked around the brightly-lit dining room, at the tourists who'd arrived, many with young children clamoring for tables with a good view of Sailboat Bay. "It's like none of it ever happened." Then he changed tack. "Maybe I can take you to Joe's some time, seriously."

"When stone crab's back in season. I'd like that." She glanced out the window, across the bay. "There are two kinds of people. The ones who eat their stone crab cold with mustard. And those who like them hot, with melted butter. Which one are you?"

"You'll have to wait to find out," he said. "Stone crab season starts in October."

ABOUT THE AUTHOR

Karen S. Gordon is an emerging author of action/adventure thrillers. If you enjoyed *The Mutiny Girl*, or have comments you'd like to share, she would appreciate you leaving a review. *The Mutiny Girl* is the first installment of the Gold & Courage Series.

The adventures of Vance Courage and Lauren Gold continue in *Scorpion Girl*, coming in 2020.

Please sign up for Karen's newsletter at karensgordon.com.

Thank you. Without you, the reader, none of this would be possible.

Made in the USA
San Bernardino, CA
25 February 2019